SOVEREIGN

Book Two: Give Me a Child

JOHN L. PATTILLO

SOVEREIGN

Book Two: Give Me a Child

ISBN: 978-0-9828365-1-4

Published by Windswift Press
www.windswift.net

The characters and the events in this novel are the creation of the author. They do not refer to real persons, living or dead.

Text design and cover layout design by Kimberly Martin

"But the mind is the captain and
the master of the life of mortal men."
(Sed dux atque imperator vitae mortalium animus est.)

– Sallust, *Bellum Jugurthinum*

Contents:

Part III: Wipe It Out, Start Over

Part IV: A World Enlightened

The Churai and Other Chugrans

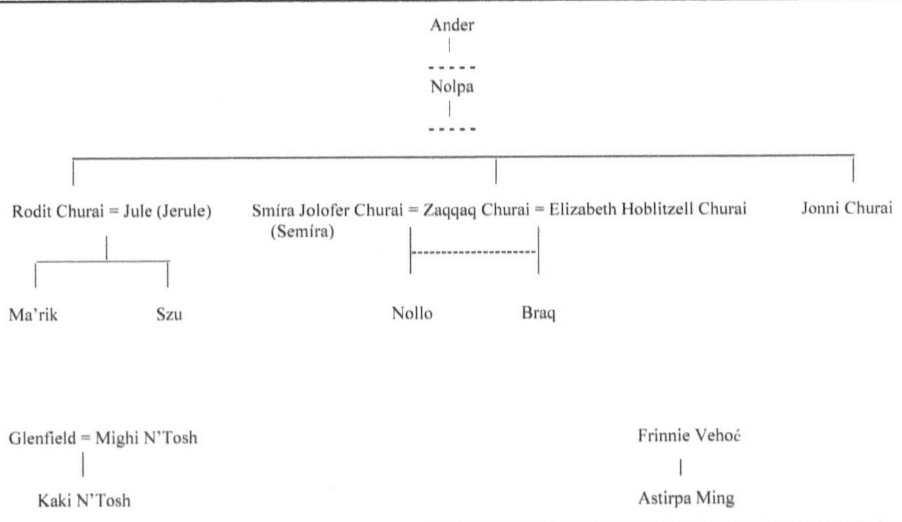

The Atelier Derosch

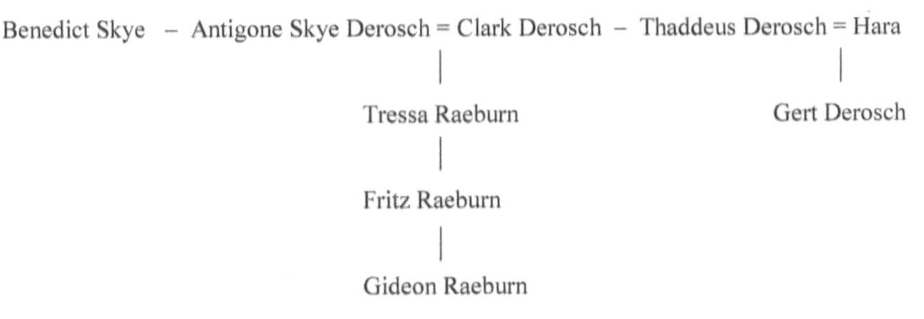

Bevol Stagri - Mila Merani

BOOK TWO
Give Me a Child

PART III
Wipe It Out, Start Over

CHAPTER 25

Interlude: The Last Painting – More Preparations.

The Painter was ready now for the linen. He rolled the huge piece of fabric out on the floor, and then placed the frame of stretchers on top of it. Allowing a generous overhang, he cut the linen, enjoying as he always did the soft chirp of the shears against the new fabric. He tacked one of the long sides, in the middle only, a single tack.

He had debated hiring an assistant for this stage as stretching a large canvas was a cumbersome job, but to preserve the sanctuary of his secluded studio, his "impregnable wall," as he called it, he decided to do it himself. Clasping the opposite edge of the cloth with the special canvas pliers, he pulled it against the wooden member and tapped another tack in place. He then turned the frame lengthwise and did the same with the two short sides. The large rectangle of fabric now hung loosely attached to each side, barely holding on with a single tack per side.

He should now have immediately carried on hammering scores more tacks on each side till he reached the corners, but he suddenly stopped and walked across his studio to look at his drawings again.

He had changed his original composition: when he first conceived it, there had been two brothers – Otos clasping Hera, Ephialtes embracing Artemis. Two mortals seeking union with goddesses. Now his focus had switched to another part of the myth, the one wherein Artemis beguiled and seduced the god-like men, running past them in a wood disguised as a beautiful white deer. The two brothers, immortal unless destroyed by their own hands, were entranced by the wiles of the goddess: they loosed their arrows at the same time. The shafts missed the hind, passed each other in flight, and killed each a brother – the white deer, Artemis, escaping.

The Painter's composition was simpler now than it had been: Hera was out, leaving just three figures, not four. It was too simple though, too symmetrical: a brother on each side, the white deer in the middle. He had tried various ways of relieving the inert equilibrium. And still it did not have enough tension – even though one could see that the one brother was in a more violent pose, more aggressive, almost as if he knew where his fateful arrow would strike.

No, this would still not be his final drawing of the composition of the painting. The Painter shrugged; he walked back to his canvas. He studied what he had done so far, lightly tacking just once on each side. It was such a big job, putting a whole project together like this. The preparation of all the materials, the extensive drawings, and still more drawings, revision after revision, and then the execution. And, yes, he could have sought help with stretching the canvas, but as for the rest...there were certain things a person could only do for himself. It was in the nature of the job.

There was still a long way to go. Undaunted, he picked up the hammer and a handful of tacks.

CHAPTER 26
Uprooted

Braq pressed the corner of his nose and the pads of the five fingers of his hand against the cool car window. He gazed fascinated out the right side of the car. Fall was over, but winter had not yet begun. It was that indeterminate period when the world, after its last desperate chromatic burst, finally gives up and leaches out all of its color – into the ground, or the air, or wherever color goes for the winter – and resigns itself to a scumble of three or four puny shades of gray. Braq's sketch pad lay unused on his lap, but not for the absence of color in the world. He would not have been trying to capture that deceitful troublemaker, color, anyway. But his usual polar friends, light and dark, that played their gay drama in his drawings under the command of his charcoal, or chalk, or pen, were also missing from this landscape of limp shapes and anemic shadows scudding past his window.

An artist surely would have been depressed at the thin gruel the visual world was now niggardly offering. Braq was not depressed. He was mesmerized.

The car, an old red station wagon, was hurtling along seemingly endless ribbons of roadway, nestled in among countless other vehicles – cars, trucks, vans – all evidently bustling to get somewhere and do something. Did these people in the cars have anything to do with those glittering buildings of glass and steel he kept seeing? Like crystalline structures extruded from the earth, the office buildings kept popping up around each curve of the road.

Now, what was this?! He leaned even more intently against the window. It looked like the masts and spars of a great pirate ship – no there was a whole fleet of them! They floated just behind a gray mass of trees. But how could such ships be here when there was no ocean? At least, he *thought* there was no ocean this close. Then, he saw lines running from one ship to another and realized that these must be much greater versions of the primitive electrical transmission towers he occasionally had seen back in Fulon.

And now he glimpsed, far away, a grayish-white spire. It stood out as a lone shape – individual and austere. Then it vanished. It was a monument to one of the country's founders, but Braq did not know this. He only knew that it looked like a benevolent beacon. He kept waiting for it to reappear.

There was so much for Braq to take in outside the window. What else is a child for but to sponge up his new world; Braq was sponging. Inside the car, two things drifted imperceptibly into his consciousness, and came to rest, perhaps to be examined at some later date.

The first was Jule's questioning of the driver. Jule sat in the front seat, sending a steady stream of questions to the driver as they wound through the Virginia and then the Maryland communities ringing Washington, D.C. On her request, he took a meandering route, on and off the great superhighways, now detouring along picturesque rural roads, now through busy commercial districts. The driver was a young man named Bucky, who seemed to be Chugran, but who spoke English the way Braq's mother, Liz, did. Braq assumed that this was the American dialect. Bucky was a neighbor of the recent immigrants, Jule and Rodit and their children. He had offered his help in picking up the two newer arrivals, Nollo and Braq.

Jules' questions were crisp and purposeful. "What is the name of this community?" "How much do these houses cost?" "How long does it take to get to Annapolis from the airport?" "How much do those pants you're wearing cost?" "Where do you buy them?" "Do Chugrans here shop where everyone else shops?" Even had Braq been paying attention, it is unlikely that he would have divined Jule's purpose in asking all of these questions. It was more her manner than the actual questions that might have struck him. In Chugrana, Jule had, if not hidden her light, certainly dimmed it under some bushel basket of deference to Rodit, at least publicly. Now, her light seemed to be flaring brightly and unapologetically.

The second thing that Braq might have identified was Nollo's nervousness. This had commenced, really, as soon as they lifted off from Chugrana.

Over several nights and days their trip had crossed mountain ranges, lakes, vast forests, arid expanses, occasional cities, green and ochre farmlands. Much later, when they tried to reconstruct where they had been, they decided that some of the domes and spires rolling backwards underneath their plane must have been located in various European cities. At the time, though, Nollo became sick almost immediately. For the first twenty-four hours, he was not able to keep much food down. Some pills from the steward helped finally.

When he regained some alertness, he began to nag the steward endlessly. "Where are we going?" "I want some water." "What plane is this?" "When can we eat again?" "When do we land?"

He asked these questions of the steward almost rudely, as if the man had no other purpose in life but to be there for Nollo. His questions were not just childish – or even adult – curiosity, but seemed to come from some profound uneasiness. No doubt this was to be expected under the circumstances – suddenly and violently uprooted from his home and parents. Yet there was something more to it than this. After all, why did Braq not behave even more anxiously than Nollo? He was four years younger, and to all appearances, knew less of the world. Later, Braq told Bevol Stagri that for much of the trip he had Zaq and Liz before his mind's eye.

"Not so much their faces, you understand," said Bevol, "as some strong impression of their persons. He saw them as someone might have painted them – some essentialized representation of how they faced the world. And this was partially because he had fresh in his mind Liz's words to him and Nollo. 'Remember – you are Zaq's and my sons. Stand up to this danger bravely, and to everything else – as we have taught you. As we do. Be like Zaq.' (I think Liz had actually said, '*Think* of Zaq,' but Braq heard '*Be* like Zaq.')

"He didn't know then, on the plane, not consciously, that he was seeing a comparison between the idols of his early childhood, and making a choice between them. That – even as he traveled further away from them – he turned now toward Zaq and Liz, and, as it were, somewhat away from his Big Brátano. For now, though, he only felt that this image of his parents, and especially of Zaq, was before him as a concrete guide to a whole way of acting, and that the behavior he saw now in Nollo did not fit with this image" said Bevol.

As for Nollo, it was only after they had landed in America and Jule had collected them, that he began to resume some of his normal behavior and his brash sense of control over his surroundings. In the car, he began chattering a stream of words so fast that he almost couldn't be understood. It was as if he had to catch up with someone or something, as if he were trying to find safety by means of the torrent of his words. He couldn't get them out fast enough. He was describing their trip, and to hear it you might have thought that he practically flew the plane himself, planned their route, and charted the topography of the earth besides. He said nothing about his sickness and disorientation.

Suddenly, a huge truck pressed up an inch from the tail of their car and blasted an air horn at them. Bucky seemed unfazed by this, but Nollo screamed, and, as the truck whooshed by their side, he yelled above its roar, "Did you hear that? Did you see that? Did you hear that?" until finally Jule had to tell him to calm down.

Braq, in the meantime had returned to pressing his face against the glass. He was filtering certain facts, only half-understood. He had noticed, for example, that the barriers and inspections they always had to pass, back in Chugrana, had not yet appeared here. Other than the inspections at customs and immigration at the airport (and even there everyone went through the same lines, unlike in Fulon where Chugros and Dryrugers were segregated), they appeared to be free to drive wherever they wanted. And Bucky – there was some intangible difference between him and the Chugrans Braq was used to. He seemed more relaxed – was that what it was? – less guarded, more at ease in the world.

The strife, the tension, the atmosphere of Chugrana – which the young Braq had only just begun to absorb and try to understand – was that really just peculiar to Chugrana? There was something to be feared in the air in Chugrana. He had left his home fearing some sudden, inexplicable, forcible separation from his parents – by some unnamed predators.

Was he safe here from these predators? He could not yet tell.

***

Lew Antilles looked out of the twentieth floor window of the office building at the gray landscape below. His eye caught a small spot of color. An old red station wagon climbed the exit ramp from the highway below and then disappeared under the web of barren branches that gradually blended into the featureless countryside. He had stood up from the polished conference table and walked to the window to give himself a break from the contentious discussion. The Board of Directors of Suffer the Little Children was trying to reach agreement on a matter of policy concerning adoption. This, after all, was its mission, to serve the welfare and the adoption of children from all over the world, children of all races. Their mission was mired.

An American Negro man had married an American Indian woman. This grave racial misfortune had occurred while they were both attending college. They compounded their lack of wisdom by bearing a child, a girl, whom they persisted in loving beyond all measure. Their effrontery knew no bounds. The two parents were killed in an auto accident. They had no close relatives, and, as it happened, the more distant ones had disapproved of the marriage anyway. Now that the child was up for adoption though, two ethnic communities of relatives were each trying to claim the girl for their own. She was currently in one of the orphanages run by Suffer the Little Children.

The organization's policy had always been a mushy insistence on placing children with "their own race, to whatever extent possible." The policy was mushy because of an insuperable problem: the number of orphans of any particular race never matched the number of prospective parents of that race – even if the organization could identify what was meant by "that race." If there were not enough parents of the "proper race," their policy, if enforced, would mean permanent orphanages for a large number of children.

As usual, they were at ferocious loggerheads over this.

As Antilles turned back to the room, he saw that things were about to get much worse. An absent Board member had just entered the room.

When he was a young man, the Chugran-American, Pranti Ku, had passed through a period of being horribly self-conscious about being "in a racial minority." So, to appear "less Chugran," he had gone to a surgeon to have his eyelids re-shaped, and his skin color altered. The whole business was rather ridiculous because, as the surgeon tried to explain, there was no agreement about the shape of Chugran eyelids anyway – like most racial features it varied both within the Chugran spectrum of individuals, and also within the non-Chugran population. And Chugran skin tones ranged widely also.

But Ku had insisted, and the surgeon was happy to take his money.

A few years later, Ku had swung to the other pole and now wanted to stand for "Chugran pride." He went to a second surgeon (since the first one had obviously, he thought, "exploited" Ku's "racially imposed shame"). He had his eyelids re-shaped again. He had his skin chemically treated one more time.

All of this cutting, stretching, shrinking, and pasting of the fibers of orbicularis oculi, levator palpebri, orbicularis palpebrarum, procerus, and corrugator supercilii resulted – as Bevol Stagri, a different type of

"Chugran-American," uncharitably pointed out in one of his anatomy classes at the Atelier – in eyelids that drooped heavily over Ku's already bulging eyeballs, giving him a perpetually drugged or stupefied look, not to mention the piebald skin that suggested that the poor man had contracted some tropical disease.

Ku's coif shot out at all angles, in a kind of hirsute affront to haloes, like some seedy lion whose mane, munched by moths, was now in pathetically irregular strands. His barrel chest had the unnaturally large and pumped up look of a person with emphysema, though he did not smoke and his lungs were in fact quite clear. Beneath this balloon-like chest, floated the somewhat larger dirigible of his stomach, which, as he walked, swayed back and forth, pushing aside the air in front of him. His short arms were crooked at the elbows which he held snugly against his sides, leaving his forearms to dangle at limp and rather useless right angles in front of his girth. He wore Chugran robes or silk business suits, variously, according to the impression he wanted to create.

The total effect of his appearance was far from accidental. He entered a room, a crowd, a space – the world – with studied offensiveness. He loved seeing the reactions.

"Ku" was a shortened form of his real name, he claimed. The full version was, by his assertion, "Kuro." He pronounced this with an astonishing *accent* which he slipped into from time to time, and which he intended his listeners to take for "Chugran." But Ku had been born in America, and had spoken only American English from infancy. And, like many Americans, his ear for tongues was not very good. What he took for an imitation of a Chugran accent came out as a mixture of Italian and Yiddish, or occasionally and startlingly, Japanese. In any event, the name "Kuro" was his own modification of a much more prosaic and commonplace name that he never used, and even was at some pains to conceal.

As to his language, words fell into his sentences from a sense of mere approximation. If it sounded more or less like the word he wanted, he used it – it was for his listeners to decipher what the more appropriate word should have been. No one had the temerity to call him on this, because few Americans knew much about Chugrana or its linguistic traits, and more particularly because they were afraid of being labeled a racist, or racially "insensitive."

Ku held positions in many organizations such as Suffer the Little Children, but he liked most to present himself as a member of the faculty of that educational institution known as the Schaal Chugrana, outside of Annapolis.

Now, as he entered the room, his paunch swaying before him, a member of the Board of Suffer the Little Children was saying, "To allow this orphan to go to the African-American community would be – "

Ku's voice boomed over the table, as he took his seat, "– communital genocide!"

He looked around the table with complacent umbrage and self-satisfaction. "It was so easy," he thought, "to make these people squirm."

"Have we not agreed," Ku continued," that our aim should be to preservate the sanctity of the ethnicities and the tribes, to safeguard the inalienable value of each culture? Yet here we are, proposing to snuff out this unique and endangered Native American culture by placing this girl with some alien group."

A member who opposed Ku jumped in. "Why isn't it genocide against the African-American community? She's just as much African-American as Native American!"

Ku was unfazed. "I think," he said condescendingly, "you will find in our research papers that her blood quanta are much more heavily weighted in favor of the Native American strains than the African-American. Both paternal grandparents were Native American, but only the maternal grandmother was African-American. Her mother's father was a Caucasian. More rape of the black race by the white, no doubt, but that can't affect our scientific judgment of her blood admixture."

This brought murmurs from around the table: "You've gone too far, Ku!"… "Unwarranted!"…"Unnecessarily inflammatory!" All of these objections were pronounced as if it were merely a cocktail party difference of opinion, nothing more.

Ku, unflappable at having stirred up this gnat's nest responded with, "Gentlemen! Ladies! Please! Let's lower the decimal level of our discourse. It's these race-mixing, race-raping, race-exploiting practices that are flammatory. The maternal grandfather was never identified, so I merely make a reasonable presumptuousness as to his race."

Antilles asked for recognition and then said to the table at large, "We know that there are many so-called white families – European, Mediterranean, Slavic, Jewish, whatever they may be – dying to adopt a child. This girl would go to a loving father and mother. Instead, if you insist on race-matching, then we're going to have to turn her over to an ethnic foster home, as a permanent orphan. What if someone *here* had given birth to this child?" He looked around the table at each of the members. "If it was *you*, wouldn't you want to find a pair of loving parents for your child? Why are we doing this?"

Ku jumped in before anyone else could answer. "I will stake my life's researches and experience and knowledge on the fact that no white couple – be they ever so noble or pure in motives – could ever hope to know what unconquerable barriers a native American or an African American child – a child of color – must inevitably face in this society. They have not had to bear the blunt of the storm. After all, you can lead a square pig to a round hole, but you can't make him drink from it."

No one at the table could bring themselves to come out and ask Ku just what "life researches" he had conducted, though several posed the question to themselves with cynical amusement. Nonetheless, Antilles pressed further. "Aren't you just duplicating here the travesties you've described and that we have read about in the papers from your own homeland, Chugrana, where families are now being shattered over this issue?"

"That is entirely different," retorted Ku. "I am talking about endowing these children with a necessary sense of racial identity, crucial to their very survival."

A newer member suddenly interrupted. "Why don't we just conduct a race-matching test to find out who would make the *best* parents – give a test to the prospective parents to find out who is best equipped to inculcate these cultural values in the child?"

There was an embarrassed silence around the table. The member who had said this had no idea why.

Finally, the chairman explained. "We tried this a year or so ago. We devised a screening test to sort out the parents for each race, tribe, ethnic group. We had questions on how much they knew about parenting, about each culture, their degree of ethnic sensitivity, the stability of their household, the responsibility of both parents, and so forth. Our presumption was that the test would automatically assign the best Negro parents for Negro children, Indian for Indian, Mexican for Mexican, Polynesian for Polynesian, and so on.

"But on every test we devised, no matter how we pre-selected the groups, it turned out that the most highly qualified couples were always the Chinese who came from Hong Kong. They scored higher on every category. They knew more about black history than blacks, more about white customs than whites, and so on. They studied, you see. They were motivated to do well, no matter what criteria we set up.

"It was amazing to see how many of the couples in all sorts of ethnic groups were utterly ignorant of the appropriate cultural and ethnic features of their own kind. There were Negroes who knew nothing about black culinary habits and holidays, Spanish-surnamed couples who didn't even know what "Adios!" means, Jews who didn't know how to serve gefilte fish."

Ku snapped, "It was a ridiculous set of tests! Should never have been given anyway! It's not 'cultural competency' we're after, but cultural security!"

"What about the security of the child?" asked Antilles.

"The welfare of the race is paramount!" said Ku.

As they argued, Asa Menzies negligently flipped through some papers in front of him. He ran his fingers through the silky white hair that along with his patrician features caused people to call him "distinguished looking." From time to time he looked down the table. He did not overtly examine his fellow Board members. This might have implied a greater concern than he in fact felt. Instead, his gaze wandered complacently around the table, lighting almost by chance on this member and that. He asked himself why they were being so stupid about all of this. They were so strident, taking such impassioned positions. Even Ku was getting hot under the collar, as if it really mattered to them all, as if they were sure they were right. As if there *could* be certainty – and right.

It would be a mistake to think that such complacency betokens a lack of conviction. Menzies had a conviction, and it was this – truth and right were the products and property of a community, which may make up and change its mind from moment to moment.

Perhaps one should pause and reflect. Is this possible? A conviction that convictions come from the changing whims of the herd seems hardly worthy the name "conviction." One might almost deem it a self-contradiction. To be sure, while the animating principle of *some* souls is like a taproot – deep, strong, and solitary – not to be pulled up save with dynamite (and perhaps not even then), the guiding principle of others disperses through thousands of meager rootlets in the uppermost inch of the topsoil of their minds. Such beings are ready to topple when a wind comes from just the right direction.

Be all this as it may, and whether you think it a conviction or not, Menzies believed in nothing if not this – that the group was the source.

The Board finally voted on the question of interracial adoption. The individuals in question had already voted on the topic at hand many times in the past, but it made no difference. Soulmates of Menzies, they felt, and they had been taught, that principles were flexible, to be decided on the basis of the facts of the moment, and changed in the next moment – that they should not be rigid or dogmatic. Thus, such votes could be taken as often as they felt like, and they could change their votes with easy consciences. When the vote came round to Menzies, he looked up as if it were all of no importance, as if they were interrupting him from something else (really it didn't matter what) that was obviously a weightier matter he might have been considering.

Calmly and complacently, he said, "I think you're all making a mountain out of a molehill. Surely, we've gotten past these superstitious mantras about the individual. How childish. It's so…outdated. All of these poor uprooted children should be brought up by their own communities."

With a languid and somewhat dismissive wave of his hand, he voted for the policy of strict race-matching of child to parent.

CHAPTER 27

The Schaal Chugrana

Bevol Stagri's students waited for him to pick up the thread of his story. He had paused for a moment. He sipped his favorite drink reflectively. Now he looked away, up through the atelier's great skylight, as if he were seeing something on a vast landscape visible especially to him. Then, he looked at the young faces around him.

"You cannot be better than your ideas.

"If you absorb and accept noble ideas, you will breathe out a nobility of spirit that will seem to be nothing but your very person. If you absorb and accept corrupt ideas, *that* will be your person. I say 'absorb,' but you realize, don't you, that these ideas may come from outside of you, or from you yourself. After all, it's not just the wheel that gets reinvented from time to time, but also virtue or vice which each individual rediscovers throughout his or her lifetime.

"Braq and Nollo, for example, had some great influences, as far as external ideas, and they had some terrible ones. For starters, Zaq and Liz were the kind of parents you could wish any child to have. But their time of influence was short – their molding of these two children was interrupted by the events in Chugrana. But even so, you could tell that these two boys brought each their own minds to bear on what Zaq and Liz gave them. And they took away – they reinvented – very different 'wheels.'

"On the other hand, they both came under the influence of the Schaal Chugrana, and its variegated faculty. They each reacted differently to the Schaal. Their lives...diverged somewhat...to what outcome...?"

After another pause, he resumed.

"Some of you know where the Schaal is – just down the way, really. Go down Old Rolling Road a few miles and turn left where it dips into the hollow. But then you can still miss it, the turnoff is so inconspicuous. Most people don't even know there's a Chugran community there – or a school.

"Jule asked Bucky to drive the boys past the Schaal before taking them home that first day, so they could get a glimpse of where they might be going to school. He drove them along the country road, and suddenly turning the corner of a lane there it was in front of them.

"Braq told me later that he got a very funny feeling right away when the first thing they saw was a baseball diamond with two teams. He had never seen the game so he didn't know what it was, but what bothered him was the fact that all of the players were wearing short colored tunics that made it seem as if they had just come from Chugrana. And that made him feel as if he were back *inside* that country, back in the midst of all the strife, the tribes, the chieftains, the riots. I think it must really have been a shock because this part of Maryland's landscape apparently resembles sections of Chugrana that Braq was familiar with.

"But it was just a baseball game, and he got over his initial unease. For the time anyway.

"You see the Schaal was going through a change. Originally it was a product of some of the better aspects of Chugran culture. I've told you about 'Let mind speak to mind.' The Schaal came from that spirit. The original Chugran immigrants wanted to ensure that their children would be educated properly. The more recent immigrants were, if anything, even more fanatical about it."

For once, Bevol's class was grateful for Toby Smaph's perennial confusion, because he asked what many of them were also confused about. We are sometimes happy, thus, at someone else's ignorance.

"What do you mean when you say 'original immigrants' and 'more recent immigrants'? How far back do the Chugrans in America go?" Toby asked.

Bevol was not surprised that the students knew so little of the history of Chugran immigration to America. After all, why should every American know the history of every one of the hundreds of immigrant groups to come here, especially one so obscure as the Chugrans?

"When slavery ended in Chugrana, in the early twentieth century, a small number of Chugrans decided to get out, and found their way to the United States. They settled in Maryland, near Annapolis, because a handful of Chugran families *already* lived there – flotsam tossed on the shores of the Chesapeake from a *previous* migration from South America, many decades earlier, where one of the very few clusters of Chugran slaves ever transported to the Western hemisphere had finally been liberated. Those freed South American Chugrans had made their way north, and settled, God knows why, considering their hostile reception, in Maryland. It was not the first time in history that a group of persons intruded on the privileged sanctuary of people already established. No doubt it would not be the last. In time came the newer immigrants from Chugrana itself.

"Their long-rooted brethren refrained from doing what many immigrants have done throughout history. They did not scorn the newcomers as if they were brash, dirty, and uncouth embarrassments. They welcomed them, even though two centuries and an ocean had sundered them. Perhaps it was because there were so few of each of the two groups. People are so much more accepting of 'aliens,' even ones like themselves, when they intrude in but small numbers.

"The two groups melded.

"The sanctuary in which both groups were 'invaders' comprised handfuls of random acres of neglected, unattractive tidewater land Marylanders had scorned for centuries. The Chugrans' offensive behavior was to work this land productively and turn it from nondescript marsh and scrub into attractive farm smallholdings.

"Such an insult could not go unpunished.

"Leaflets appeared, tacked to tree trunks, screaming about 'hordes of Chukers,' 'shanty Chukes,' and 'cheap Chigger labor,' and 'No Chukes Allowed.' A local newspaper editorial bleatingly decried 'the Chugran peril,' and opined that the last thing they needed in bucolic Maryland, with its gracious horse farms, was a 'mob of Bochunks,' dirtying up the place.

"The usual physical harassments occurred.

"Why usual? Because the 'good' people said nothing.

"And what was 'the usual?'

"Cars driving by with shotguns and rifles branching out the windows at odd angles, shattering the still country air, with their blasts of welcome. Trash dumped in Chugran yards. Chugrans shoved off of sidewalks. The occasional rape, unprosecuted.

"The local Negro population said nothing. Occupying their own world, all over rural Maryland in unseen pockets and enclaves, eking out an existence where and as they could, excluded by most of 'white' Maryland from most of public view, they had no desire to come to the succor of these newer wretcheds, when they were hard pressed even to provide for their own. It would be comforting to hear that – persecuted so long themselves – they became the shield for these newly arrived unfortunate ones. Alas, they did not…

"It would be especially reassuring since the Chugrans were in certain ways similar.

"But, then, they were similar to so many people on earth.

"And, again, they seemed so different.

"So, late in the nineteenth century, some farseeing Chugrans created the Schaal Chugrana here in Maryland. And one of the first things they did was to emblazon the front door of their first building with a sign: 'Let Mind Speak to Mind.'

"As the years went on, the newer Chugrans who departed Chugrana and those who had already spread out elsewhere in the U. S. supported it with pride and enthusiasm. In Chugrana, as I have explained, a Schaal might be so modest an endeavor as a single instructor teaching a child a single thing. But here, they went all the way – a full school from first through twelfth grades. And they made it rigorous. They wanted no halfway measures, no mere 'enrichment,' but hard-core, demanding instruction. And they held the children to it. Anyone who misbehaved, for example, was out the door – and their parents ostracized. That happened rarely.

"Their academic standard was so high that graduates of the Schaal Chugrana did extremely well in college – once the colleges admitted them. When word of this filtered around, the Schaal even had some non-Chugran parents ask if their children could attend. And, for a brief time, they allowed it. They were, during those days quite open to such things. They were a small school, and dedicated to their own Chugran community to be sure, but in the name 'Schaal Chugrana' the greater word was 'Schaal.' They *happened* to be Chugrans struggling to make a success of their lives, as people all over do, but the education of children was the supreme value. They were happy to take in a few non-Chugrans who were bright – I would even say they were proud that their school was so regarded.

"But that was all some time back. By the time the two Churai boys arrived, a new tone had crept in. It was like sewage seeping from the septic tank of the whole culture of that time. 'Chugran pride,' and 'Chugran awareness,' and 'Chugran-ness,' and 'Chugritude.' You've heard it all, and not just for Chugrans.

"As if the older Chugrans hadn't had *pride*, they who under the worst of degradation had borne themselves with the dignity of kings and queens.

"The specific conduits for this sewage were certain of the faculty.

"There is no doubt that Ku was one of these, but only one. At any rate, by the time Braq and Nollo arrived, the 'Movement,' as some liked to call it, had begun. Some of the students were now wearing Chugran clothes, and at lunchtime ate Chugran food, and sang Chugran songs. Most of this stuff had disappeared from the Chugran American community in the days of their great great grandparents – especially as many of these had intermarried with the population at large. Now the students indulged these ethnic peculiarities with an air of vindictiveness, as if the residents of Maryland, or even America as a whole, had forbidden them. But of course it was just that their great great grandparents had decided that all this hand clapping and foot stomping to ancient tunes, after donning the tiresome tunics, was perhaps just not worth preserving year after year. Many of these students now being dipped in the dye of Chugritude also belonged to one sect or another of the Chugran religion, and wore *its* symbols. And then there were the half-hearted who might wear a shirt or dress of Chugran design, but engage in nothing else.

"Some participated in none of this. *Their* parents were disturbed that the Schaal seemed to be instilling a kind of murky tribalism within the children. But these parents tended to be the less vocal ones.

"The Schaal Chugrana had its own miniature culture war going on now.

"That first day the two boys – newest of Chugran émigrés – were shown around and endured the gawking of the students. They only stayed a short time before going on to Jule's and Rodit's home nearby in the Chugran neighborhood. Some people had taken to calling the area – that is, the small community and the Schaal – 'the village.' As if they were all living in some thatched hut enclosure or other in the middle of rice paddies. Most of them, of course, had never in their lives seen such a thing as a 'village'.

"When, on the next day, the two boys returned for their first full day of school, Braq was hit with the full force of what Pranti Ku had christened, 'Chugranata.'

"Many of the students wore brazen racial markers, a tunic, a cap or hat, a scarf, a necklace. Even the expressions on the faces of these children – *children!* – impressionable and anxious to impress – was emblematic. There was a self-consciously militant yet unselfconfident atmosphere of mutual comparison. The militancy was indicated by pouting, clenched, and faintly bellicose mouths. The lack of confidence by eyes darting left and right to test the reactions of the other children.

"Even in Chugrana at its worst, Braq had never felt such an unsettling atmosphere. When his Uncles, Rodit and Jonni, raised an issue which became the subject of a haranguing debate with his father, the temperature rose indeed. But before and after life went on. Yes, Chugrans had to be careful not to transgress Dryruger restrictions, but so long as they heeded these, the rest of their hours and days were pretty much filled up with the normal concerns of people everywhere. They were not submerged, saturated, enveloped, smothered in – race.

"For this reason, as the days went on, Braq found that his lone enjoyable class at the Schaal was arithmetic. Only here did the issue of race vanish, and a clean clear object to study stand before his bright mind. It helped that the arithmetic teacher was not a supporter of 'Chugranata,' but just seemed like – a plain human being.

"On the other hand, his least favorite class – well, the way he put it to me was, 'the class I hated was Ku's 'Chugranata.'

"This was an 'interdisciplinary' field of allegedly scholarly scientific inquiry Ku had himself invented, or 'discovered.' It covered a little of Chugran history, a little linguistics, some politics, a lot of theology, some sociology, some outrageous and unverifiable autobiography – all wrapped up in Pranti Ku's flamboyant personality. He even got a couple of articles published by journals eager to appear racially 'tolerant' and 'inclusive,' and who were also terrified of being accused by their peers of being racially insensitive. So they assisted Ku in smutching the shield of academic research.

"These articles tried to prove – well, 'prove' is the wrong word – all kinds of exaggerated things about Chugran history and Chugran accomplishments. It was not for Ku to be satisfied with detailing the modest mathematical or astronomical or musical achievements of a handful of ancient Chugrans. He had to say things like, 'It isn't at all clear that Archimedes, centuries before Rome was invaded by the Aryan Otoliths, was not a Chugran. After all, we have only the reports of white European and American 'scholars' to say otherwise.'

"Incidentally, he made his 'scholarly' article even worse by deliberately but inconsistently lapsing into that silly archaic Chugran mode of telling a story. So he would suddenly say things like 'And Chugrans will invent the diatomic musical scale.' He would go on in that strange future tense for a while, then get tired of it or confused even in his own writing, and suddenly he would be speaking in the past tense again.

"Braq said he even heard him do this kind of thing in front of his own class, and that Ku was oblivious to the fact that the boys laughed at him behind his back for it.

"When he was criticized for this, he replied, in a later issue of the journal which had published him, that his critics were only showing their cultural insensitivity and proving how impossible it was for 'two such different peoples' to understand each other. This was a point he returned to often.

"But the fact is that no one could explain just what he was talking about in these articles. They were just so much soup of Ku.

"Ku often lashed out this way at his homeland – you understand I mean America. Oh, yes! There's no doubt that he was born here, however much he tried to suggest otherwise, although his *parents* were from Chugrana. His lashings seemed so reasonable, looked at a certain way. But he took every act of discrimination – whether against blacks, or Jews, or Asians, or anyone at all – as equivalent to persecution of Chugrans.

" 'The white establishment has been content for all the darker children of the world to grow up ingesting corn pone and chilblains, regardless of the effect on their health – has allowed them to bathe in unsanitary streams where they develop tricky noses and are deformed for life.' (Yes, he actually said this, in print! But woe to anyone who tried to correct his abuse of English. They would be accused of that moral atrocity: racial insensitivity.)

"But what he really could not forgive was the fact that America – everyone in America – did not bestow laurels on him for merely being a Chugran. He could not stomach the fact that, to achieve respect, he would have to be – an achiever.

"When the two boys enrolled in the Schaal, Ku was ecstatic. Here were two fresh émigrés from 'the true homeland' – 'the Chugran patriae' he called it. 'Victims of oppression' he gushed unctuously to the class. And victims they certainly were. Who could deny it?

"But, as usual, he couldn't rest with a simple statement of fact, or of a simple statement of value. No, Nollo and Braq were 'true Chugrans,' 'authentic,' even 'unmixed, regal blood.' (He just blatantly sailed over Braq's maternal parentage, for the time being. Later he would make quite an issue of it.) And now, with Nollo and Braq standing there in front of the class, he launched into one of his obscure linguistic derivations, alleging that both 'Churai' and 'Chugran' came from an 'ancient stem,'

'Chu(g)–' (he wrote this on the blackboard) meaning, he claimed, 'man' or 'human.' Also, he said, some scholars believed it might mean 'real people,' 'true people,' 'authentic,' or 'chosen.'

"And, without batting an eye, he said, 'Another form of the stem is – ' and here he wrote on the board, 'Ku.'

"Of course, there were no such scholars. He just made it all up on the spot.

"Nollo was elated at all this attention and at Ku's blather. With Ku – with everything about Ku – he felt, somehow, at home. I don't think he was ever *taken in* by him. If anything the contrary. But he was the kind of person Nollo wanted.

"Braq, on the other hand, was stupefied by Ku's appearance and baffled by his behavior and words. As to the appearance, he told me that he thought Ku was made up for some grotesque theatrical performance – Braq didn't know then about all of the surgery – and he was dismayed to see day after day that this was Ku's 'normal' look.

"But there was no way under heaven that Braq could ever become one of Ku's protégés as Nollo did.

"One day, after they had been there awhile, during one of his classes, which was made up of children of different grades, Ku brought up the matter of the tunics some of the children were wearing at Ku's instigation. By now, Nollo had started wearing one too, but Braq had not. Ku looked over the class and said, 'So inspiring! To see so many of you declaring that you belong to the Race. The Race is proud of you. It would like to be proud of *all* of you.'

"As he said this last, he looked somewhat sternly at Braq. Then he went on, his eyes narrowing reflectively, 'So many Chugrans intermarry. Gradually our gene pool is being filtered into every other race. And since we were not numerous to begin with, soon – no more Chugran Race. We will have disappeared. The rapes by the slave masters, and the voluntary intermarriage by our own people will extinguish us. The genocide that began with murder will end with sex.'

"Braq raised his hand. He said, 'Well, then we will just be people – humans – right?'

"Ku got very hot. 'No! That's terrible! We Chugrans – ' here he smacked his thick chest '– will have no identity. We must belong to our own people!' He practically shouted this at Braq. He was standing now directly in front of the boy. But Braq had this derangement in his soul, that when someone said 'Chugran,' he thought first of Zaq. Ku's implication that Braq and Nollo should think of *Ku* as an exemplar of 'the Race' struck Braq as fantastic and inconceivable. But there was an even more fundamental barrier to his acceptance of the claim Ku had just made.

"When Ku said, 'We must belong to our people,' Braq answered with these words: 'I belong to *me*.'

"If Ku wasn't already suspicious by now of how the land lay, I'm sure this statement set all of his antennae twitching.

"Ku drew himself up and said, 'That is the white man – or perhaps the white woman – talking. The white man's philosophy. The white corruption. *Selfishness* – the white way of thinking.'

"But Braq would have none of this. And, fresh from arithmetic class and the arithmetic teacher, he said to Ku, 'Don't Chugrans and whites both believe that two plus two is four?'

"Taken aback by this youthful Socratic interrogatory, Ku could only reply, 'Yes.'

" 'And when Chugrans and whites draw, don't they hold their chalk with hands and fingers that are the same?'

"(My guess is that Braq, a Chugran born, had heard the Shakespeare-an cadences, had probably heard the very words, 'If you prick us do we not bleed…?' Whether or not, he was heading for the same point.)

" 'And when my beloved father says he loves me, does he mean something different from a white father? Or from my white mother?'

"Here he had called up strong artillery indeed, because even Ku knew and had to respect the name of Zaqqaq Churai. He had even spoken, with pontifical praise, of Zaq during one of his classes. Nonetheless, he retorted lamely, 'White people and our people do *not* see the world the same way. There is great and mutual repulsion between us.'

"Braq said nothing to this, and Ku pressed his point: 'How do you explain that, if we are all one?'

"Braq thought for a minute, and while he was reflecting, Ku added this: 'Someone is working on you, Braq – you may not know it, but someone is corrupting you.'

"Braq was so incensed. Ku was, as it appeared to the boy, implying that Braq had no ideas of his own, that he could not think for himself – that some 'outside influence' was governing him. He immediately shot back, 'Maybe the mutual repulsion comes from bad ideas from our teachers.'

"Ku, a pout on his mug, stiffened. Then he leaned his offensive bulk over Braq and said tartly, his nose pinched up, the blotchy face even more hectic, 'Do you mean me?'

"But Braq could be very stubborn. He just stared back at this grotesque mask that was trying to intimidate him. He gave a short shrug. You might have thought an eight year old would be cowed by this blustering behemoth, but he wasn't.

"He told me later, 'I just couldn't take him seriously. He didn't seem like something real.'

"I loved this boy for that kind of thing – and I was sometimes afraid for him too. Ku was, you must understand, not innocuous."

***

The exchange between Braq and Ku had caused someone else consternation too. Nollo, sitting in the class with Braq, saw his brother raise his hand to challenge Ku. Nollo clamped his lips shut in irritated anticipation. He thought, "Oh, no! There he goes, he's doing it!" What "it" was he didn't know, but another thought flashed through his mind – "Why does he have to be different? Why does he have to shame me in front of my own…group of people?!"

CHAPTER 28

Never the Twain

When Braq and Nollo first came to the Schaal and Ku found out who they were – Zaqqaq Churai's two sons – he tried to ferret out everything he could about the boys, about Zaq, about their uncles, and about what was going on in Chugrana. Of course, the boys knew very little, Braq especially. Nollo pretended to be a big shot, but Ku could tell that he really knew next to nothing.

He made the boys tell over and over the story of their escape, both for its inherent drama and because it gave him more openings to cross examine them on who had made it possible. It seemed of special importance to him, so detailed were his questions. Unfortunately for Ku, they could give him few details. They did not know the name of the man who had taken them from their mother and driven them into the hills, what kind of airplane or airline it might have been, or the name of the pilot or the steward, or any of the other people along their route who aided in their escape. The two children might as well have been parcels, so efficiently anonymous had been the machinery of their conveyance from catastrophe to safety.

During one of these interrogations, Ku asked, "Did you encounter Vasc Sulam?"

The boys shook their heads, although Nollo added, "I've heard that name."

"When?" asked Ku.

Nollo was unsure. "Maybe from father. Or Uncle Rodit."

Ku finally let the matter drop.

Later that day, the president of the Schaal, Pakker Carroll, in his office, head down, felt a presence. Carroll was studying a report. He was concentrating intently, but he suddenly felt it. Without looking up, he knew who it was – that damned Ku!

President Carroll was not a mystic, he did not believe in extra-sensory perception. Nonetheless he wondered how he had intuited that Ku was standing in the doorway. Well, the obvious answer was that this is what Ku always did. It was so annoying. He did not knock, or clear his throat, or shuffle his feet to make a noise. Suddenly his bulk was just there, filling up the opening of the door silently. It wasn't threatening, exactly. It couldn't really be called rude. It seemed, in some perverse way, to be respectful. Yet it also seemed to demand that the other person surrender his time and attention.

Finally, his concentration broken, Carroll looked up. "Yes, Pranti?"

"I didn't want to disturb you," said Ku, moving now fully into the room.

Carroll said, resignedly, "No, no, go ahead."

Ku planted his mass on the two stanchions of his legs near one corner of the president's desk. As he spoke, his hands flapped limply and spasmodically up and down on his stomach like freshly caught fish on the deck of a fishing boat.

"I finally got an appointment with his high and mightiness, Vasc Sulam."

Carroll objected weakly, "I wish you wouldn't refer to him that way. He's been a big source of support in the past."

"In the *past*," emphasized Ku. "But not for some time now. I guess he's gotten too independent of us lowly Chukes."

Carroll winced. He hated that word, even when it was used by other Chugrans. It seemed to denote a kind of self-contempt, even though such people protested that they only used it sarcastically. But he wasn't going to get into that again with Ku today. President Carroll had a sculpted, patrician head, and a dignified bearing at all times. His clothes were neat and immaculate if somewhat threadbare and out of date. "When is your appointment?" he asked Ku.

"Tomorrow. I was given no choice in the matter. A royal edict. Tomorrow at eleven a.m. in Delaware, at his corporate headquarters."

Carroll asked, "What exactly did he say?"

"Oh, you don't think I got to speak to his highness himself do you? His secretary said, 'Mr. Sulam can see you at eleven o'clock tomorrow morning. Then he's leaving the country.'"

Ku imitated the secretary's voice with a sneer of condescension, as if it was an insult to him that a person might be "out of the country," when Ku was there requesting an interview. Or for any reason, really. As if people would be better off staying put just for his benefit.

"Well," said Carroll, "I wish you well. God knows we need the money. And he's got it."

"Yes!" exclaimed Ku, "and off the backs of his fellow Chugrans – not to mention countless other exploited races."

Carroll rushed to interrupt Ku. "Whatever you do, don't take that tack with him. You'll get nowhere!"

"I know, I know," said Ku. "Not to worry. Eggshells. I'll walk on eggshells. I'll take this abasement on myself – for the sake of the Schaal, and for the sake of the Chugrans. Worms won't melt in my mouth."

Carroll squirmed. He wished Ku wouldn't go on this way. It was just a matter of asking for a donation! Why did Ku have to turn it into the Exodus from Egypt?

"Was there anything else, Pranti?" asked the president.

"Yes," said Ku, obviously in no hurry to leave.

"I've been speaking to the Churai boys. Nollo is going to be a great asset to us, he's just such a pure Chugran. I've asked him to spearhead the plantchi project."

"The – what?" asked Carroll.

Ku stared at the president imperturbably. This was his brand new little idea, but what he said was, "Surely you remember discussing the fact that so many of the boys want to learn how to play plantchi – their revered game that was stolen from them here in America and replaced by this white boys' game of baseball."

Carroll fell once more into an objection, knowing as he did that there would be no end to this discussion if he pressed the matter. Such discussions with Ku never produced any enlightenment or agreement, only an eventual concession by Ku's adversary just to avoid a scene. As the words were escaping his lips, he was kicking himself. "Well, surely, baseball is played by all kinds of people, not just whites?"

"Yes," conceded Ku rhetorically. "After they first genocidally obliterate those peoples' own indigenous sports. Then they suck them into the common stew, so they can pretend to be tolerant."

Carroll wanted to drop the whole unsavory discussion. Besides, he had no recollection of any such conversation as Ku alluded to. The fact was that only one boy had expressed any such interest in plantchi and then only after some heavy-handed hinting from Ku. Now, Pranti Ku launched the suggestion at President Carroll as if there were a tidal wave of interest in this "neglected" sport.

"And it will serve as another large brick in the wall of their renewing pride in the culture of Chugrana, in the edifice of self-respect we are restoring in them" he intoned pompously.

Carroll thought back to the time when *he* had been a student at the Schaal, and he and his classmates had proudly graduated and gone on to productive careers. They had been eager and hopeful – with no lack of self-respect, even without the concept of "Chugranata." What had changed, he wondered. Who had made it happen?

Ku went on. "The problem is with the equipment. It's almost impossible to find the plantchi rods and plamballs here. But I have in mind that Sulam may be able to help us. With all of his contacts."

President Carroll nodded somewhat uncertainly. "Just make sure that you keep to the major issue of his donation."

Ku sighed as he prepared to heave his bulk into the effort of leaving the office. "Yes – it's a shame and a disgrace that we have to go hat in hand to these predators, begging for alms. If this were a just society, the funds to preserve our unique culture would be on the doorstep already."

With relief, President Carroll at last watched Ku's form exit, bulging, through the doorway.

The next morning, a complacent toll-taker in one of the tollbooths on the great north-south highway that linked the cities of the east coast was startled out of her wits when a small car pulled up to her booth. The car window came halfway down in jerks of irritation and a large motley face ringed by a mangy balloon of hair glared out of a small opening. The occupant of the car was struggling to get at the money in his pocket, but he was so squashed into the tiny car by his girth that he was having great difficulty. The car rocked from side to side as the driver squirmed inside his oubliette. Finally a hand slithered out the window in her direction, waving a bill petulantly.

The toll-taker made change and then watched in disbelief as the seething capsule slowly gathered speed again and finally disappeared to the north.

Ku was genuinely affronted that he should have to go through such humiliations as this. Why couldn't he have a limousine like any proper executive – probably like Sulam, for example? Why couldn't his way be paved for him? Just in general, why didn't the world give him what was coming to him?

And why wasn't Sulam coming to see Ku instead of the other way around? Who was he anyway?

Vasc Sulam was born in Chugrana, parentage commonplace. His childhood and adolescence were unremarkable, although if you *had* paid attention to him, which few did, you would have noticed that he had a kind of obsession about Chugran cloth. His curiosity about it was insatiable. By his mid-teens, Vasc could have told you every design, every color combination, what types of threads and how many in the weave, what kinds of dyes and where they came from, how the weaving was done, what types of archaic looms and methods were used, how long each weaver worked and how laborious he or she found it, who cut the cloth, who transported it, how the middlemen conveyed it to the end users, what those fabricators did with it – a profusion of skirts, shirts, scarves, robes, tunics, headdresses. He also could have told you the cost at each stage. He knew all of this in part because by this time he had become a middleman himself. A teenager, his comprehensive curiosity nonetheless gave him the knowledge of someone who had been in the business for years. He recognized bargains and bought them. This, among the many groups he dealt with, led eventually to a reputation for shrewdness. Which is another way of saying that it led to envy. Which is another way of saying that it led to hatred. Each tribe, clan, or village resented the fact that Vasc did not give them a better deal than he gave the next tribe, clan, or village. Of course, they really didn't know – rumors and lies were rife in such things, and they just *thought* he must be paying more to the next village, or tribe – which lied anyway about what *it* had received, just as the first village or tribe did. What really made them nasty was that Vasc bypassed their clannish leadership front, and went to each weaver's place to inspect individual work. He talked to individual workmen *about* their work, which they enjoyed. But one did not do this. One bought only from the council house where everyone brought their work, to be turned over to the supervision of the council. Vasc did not go so far as to try to buy directly from individuals – that could have gotten him killed. But he filed away in his head the exact names and locations of the best weavers.

Actually, the only thing that overcame the chiefs' resentment of his whole manner was his *whole* manner. He was scrupulously accurate, honest, and responsible about money. He gave credit to the creditworthy – and he knew who such people were. He knew to the penny margin what price would overcome suspicion and resentment, and he paid no more than that marginal penny.

In short, by the age of seventeen, Vasc was a consummate businessman. He would have been a big success on the Silk Road, or dealing with spices in Renaissance Venice, or trading in dry goods in 1850 Chicago.

Then, for a couple of years, no one saw him in Chugrana. Sulam had gone to the U. S. and hired out as a low level worker in the garment industry. By the end of his second year, he knew most of what was worth knowing about the way this industry worked in America. He sank his earnings from his years in Chugrana into his own company, in partnership with an American who was adept at jumping the numerous legal hurdles, although for an American businessman these hurdles were trivial in comparison to those within Chugrana itself, or, for that matter, most countries. After a few more years, Sulam had bought out the partner, and become an American citizen.

By now he had some of the best weavers in Chugrana working for him. No one knew quite how he accomplished this. One day the weavers of a tribe would be going about their business as they had forever; the next day they found one of their benches empty. It had belonged to their most skillful and productive weaver. The same happened with the cutters, and the men and women who supervised the dyeing.

Their passage from Chugrana to America was also a mystery. Emigration was tightly controlled in those days, but it made no matter. It was as if a genie had whisked them away, suddenly to appear in the States, properly documented for the authorities. They became not the low-level workers but the supervisors and foremen and women of automated plants Sulam built all through the South and West. Already speaking a brand of English, quaint though it may have sounded, the language was not a problem.

Some of the river of cloth that flowed from these plants went to American markets, in the form of cheap bags or fashionable accessories. The most popular line was the dresses, or "frocks," modeled after those worn by the Chugran women – simple in design, with brilliant gemlike colors, they caught the motion of the women's' legs, swirling like an Arabian veil around calf and thigh. They were easy to wear, and intoxicating to watch. Since America was heading into the look known as "grunge," these dresses were less popular there. Elsewhere in the world, and especially in Europe, they sold very well. In time, Sulam reduced the U. S. manufacturers, replacing them with more efficient and economical plants in various parts of the world.

Outsiders accused Sulam of running a "Chugran Mafia." It was not strong-arm tactics that brought his phenomenal success though it may well have been the tactics of a strong mind. He did have a substantial core of Chugran employees because they had started with him in the early days. They formed his cadre of management. Having hired with good judgment, many were still with him. As he ventured into further regions of the world, others came on board, if they knew their stuff. It sometimes happened that he needed people who knew the local language and customs. He hired them not out of "ethnic fairness," but because their "ethnicity" was of use to him. His only criterion was: "Can this person do the job for me?"

His chief financial officer was a Chinese from Guangdong, his marketing chief a Gujarati from India. Unlike the tribal chiefs of Sulam's childhood, and unlike the race, caste, and clan societies they all came from, Sulam's chiefs – corporate officers – had not come by their positions through the coercive totem of blood and family.

Sulam's private secretary on the other hand was a mongrel made up of about six nationalities – well, to be exact, he was an American.

Producers in the Deep South chaffed Sulam for not joining them in lobbying for tariffs to protect them. Chugrans in the garment trade screeched because he did not locate his factories in Chugrana. Chugran activists in the U.S. joined in the din because he did not invest in the "Chugran community" or its banks. He was vilified by non-Chugrans for "hiring only Chugrans," and by Chugrans for "hiring non-Chugrans" and thereby "betraying the Race." He was attacked by unions and by various state governments for moving his operations to lower cost countries. In the meantime, Sulam's enterprises now employed over one hundred thousand workers worldwide. In each country they received higher than that country's prevailing wage. Sulam wanted and got the best workers available. There were long waiting lists of prospective employees.

Sulam dealt with all of his yammering critics only through his lawyers. He had never made a public appearance. Since he had no stockholders save himself, he held no public meetings. Outside of a few industry insiders, not many people knew the name or the man behind these enterprises. Fewer still knew that Vasc Sulam was one of the richest men in the world.

Only the smallest handful knew that the Underground Railroad, which spirited people out of the tyranny that was Chugrana, was Sulam's personal creation. Braq and Nollo were passengers on this railroad. Sulam had been all too happy to help these particular refugees. His tie to Zaqqaq Churai was of long standing. It was Sulam who had financed the printing equipment of the Sovereign. It was also Sulam who, from his network of contacts, had learned in advance of the danger to Zaq's family, and alerted him. At this time, he had offered his services to Zaq in getting his family out. He understood and respected Zaq's and Liz's decisions to stay. He kept open the escape hatch for the children.

On the other hand he had earlier declined Rodit Churai's overture to do business with him: he knew that Rodit was an incompetent, and that to deal with him would be a complete waste of time and money.

Once, Sulam had made a generous bequest to the Schaal Chugrana. This was fifteen years before the time of Ku's trip to Delaware, when the Schaal still held to academic standards that were the envy of every school in central Maryland. He had made none since then.

Now, Pranti Ku pulled his car into the parking lot, glanced once more at his watch, and noted indifferently how late he was. Well, it wouldn't be the first time he had made people wait for him. And two could play this game of condescension. He looked forward to plopping himself in the great Sulam's office and applying his cajoling suasions. He strolled into the office complex. He could not tell if these buildings belonged to Sulam, or one of his corporations, or someone else altogether. He really knew nothing of "the ways of capitalists"; *that* was a tribe utterly foreign to Ku. He found the office number he was looking for, but he saw no name on the plain door. The reception room was also quite bare, with one secretary who looked up as he came in. He immediately checked out her race, but he could not tell if she was a Chugran or not. "Perhaps," he thought, "some kind of mixed breed – wouldn't you know."

She did not give him the usual satisfaction of being startled at his appearance, but barely raised an eyebrow as she asked, no more than if he were a deliveryman, "May I help you?"

Miffed, Ku flapped a palm at her. "I have an appointment to see Mr. Sulam."

Still matter of fact, the secretary said, "Name?"

"Pranti Ku," he said with annoyance. From the side of his stomach, he flapped another hand at her desk. "I'm sure you have me down there somewhere."

"Yes, Mr. Ku, but you're twenty minutes late. Mr. Sulam is on his way out now. He just went to his limo for the airport. He said if you arrived in time, you could ride with him to the airport, and his driver will bring you back here."

She had risen and was gesturing him to the door. Ku was furious at being shamed in this way. In the first place, what was some stupid twenty minutes?! And how dare this woman – this woman! – and her grubby boss treat him this way? The disrespect was colossal. He was tempted to storm out. But the Schaal needed the money. He turned, and stumped after the young woman down a long corridor. He was flabbergasted. She actually had the nerve to look back at him at one point and say, "We have to hurry if we're going to catch him."

He was sweating as they burst through a door to the outside, and she waved to stop the limo that was just pulling away. Feeling foolish and demeaned, Ku ducked his head and stepped into the limousine. The door closed behind him, and he barely had time to sit on the seat facing backward toward Sulam as they sped away.

The man Ku found himself facing was lean and slight of bone, a small man of whom, perhaps, three could have fit into Ku. From a gaunt face, the darkest he had ever seen, large eyes bored into Ku. Sulam's slender fingers were held, arrested, above a keyboard on his lap, a modern piece of equipment Ku had never seen. Sulam's hands waited in midair as if Ku might disappear and Sulam could return to the work from which he had been interrupted.

Beside Sulam sat a man holding a notepad and pen, waiting for Sulam's instructions. Ku noted the man's light skin color, but could not determine his nationality.

"Couldn't you have waited?" puffed Ku, still out of breath.

Sulam let a moment pass, during which Ku felt a prickle go up his neck. Then, Sulam said, "No."

His voice was deep and resonant, penetrating even over the hum of the car. "I suggest we get down to business. We will be at the airport in just a few minutes. Then I must leave you."

Ku swallowed his pride and humiliation. He began, "I am here on behalf of our beloved Schaal Chugrana, the institution that is the guarantor of the life of the Chugran people in America."

Sulam cut off this stream. "Graduates of the Schaal now score in the lowest rank of applicants to the state colleges. They used to score at the top."

Ku floundered a reply. "Yes, well, that's why we need more money, to help enrich…"

Sulam cut in again. "The scores began dropping when the curriculum was 'enriched' by all these academic frauds like 'Chugranata.' And – are you the Ku who said that Archimedes was a Chugran?"

Ku flapped both of his hands dismissively. "*Might* have been a Chugran, *might* have been. But I don't see why we should go into that now…?"

Sulam said shortly, "No, we shouldn't. Ever."

Ku felt humiliated that Sulam was taking this tone in front of "the white man," if that is what he was. He tried to regain a ground he had never held. "But how can you turn your back on the Chugran people and its traditions? Especially on the Schaal – 'Let mind speak to mind,' after all."

Sulam answered, his eyes unrelenting. "I understand that you have installed a new sign above the main entrance door – below the one that says, 'Let Mind Speak to Mind,' – that the new sign says 'Let Race Speak to Race.'"

"Damn!" thought Ku. Sulam was up on everything. Ku had just had the sign nailed in place a few days ago.

He said, his voice beginning to rise, "The Chugran race has a message for the world. Our Race must be allowed to speak that message to the white race!"

Sulam said, "You mean *you* must be allowed to speak, as if *your* message was that of every Chugran. It isn't."

They were pulling into an access road of the airport now, and Ku felt his anxiety increasing. This was not going at all as he had anticipated. There was almost no time left. He had to bring up the plantchi matter. He didn't know why, but he felt urgently that he had to.

"Won't you at least consider a grant to help us acquire the equipment for the restoration of plantchi to these children? They voted unanimously for it."

(This was even more brazen than the lie he had told President Carroll, but these kinds of things just slipped out of Ku. He couldn't help himself. He knew no other way of speaking. Besides, he saw no great difference between 'one child,' 'some children,' and 'all children.')

Sulam said simply, "No." Desperately, Ku felt as if Sulam's attention was now receding from him, as if he, Ku, were a phantom becoming ever more ethereal to Sulam.

Ku whined supplicatingly, "Won't you even help us to *locate* a supplier for the plantchi rods and plamballs? They're hard to get."

Sulam's eyes flashed. Afterwards, Ku reflected that he had never felt in such danger in his entire life as in this moment. But Sulam's steely voice was low as he said, "When you've restored the academic standing of the Schaal, you can come talk to me of those damned sticks and balls."

In only a few seconds the limousine had come to a stop and Sulam was out the door followed by his secretary with not so much as a further word to his visitor. Pranti Ku was still gaping out the open door, one limp hand hanging in front of his stomach, a sentence stuck in his throat. The driver shut the door and took him back to the office parking lot.

When he returned home, and over the next few days, Ku put the finishing touches on an article he was preparing for the Journal of Racial Studies. The article was entitled, "Eminent Chugrans of the Twentieth Century." Though he very modestly stated point-blank that he would not put his own name in this list, as if anyone would have suggested such a thing, he nonetheless managed to sprinkle the article with many irrelevant details of his own life. He included a small entry on Zaqqaq Churai, including misquotations from Zaq's speeches.

His article made no mention of Vasc Sulam.

Over these several days, Ku found himself muttering under his breath, more than once, "I must speak to Mister Menzies."

CHAPTER 29
Humanitarians

Pranti Ku arose early this spring morning so that he could be one of the first to arrive. He punished his little car through the Washington suburbs, oblivious to a Maryland countryside busy with the purposes of man and nature. Ku had purposes too. For one thing, he wanted to get there before the others so he could park his decrepit auto in the back of the building and avoid the shameful comparison to his fellow board members, pulling up in their chauffeured limousines. More importantly, he wanted his pick of seats in the Board room.

As the Board members of Suffer the Little Children entered the luxuriously furnished room, Ku was happy to see that Asa Menzies was present for a change; he had missed the last several meetings. Ku contrived to sit beside Menzies, who was occupying his preferred seat at one end of the conference table. Menzies returned Ku's fulsome smile of greeting with a complacent nod of his head. Ku wanted to be able to keep Menzies in view, to chat with him, and simply to be ready to take advantage of any little opportunity that might arise.

It did not take long for the Board to get into one of its unpleasant fracases. "Oh, God! There goes that damned son of a bitch, Antilles!" thought Ku. "Why is he even here? Why doesn't he just drop out?" He felt that Antilles didn't belong, that Antilles' way of approaching things came from a different way of thinking.

Lew Antilles had proposed that Suffer the Little Children declare its support for a boycott of the Sulagasy Republic, another petty tyranny like Chugrana, located in a similarly remote fastness. Even the way he spoke of it was offensive to Ku. Running a hand through his ash blonde hair in a gesture of exasperation, Antilles described it as "this primitive country which at the end of the twentieth century still engages in the practice of slavery in its God-forsaken corner of the globe."

Ku jumped into the fray. "Don't you think it's condescending and egotistical for us to call another country 'primitive'? Are you suggesting that we are superior to others?"

Antilles answered him. "I think a country such as ours which proclaims the rights of the individual is superior to one which has never heard of rights. I think a country that protects rights is superior to one which practices slavery. I think a country which upholds objective laws is superior to one whose law is nothing more than the dictator's latest whim. And I think, if we really care about 'the Little Children,' that we should work to ensure every citizen of Sulagasy the same *selfish* right to life that we have. I, therefore, move that we declare our support for our government's boycott of Sulagasy until they end slavery."

There was a welter of arms and hands seeking recognition in order to attack Antilles' proposal. "It is not our job to dabble in politics." "We care only about the welfare of the *children* of the tribes, not the national government." "It would be arrogant for us to impose our values on this unique race. Each race has its own idea of what it should be and how it should be governed." "Let them work out their own racial destiny, free of outside intervention."

Ku waded into the stream of invective against Antilles. What he brought up was not really germane, but Ku never scrupled to hijack a conversation. He ostentatiously removed a letter from an envelope, rested a pair of glasses on his nose, and, looking over the rims at the table, said, "This is a communication from one of our agencies which handles my own patriae, Chugrana. It concerns a pitiful girl," – he inspected the letter through his glasses – "one Astirpa Ming." He again looked over his glasses at the table, with an unaccountable air of belligerence, as if someone at the table was guilty of some personal affront to him. "She's a teenager – been in one of our orphanages for quite a time, the Merlikorn Orphanage in Fulon, but has yet to be adopted – allegedly because of our policy of race-matching, which, as you know, I strongly support...but really she's still stuck there because of the poor public spirit of some Chugrans."

Asa Menzies usually listened to Ku with boredom and, therefore, less than acute attention. But, at a certain point in Ku's blather, Asa's breathing had suddenly stopped. The muscles which automatically moved his lungs day in and out without conscious control had simply frozen, as if paralyzed.

Ku went on. "I think that some of us should remember that, as the saying has it 'Pride – Go west before the Fall.' Far from standing in such superiority to the less fortunate races of the world, I would think that some of us" – he looked at Antilles – "would remain quiet in humility, if not shame, at such tragedies as this poor girl's – another of the scourges of Chugrana, and its history of rape by the white slave masters, who have left thousands of orphans behind them, and thousands of innocent women forced into prostitution. This girl's mother was such a prostitute known only as" – he scanned the letter again – "Frinnie. The girl, Astirpa, thinks her father was white."

As Ku went on (with genuine pleasure because he loved to see the white Board members squirm), Asa saw the whole room go out of focus. Bright flashes of light jiggled in front of him – because his thumb had slipped off the side of his cheek bone and was gouging into the side of his left eye. This occupied only a couple of seconds. The pain finally broke through, and Asa began hectically rubbing his eye.

"Something wrong, Asa?" inquired Ku. His tone was not sarcastic, merely solicitous, but Asa knew that Ku was needling him.

"No, just something in my eye," he responded irritably.

Ku filed this moment away, and then finished the letter. He concluded, in a self-righteous tone, "I think the whites have done enough to torment and persecute my people. Every Chugran child should have the right to Chugran parents, a Chugran upbringing in a Chugran home. And we should stop trying to meddle in the affairs of each race, imposing arbitrary rules. We should let each one develop itself – develop its own racial essence. Above all, the Chugroid should not be forced to mix with the Aryoid or the Sinusoid."

There were several guffaws from around the table, but Antilles, ignoring Ku's racial needling and his outrageous neologisms, said calmly, "As to the Chugran girl, if you're assuming that one parent was 'white,' then the girl is just as much 'white' as she is 'Chugran'. Or are you accepting the traditional racist's 'one-drop rule?' which says that one drop of 'non-white blood' makes you 'non-white?' "

Looking up and down the table, he went on, "If I may bring us back to our previous discussion, as for not 'meddling,' if we were truly concerned with the welfare of the children, we would be passionate advocates of individual rights, capitalism, the freedom of the mind. *These* are what have lifted men's bodies and souls from the oppression of centuries, and produced the common man's wealth undreamed of by caliphs of old. What can we lose by adding our voice to all of those who are demanding that Sulagasy declare the unalienable rights of its citizens? That they do away with their internal passports that hamstring every individual. That they end emigration restrictions that entrap the whole population. Or at the very least that they get rid of their petty licensing laws which favor entrenched groups over the inventive individuals who could spark an economic explosion? For that matter, we should do the same thing with Chugrana too."

Another member responded with dismay, "We have never taken a stand like this before, and I don't see why we should now. We should be pragmatic and bend with the breezes of each country we have to deal with."

Antilles put this question to the man: "Shouldn't the individual in Sulagasy have the right to freedom of speech?"

The man replied, "Why do you think you have the absolute answer to everything? These principles should be malleable."

Antilles pressed him, "OK. Do you think *you* have the right to freedom of speech?"

The man spat back, "That's different!"

Ku jumped in. "All of this is irrelevant. Mr. Antilles' suggestion hasn't even been seconded, so by strict rules of order we shouldn't even be discussing it."

"Yes, Yes!" and "Here, here!" and "Let's follow some strict rules of order." All this burbled around the edges of the table from people who had never followed "rules of order" in their lives, and who a moment before had been eager supporters of pragmatic flexibility. The Chairman asked, "Are there any seconds?" No one on the Board wanted to discuss Antilles's proposal. They started to move on to other business. But Antilles stood up. A strand of hair fell across his forehead, and his cheeks were faintly pulled in scornfully. He said, "So this is what we stand for: 'To hell with the adults who are enslaved, tortured, and murdered – suffer the little children to come unto us to be fed and clothed so that they can grow up to be enslaved, tortured, and murdered by their government.'

"This is what it means to be a humanitarian today.

"Gentlemen, I'm resigning from *Suffer....* I'm going to find some other way to help the little children."

With that he walked out.

After Antilles shut the door behind him, Ku shrugged, and said sarcastically, "As for freedom of speech, it's too bad that *everyone* must be given that right."

The only person in the room who had not followed all of this was Asa Menzies. For the rest of the meeting, he kept hearing in his mind, like a murmured cadence, his name. Not the name the world knew him by, but a slightly different one. Now, as the meeting concluded, Menzies stood up to go. He started to put a hand up to his eye. Ku, at his elbow, said, ironically, "Is your eye still offending you Mister Menzies? Perhaps you'd better have it out?"

Menzies stared at Ku, trying to assess what this hateful individual might or might not know. He kept his own face impassive. "What do you mean?"

Ku said pedantically, " 'If thy right eye offend thee, pluck it out.' "

Annoyed, Menzies nonetheless shrugged and replied with a placid smile, "Nothing 'offends' me."

"Nothing? Perhaps whites have less conscience than I thought."

Menzies looked at Ku warily. He asked, "Now what?"

Ku replied, "Nothing more than what we have discussed before – atonement. The white races should make a substantial effort to reparate the harm they have done to the dark races. They should try to sanitize the scourges they have created."

The fact is that Ku knew absolutely nothing about Menzies' affairs in Chugrana. But he, grinning fulsomely, had an instinct for vulnerability, for weakness, for openings in men's armor.

"Dark institutions," he went on.

Menzies shifted his weight uneasily. He was disturbed by the implications of the phrase.

Ku continued. "The institutions of dark races need nurturing. Like the Schaal Chugrana. We lesser races fall by the waysides of the purse strings of benefactors."

Menzies began to relax. Perhaps this man was nothing more than a charlatan. "How much do you need?"

Ku answered, "Let's not say 'need.' Let's say, how much are we owed? And then leave it to your sense of generosity and justice."

Menzies sat down and took a checkbook from his briefcase. With a cold, gray expression, he made out a check. He stood up and handed it to Ku.

Ku caught his breath. He choked off a laugh before it could break out of his throat. The amount was far larger than anything he could have mustered the nerve to ask for. He wanted to snicker in Menzies' face. This check had to come not from generosity but from guilt, he thought. He appraised Menzies brazenly. He said, "President Carroll will be very happy to receive this. And all those little dark children will be blessed – by their white benefactor. Thank you, Mister Menzies."

CHAPTER 30

What's in a Name?

Jule Churai worried about Braq.

She realized now, a year and a half after their arrival, just how difficult a commitment she had made. And Jerule Churai took her responsibilities seriously. She had promised Liz and Zaq that she would take the best of care of the two boys, not out of a blind sense of duty to family, but because she genuinely loved and admired her brother-in-law and his wife, and their two children.

It was all well and good for Rodit to say his whole life long that family came first, that they all had to stick together, and watch out for each other. That had a nice, vague, warm sound to it. But when it came down to practicalities, how did it put bread on your table or a roof over your head? And at what price? Jule had had enough of this family tyranny, whose indenture never ended, in Chugrana. In practice, it meant that the freeloading relatives – and every family had some – whether lazy or incompetent, were forever spared the necessity of becoming productive. The able ones had to take up the slack. So it was, in practice, a one way street: only the able were required to conform to it.

Or worse. Jonni could become an unemployed bomb-thrower while Rodit was left to support him, and then to be implicated *as* his supporter.

And in the meantime, the very productivity of the able, that kept the family going, was hobbled by the constant necessity to consult, to request, to talk, to defer to the rest of the extended family. At first, she too had been critical of Zaq and his notorious independence, which included freedom from these chains forged by kith and kin. It was not something she had thought deeply about. Like most people the world over, Jule absorbed, imbibed, swallowed, accepted the norms of her own society without too much reflection.

But Jule had a sort of handicap in her character. What was this defect? Simply that she had a mind which could see the facts before her, and the course of action that would bring results. Such a mind, by its very nature, carries within it a certain amount of self-confidence. To see and to think are acts of assertion, even, at times, of courage. To say, "It is," may be a species of bravery. Especially when the world is full of people who make it their job to instill fear and reluctance in other people's minds.

A mind – reluctant to think! Such monstrosities may be manufactured. One way is to require those who can think to consult: "Respect the wishes of your family." Even when those wishes are irrational, even when they are destructive. In the crabbed world of Chugrana she had seen no way to surmount it. The crisis – the necessity to choose between his brothers, followed by the flight from Chugrana –that had crushed Rodit had lifted Jule up. Always the motor behind Rodit's success, such as it was, she could now make decisions on her own. There was no family to consult, no hanger-on relatives to get in the way or drain resources, no official edicts around which to warily dance.

Rodit himself did little now. Everything fell to Jule, and she exulted in it. Drawing on her years of helping Rodit behind the scenes, she now pooled everything – money, experience, savvy – and opened a store in a small shopping center not far from Annapolis. She called it, "The Chew Emporium."

Why "Chew?" Like countless immigrants before, Jule decided to appear as "American" as possible. What easier way than to begin with a name change? Immigration authorities used to do this for you at the country's gate, but many people elected their own transformation afterwards. And why was the name you were born with so important anyway? Important to whom? So "Churai" became "Chew," at least in the business's name. And her two children also endured a rebaptism. "Ma'rik" became "Mark." "Szu" became "Sue." The name "Jule," from "Jerule," was close enough to the American "Julia," or "Julie" to require no change. "Rodit" was definitely a problem, but the man who bore the name stayed out of the way, so it was never an issue.

As fluent English speakers, thank God, they didn't have to learn a new language. Only the accent and certain turns of speech were different, but this was a minor mark.

By five every morning, Jule was on her way to her Emporium, only ten minutes away from their home. At seven-thirty, she was back again to prepare breakfast for the family and see her children off to the local public school. Yes, the Schaal Chugrana was admirable, but she wanted her children to learn the ways of *this* country, not vegetate in old ways that they would probably never see again. Thus, over Rodit's objections she sent Mark and Sue to the public school. But when she told Zaq's boys that she might enroll them similarly, Nollo became furious. He insisted that they be allowed to attend the Schaal Chugrana. Jule relented. Braq, unsure what the difference might be between these two schools, followed his Big Brátano.

Every morning, having attended to the children, Jule with Rodit in tow was back at the store. She kept Rodit out of the public eye as much as possible, and, really, he was pretty useless. The mainspring of his motor had snapped. In Chugrana, everything this eldest of the Churai brothers did had been centered in his mind around the Churai family first, and, second, the Chugran people. Thinking of business matters independently, for himself, was something he had no experience in. If he sold so much as a sponge, in his mind the proceeds from that sponge were not just bare profit: whatever initiative he had shown was not his own self-contained action, all had redounded to the family and to his people.

Immigrants are typically described as "uprooted." But roots can find new soil. Rodit's roots hung exposed in air, unable to find soil, suitable. "Chew Emporium?" What was wrong with "Churai?" And what were these new sounds – "Mark?" "Sue?" Were these his children? There was something mystically sacred about a name, he thought. Names should not be changed. And why did not Jule confine herself to selling just within the local Chugran community? Why was she out on the main road, selling to everyone who came along? These breezy Americans who popped into the store – he didn't know them and they didn't know him. They didn't know and respect his family.

Mark and Sue, who came to work at the store after school, were unfazed by Jule's new role or the name changes or the new home. Rodit didn't know how they were able to change so quickly, but almost from the first they seemed just like other – Americans! Thus engrossed in their new lives, his family gave him little of the old feelings from Chugrana. The only one who struck these chords for him was his nephew – Nollo, the hero who had saved the floumiix from the fire. Rodit felt a pathetic nostalgia when he now heard Nollo evoke its twanging tones. Nollo who reminded him of his lost Museum. Who reminded him of his own brothers. Poor Jonni!

Braq, on the other hand, was no such provoker of consoling memories. He was just off somewhere, as he always had been, in his own world of drawing, and of being a child. What use was there in that? Certainly no use to the family! Rodit just did not know how to behave with the boy. Each day, late in the afternoon, Jule left the store to a trusted employee, drove Rodit home, and prepared dinner for the family. Then, leaving her two nephews, who had walked home from the Schaal, in Rodit's care, she and Mark and Sue returned to the store. Rodit was then supposed to supervise the boys.

They went out to play often, and that seemed OK. Or Braq went off to draw, and that was not OK. But Rodit's religious objections met no support from Jule. She gave him a sharp rebuke when he tried, feebly, to object to this "making of images." "We are caretakers of these children, not their parents," Jule said to her husband. "I promised Liz to do everything she would have done to promote and encourage Braq in his talents. If you're so big on family, I think you will honor that request, not get in its way." In the clash between Zaq and Jonni, he had – at the terrible cost of the unity of his soul – sided with Zaq. Now, Jule threw a new clash in his face – his religion or his family. He hated having to endure another such crisis. He chose family. At the Emporium, his wife darted quickly up and down the aisles in her cobalt blue Chugran dress, her voice now coming from the racks and shelves, now from the cash register, chirping like a cheery little Chugran bird supervising her seed. But in confrontations such as this one between Rodit and his diminutive wife, he heard the snap of an eagle's beak. He gave in.

Thus, Jule Chew tried to protect her charge, Braq. Yet she knew that protection was not enough. It was clear to her that he was not happy at the Schaal. She had little time to get involved in whatever those strange doings were over there, but she somehow discerned that it was not the right place for Braq.

One day, Jule discovered that there was a small museum of art close by in Annapolis. There happened to be a small traveling exhibit there that week, containing among other things, some Rembrandt etchings. She took Braq there, and, of course, his eye lit on these immediately. He would have stood there all day, but Jule quickly got bored and made him leave.

"Quickly." Your sense of time and, therefore, of "quickly" is affected by your values. Measured by an accurate chronometer, they were there for half an hour. Jule thought it was three hours, Braq five minutes.

Jule had also found an art supply store, and had started to replenish some of the materials Braq had had to leave behind in Chugrana; that seemed to make him happy. He went through his materials so quickly though; she thought she could have papered the walls of the whole basement with his drawings.

This basement was the boys' bedroom. Rodit and Jule had a small house, with only three bedrooms. Only three! What a luxury that would have been in Chugrana. But Mark and Sue, both well into their teens, could not share the same room. So their parents had found an inexpensive home with three small bedrooms. When the boys arrived though, they had to go to the basement. There was no other space. The family made it as cozy as they could. Perhaps it was too cozy. The room was small, merely a space scooped out next to the furnace. The lighting was poor. The boys shared an old bureau. Two rickety beds served their sleep. And Braq missed, realizing for the first time that he had possessed it, the sense of privacy he had owned in their home in Chugrana.

This sense of privacy had not been an accident. Zaq had consciously gone about making sure that each of his sons had their own room. He believed it was an inestimable value for anyone, child or adult, to have privacy – to think, to dream, to work, to muse – without the constant and unpredictable yammering or nattering of others. It was a luxury Zaq and his brothers had not had when they were growing up.

Now, at any time, Nollo might come pounding down the stairs to needle or interrupt Braq in his drawing. He had also begun to bring pals from the Schaal down with him.

Jule knew all this only on the margins of her mind; every spare minute went to the business. It may seem a simple thing to say, "So and so moved to a new country and became a success." But the details of such a "simple" triumph would stagger you – unless you are yourself one of the immigrants who have accomplished such a titanic labor. The countless hours, the concentration, the dedication, the determination. The success of the Chew Emporium over two years was impressive. It was not on the scale of one of Vasc Sulam's enterprises, but in Jule's context it was a huge achievement. Though modest by some standards, it was the kind of enterprise Sulam would have enjoyed investing in, whereas he had had no interest in Rodit's incompetent snuffle of a business in Chugrana.

But all this left Jule with scarcely any morsel of time to really study the problem of what to do with Braq.

Liz's words to Jule in Chugrana ignited the chain reaction that led to the solution – Liz's words and also Braq's blazing doggedness. Some might say it was chance that brought all of this together. But successful people make their own "chance."

When Liz was giving Jule instructions before the flight from Chugrana, she mentioned that she had once taken a superb summer drawing course, given in Boston by a visiting teacher, Antigone Derosch. Liz believed that this person had a school "near Annapolis, or somewhere there in Maryland. If you can't find her," she urged Jule, then, "please find *someone* good." In one of the letters that Liz tried to mail from Chugrana, she repeated this. However, this letter never reached Jule. The mention of Braq caused the censors to destroy the letter. He was a corrupt product of an illicit relationship. They would not give this woman the satisfaction of corresponding with anyone about the brat.

Her sister-in-law's remonstrance was far in the back of her mind the day Jule pulled into the parking lot of a large local shopping center, just down the road from her own business, to scout out her competition. She was looking at the signs on the storefronts when she saw a banner proclaiming, "Exhibition and Instruction: The Atelier Derosch." The banner was in the front window of a small art gallery which had two exquisite paintings on display beneath the banner.

Derosch… Derosch?? Wasn't that the name Liz had mentioned?

Jule parked and went in. She did not know quite what she was expecting, but upon asking what the Atelier Derosch was, the clerk directed her to the back door. Jule walked through this door and saw on a grassy space a gaily striped tent, with a throng of people walking through it. It turned out that this was an annual event, sponsored by the gallery and the Atelier. Inside the tent were many paintings, drawings, and sculptures by the faculty and students of the Atelier. More interestingly, there were instructors giving demonstrations. It was late in the day, but Jule ascertained that the exhibit would still be there tomorrow and the next day. She took some brochures and went home. She told Braq about it. He was very interested, of course, but, after all, what did he really know? That it would change his life? It seems unlikely.

The next day was Saturday. Jule took the family to the shopping center.

"I wish I had been there," said Bevol. "I was away that weekend, so I wasn't privy to it. But Benedict, Tressa, and Fritz told me all about it. How this little boy came in, and stood there …as if he were a statue…for the longest time, just staring…transfixed at the drawing that Benedict was working on.

"After a while, Jule had left him in the care of the older children. She and Sue went on to the store with instructions for Mark to call when they were ready to be picked up. Apparently, at one point there was quite a row. Mark and Nollo wanted to leave, but the little boy would have none of it. They might as well have tried to lever the Statue of Liberty with a toothpick as dislodge Braq from his spot. Finally, they must have placed a call because his aunt suddenly appeared again and tried to take in what was going on.

"She said something like, 'Braq, it's time to go. You've been here for an hour.'

"But he turned a face to her that she had seen before. It beamed a kind of holy rapture.

"When she had seen that expression on Braq's face as recently as several years ago in Chugrana, it had struck her as bizarre and unnatural. Now, this rapture had appeared, and even more than once, on Jule's own face, as she busied herself in the affairs of the Emporium. But when Braq turned this glowing countenance to Jule and said, 'I'm staying,' she was just floored. He said it like it was an immutable law. 'Twice two is four.' 'Water boils at 212 degrees Fahrenheit.' 'I'm staying.'

"They huddled and Jule finally went back to the Emporium, taking Nollo. He was beside himself – embarrassed at Braq's intransigence. Jule left Mark with Braq. Mark was also disgusted at having to watch this little boy, but, somehow, no one dared to counter Braq. He was just this little law of nature – impervious to the mere wishes of humans.

"It was then that someone, I think it was Fritz, thought to look inside this boy's sketch pad. Braq had had it under his arm the whole time. Fritz stared at the first page, in disbelief. Then the next. Then another. He took the book to Tressa. She examined it. She looked at Braq. Then, she and Fritz came over to Benedict, where Braq stood watching. They interrupted Benedict's drawing demonstration and showed him Braq's pad. They didn't ask Braq's permission – an egregious violation of respect and propriety – but I can't say I wonder, or blame them. I would've done the same.

"Benedict studied the pad. He turned and looked at the boy. 'How old are you?'

"Braq said, 'Nine.'

" 'Where did you learn to do this?'

"Braq said, 'In Chugrana.'

"Who taught you?'

"Braq shrugged and said, 'Mother…and I taught myself.'

"This grilling continued for a while, and finally let up. When Jule came back, after several more hours, everyone – I mean Benedict, Tressa, and Fritz – ganged up on her. They avalanched her with insistence that Braq be allowed to come to one of the evening classes at the Atelier. They had found out that he attended the Schaal, and they had no intention, then, of interfering with that. I suppose they thought at first that he must be very happy to be enrolled at the Schaal. Most people outside knew very little about what was going on there.

"Jule did not need a lot of persuading. Within a day or two, she visited the Atelier, with Braq, to make sure the place was respectable. Respectable!

"She was proud to have discovered on her own the very place Liz wanted, and to learn – who could have believed it – that it was actually very close by. Jule had never noticed it in driving about the area because there was no sign, just a number on the old gatehouse. Some establishments need no signs. People find them without benefit of an advertisement. Jule had probably driven by the place more than once, but didn't know what it was. After her visit, Jule took a brochure with her to mail to Liz. At that time, given the state of affairs in Chugrana, there was no guarantee that Liz would receive it. It so happens that she did, perhaps because Jule sent it with no mention of Braq; she cleverly put it in with some other literature about points of interest in Maryland, as if she were just letting Liz know about their new home. But she knew Liz would grasp the significance of the brochure for *the Atelier Derosch.*

"Braq, of course, was as excited as could be about getting true art instruction."

***

The one person who was out of sorts about all of this was Nollo. It was not so much hearing about the effuse praise for Braq's talent. He had had to put up with that stuff back in Chugrana. Back then Braq's worship of his Big Brátano had rubbed salve on the sting of envy in those situations. What rankled now was that Braq was about to step out from under his wing, his oversight, perhaps even his suzerainty.

Nollo's first action was to needle his Uncle Rodit. When Jule and Braq returned from checking out the Atelier, Nollo said to his uncle, "Guess we'll have whole mountains of images now." Then, a bit later that evening Nollo came down with a terrible headache and even threw up at the dinner table. They put him to bed, and though he was not much better the next day, he insisted on going to the Schaal anyway. He moaned to his friend Pranti Ku about his headache, but then unloaded the whole business about Braq going to the Atelier. Ku remarked disparagingly that he had "heard of the place – some artsy hole in the wall." He added, "It appears that my tutelling is inadequate for the little prince." Thus they stoked each other's resentments with fine and devious innuendo.

Over the next few days Nollo cooked an idea which he served up at the dinner table one night. He had waited for an opportune moment which came when Jule fretted, almost as to herself, that Braq would be in "a strange environment at the Atelier all by himself." Into the conversation popped Nollo with "I could go with him." Everyone stared at him in some amazement. "Well…I draw too, you know," he said with a little resentment. "Maybe I could take a class too, and that way I could be Braq's chaperone."

The suggestion met with ready acceptance. "That would be fun, Nollo," said Braq who, already brimming with eagerness to start the evening classes, was now even more excited at the idea of having his Big Brátano, the greatest chum in the world, go with him. Jule liked the idea of the chaperone. It would keep both boys out of trouble in the evenings. And it was reassuring, Jule thought, that Nollo was not behaving jealously and making a fuss over Braq's getting this special attention.

As for Braq, it was time.

For the year and a half that he had been in America, at the Schaal, he had gone on drawing, every day, so that was good, of course. But geniuses need guidance too, and he was getting none.

Bevol could not keep the scorn out of his voice: "Did I tell you that, when he first went to the Schaal, he found that Ku fancied himself an 'artist'? He did 'native Chugran art,' that is, paint applied to something or other, with bits of old Chugran pottery glued in here and there, gratuitously – well, how could it not be gratuitous? He insisted on calling these things "sculpturessents.' Only God and Ku knew why, and neither deity ventured an explanation.

"These 'works' he was anxious to show to the precocious young artist, Braq, when he first arrived, thinking that he would impress the boy. Braq just looked at them blankly, as if he were looking at some unmarked piece of paper. I don't think he showed any reaction at all because he honestly could not comprehend such a total absence of talent, creativity, or honesty, all of it being paraded as an achievement. The boy had never really encountered pretentious fraud before. There had been nothing like this in Chugrana. Probably just as well that he hadn't seen such a thing. It meant that he did not give Ku the scathing look of condescension that, in later years, would have inevitably blossomed on his face.

"But the ban on human or religious images by that faction of the Chugran religion that abhorred them meant that the Schaal had no art instruction. Geometric and abstract designs had always been the core of Chugran artistry, woven into their fabrics and fired into their pottery. And now, at Ku's prompting, at the Schaal there were Chugran craft projects. Braq, after five minutes of stultifying boredom, walked out of the craft class and did not return. And this was one of the few blessings of the new 'do your own thing' atmosphere of the Schaal. It left the brighter children free to get out from under some of the inanity that was now passing for education."

Braq and Nollo resumed some of their old habits from Chugrana. Braq would go out by himself with his sketch pad, or he would tramp around with Nollo, learning about their new world. His older brother had found a route between home and the Schaal. Nollo led Braq down to the Severn River and along its bank for a short distance. Then he struck up a hill and around a massive pile of rocks. Coming around the side of this pile, a space opened up in the base of the rock, forming a sort of grotto. A large slab of rock some fifteen feet above overhung its dank walls as a ledge. Nollo took Braq through this grotto and clambered up a series of ledges he had reconnoitered when he first discovered it. They emerged on top of the ledge and from there it was an easy jog to the new plantchi field.

This route didn't really take less time than walking along the road, but it was far more interesting, and "secret," so it seemed like a shortcut, especially since they would race each other, Nollo barely beating Braq to the field.

These adventures were not the same with Kaki no longer part of their band, but some of the other boys from the Schaal joined them. Nollo was now in charge of teaching the other boys plantchi, and a kind of following was growing around him. Ku's plan was moving ahead; he had completed transforming the baseball diamond into a plantchi field. All the boys admired the beautiful, athletic Nollo's prowess at the unfamiliar sport. Or what they took to be prowess. In time, some of the boys surpassed him – the ones who took it seriously and practiced. In the meantime, Braq was so proud of his Big Brátano, seeing everyone else looking up to him.

These children had not seen Nollo the night of the Museum fire, as he and Kaki had. Braq loved to tell them the story. He re-enacted Nollo's dive through the window into the flaming building – as he imagined it. Braq's lanky little frame would arc through the air and land on the ground with a thud, to the amazement of the other children. Their glowing faces would then turn to Nollo, as if he were a lord among his vassals.

The lord was made uneasy by all of this. The theater piece he had contrived was no longer of value to him – it had accomplished its purpose at the time, then dropped off the cliff of his awareness, to be forever buried in the rubble at its base. At the time, he had not thought beyond the event and its immediate aftermath – not thought that it would go on and on, a persistent spectre, ever leering over his shoulder, waiting for him to make a slip in remembering just what happened. Its sole present value was a furtively pleasant sense of having gotten away with something. Except....

If only Braq would shut up about it. Especially when he got to the part of the story when he said, "Then I saw Nollo ride his bike through the stream, and off toward the Museum. Then, a while later, Kaki and I saw smoke coming from the Museum."

Why couldn't he leave out the damned stream?!

If any of the children asked who this "Kaki" was, Braq might say, "Our friend," or sometimes, "Nollo's girlfriend." Nollo described her as "my girl," and, once, with a snicker, as "my wife."

Flipping through his sketch book on occasion, Braq would stop on one of the pages with a drawing of Kaki. He stopped on pages of Zaq or Liz too. There was no one who gave him the same sense of the world that these three had. But, at least, if he could not have their reality, he could have their images. The images of the kind of people he wanted in his world.

"I was happy to learn later that he hadn't skipped classes altogether," said Bevol. "The Schaal did still have a few good teachers, and also Braq went to the school library – quite a good one from the old days. But much of the time, he worked on his own. As for his art, he just went about drawing whatever he liked – well, that meant the whole world. He would take up little obsessions for a day, like doing detailed pen and ink drawings of bugs or snakes or mice he found in the basement. Well, of course, he was a boy and such are the fascinations of boys – or scientists – or artists. But his lifelong obsession with bodies and faces was still intact. He was always on the lookout for interesting faces, like any artist.

"One day he saw an old man shuffling along the side of the newly reconstituted but empty plantchi field. The old man was sweeping and occasionally bending over to pick up a scrap of paper. His face was creased with age, and other cares. When Braq approached him, the man began bowing and ducking his head, as if Braq was a kind of overlord. Braq asked him if he minded if he sketched him. The old man bowed again, and said he didn't mind.

"Braq took a piece of chalk out of his pocket, and his sketch pad."

Bevol surprised his students by saying, "I own this sketch because I bought it from the old man. I went hunting for such things, like a deep sea diver looking for lost treasure, and I purchased them whenever I could. I'll show it to you next class.

"His sketch conveys a man weighed down by some lifelong burden. The pain and the suffering of this burden have etched deep furrows in his face. One saw all of this in the man himself, and one sees it in Braq's drawing. But in the drawing, there is something more, some intangible compassion for this old man which says that his degradation was not entirely of his own doing, that in some other place or time or circumstance, he might have stood upright and looked at the world with more satisfaction and more self-respect.

"Was this really part of the old man's visage? Or did Braq project something of his own values into the drawing? Would *you* have seen the same thing if *you* looked into this old man's face? I can't tell you that. How you see your fellow man is part of *your* soul. I'm not sure that *I* saw it when I met the old man. All I can tell you is that, through his art, Braq was only capable of elevating people. That was one of the reasons I loved him." He stopped. He corrected himself, his voice dropping solemnly… " – love him."

That day, by the plantchi field, when Braq finished the drawing, he showed it to the old man. The man studied himself in the drawing for a moment and then said, "That's a fine drawing, young man. You must have a proud father."

Braq smiled and nodded. The old man said, "I'm a proud father too." He looked off somewhere into a distance as if he were seeing that child he was proud of.

Something about this old man and his gentle benevolence, darkened by some sorrow, touched Braq. He didn't know what the man might do or say, but his own ingenuousness prompted him. He was like that. His own good nature just bubbled over and out of him. He tore the page out of his sketch pad and handed it toward the old man, saying, "Would you like it?" The old man was about to nod in assent, but Braq drew his arm back, saying, "Oh, I forgot, what's your name?" The old man told him, and Braq printed "Henry Crow" near the bottom corner, and signed his own name below that. Then he handed it to the old man, who thanked him, bowing several more times.

Braq turned and began trotting away. Something made him look back. He saw in the distance, across the plantchi field, the old man still stooping, looking down at the drawing in his gnarled hand.

CHAPTER 31

Antigone Skye Derosch

As a young woman Antigone Skye, after just a few months in any class, managed to know more than her teachers did. Born in the early part of the twentieth century, as a young woman she had briefly attended several art schools until, at last, she transferred to the Chamberlain Art Institute, a division of the prestigious Chamberlain University. She did this in order to study under the great painter of the human figure, Isaac Choate. He was an exacting teacher, unendingly patient, but without an ounce of mercy. He would require a student to sand out a painting he had spent three months on and start over, if it was poorly conceived.

Choate was overjoyed to have Antigone in his department. He, who had had no favorites, unapologetically placed her above all others. Dreary university chores notwithstanding, his spirit lifted every time the tall young woman came into the room. He could not bear the thought that she would graduate and go elsewhere. But two years into her four-year program he looked at her and said, "Ann, you must leave."

Her eyebrows lifted, and she frowned slightly, as if to say, "Well?"

"You are wasting your time studying academic subjects. Drawing, anatomy, composition – you excel in these already. Yes, you can learn more from me, but you will learn those things for many years to come. In the meantime what will really help you is to study the great masters. There are so many techniques, such magical things, and only a quarter of them are in this country. You have no idea what awaits you in Europe. Looking at these pictures in books is worthless – to a painter. Nothing beats standing in front of the painting, with your eye glued to the canvas, and the guard shooing you away. Standing two inches to the left to see that light, and then one inch to the right to see a different light.

"You need to go to Europe."

They discussed several plans. She selected the one that came with his letter of recommendation to a friend at the Louvre. She moved to Paris and went to work in that great museum's department of restoration. Here she was able to get under the skin of the great paintings. She was able to see each layer of a Rembrandt, to see exactly how Rubens applied his paint, to discover how Bellini used his medium.

She began a project to discover how the great artists had created that medium, that special substance that when mixed with their oily pigments gave their paintings an unparalleled luster, translucence, and luminosity. Each painter had jealously guarded this secret. Each one only grudgingly passed it on to one or two of his apprentices. This secret of the old masters had been lost after the time of Rubens, with the collapse of the atelier system. Many of the great paintings done after that time began to crack and to turn muddy. A few painters by chance and luck avoided these pitfalls, but not many.

Antigone set herself to rediscover the secret by reading obscure diaries, journals and manuscripts. She read works by and about the great innovators: the Van Eyck brothers, da Messina, Titian, Bellini, Leonardo, Rembrandt, Rubens. She undertook chemical analysis. She conducted experiments with various oils, metals, and earths. After many attempts at heating linseed and other oils, mixed with litharge, an oxide of lead, she succeeded in producing a medium that seemed to come close to producing those masterful results that had made paintings from the time of Bellini and Titian through that of Rubens glow like none before or since.

In the meantime, whenever she had the chance she traveled. She went to each of the great museums of Europe. She went to the cathedrals and churches, not out of interest in religion, or even architecture, but because many of them contained unsurpassed paintings. On one trip she rented a car, and drove through the Italian countryside. She marveled that each little town she came to, no matter how insignificant, had a church near its center, and in that church one might find a masterpiece by Raphael, or Giotto, or Massaccio, or Mantegna, or any of scores of other great artists, each with something to say, some technique for her to study, some composition to admire. Sometimes she would spend an hour with one painting in one church. It took no effort; the effort was to leave.

There was hardly a locale she did not visit – in France, Italy, Germany, Austria, Poland, Czechoslovakia, Belgium, the Netherlands, Spain, England. She even slipped inside Russia, to visit the great Hermitage Museum in St. Petersburg (then called Leningrad). She managed this with the help of some of her associates at the Louvre, even though Russia, then the Soviet Union, was well into the darkest hours of its millionfold slaughter. Nazi Germany had not yet reached its own similar nadir, but was headed in that direction.

The trips to Russia and Germany were depressing. Glorious though the art in their museums, the collectivist culture and politics of these two countries were appalling. Their contemporary art – propaganda art – was dismally lifeless with no shred of individuality. And the people were fearful ghosts. She was walking through centuries of artistic glory, but she longed for the fresh air of America. The approach of war pushed her to the point. The Italian invasion of Ethiopia and the German invasion of the Rhineland signaled more to follow: the fall of Czechoslovakia, the German-Russian partition of Poland, and the final total conflagration. Antigone got out before the betrayal of Czechoslovakia.

After five years abroad, she returned to the U.S. She had learned much about painting techniques, but also about ideologies which brought to fruition their hatred of the individual and his rights. As her mentor had hoped, she had absorbed huge amounts of visual information from thousands of paintings. At Choate's insistence, Chamberlain University's Art Institute immediately hired her as a full Professor. She was happy there, for twenty years. She applied her prodigious knowledge to her own paintings and to teaching. She continued to learn from her mentor.

Like any great artist, Isaac Choate's style was unique. He planned his paintings with great care, but the bold vigorous strokes seemed to have come from a spontaneous emotion, so sure was his technique. He did not take his paintings to a high degree of finished detail, but preferred to let the large strong forms carry his subject.

Antigone's favorite work by Choate was his depiction of Prometheus bringing fire to man. The painting hung in the entry foyer of the Chamberlain Institute of Art. In Choate's rendition, the fire Prometheus brought was – a book. In a larger than life canvas, the Titan leans over a gaping precipice, out of the darkness, arm outstretched, holding an open book. The book shoots illumination from its pages, ineffably, into the atmosphere surrounding it; the glow lights the face of Prometheus. Slightly below him, a man of strikingly noble countenance, the recipient of Prometheus's gift, reaches for the book. Dimly suggested, in the obscure background, the vulture approaches with chains in its beak, Zeus's punishment for Prometheus's insult to the gods.

His painting was entitled, "The Light He Brought to Man."

Antigone and Choate were two sides of a coin. Had the obverse and the reverse been forged at the same time, they might have married. As it was, he regarded her as a daughter – more than a daughter, as an heir. They shared information with each other. They shared techniques. They shared critiques. It was not romance, but part of what a perfect romance would be, a marriage of minds.

Romance in its completeness came when she met Clark Derosch. She knew of the Derosches, a family of artists. She had seen paintings and woodcarvings by his forebears. She had never heard of this particular member of the family until she returned to the University. One day she heard his name mentioned in an inconsequential conversation. Clark was, at that time, a financial officer of Chamberlain University. She asked Choate if he knew who this Derosch was, and if he was related to *the* Derosches. On learning that he was, and that he was the brother of the sculptor, Thaddeus Derosch, but that he was himself no artist, she shrugged him off as of no further interest.

A few years after returning to Chamberlain, she presented a showing of some of her recent work. At the exhibition, as the throngs milled and swirled, and she circulated through the usual boring round of chatter and well wishing, she saw one man, a large, sturdy man who stood alone for the longest time in front of one painting. An hour later, she noticed that he was reinstalled in front of a different one, but still just as immobile. When she saw him growing roots in front of a third painting, she went up to him, and stood alongside, looking at the painting with him.

After a moment, she said, "You find these interesting?" He looked at her, and for a few seconds said nothing. He just stared at the most commanding face he had ever seen. Later, he would tell people that he thought he was in some mythological army, and that he was standing next to the great commander of that army, and that if she had suddenly handed him a packet of dispatches, saying, "To be delivered to the front," he would have run straight out the door with them, though he knew not where "the front" was. Though he was taller than Antigone, it seemed to him that she stood high on the prow of a great sailing ship, or over one of the portals of a Gothic cathedral.

Finally, he said, distractedly, "I didn't know there was anyone still capable of doing things like this." He continued to stare at her.

With the scarcest lift of one eyebrow she asked, "What's the matter?"

"Someone should paint you," he said.

"Why?" she asked brusquely, as if he had been impertinent.

"So people will know what you were like, three hundred years from now."

She laughed easily. "Let's hope the painter knows what he's doing," she said, dryly.

"Why not get this one?" He gestured to the painting on the wall, reading off the signature, " 'A. Skye.' He seems to have the knack."

There was a glint of amusement in her eye. "This painter is I."

By the usual standards of feminine beauty, Antigone was not regarded as beautiful. There was something knife-like about her profile. Looking into her face made most men uneasy. There was decidedly something ascetic about the merciless eyes, the slender, straight nose, and the vertical planes of her cheeks.

Men and women both felt anxious under her cool, unwavering gaze – unless they were innocent and talented. With her students and with herself she was ruthless. She was the same with strangers, too. Occasionally, at an exhibition, or at a public gathering, an unsuspecting artist would ask her to give an opinion of his work. Those who did this were accustomed to people saying very nice things. Or at least nice things. Why "nice" satisfied them was a mystery since it implied the viewer's inability to find a single positive thing to say about the work.

Antigone would give this person her "opinion."

"You can't draw," was one.

"Why are you trying to do this, if you can't draw?" was another.

"You should stop wasting all this paint and canvas until you learn to draw," was still another.

Not surprising, as the twentieth century had abandoned drawing as a criterion for an artist. There were lawyers who could do excellent sketches; there were doctors and dentists who were adept at drawing anatomical features; there were a few accountants and engineers who could produce something resembling artistry in the rendering of some object. But the *one* class of professionals guaranteed *not* to be able to draw was that of artists. They had long since abandoned this skill. It was beneath them. For Antigone Skye, it was not. By her lights, it was *the* cornerstone of the visual arts. "If Michelangelo thought it was the most important skill for an artist, who is the twentieth century to have an opinion of its own?" was the way she sometimes combatively put it.

"The values are all wrong," was another comment she frequently made about the work of aspirants. Though it had been one of the most important discoveries of the Renaissance, artists of the modern era had little comprehension of how to employ a rich value scale of light and dark to bring their subjects and compositions to life.

Antigone was not mean about these critiques. It was just that facts were facts – either the person could draw or he couldn't (and she was endlessly patient with anyone who was willing to work endlessly to improve themselves). If she judged that they just did not have the talent, she told them so.

Surprisingly, very few went away angry. There was, curiously, nothing personal about it when she said to a prospective student, "You're going to have a long hard road ahead of you before you achieve something. Unless it's your passion, I think you should look for something else." It was as if she had looked at the person and said, "You have blonde hair." It was just a fact. How could one take offense? More than one thanked her, and changed their field of specialization, to their great satisfaction.

She had little interest in people who just dabbled in art, and scarcely more in artists who were less than fanatical in their dedication. When a painter she knew decided after thirty years in the profession that he was tired and wanted to retire and do something else, she said, "Ah…then he wasn't very serious about art after all."

If someone had talent, but was morally tawdry, he fared even worse. If a fledgling (or established) artist copied someone else's work and called it his own, if a girl did not work and yet demanded praise, if a novice flaunted his few puny feathers of knowledge as if he were a peacock of learning, then it was not just Antigone's profile which suggested a knife. Her words would come – few, sharp, and unsparing. The person would remember the sting of it years later.

Such mercilessness is not seductive – to most men.

The icy passion belonging to the original Antigone, immortalized by Sophocles, was not usually seen as erotically arousing. But there *were* a few men. Clark was one. He looked at this woman with her single-tracked passion for her work, and her unswerving perceptiveness, and wanted no other woman on earth.

Bevol Stagri was another such man – but Clark and time had beaten him to the prize.

Antigone Skye married Clark Derosch. In so doing, she married into the Derosch family of artists. The Derosches had been involved in the arts for many generations. Clark's great grandfather, Penger Derosch had been a famous landscape painter. Penger's cousin was a famous watercolorist, and his nephew a woodcarver employed by Rockefellers and Astors to build the elaborate staircases and mantels and libraries of their mansions. Each generation had produced people who had not only a passion for but excelled in some area of the arts.

But not Clark. He was a Derosch anomaly – seemingly possessing not even a tincture of artistic talent.

Antigone was indifferent to her husband's lack of artistic ability. She loved his level-headed common sense, his unquenchable optimism. Clark's immediate response to any suggestion she had was "How can we make it happen?" followed by a crackerjack solution, usually one she would never have thought of. His sense of life clicked perfectly with her own love of science and art.

Science and art! How could these two be affianced?

This question might well not have occurred in the past. But in the latter half of the twentieth century an aspiring artist, say one of Antigone's students at the Chamberlain Art Institute, might easily have come to his craft with the following idea, spread endlessly throughout popular culture – that science and art were opposites, even enemies. He might easily have been led to believe that a painter, unlike the "coldly analytical" man in the laboratory, approached his work without logic, in a mystic emotional fit, grabbing any materials at hand, by whim, to slather away at canvas in a kind of convulsion of creativity, free of any constraints, laws, principles, rules and certainly free of science or reason.

This had not always been the common conception of art or of artists. For many centuries an artist was considered to be an artisan, one who labored for a lifetime to master a narrow set of skills, eventually becoming a master at his craft. The great revolution of the Renaissance did not contradict this conception, but added to it two bodies of knowledge it regarded as harmoniously related – science and the study of man. Artists in Italy, Germany, and the Low Countries eagerly applied discoveries in mathematics, geometry, anatomy, and optics, to name only a few. They saw no conflict between their art and the new science. Where the Dark Ages had damned scientific inquiry as evil, as "the lust of the eyes," the Renaissance and its offspring, the Enlightenment, saw science as man's glory. Artists reflected that glory. They reveled in it. They shared in it. They made use of it. They depicted it. They saw no conflict, no antagonism. Reason and creativity were friends.

Reason being the tool for integration, if one rejects reason disintegration follows. In the twentieth century's Age of Unreason, disintegration ran rampant. Friends became enemies. Many chasms cracked open. Between the thing as it is, and the thing as it appears. Between the mind and the world. Between pure mathematics and applied. Between pure science and applied, and then between physicists and engineers. Between science and the humanities. Between science and art. Between reason and emotion. Between reason and morality. Then between men and men. Between race and race. Between class and class. Finally, even between man and woman. Between any two groups whatever. And, above all, between the group and the individual.

On one side of this new chasm between reason and art stood the artist – now cast as a vessel of inchoate mysteries, a high priest of intangible and untouchable feelings. The chasm cloven between him and his one-time brother, the scientist, was absolute.

Antigone Skye Derosch stood athwart the two sides and saw no chasm – perhaps because there was none. She saw that the mind was the fountainhead of both. If that mind displayed itself in different ways, it implied no clash. There was no clash in her approach to art nor in her estimate of another person. She was expert at art; Clark was not – to Antigone this meant nothing. Clark could solve practical, mechanical, financial, or organizational problems in a trice; she could not – to Antigone the difference was of no matter. Where some would have seen an opposition, a conflict, a negation, she saw harmony and unity. This ascetic unyielding woman, this acolyte of art, knelt before the man who was Clark Derosch, and reveled in the ceremony wherein she kneeled.

But the cultural clash did matter to her; the chasms dividing man from man mattered. She had seen them often. The twentieth century creating so many chasms, gargoyles leered from them. When one of these – the Unknowable – confronted her, Antigone Skye Derosch abandoned Chamberlain University and created the Atelier Derosch.

CHAPTER 32

Bloodless Bloodshed

The Unknowable…

Forty-odd years *after* the founding of the Atelier, the dictators of Afghanistan – Islamists known as the Taliban – ordered the destruction of massive stone sculptures of Buddha at Bamiyan in the Ghorband Valley in central Afghanistan. Other Buddhist images around the rest of that country also fell under the sledgehammers, wrecking balls, and dynamite. It seems that to stand inert and silent for a millennium and a half is an unpardonable offense.

A torrent of world condemnation and supplication poured into Afghanistan to try to save the statues. To no avail: the war of this religion against art raged on, and, at least in that time and place, prevailed.

Religion is a way of viewing the world. It is a way of viewing human life, human action, and the human spirit. As such, it is a reflection of the minds and souls of the individuals who subscribe to it. Especially so are the world's great historical religions – Christianity, Islam, Judaism, Buddhism, and Hinduism – because of the scope of their conceptions. Even though these great religions, being religions, are repositories of mysticism, they also boast in their crowns diadems of philosophy and mythology.

Then to physically destroy the symbols of a particular religion – such as these 1500 year old Buddhist statues in Bamiyan – was to attack the minds and souls of the millions who held to this particular religion. It attacked them not through the use of reason and persuasion, or even through proselytizing, methods which would have left individual Buddhists free to choose, but instead physically destroyed their own image of their thought.

More than that. It attacked the minds and souls of anyone who disagreed, whatever their religion or even secular belief. There can be little doubt that the Taliban would have destroyed statues of Christ, of Moses, of Vishnu – or of Thomas Jefferson – just as eagerly as they did the statues of Buddha.

Sandstone images one hundred and seventy-five feet tall, crafted by artists, reflecting a mixture of influences from Asia, the Middle East, and the Mediterranean, these statues were the meeting point of cultures as diverse as Rome and India. Works of art – specific, individual distillations of vast abstractions – in their cliff enclosures, they stood for the thoughts which otherwise would require countless volumes of words to explain. The years to grasp the thoughts contained in Bible or other revered work can be condensed, by artists, to a specific image of their meaning. As sculptors condensed ancient Egypt to the Colossi of Abu Simbel and as Daniel Chester French condensed an American ideal to the statue of the Minuteman.

Those specific Buddhist images – reductions of thought – were in turn reduced by the Taliban: to rubble. Religious mysticism drew support – from dynamite. It is irrelevant whether one sympathizes with Buddhism or even any set of religious beliefs. To destroy a work of art in such a manner, as the Taliban did, was to attack the individual mind in one of its most fundamental aspirations. An evil even wider than religious intolerance, dynamite attacked the very essence of what it means to be a human being – grasping the world, and then objectifying that grasp in a specific word or image.

Men and women everywhere were aghast. The world which clapped its hands over its mouth in horror at this sacrilegious destruction thought it had been transported back to some primitive, barbaric era; it blanched to think that cultural monsters had re-surfaced from coffins interred for millennia. The world was mistaken. It had *not* been thousands of years. Monsters had been among them much more recently.

Less than fifty years earlier, upon the death of Isaac Choate, gargoyles foreshadowing the Taliban of Afghanistan emerged at Chamberlain University.

Modernism was in the full flood of its advance; artists shunned the depiction of anything recognizable. If you could identify any object in a painting, the painter felt he had failed. The credo, to the extent that it could be discerned, was this: only *process* was important; any process was as good as any other; and none of it meant a damned thing. Modernists who did engage in the now discredited practice of painting reality made up for this sin by distorting it . The human figure especially they rendered ugly, grotesque, deformed, loathsome. At Chamberlain University, the modernists being generally under the age of sixty, they thought of themselves as "young." Hence they adopted the party name of the "Enfants Sauvages."

They meant it. Their "paintings" and "sculptures" were as if created out of the primitive rage of two-year olds, or of bestial monsters. But they went further than this savage "creativity" in respect to their own new "works." Installed as heads of university art departments, museums, and galleries, they removed, discarded, and demolished traditional works of art.

The more beautiful and man-glorifying a work, the more suspect it was. The more innocent and benevolent the desire of artists and spectators to see beautiful bodies, incarnating the man-revering pagan philosophies of Greece, the Renaissance or the nineteenth century – such as "David," "Orpheus and Eurydice," "Andromeda" – the more the Enfants hated it. The Talibans of modernism struck quietly and furtively. Doors to galleries were bolted. Like Macbeth's murder of Duncan, the deeds were done quickly. When the bolts were unclasped, canvases had disappeared, statues, casts, and molds were gone. But no bloody knives needed to be explained. Sledgehammers, after all, do not reek with gory evidence.

Impossible! Incredible! Such atrocities could not happen in a civilized country. Nevertheless, they did.

Not just in Renaissance Italy were there "Bonfires of Vanities." Ask the curators of such repositories of art as the Peabody Library in Baltimore about the unaccounted gaps in their inventory. Then weep for what will never be seen again.

We have seen this before; how many ancient statues display broken arms and heads, defaced by nihilist tribesmen? From our perspective, the motive of the modernist destroyers was worse than that of barbarians in the ancient world who destroyed works of art. After all, those ancient barbarians had no college degrees. History records no Visigothic universities or Hun estheticians; it has translated from the ancient Latin no theories of art like the modernist ones: sophisticated as snake oil salesmen. The original Vandals, and other barbarian looters, made possible only by the inability of Roman civilization to defend itself, were symptomatic of nothing more than their own primitive churlishness. They did not stand at the apex of thousands of years of the advance of civilization, as did the "Enfants Sauvages."

Even so, what could be farther apart than these two grotesque gangs – on the one hand, the Islamic fundamentalists of the Taliban, throwbacks to eighth century Islam, as primitive surely as the ancient Vandals, and, on the other, the subjectivist, relativist avant-garde of the twentieth? Surely there could be no affinity between such poles?

And yet….

A religious fundamentalist, who is hostile to art which depicts gods of *other* religions, may yet go further: he may oppose the attempt to depict *any* object of religious belief, even *his own* belief.

Why?

Such a depiction is an attempt to know. It is an attempt to give identity to the objects of belief. Even to name God is to try to know him. Therefore, to preserve mystery one must prohibit even using God's name. Barbarically primitive as it seems to modern ears, such priests, rabbis and imams are, from their fundamental premise, *right to do so.* A name, or a word, is a product of the mind. Every aspect and component of language comes from intelligence. To say "God" is to say something to which you ascribe meaning. Once formed, a name enters the realm of logic, of identification, of reasoning. To name someone "Socrates" subjects him to an eternally pedantic indignity:

"Socrates is a man. All men are mortal. Therefore, Socrates is mortal."

Poor Socrates. To be the subject of so many syllogisms. We cannot expose God to the same insult, and this same threat. For, if something has a name, the belief – if not the believer – is at risk. Other men may challenge this name or this concept. They may have the effrontery to find contradictions within it. They may say you are mistaken, that you are trying to describe a phantasm. Or that you have ascribed characteristics which are impossible. Impudently, they may ask you for your evidence. Imagine! Trying to apply logic to God! Give this ineffable being a name, and you may now encapsulate him in syllogisms of reasoning.

The presumptuousness of such persons must be prevented, then. Easy enough. Prohibit them from giving God a name. Without a name, there can be no syllogism. Nothing can be denied. Of course, nothing can be affirmed either, but that is a logician's quibble, and who is concerned with *him*?!

To utter God's name is, therefore, an act of heresy.

Thus, religious mysticism frequently walled itself off from the searchlight of the mind, safe and secure. It is an easy step from there to say that not only words but also sculpture and painting must be proscribed. Dostoevski, no censor himself but nonetheless dismayed at the demise of religion, cited Holbein's painting of the entombed Christ as an image "*which could rob men of their faith.*" Images – paintings – give identity to what should be a mystery; images *of any kind,* then, are likely to be branded sacrilegious.

But there is another way to protect the irrational.

Instead of proscribing it by force of law or dictate of religious authority, you can protect your sacred untouchable dogma, or your whim, by putting it behind a veil.

Make it deliberately incomprehensible. Make art utterly unrecognizable, but then reserve to yourself the power – to recognize it. When people attack this "new art" as incomprehensible, you are safe – you declare *them* to be philistines, and the proof of *their* worthlessness, the proof that *they* should not open their mouths is the fact that *they* admit to being unable to comprehend the incomprehensible.

Once reason and the evidence of the senses have been proscribed, only feelings remain.

But with feelings religion is wholly comfortable.

And not just religion.

At the age of thirty, Manoel Slovomir, Professor of Philosophy and Esthetics, became the Dean of the Chamberlain Art Institute. Slovomir proclaimed to have "no hard and fast beliefs" in anything. He was "not a dogmatist." He was not "a Believer," though he was "tolerant" of religion. Slovomir was the theoretician of the Enfants Sauvages.

Against the tyranny of the objective world, he held that what an artist does is not subject to rational comprehension. "Art and reason are opposites," he said. Art comes purely from the artist's "spiritual self." It has "no meaning expressible in words." "Art comes from feelings, and only from feelings, and, therefore, cannot be an object of comprehension of the mind. Don't seek to 'understand' a painting or a sculpture. Only philistines make such an attempt."

In his inaugural speech as Dean of the Institute, he stated the nature of the unknowable even more lucidly. "The Law of Identity, that outmoded straightjacket of the unimaginative, has been repealed. Anything can now be anything else. Anything – including nothing – that occupies the space of the canvas, or even the frame, or even the room – well, why don't we stop shilly-shallying and just say the whole world – is acceptably a work of art, if the artist says it is. All subjects, or absence of subjects, and all techniques are equally valid. All media may be mixed. In fact there *are* no distinctions between media. Charcoal, pen and ink, oil are all superficial, even arbitrary, manifestations of the one underlying so-called reality. And all 'mixtures' and 'methods' are equally valid.

" 'Beauty' – if it even matters – is strictly in the eye of the beholder and in particular in the eyes of the group to which the beholder belongs."

Privately, to his students, he said, "Art is really what *we* say it is. Our generation has finally realized that this representational stuff" – he gestured off somewhere – "is just self-indulgent egotism.

" 'Look at me! – How skillfully I can draw, paint and sculpt these objects!' – is all that a Michelangelo or a Raphael was saying, or capable of saying. When will someone rid us of these self-glorifying anachronisms? He would do us all a favor."

As he said this, he looked straight into the eyes of two of his favorite acolytes.

That night Choate's painting of Prometheus, "The Light He Brought to Man," was extinguished. It disappeared. So did several classical marble statues, which had stood throughout the hallways of the Institute. When people arrived the next day, they found a large thing of Slovomir's hanging in the entry foyer where Choate's painting had been. The new thing was a raw slab of wood with four petulant smears of clashing color oozing across it.

Choate was no longer there, to witness what the art Taliban had done; he had died several years before.

To all inquiries as to what had happened to Choate's painting, the answer was just that it had been sent out "for restoration." Antigone Derosch knew that the painting needed no restoration. It was as fresh as the day he had painted it, because Choate had used the techniques of the oil medium re-discovered by Antigone. She finally cornered one of Slovomir's students, who cowered before her blazing eyes. He took her to the back of the Institute, where, in a large trash bin, she found Choate's painting, out of its frame, with a vicious diagonal gash in the canvas from one corner of the stretchers to the other. Close by, she saw a heap of marble fragments: the day before beautiful human figures, now rubble.

She walked with the painting to the President of the University. She walked past the offices of several subordinate deans, and an open-mouthed secretary at her desk, straight into the President's office. She stood the painting on top of his desk with a bang.

"Either Slovomir is fired, or I leave."

The President was dumbfounded. He tried to placate her, and at the same time figure out what the hell was going on. He promised to investigate. Later that day, he reported to Antigone that "no definitive proof" could be obtained to show that Slovomir had any hand in the vandalism.

On the next morning, the painting students found several offices empty. Ann had gone, taking all of her work and her collections with her. The chief financial officer of the University, Clark Derosch, was gone also. Over the next several days, a handful of other professors left too. But most just shrugged. One professor said, "It's just sour grapes over the fact that her day is past. That old-fashioned representational stuff is passé." A member of the philosophy department said, "There is no proof that Professor Slovomir was responsible – who can be certain?" Another scholar said, "Derosch wanted Slovomir's position – she probably slashed the painting herself just to pin it on him. He doesn't really mean all that bilge he spouts. It's just philosophy." Another said, "Well! At last we can be a collective of artists!" One of them, a woman who had made a name for herself doing "ethnic art," said "I was tired of that damned painting of Choate's anyway – glorifying the individual intellect and ignoring the racial instincts that have produced the great civilizations."

When a person is murdered, his life snuffed out, how do you bring him back to life? You cannot.

When a marble statue is smashed, demolished, how do you recreate it? Brilliant craftsmen, of whom the world has few, might just be able to do it.

When a painting is slashed, how do you restore it? Such a miracle is possible. Antigone took Choate's painting with her. Having worked for years in restoration at the Louvre, knowing to her fingertips every detail of the painting's identity and nature, she knew that she had the skills to work this miracle. But, to restore Choate's great painting, and to continue her own painting, she needed a place to work.

CHAPTER 33

The Atelier Derosch

Chamberlain University and the community which shared its name lay in the center of the triangle whose apexes are Baltimore, Washington, D. C., and Annapolis. The white columns of its colonial facades, or what is left of them, hearken back to the time when the Maryland countryside was dotted with plantations. Historians call it a "border state," but acknowledge that its sympathies were with the South. Its sympathies lingered long after that conflict was over, though one by one the plantations died: some sank into bankruptcy; some were subdivided into smaller and smaller holdings, sold off piecemeal to people with the rude names of newly arrived immigrants, or even sold to ex-slaves or their descendants; some just decayed.

One such was the estate known as Cockey's Delight, situated on the Severn River, east by southeast of Chamberlain, between the University and Annapolis. Once the pride of the colonial slave owner, Llewellyn Cockey, one of the numerous Cockeys of Maryland, by the 1950's it was near that pathetic stage of collapse in which a property must be, in the lugubrious expression, "condemned." The walls of many of its buildings were atilt. Their roofs had been pierced by missiles which were branches hurled by trees contemptuous of the Cockey name. The once spacious gravel drives were overgrown with mats of weedy interlopers. The south gatehouse of the plantation gazed with one decrepit and morose eye onto the thoroughfare of Old Rolling Road, down which tobacco hogsheads had once rumbled from Cockey's Delight to the Severn River and thence to the seabound vessels which were part of the slave trade.

If, at the time that Antigone Derosch quit Chamberlain University, you had debouched from Chamberlain by its back roads and explored south and east, you might have happened upon Old Rolling Road. Continuing still southeast, you would have then driven, or walked, if such was your pleasure, past the senile sentry of a gatehouse at Cockey's Delight, little suspecting what ruin lay beyond it. But Clark Derosch had an eye for possibilities. He had scouted the area, and when he saw the auction notice in the newspaper, he went out to Cockey's Delight. He explored the grounds. Then he took Ann there.

For a relatively small sum, Clark and Ann acquired the ruin built by Llewellyn Cockey. The main structure on the plantation, the manor house, they gutted and re-designed. Its many wings became in time the living quarters of various Derosches, and other faculty.

The house paralleled a branch of the Severn River that pointed due north. The north wing of the manor house became Ann's personal studio. Into the puncture of the decaying roof, they engrafted a slanted window to flood her studio with light.

But this was nothing compared to the skylight of the Atelier's main classroom. To create this classroom, they uprooted the barn of the old plantation, moved it near the north wing of the house, to which it was to be attached by a peripatos, turned it upon its axis so that its length faced north, wedged it in at a right angle between the manor house and the old customs warehouse, and then installed along that entire northern length of barn a shield of skylights sixteen feet high and eighty feet in length. Here the students and faculty could paint the whole day long under the gentle and constant northern light that bathed the huge room.

The old customs warehouse became the sculpture studio. This, Thaddeus Derosch's domain, received a skylight too, and a winch for manipulating the larger works. They converted the smokehouse into a laboratory for Ann's continuing investigations into pigments, the oil medium, and ways of preparing canvases.

The rest of the buildings became dormitories for many of the students. Not all lived on the grounds of the Atelier. Some of them commuted from nearby communities, or even from Baltimore or Washington, D. C. But Ann and Clark restored the remaining outbuildings for those who could manage to live "on campus." These outbuildings were, originally, the gatehouse, a spinning cottage, a forge, a carpenter's shop, and several slave quarters. These last were, when the Derosches bought the plantation, one-room cabins, each with a single low doorway, one small window and a rude fireplace; a small stairway in each cabin led to a shed-roofed attic. Clark and Ann refinished each of these cabins and built skylights into the attics. The cabins became the prized dormitories for the upperclass students, their own private studios in which to live and work uninterrupted. Formerly the cramped confine of a slave, each was now the cell of an anchorite artist punished with – utter freedom.

The new owners of Cockey's Delight cut down trees which blocked several of the skylights. They cleaned out and brought back to life the old flower and vegetable gardens, which over the coming years would supply many a student's still life with its subjects. They hired a fulltime gardener. The students often assisted this gardener. The Atelier was not a commune – they merely loved contributing to the beauty of their own Eden.

The Atelier Derosch opened its doors. Then Ann and Clark triumphantly hung Choate's painting of Prometheus, after months of restoration, in the main studio.

One by one they assembled their extraordinary faculty.

Among them were such individuals as Benedict Skye, Ann's brother, a renowned medical illustrator and animal painter. Benedict had made a painstaking and prodigious study of human and animal anatomy. He had an unsurpassed ability to see an object, such as an eagle's claw, once, from any perspective, and then envision it in any other position and draw it with uncanny accuracy. He knew how to draw any possible gait of horses, or dogs, or leopards. He could quickly sketch hair, feathers, or scales, and tell you the different types of each among the species. He loved illustrating any living creature and what Aristotle called "the parts of animals." At the Atelier Derosch he taught anatomy, drawing, illustration, and composition. He had little patience for students who were lazy. If one complained to him about the workload at the Atelier, he would fix them with an unyielding gaze, and say, "It's worth it." This stopped them in their tracks, but he would have already turned his back and walked away. Abrupt terminations of conversations were common with Benedict. Did the students love him? No, he was rather cold. But it was strange that they felt excited, challenged, energized – well, *warm* – when he came into the room.

Ann and Clark had had one child, a daughter – Beatrice. It had been Clark's desire, not hers. Ann would rather have devoted herself to art exclusively, but, on the other hand, the thought of a family workshop with artistic synergies, reminiscent of those of the Renaissance, attracted her. After one child, though, she said "Enough." She loved her daughter, and was not inattentive, but her main passion, day in and out, was her art and her teaching. When Tressa was young, Ann decided to give her a small set of watercolors. While many people found the medium of watercolor more difficult than oil, it was physically much easier to work with. It required no grinding and laying on of pigments, nor the lengthy, messy cleanup. Also, it was easy, day to day, to set up and get going. These things made it ideal for a child to dabble with. Ann gave them to her daughter with the idea of "We'll see." She showed her how to use a can of water to liquefy her pigments, and drew a few simple shapes for her. Then she left her to her own devices. Tressa stroked the brush back and forth across the paper, making some pleasing shapes for herself. Did they show talent? Who knows? She enjoyed herself. After a while, she set it aside, and ran outside to play. Ann shrugged. It would happen or not. All she could do was to put riches in front of her daughter; she could not force her to value them. But every few days, or weeks, Tressa would take up the watercolor palette, with its opaque blobs of color, splash water into them, see them go translucent on the white plastic mixing tray, smile, and begin daubing. When this happened, if Ann was around, she would stop beside her daughter and say, "May I?" then take the brush which Tressa proffered and make a stroke or two which, distilling some essential shape or color, suddenly gave vigor and clarity to the painting. She would cup her hand with affection around the back of her daughter's head and then walk away. Tressa would study her mother's marks, after she left; later Tressa's own marks were more confident, and better. Tressa rarely saw the tartar that other people encountered in Ann. What she felt was that she was skipping down an endless garden path, filed with pleasures, and that a strong guide was there for her, if she happened to stray into brambles. As Tressa grew, she eventually was introduced to all the other media – oil, chalks, charcoal, sculpture – but her love remained watercolor. As an adult, Beatrice Derosch achieved renown as a watercolorist. The drabbest landscape became a scene of wonder and joy, as she washed a few seemingly simple translucent strokes across the white paper. So it was inevitable that when Ann formed the Atelier, she turned to her daughter to teach this particular medium.

Beatrice's husband, Tony Raeburn, had no connection with the arts. He died rather young, and Beatrice used "Tressa Derosch" as her professional name. Her son, Fritz, kept his father's name. Fritz Derosch Raeburn was an oil painter. Technically skilled, but undistinguished, he was a thorough, solid teacher, on the Derosch faculty.

Fritz's son, Gideon Derosch Raeburn, on the other hand, showed enormous talent. At the time that Braq enrolled in evening classes, Gideon, a year older than Braq, was the precocious star of the Atelier, and the heir apparent.

Everything at the Atelier Derosch dovetailed. Philosophers have said, "All is one," and "The Whole is the true." The Atelier Derosch exemplified these precepts. Each subject meshed with, complemented, reinforced, illustrated all of the others. There were no clashes. The drawing class helped painting. Sculpture helped drawing and anatomy. Anatomy helped portraiture. The teachers did not have to consult one another about this. The connections were seamless and obvious to all. While techniques might differ, the underlying principles did not. "Observe the world." "Learn from nature." "Respect facts." But then – "When you have grasped the nature of reality, recreate it, transform it, by the light of your imagination." "Don't just copy; show us what *might be*!"

The "might be's" of sculpture at Derosch came from Clark's brother, Thaddeus Derosch. His works were in private collections around the country, but in few public settings. The age of exalted sculptural figures for public monuments had long passed. The hallmarks of Thaddeus's sculptures were the living, glowing plasticity of his nudes, which made everyone want to caress them, and the strenuous vitality of their actions, which, on close inspection, seemed impossible – but you forgot about that as you stared raptly at the tense elasticity in their animation.

Thaddeus's wife, Hara, had mastered the antique art of fresco. This was a demanding skill, requiring total mastery of drawing, and only a few students took it up with any knack.

Occasionally it happened that other members of the Derosch family would try to cash in on the family connection, and seek to become part of the Atelier. Mediocre artists or mediocre teachers, they nonetheless assumed that being "a Derosch" entitled them to regard.

Ann was uncompromising about barring such camp followers from the faculty.

When a student said to her, "Clark's cousin, Louis, dropped in this morning to watch us and he told me to use raw umber for my under-painting," Ann gave a cough of disgust. She growled back, "Louis is a moron. He can't even draw, and his knowledge of paint would not allow him to teach finger painting. If he comes by again, ignore him."

Thaddeus and Hara had a daughter, Gert, who was accomplished in nothing. Gert's shape suggested a family resemblance: the cello family. Unlike several other members of the Atelier, though, she could play no instrument. She had smatters of knowledge in many fields, and pretend-ed to some expertise in decorative arts. It would not be true to say that she had no talent. Perhaps it would have been better had she none.

Instead she had just enough to be always pregnant with pretension. Though she wanted to be accepted as one of the faculty of the Atelier, Ann simply looked at her and said, in amazement, "You can't do anything well." That ended the matter.

To her brother-in-law and his wife, Ann said, "I hope you understand." Thaddeus and Hara did understand. They loved their daughter, incompetent as she might be, but they knew that she just did not have the kind of skills that the Derosch faculty expected and required. Ann allowed her to hang about, and eventually Gert filled, resentfully, the role of a kind of receptionist and supply clerk.

Thus, Antigone Derosch distilled her faculty, and her family. History has seen artist families before – the Holbeins, the Carracci, the Peales. But none who banded together to keep alive the very meaning and purpose of art itself.

CHAPTER 34

When Wolf and Grey Wolf Meet

Not all of the faculty were relatives.

Fifteen years after Ann and Clark left Chamberlain, another professor fled the University, under similar circumstances. To the catechism of modernism, the University had by now added post-modernism and multiculturalism. The first of these allowed that it was now occasionally all right for art to be representational – for those artists who so chose – as long as everyone agreed that it was not reality that was being represented and that the reality so represented was – repulsive. The second was the doctrine that all cultures were absolutely equal – alike those which had discovered the rights of man and the freedom to make of life a prosperous joy, and those which had distinguished themselves by practices such as cannibalism, human sacrifice, torture chambers, and utter stagnation. Having first stated that they were all equal, and gotten away with it, these scholars now proceeded to say that the European and American cultures were alone intrinsically suspect and corrupt.

In the visual arts, the knowledge, skill, and *artistry* that enabled artists to draw were still deemed déclassé. In another bout of fury, the now not-so-enfants sauvages smashed a number of plaster statues and casts. They alleged that as "dead white males tyrannized over the modern world," so "dead white casts" did likewise over the world of art.

Bevol Stagri, a lonely outpost of reason within the Chamberlain Art Institute, quit in protest. When friends asked him what he would do next, he said that he had in mind to apply to the Atelier Derosch.

Stagri was a Chugran American. As far as he knew, his forebears were all Chugran, but he was not much interested in genealogy. His grandparents had immigrated to America from Chugrana. Because Bevol had grown up in a Chugran community, he knew all of their customs, their religion, their traditions. He had also studied their history. But he did not think of himself very often as a "Chugran." Only when someone accosted him that way, such as the police, or when people remarked the fact in conversations.

Now, cynical associates told him that the Atelier Derosch was a "white bastion," that the Derosches were artistic reactionaries and, therefore, probably, racists. They predicted that he would not be hired, or not given a fair chance at a position, or that, if hired, he would only be a "token," and that he would not last. At the very least, he would be a "problem" for the Derosches. On the other hand, his good friend, Andrew Jaeger, disagreed with these cynics. "Apply and find out," he advised. This much was true: the Atelier had never before hired a teacher who was other than light-skinned.

When Stagri arrived at the Atelier, he was directed to the main house. Behind the antique reception desk, burnished with long use, Gert Derosch scrutinized him warily. Though many Chugrans inhabited that same small corner of the world in Maryland as the Atelier Derosch, Gert had had little contact with them. She went up to Mrs. Derosch's studio where Antigone was sitting working at a flat drawing table and said, "There's a Chugran here with an attitude. He won't say why he's here. He insists on seeing you. Should I call the police?"

Antigone raised her eyebrows, and said, "Why?"

Gert shrugged and said, "Well, you never know about them."

Antigone said, rather curtly, "Does he look like he's going to attack me?"

Gert said, with reluctant uncertainty, "No…."

Antigone said, "Show him in."

This is how Antigone Derosch and Bevol Stagri dealt with their "race problem": –

When Gert showed Stagri in, Antigone was sitting behind the drafting table working on a large drawing. Bevol shook hands with her, saying, "I'm Professor Bevol Stagri. Until yesterday on the faculty of Chamberlain University, teaching artistic anatomy."

Antigone cut him off sharply. "Yesterday?"

"I quit, resigned, left."

She leaned forward. Again, sharply, she said "Why?"

He answered, "I could not stand to see them destroying everything I love." He leaned slightly toward her. "Why did *you* leave?"

She felt that she was now the one interviewed, or rather, interrogated. There was nothing hostile about his manner or his question, neither was there anything pleasant. It was, in some intangible way, pointed and insistent.

She asked, "You know about me?" He nodded. She continued, "I left because Chamberlain University was supposed to be dedicated to learning and the Chamberlain Art Institute was supposed to be dedicated to art, but both institutions hated the mind and the products of the mind."

She reasserted control of the interview. "Do you know what a human mind is?"

His reply came back immediately: "The most glorious creation in the natural world – along with the human body. Do you know what the human body is?"

This time, she felt the reply as a deliberate thrust.

She said, "The most beautiful object in the world to paint – and the most difficult. Do you know why?" she counterthrusted.

He answered, "So much complexity to be simplified – so much divinity to be humanized – so much of the human to be deified." He changed his attack. "What do you do here?" The wave of his arm took in the whole school.

"We teach an artist to take the abstract and make it concrete, to show us on canvas or in clay how his soul views the world." She struck on the new flank. "What *makes* a good teacher?"

Without a moment's hesitation, countering her enfilade, in a manner that convinced her that he had thought deeply about this, he answered, "Present the *essentials*, then emphasize the *essentials*, then drive home the *essentials*. What do *you* think teaching involves?"

She flashed back at him, and though there was passion in her voice, there was no heat directed at Bevol. "Making each student feel that the game is worth the candle, and that the candle is within his reach." She pressed on, still probing. "Is there anything *objective* to teach?"

He practically snorted. "Is there anything not? Do you think it's in the nature of an arm to grow out of a head? Or that a muscle can move and not move one and the same bone at the same time and in the same respect?" His voice now was contemptuous and dismissive.

"And if," she queried, "a student wants to draw men as beings with arms attached to heads, and if that student says, 'After all, I have a right,' "?

Stagri replied, "I would say that my art class is not a republic...nor am I his slave. I would tell him to go draw his arm-headed man elsewhere, and that it was never my decision to dedicate my life to teaching fools."

Antigone leaned forward over the table, and extended her arm. Her index finger struck her drawing on the table halfway between herself and

Stagri with a resonant pop. "What if you and I disagree – who gets to win?"

He shrugged. "If it's about something here to do with the Atelier, you're the absolute ruler. If it's an intellectual or artistic issue, I guess we'll argue, discuss, reason, wrestle, and throw intellectual cannonballs back and forth. We'll both win – but the only absolute ruler is reality."

She stayed at him, refusing to release her grip. "But who will decide?"

He was unflappable. "We will both listen to each other. We will both rethink. Then, one or both, or neither, will change his or her mind, and we will keep on thinking. Some issues take time. But no person 'decides' for another – except popes – and I kneel to no pope."

Antigone got up and walked past him to the door into the hallway. She opened the door. Then she gestured, with a slight inclination of her head, and the barest hint of wryness in her voice. "The anti-Pope, Ann, would like you to attend her."

He followed her down the stairs. When she stopped at the reception desk where Gert was sitting, she turned full toward Stagri, her figure half blocking Gert, who had to crane her head around Ann to see what was happening. "It's 'Bevol' isn't it?" Ann asked.

He nodded. She said, still not looking behind her, "Gert, this is Dr. Bevol Stagri – Professor of Anatomy at the Atelier Derosch. Dr. Stagri, you can order supplies through her." There was nothing tangibly contemptuous in the way she said "her," but her back was still turned in a way that suggested Gert was a piece of furniture. Ann leaned in toward Bevol as if she were going to whisper a confidence, but her voice did not drop. "She sometimes has an attitude, Bevol, but I hope she won't stretch our tolerance too much farther." Then she took Bevol through a doorway into the peripatos, a glass corridor sparkling with sunlight. At the end, they reached a slightly enlarged entryway in the center of which were double glass doors which Ann threw open. She strode to the middle of the vast cathedral of light which was the main studio. She got everyone's attention. She said, "Dr. Stagri, these are your students. And this" – she paused ever so slightly, gesturing in his direction – "is Dr. Bevol Stagri, late of Chamberlain University, now of the Atelier Derosch. He will teach you anatomy, and enlighten you as to what a human being is."

Bevol Stagri became the Atelier Derosch's explainer. When any of the students were confused on any issue, they went to Bevol. It was not just that his knowledge was encyclopedic – art history, the origins and derivations of concepts and words and tools and materials, perspective, general history, philosophy, and, of course, his specialty, anatomy.

No, it was something further about the way his mind took hold of the world. Cadavers were not the only things Bevol had dissected. He could tell you what was fundamental and what was minor. Bevol figured out the best order of presentation for his subject, and could advise other teachers for their subjects also. As a cadaver had to be dissected in a certain order and with a certain method, so too did a subject. Bevol was a master at discovering that method. He could divine just the right aspect to present to an individual student to clarify whatever was puzzling that person. It was as if he could see into the structure of a person's mind and know just how that person had organized the "furniture" of his mind. He could then see just which chair to re-position, or what new piece of furniture was needed.

Bevol fascinated the students and faculty of the Atelier. Ethnic types always fascinate artists because so much of ethnicity resides in the facial features, and scarcely anything is of more interest to artists than the face. And not just to artists. Bevol did not mind this curiosity. Though he was as characteristic, physically, as anyone of the Chugran racial type, yet being a man of self-made character and personality, he thought of himself as a citizen of the world and its great civilization; if asked about his race, he would invariably say, "I'm an American."

His Chugran-American parents, simple, conventional, unintellectual, had exposed him at an early age to the Chugran orthodox religion, but he was an atheist.

He had had several romances, but his current passion with a Philippine-American full of joie de vivre, Mila Merani, looked like it might become permanent.

Though familiar with Chugran music, it harmonized with nothing inside of him. His passion instead was songs of love. He had a large collection of lieder, art songs, and ballads. The collection included geniuses such as Schubert, of course, but also popular composers from all over the world. While discussing the features of a human skull in anatomy class, he might say, "Notice the shape of the orbits on either side of the nasal bones…" He would stop, and stare as if transfixed by the visage of the skull he held in his hands. Suddenly he would sing out in a clarion baritone, "Believe me if all those endearing young charms, which I gaze on so fondly today…," and then, with the barest pause, having stupefied his class with this line from the old ballad, continue his lecture by saying, "Those endearing young charms you must grasp so that you can draw them even when there is no model in front of you."

On another occasion, having just listed all the differences between the male and female skeleton, he broke up his class, by putting an arm around the skeleton and singing, "I want a gal just like the gal that married dear old Dad." Braq, especially, laughed convulsively – though he was not familiar with this song.

Bevol had never played plantchi. His sole concession to ethnicity was his fondness for "frishy." Chugrans had, for many generations, drunk this spry beverage, made of certain fruits, herbs and a teaspoon of cream, and infused with crushed ice; they traditionally drank it from a glass vessel of old Chugran design. Bevol had grown up drinking frishy in the beastly summer days on the Atlantic seaboard, and even now, unexpectedly, wafting out of the vessel would float fond reminiscences of his youth, of his parents, of his childhood home and haunts. Frishy was his only thread of feeling or nostalgia for "things Chugran," and it was only that it was a part of his personal history rather than being due to any ethnic loyalty. If you had revealed to him that frishy was really invented by the Eskimos, he would not have minded, nor would it have changed his emotional attachment to the fizzy drink and its vessel.

The students in the Atelier's anatomy classes typically saw before them, perched on one haunch on the edge of a table in a position of impossible equilibrium, reflectively sipping his flagon of frishy, a middle-aged man with a sharp, observant eye that for some reason made them feel they should sit up straighter. Perhaps it was just the expression on his face, slightly ironic, that held each of their glances and suggested thereby that they were there in that classroom for a specific purpose and shouldn't they focus on what that purpose was.

He was slightly above average height with a build that suggested athleticism when it was not suggesting a dancer even more. When he was lecturing on the countless positions a body could take, he was able suddenly to strike a pose to illustrate the exact position of the figures in hundreds of paintings or sculptures which the students immediately recognized. When he did this, he often made use of a skeleton he had specially designed and cast from synthetic materials, which was fastened at various joints and junctures so as to allow him to lock the skeleton in any position he desired. This skeleton was Bevol's pride. When he stood in a pose mirroring that of the skeleton, the students could study both it and him as alter egos. He refrained from posing nude. He was in no way ashamed of his body, but he was so far not a modern as to surmise that the students might lose some respect for a teacher who was always popping in and out of his clothes in front of them. Instead, he used life models – men or women from various walks of life who, whatever their motives, had no reluctance to pose nude for artists.

"Nothing differentiates people like nudity," Bevol told his class. "I don't mean that the nude bodies are different – that is so obvious as not to require mention…well, if you insist, go ahead and mention it!

"I mean the way people *react* to the nudity in front of them.

"If you think there are conflicts between people who paint healthy, unblemished apples and those who paint apples that are rotted, imagine the strife between a man who paints a naked body healthy and beautiful and one who paints it distorted and leprous."

He suggested that they take time during the next life drawing class to study the different ways that each person there depicted the model. "I particularly urge you to study what La Maestra is doing."

The next life drawing class arrived. A young woman lay on a pallet in front of the class.

She was naked.

She was also fat.

Several of the men in the room groaned to themselves at the girl's obesity. One muttered under his breath to his fellow, "Oh, God! How would you like to date *her*?!" They wanted a Venus less hefty. Some of the women smiled complacently to themselves, with relief. Had the young woman been a goddess, jealousy might have unsheathed claws instead of paintbrushes. Did this young woman know that her ample forms were producing these less than complimentary observations? Evidently not. She seemed quite at ease, even pleased to be displayed this way. But no one asked life models such a question. From the viewpoint of religion, a devout Christian, Jew or Muslim might have rushed to cover her with veil, shawl, or burkah. If he did not instead stone the girl to death. Or at least give her a death of looks. Did the girl experience shame as a religious person might? Again, no one asked her. It seemed unlikely. Else, why would she lie there in the first place as nature made her?

Bevol Stagri studied the girl's body, noting how the underlying forms of bone and muscle were dissolved, rounded out, transformed by the layers of fat; he studied the anatomy of cushions.

Thaddeus Derosch, discounting her girth, thought the girl's charming pose was just what he wanted for a statue he was planning, and wondered whether or not he could use her for that purpose even though he did not want a statue of a fat lady.

Gert Derosch paused on a skulk through the room, and looked at the girl with embarrassment. Through her mind flitted this: "Doesn't she know how dreadful she looks? She's a disgrace to white women. And look at that black lecher Stagri ogling her. That girl should be forced to lose weight. That's no way for a proper Caucasian to look. She should be made to go for a long hike!" It would have been useless to point out to Gert that her own figure was far from svelte: "*I,*" Gert would have promptly replied, "am not baring my figure for all the world to see."

A student created a drawing in which, amazing to say, the model appeared even fatter than she was in reality. This was not due to any inaccuracy of eye, or lack of skill in his hand. Rather, it was appealing to this young man to portray his fellow human beings "with all their warts," as he liked to say. He ignored the fact that these "warts" became exaggerated and occupied a more prominent place in his renderings than they did in the original.

Antigone Skye Derosch curled her brush deftly over her canvas, murmuring softly to herself, "Oh, my God! If only Rubens were here!...these beautiful forms…He would paint a goddess." Enthralled by her own vision, she worked swiftly and expertly. Watching the figure appear on Ann's canvas, you would certainly have recognized that girl; Ann did not transform her into a slender nymph. But you would have thought, "How beautiful the human form is, no matter the specific measure," because Ann was using the model as the raw material to show you her vision of a human being.

And here lay exposed the core of the Atelier Derosch, the core of Antigone Skye Derosch.

Antigone knew that many of the students she got now came from years of exposure to modern schools of art and modern views of man – man seen as an animal who had, presumptuously, crawled out of a sewer. She knew that many students thought that the artistic portrayal of beauty was shallow, naïve – and, therefore, easy.

"Nothing!" she exclaimed, "Nothing harder than to depict beauty!

"One slip of the brush and you have botched it. One misjudgment of proportion. Or one lapse of taste. A line too thick, or too thin, a stroke too heavy-handed, or too timid, and your figure is a freak – or a drudge.

"And the slip of the hand or eye is the least of the challenges. The intellectual cataracts that grey your conception of what a beautiful person might look like are far more destructive. Before you can draw a beautiful neck and shoulder, you must think! You must decide *what* beauty is!"

At other times, she would say, "You moderns!" – this scornful description she aimed at those like the young man drawing the model fatter than she was – "you moderns think man is sordid, contemptible, flawed, with feet of clay. If he is all of this, why show him to us in the first place? What is your purpose? If we – all of us or some of us – *are* beautiful and virtuous, do you want your art to make us feel *ashamed* of our beauty and our virtue?"

She was just as scathing to the students who tried to follow a formula. She would say in the quietest tone, with a tinge of sadness in her voice, to a student who was merely copying Ann's own work without thinking about what he was doing, "This is not what I'm training you to do. You are giving us a Derosch stereotype – a repetitive ideal of a human body – just as the Nazis gave us a depiction of a racial stereotype – an ideal Aryan – and the Communists gave us a class stereotype – an ideal Proletarian.

"None of you gives us an individual person. It's all propaganda art.

"Look at what the Greeks achieved instead – what no one had before, and few since – depicting the most beautiful race on earth – the human race – but still as *individuals*, not merely abstractions but an abstraction as a *particular* person, and at the same time a concretization of the widest characterization of what it means to *be* a human. The abstraction as specific; the individual as abstraction. The many in the one, the one revealing the many.

"Polykleitos, Praxiteles, and later Michelangelo (a 'Greek' in spirit though he was from Florence) each carved a beautiful man's body in marble. Each depiction was unique. Each could have been a real individual. But each of these artists said – through the individual creation – '*This* is what I think of the human race – a race of divinity.'

CHAPTER 35

The Late Bloomer

Antigone Derosch became furious with anyone who put limitations on what a person could accomplish, unless they were certain whereof they spoke. That is why she said to an untalented student, "You will have a very hard time," but did not say "You will never make it." She knew too well what determination and time could do to supposed limits.

One hundred and fifty years earlier, people would have said of the Derosch family's artistic abilities, "It's in their blood." Now such people were enlightened. They scoffed at such a primitive, silly view. Instead, they said, "It's in their genes." On such a view, Clark Derosch was, evidently, a genetic freak, although when someone joked that Clark was a refutation of Mendel's genetics, Benedict Skye bellowed at them derisively that Mendel had never posited a special gene for painting. In any event, Clark seemed devoid of art. When he tried to draw, his people were feeble stick figures. His horses looked like cartoon dogs, and his dogs looked like boxes with mop tails. Since he concluded at an early age that he was dreadful at it, he stopped trying. Infrequently, he would pick up a pencil or a piece of charcoal in his stubby, laborer's paw of a hand and produce another hapless drawing. He would give up for another five years. This went on for decades.

"I could as soon be an artist as a brain surgeon," he said.

It is a curious fact that, if you had asked Clark this question: "Can a man take one piano lesson and be a concert pianist?" he would have laughingly said, "Of course, not!" Had you continued, "Could a woman take one tennis lesson and carry away the U. S. championship?" he would have seen the absurdity. Yet, like many people, in regard to *himself*, based upon single, isolated, tentative gropings which ended in failure, he unthinkingly denied the existence of any shred of talent, as if he thought he ought to have emerged from his mother's womb drawing masterpieces; since he did not, he must have no talent; it was obvious.

He would have been surprised to find that great artists throw out many botched paintings or drawings, great writers can compose worthless prose, and great athletes can at times be awkward. Surprised to find that the road to many great accomplishments was long – begun even in ineptitude, and false starts. None of Clark's misgivings were convictions. He had not studied these matters. It was just an unexamined feeling. Many of us harbor such ideas, lying dormant yet perniciously destructive in our psyches – waiting for the day when they either dissolve in the light of reason, or ensnare us in their stranglehold.

But Clark could *manage* artists and their business. When Ann decided to leave Chamberlain, to set up her own school, Clark undertook the Atelier's management. He contacted all of Ann's former students and colleagues, who immediately began spreading the word. The first class, and every class thereafter, was overenrolled. He worked out the financing and the plan of operations. He helped her find the perfect site for the Atelier. He oversaw purchasing of equipment and supplies. He sought sponsors of scholarships.

Clark regarded life as a practical affair, which it was his job to solve and get on with. He solved it. He got on with it. He knew what his talents were and were not. He could not wait upon the things he could not do. The things he *could* do occupied him. He did not mope unrequited for the things out of his reach. Which did not mean that he had no aspirations.

One day, Clark changed. He suddenly grew, contrary to the laws of genetics, some new genes. Or so it seemed. In fact, it had been building for months, perhaps years. On one level he had said, "I cannot draw. Forget it. Case closed. Forever." On another level, he kept looking. At the techniques of those who could do it. *How* did they do that? How did Ann do it? It was fascinating. Mysterious. And wonderful. But not for him. And yet...

Years went by. He kept staring, peering, squinting, beguiled by those incredible masters of the Renaissance – Michelangelo, Leonardo, Raphael. The beautiful heads and faces. And especially one portrait Ann had done. It was a lyrical painting of a woman's face against a dark background, the deliciously subtle contour of her cheek emerging from the darkness, in a way that made you want to reach into the canvas and touch that cheek, to caress it. He kept marveling at the tender subtlety of it. He would shake his head. "If only I could," he thought with blithe wistfulness. It seemed like black magic to him.

One particular day, and there was absolutely nothing special about it, he looked at Ann's painting again, for the thousandth time. Its contours and shadows were so vivid, more real than an actual person.

Clark forgot that he could not draw.

He took the picture to an unused room. He took paper and a drawing board – as he had seen the students do so often. He took a pencil. He drew a contour, which was part of her head. He began shading, creating in pencil the shadows that defined the face which Ann had created in paint. He worked for an hour, unconscious of anything outside of the painting and his drawing. When he was done, he studied it. He stood back from the drawing board and compared the drawing with the painting. He made a few corrections.

He walked out of the room with the drawing, and went to find Ann. She was in the kitchen, making a cup of tea. He walked up to her and, without speaking, held the drawing up for her to see. She looked sharply at him.

"Who did this?"

"I did," he said.

She was silent for a moment. Her eyes narrowed. Finally she said, "What took you so long?"

He grinned broadly. "It's good isn't it?" He said it without boasting. She inspected him, as if he were a phenomenon she had never seen, cocked her head, and raised her eyebrows as if to say "Of course." But she said nothing. She merely leaned forward and kissed him.

Clark went to the library and looked through a book of master drawings. He began another copy of a face. Again, after a couple of hours, he took it to Ann. She placed her hand over it, her thumb and little finger spanning a distance between the chin and the brow. "Check this distance." He went away, compared the drawing and his copy, and saw what she meant. He fixed the inaccuracy, marveling that she knew the original so well and knew exactly what was wrong with his. He brought it back to her. "Better," she said. This time husband kissed wife. He thought that he was lucky to be her husband – the students could not claim the kiss when they did something good, only a soft grunt, and a nod.

Ann wanted to add a word of advice on drawing technique, or on where to go next, but resisted. She was too happy with this new, seemingly uncharacteristic, aspect of her husband. She did not want to upset something fragile being born in front of her eyes. "Plenty of time," she thought.

Clark did not join the faculty of the Atelier. His newly uncovered skills were fledgling. He would not have dreamed of winging it as a teacher. Besides he was quite happy to be the Atelier's chief of operations. But now he was also one of its happiest students.

***

The Atelier ran in a no-nonsense fashion. The sometimes manic eccentricities of a colony of artists Antigone Derosch – La Maestra – benevolently tempered. "Get that dead cat out of here," she said to a student – "We have plenty of stuffed animals for you to draw!" For a person who was obviously an individualist it was curious that she seemed not to mind sharing with scores of other people what was after all her home: having sundry students walking in and out all day, sitting down at the huge dining room table to grab their meals at all hours, or working on their latest drawing composition at one end of that same table while La Maestra sat at the other end having her breakfast.

If she often spoke with the spareness of expression of someone from, say, New England, it was only because she had no time to waste. But as her discussions of the meaning of art with her classes indicated, she could hold forth when the occasion warranted. When Gert could find anyone who would bother to listen to her, she might remark pontifically about her aunt, "It's surprising how few words she uses – considering that she's of German extraction, and you know how wordy the Germans are."

Thus, in one sentence, Gert managed two incorrect stereotypes. Apparently, she thought that since the Germans used certain long compound words, this meant that they were "wordy." And that since Ann did not waste words, she was untrue to her "ethnic type." It was certainly the case that Ann *was* German – one eighth German. Except that the one eighth ancestor came from the time when there was no such country as "Germany." In any event, "unGerman" or "German" as she might be, pith characterized her speech.

"We're admitting people who can't draw?" she said to Benedict, looking over a less competent newcomer's work.

"It won't work – wipe it out," she frequently said to students starting a painting ineptly.

"You're not ready for such a complex still life," she said to another. "Paint just *one* spear of broccoli – nothing else."

"No anatomy," she said to a life drawing student.

"Do it again," she said to another.

"Meaningless," to a third.

And once, to the faculty and students who were all in the main classroom, a short bark, "Stop him!!!" This from La Maestra about a student who was trying to copy Michelangelo's entire Sistine Ceiling onto a two by four canvas.

There was absolutely no malice, no sting in her remarks, they were utterly factual and spontaneous evaluations of the worth of what was being done, and always with an eye to practicality – how to make it better. The students loved her – they accepted the objective brutality of her manner. Then they would repeat her criticisms to each other afterwards with affectionate humor and admiration for this woman who was unconcerned with "public opinion," or with trying to make people "feel good" about their work, by means of false praise.

She could paint or draw anything expertly and quickly. She was a master of still life, landscape, portraiture, and figure painting.

She wanted to be called Ann, but faculty and students insisted on calling her "La Maestra."

She was concerned only with talent and with an individual's degree of dedication to his craft. If someone did not want to work, to accept criticism, to persevere, she had no use for him. That type did not last at the Atelier. This was no problem; there was a waiting list. Word of mouth kept the list long. The Atelier had never had to advertise.

If a student had ability, that was all Ann wanted or cared to know about him or her. Be they young or old, white, black, or purple, red-haired or bald, socialist, capitalist, or utopian monarchist, she was indifferent to any such irrelevancies. Only their ability mattered.

One new student at the Atelier learned this the hard way.

Braq's sketch pad and ever present stick of chalk being conjoined to and part of his anatomy, the rowdy crew of American students nicknamed Braq "the Chalk" because he seemed to have six fingers – the usual five plus his stick of chalk ready at hand to draw. Thus, as one famous artist in the past had been called "Squinty," and another "the Fist," Braq was "the Chalk." One evening a new student was sitting near La Maestra in the main studio during portrait class. This student asked, "Who's that?" as Braq walked by in one of his funks of concentration.

Another student said, "Braq, 'the Chalk'." The new student said, with a smirk, "You mean 'the Chuke?' "

There was a sudden stillness in the room. The new student felt his intestines churn. He glanced, unsure why, at Antigone. She was looking at him in a way that, months later, still frightened him, and, years later, still made him feel shame. She said, quietly, more quietly than anyone normally heard her speak, "You'll be out of here in three minutes, with your things." He sensed that argument would be useless against this implacable face, but he gestured helplessly at his work space, and whined softly, "But I can't take all that with me now."

"If you don't, it will be in the incinerator."

Three minutes later he was standing on the roadway, by the gatehouse, in the midst of his pile of stuff. To the student who helped him carry everything out he said, sneeringly, "What is she, a Chuger-lover?" The student replied, "No, a Braq lover and a racist hater. Congratulations! You scored twice in the same breath." Turning away from the outcast, he walked back through the gateway into the world of the Atelier Derosch.

CHAPTER 36
Abstractions

Braq stared intently at the eye.

The iris was incised on a large orb overhung by a long curving eyelid under a generous brow ridge. The large eye was a plaster cast that had been drawn by hundreds of students. It was seven inches square, copied from Michelangelo's "David." It was to be Braq's first drawing assignment in the evening class at the Atelier Derosch.

Long ago, art teachers had realized how perfect the Renaissance genius Michelangelo's sculptural forms were, as individualized abstractions of anatomy. So they had made plaster copies of these features – an eye, a mouth, an ear, a nose. Ever afterwards, for centuries, thousands of artists had learned portions of their craft by drawing, sculpting, and painting these features. Benedict Skye had explained this method of training to Braq and then set him up at a drawing stand, with a cast to render in charcoal on white paper. He said, "Sharpen your charcoal."

Braq felt a thrill of excitement as he picked up the sanding block and a slender stick of charcoal. Excited because he was the youngest person there, a child in the midst of adults? Excited because this fact implied some great compliment to him? No. He realized the fact of his youth as he realized that he was wearing a gray shirt – as a fact of no importance. He was too selfish to make an inference conducive to conceit. Selfishness pre-empts comparisons. Braq was too focused on himself and his delicious pleasure to be even remotely concerned with the other students. He barely noticed the people around him that first night, even for several nights. Was he proud that he had been admitted to the Atelier? No doubt, although he could have had no real appreciation of the school's reputation, or of that on which its reputation was based, the quality of its instruction. He had not been around enough. But he had certainly been pleased when, at the exhibition at the shopping center, Benedict and Tressa and Fritz had expressed their admiration for his drawings. It was the first time any professional had looked at his work and given him an evaluation.

He was pleased that their evaluation confirmed his own. He could draw.

"I think there is a certain kind of smallness of mind in some people," said Bevol, "which swells up with pride when they receive a compliment – swells because there was no independent esteem in the first place. They may even be people who have loads of talent, but they combine it with loads of doubt. They go through life cowering in fear that there will be – someone better. When they spy a better, they feel crushed, worthless. They are amazed, and even resentful, when they bump into a talent that is content within itself, that makes no comparisons between itself and others. A talent that simply says, 'I can do it,' and leaves it to historians, or critics, or whomever, to stitch emblems of rank onto the fields of its escutcheon. I think this self-sufficient person is just too busy racing on to his next achievement to sit and stitch.

"Braq could draw. The teachers saw it.

"Braq was pleased that he could draw. He was pleased that they saw it. That was the end of the matter.

"All of this notwithstanding, it's exciting to be talented and to have your talent challenged; it's exciting to be a greenhorn with the veteran's arm around your shoulder; it's exciting, being youth, to have maturity setting your feet on a steady path.

"And it is thrilling to purify your life by immersion in what you love.

"The main thing was that Braq was going to be doing what he loved, and learning to do it better.

"Thus Braq's thrill of excitement.

"He had already met La Maestra, the day his aunt came with Braq in tow to check out the school. La Maestra herself had wanted to see why we were admitting such a young person to our already crowded student body. Braq had been told to bring his sketches for Mrs. Derosch to see. I looked over her arm as she closely studied a number of pages. Then she gave the boy one of her looks, you know the kind I mean, that goes right through you. You feel as if she is scanning the lights and darks not of your body but of your soul. You all know how nervous that look makes people.

"Well, he just held his face up to her as if he were used to it, as if they were old chums, even equals. As if he had nothing to hide from this searching scan of his soul. And, I have to say, I almost had the impression that he was scanning right back, that *he,* the nine year old, was inspecting *her*, this old lady standing over him with her spine and eyes of steel.

"You might've thought him impudent the brazen way he held his face, as if he thought his face was worth looking at.

"Well, really! Can you tell me why anyone should *not* feel that way? Are infants, then, wrong? Defective? You will find scarcely one in a thousand of *that* breed who holds his or her face with diffidence, with reserve, with modesty, with reticence. Only when the adults have had their chance to jab a child repeatedly with moralistic hectoring does he begin to withhold his face behind a mask of humility, and to display what the adults proclaim a virtue – meekness."

Bevol interrupted himself to add contemptuously, "The meek had jolly well better inherit the earth – they'll never get a jot by their own efforts.

"Well, Braq was not meek. The only change I saw in his manner that day he met Mrs. Derosch and me was when she turned to a series of sketches of Kaki N'Tosh. She said, still looking at the sketches, 'What a striking girl! Who is this, your sweetheart?' I think she saw something in these drawings that prompted the question – she had spent her whole life studying how artists put their souls in front of the world.

"After a moment, she gave Braq a look because he didn't answer right away. He didn't blush, or frown, and he didn't dissemble, but it seemed that there was something. After a moment, he said, 'No…she likes Nollo.' And, as he said it, he gave the slightest nod of his head, three times, as if he were confirming it to himself.

"I didn't know then that he was thinking to himself, 'I'm married to the moon.'

"Mrs. Derosch did not pursue this.

"I barely noticed this small cloud that passed by. Only later did I think about it. In the meantime, Mrs. Derosch went on looking at his drawings.

"Other people in her situation, upon seeing this brilliant boy, standing in front of her like a gift, the kind of gift teachers go down on their knees for, might have said any number of very wise – and useless – things that, however well-intentioned, would have, alas, put a distance between them. Things like, 'You have a great gift, my boy. Don't waste it.' Or, 'I hope you're prepared to do the hard work that will give you what you want.' Or, 'There's a long road ahead; don't be in a rush.' Or, 'I hope you'll make your parents and aunt proud.'

"But the thing she said to him when she closed his books was so revealing of what an inspiration this tartar of a woman was. It showed how much she respected that each person's values were – their *values*.

"She smiled at Braq and said, gesturing to his sketch pads, 'It's fun isn't it!'

"He chuckled right back at her, and said, 'Yes, it is!'

"Seven and a half decades looked at one – and one looked back – and these two saw straight into each other."

Three sharpened sticks of charcoal now lay beside Braq. He set the sanding block down and, leaning forward in his chair, studied the eye. He was in no hurry to pick up his charcoal. Bold shadows slashed across the surface of the plaster cast. Braq noted these various shadows and their relationships. Finally, he began. Benedict watched only for a minute or so, and then stopped him. He tapped Braq's shoulder. "Get up."

His tone was brusque, but held no rancor. It was merely business-like, professional. Braq unfolded his skinny frame and got up. Benedict slipped into the chair. "Try holding the charcoal this way," he said. He showed him what he wanted and made a few strokes on the paper. Then he let Braq try it again. It was a foreign way of holding the stick, and Braq found it slightly awkward at first. Then, his arm and shoulder began to relax. Benedict watched a bit more, and was pleased to see that his judgment of this boy had been right. Braq rained a series of strokes on the paper. He squinted to isolate a shape, then followed with another batch of strokes. His thin fingers cradled the charcoal comfortably now, as if he had been doing it that way for years.

Ordinarily, Benedict might have urged a beginning student to slow down, but, while Braq worked quickly, he was extraordinarily accurate. Forms within the plaster eye began to appear as charcoal shadows arrayed on the white paper. Though he was putting marks *onto* the paper, his hand moved with such easy assurance that it almost seemed in a kind of illusion as if his hand were merely uncovering shapes that lay already woven within the fibers of the paper.

The eye he was drawing was the hardest of the whole set of features to draw. Its forms were complex and subtle. Benedict had deliberately chosen to give Braq this as his first assignment, to challenge him. He was impressed that as Braq worked, he kept coming back to reinforce the most important shadows, so that the whole picture kept its integrity. In the mass of individual strokes, he did not lose his sense of the whole. It meant that he was keeping the unity of essential forms in view the whole time – something even experienced artists sometimes lose. From time to time Benedict would sit in Braq's chair and show him how to create variety in his shadows, or his strokes.

"I watched him unobtrusively," said Bevol. "After seeing those incredible drawings, I wanted to see just what this boy was made of, to see how he worked. And whatever Benedict said, it seemed that just that piece of information was the one Braq had been starving for, and he pounced on it and made it his own. He had been working for so many years on his own, with little or no help, that now these pieces of information began to fill in precisely those gaps in his knowledge that Braq was hindered by. His genius needed this prompting, this goading, this challenge.

"Some students get testy, or defensive, when you correct them or try to change their method. You can see them bristle when a teacher says 'Get up – let me show you how.' The student stands up with a faint surliness, as if he owns the chair. Grudgingly, he allows you to touch his masterpiece. Well, of course, if it *were* a masterpiece, you wouldn't touch it. But most of these student 'works' are only fit for the closet. They seem to think that because they have put a mark on a piece of paper with a stroke of charcoal, it's now some sacred thing that will be treasured in some royal collection or at the Vatican. Little do they know how many pieces of paper they'll destroy by the time they learn their craft.

"But Braq was only too eager to receive the information we were there to give him. I did see his eyes widen a bit when Benedict made some strokes right over the top of Braq's own marks to show him how to create an effect. But it was just because he had never had anyone work on his drawings before. Far from being defensive, Braq was a being who craved knowledge. He was some kind of learning *machine*, designed to take the world into his brain, to identify the pieces, to put them together. It was a delight to watch.

"He knew about shadows, his mother had helped him with that, and he had taught himself much, but he hadn't put it all into conscious packets of knowledge. When Benedict explained it to him, it was if he had screwed the lens of Braq's understanding to a tighter degree of focus. Benedict asked Braq to look all around him within the room, to identify every single shadow his eye fell upon. Thousands of them. 'Wherever the light is *not*, is a shadow. Wherever the light is blocked, or impeded, or veiled, or obscured is a shadow,' Benedict told him.

"This was not a difficult concept, but Benedict wasn't finished. 'On most physical objects, there can be three important types of shadows.'

"He pointed to the cast, to the lower lid of the eye struck by the spotlight, very bright on its top flat surface but darker underneath, where the lid turned sharply to a downward facing plane. This was a 'change of plane shadow.'

"Next Benedict pointed out that the upper lid cast a bold shadow over the upper part of the eyeball. This was a 'cast shadow,' a shadow cast by one object on another.

"Thirdly, the eyeball itself, a sphere, curved away from the light, and so did the two lids, with a softly and very gradually deepening shadow as the sphere turned – a 'turning shadow.'

"Braq studied the eye some more after Benedict explained all this and then went away. I saw Braq give his charcoal three little snaps one after another at the eye, and I heard him say softly, 'Cast – change of plane – turning.' He repeated it as a rhythmic chant. Then he gave an impish little shake of his head with a grin as if he had just made these discoveries all by himself. Then he went on drawing.

"But, of course, this wasn't just academic trivia, and Braq understood that – he made his drawing *show* you these different types of shadows. He *recreated* their reality. He enhanced, he stressed them, with good judgment, to make you understand in a heightened way, what the light was doing to those forms, and what the forms were: the forms of this very individual eye, but also of what any human's eye was. He made the abstractions concrete.

"The eyeball began to 'pop' off the page, as we say. Its lights and darks began to glow with a kind of vigor of their own. You began to think you were seeing not just a drawing but the cast itself. It began to trick the eye, even though you knew the trick. Braq was taking you into his own world, compelling you to see the world as he saw it.

"Well… he was doing what *all* artists are supposed to do.

"With Benedict's help, he had fashioned these mental abstractions – the three types of shadows – he had given them each a moniker to remember them by and to nail their identity – and then he had used them to help him understand and organize his perceptual world. His was not the method of many students who grunt, 'unh hunh,' when they only vaguely understand something. He had expanded the vocabulary of his mind by these abstractions.

"Well…he was doing what *all* human beings are supposed to do with thought and language.

"I was just admiring what Braq had done when I heard a grunt behind my right ear. I looked over my shoulder and saw Gert Derosch staring at Braq and his drawing.

"She said, 'Hmp! He's pretty good isn't he?'

"She said this as if she and I were buddies, as if we were on some common ground. But then she did that with all of the faculty. Even so, I had the distinct impression that when she spoke this way to me there was an additional implication – namely, that she was being especially tolerant, speaking to me, a Chugran, in a way that demonstrated that we were equals. As if it showed how liberal and accepting she was that she would speak to me that way. But why did she have to demonstrate it? Demonstrate *anything* for that matter? I've often tried to figure out what it is that reveals this kind of thing about people. I can only tell you that there is an edge to their voices, they are slightly tense, ill at ease, as if they don't know how you'll react. As if they think you're some different species.

"I don't want to be suspicious. It may be that someone is nervous for a completely different reason. Maybe they're having a bout of indigestion. We mustn't psychologize. But Gert's manner to me and to Braq and to Nollo was different from her manner with others. And things would slip out, in spite of her precautions.

" 'He's pretty good, isn't he?' she said, and followed it with, 'Of course, he's going too fast…as usual, like all beginners…he should take about two to three hours on that cast, shouldn't he… and here he is already finished in half that time.'

"She said this with the mildly intolerant exasperation of someone with years of teaching experience. But Gert was not a teacher. She was indulging her usual habit of making dogmatic statements, not to mention trying to speak as an expert, which she wasn't. I couldn't help myself – she had that knack of touching one's nerve in just the right way to make it jangle. I shot back over my shoulder at her, 'Gert, we're not all cut from the same cloth. *Some* people have talent.'

"She didn't answer, but instead gave an involuntary blurt – 'Oh! There's *two* of them! I forgot.' This, as she saw Nollo hurrying up to Braq.

"I turned to face her. Letting her rude phrase hang in the air for a minute, I said, enunciating each word, 'Two *what*?'

"Her eyes darted at my pocket, then at my shoulder, then somewhere in the vicinity of my face.

" 'Um…two new students.'

"She had meant 'two Chugrans,' of course. Why is it so all-fired important to some people to identify the fact that there are two Chugrans in the room – or two Swedes, or two Chinamen, or two Turks? What does it accomplish? Unless you need to keep hanging on to these racial *inventories* at all times – if it's that important to you. I guess she forgot for a moment that *I* was 'one' also; she should have said 'There are *three* of them.'

"Gert was not just a covert racist; she was a covert everything. She was one of those people who never reveals what she *really* thinks about something. You know – the type who skirts all around the edges of the implications of a hint. Who drops one word into the pudding of a paragraph, and that one droplet of a word suggests a particular idea, but if you question them, or challenge them, they scurry back into the pudding, so that you never really know what they think. Or they clam up. If you try to make a particular point about what they said, they let you talk, but never reply Yea or Nay. Perhaps a barely audible hum from the vicinity of their throat tells you they're still conscious, but not whether they grasped anything you said, or agreed or disagreed. This gives them license to go right on thinking whatever they wish. They pretend to an open mind.

"Such pudding minds often conceal sewers, festering with vile gaseous matter.

"It wasn't worth pursuing, and anyway, I wanted to see what Nollo's problem was. He was urgently tapping Braq on the back, and muttering something to him. He gestured off down the large open space of the main studio. He and Braq trotted off in that direction.

"I followed them."

CHAPTER 37

Écorché

Nollo had stared dully at the nose. The nose, he felt, had sneered back at him. He already hated it.

When Benedict Skye had first ensconced Braq and Nollo at their work stations, he had placed them in a corner, facing in opposite directions, so they wouldn't distract each other. He knew perfectly well how students heckled each other, how they looked over each other's work, and gave unasked for advice; and he knew children (not that he needed to worry about Braq). He had taken note that the rest of his class was busy with their work, and then he had turned his attention to Braq. He could leave everyone else alone for a while, and he was especially eager to get Braq started properly.

Nollo was left staring at the nose. The large white plaster nose (the easiest of the casts to draw) hung there on the wall in front of him.

He had thought it would be a lark. He would come along with Braq, to "take care of him," to be his "chaperone." He would do some caricatures, or other drawing – who cared what. And he would just see what developed. There might be opportunities.

But this looked like work. These people were serious. They expected him to learn something, to produce something. It was not like his classes at the Schaal where he was only expected to listen to some teacher shooting the breeze. Where he could just nod sagely once in a while to imply that he grasped his teacher's every thought. These people wanted him to look at – what? An object. Light. Shadows. The real world. Facts.

It was all so remote.

He looked around the room at the other students. The evening classes included both full-time students and others who could only attend less frequently. But they were all so intently wrapped up in what they were doing. He studied them for a while. This was no fun. He looked back at the nose. Maybe he could just do a caricature of it. No, that probably wouldn't go over with these people.

Benedict had explained something or other, but Nollo still didn't know how to begin or what to…Nollo suddenly started feeling a buzzing in his ears. He didn't hear a buzzing, he *felt* it. The light around him seemed to narrow. His vision seemed to go into a tunnel. He had the idiotic sensation that he might fall off his chair.

As a steelworker walking on a girder three hundred feet up knows that an abyss gapes beneath his feet, but suppresses the knowledge, and trusting to his agility gets on with the business of focusing on walking over the girder, so the artist knows that an abyss may gape when he picks up his charcoal or brush. This abyss is failure, incompetence, an ugly creation, a bungled job. But he gets on, knowing that he will deal with it, that his talent, or his painstakingly acquired skill, will see him through. But some people focus on the abyss. Like a bird mesmerized by a snake, such a person can't take his eyes off of the chasm, or the thousand eyes waiting to see him fall. He becomes terrified. If one wants to fall *into* the abyss, this is a good way to go about it.

Nollo looked through the tunnel of light into the abyss.

It had a nose in it.

He teetered over the abyss. He picked up the charcoal.

He made a dark outline of the nose on the paper. He tried to make it as accurate as he could. He was immediately aware when Benedict approached him. Nollo's hand suddenly became very tentative. He took it away from the paper and pretended to peer at the nose with great attention.

Benedict stood there for a minute. He saw that Nollo had done precisely what he had said not to – what most beginners typically do – made a harsh outline. He took a deep mental breath. Then, he said, "Well! That's a wonderful outline you've done there. But let me show you something, Nollo."

He leant down so that his head was at the level of Nollo's and pointed to the cast of the nose. "You have only two things to work with – this white paper, and the dark marks you're going to put on it. You're looking at a piece of white plaster in front of you, with some shadows on it. If you can duplicate those shadows on the white plaster with the charcoal on your paper, we will see *that* nose on *your* paper. Don't draw a dark outline, create the shapes of shadows."

Nollo's mouth was slightly sullen now. "Well, how do I start? There are shadows all over the nose."

Benedict laughed easily, but Nollo was not in a jovial mood. He jerked his head around to see if Benedict was laughing at him. But Benedict just patted him on the shoulder and said, "There sure are lots of shadows. So here's what you can do. Squint."

He demonstrated, narrowing his eyelids a bit as he looked at the nose. "If you squint – just a bit – all the details drop out. You're only left with the largest, simplest shadows. That's just what you want to start with."

Nollo tried to squint. Benedict said, "That's right. Normally, you try to see the world as clearly as you can, don't you?"

Nollo just wanted to be rid of Benedict, of drawing, of people talking to him, making him think. He nodded his head as if he agreed. Benedict, encouraged by the falsehood, said, "That's right. You try to bring it into the most exacting focus. Isn't it an incredible thing about humans that we don't *have* to do that?!" He paused for a moment's reflection. "There's a parakeet next door in La Maestra's studio. It sees and hears the world in one and only one way, day in and day out. That bird can't suddenly say, 'Today, now, just for this moment, I'll squint. I'll use my consciousness differently, for a different purpose. I will be a bird artist.'

"But you, as a human, can.

"Every act of awareness is yours to direct. You can start with respect for reality – seeing it, hearing it, touching it – or with disdain for it. You can honor it, or dismiss it. You have to make decisions. You have to say: this is important, that is not."

Nollo said, "So I can make reality whatever I want?" His face brightened. Benedict gave him another of his probing looks to try to see just what Nollo meant. "Yes…you can make reality whatever you want *as an artist.* You can project what you would like. Of course, it doesn't make reality itself different, does it?"

Nollo didn't answer him. Benedict repeated, "Reality doesn't change just because of your imagination, does it?"

Nollo shrugged.

Benedict tried one final time. "Reality doesn't change to suit *you.*"

He waited. Nollo still just stared off somewhere past Benedict's knee. "Nollo, if you think that way, reality will destroy you. A farmer who just sits and *wishes* his vegetables were harvested and on the table will starve."

Nollo was getting more and more irritable. He snapped, "OK, OK, so you're saying I have no choice about what I put down on the paper, about what I think is important. It's just there in front of me and I have to accept it?"

Benedict took another breath and sighed in his own mind. He saw that Nollo had swung his boat from stem to stern, from one false alternative to another. He answered, "No, Nollo. I don't know if you heard me earlier when I was explaining to Braq about these shadows?"

Nollo nodded, and said, in a mechanical cadence, "Yes – 'cast,' 'change of plane,' 'turning'."

Benedict raised his eyebrows. It was obvious that this was a bright boy. How could he be so bright and so dense! What was stopping him from using his intelligence? Was Nollo just a parrot, able to associate sounds and objects, or did he really grasp the meaning?

Benedict said, "Look, Nollo. You don't *have* to do anything. It's just that *if* you use the intelligence you obviously have, you'll accomplish what you want. But nothing forces you to look at these shadows the way I'm saying. You do it because it *helps* you to understand. An eye doctor, or a physicist, or an interior decorator might each look at it differently – they have different purposes. But an *artist* focuses this way because these three types of shadow tell us all about that shape he's trying to recreate, and the kind of light it sits in."

He studied Nollo's sullen face. "It's not arbitrary, Nollo – the reality is there, but *you* have to do the work of grasping it. Only then can you decide, as an artist, to change it. I can't do it for you; the whole faculty here can't do it for you; the whole of humanity can't do it for you.

"Give it a try. Squint, that by seeing less you may see more. Identify the shapes that appear when you squint – and then block in the shapes of the biggest shadows you see. The large ones usually tell you the most. Then, go on to the details."

He leaned over Nollo's pad and quickly drew a small, rather squared off version of a nose, with shadows, to show Nollo what he meant. He surmised that at best Nollo would take a stab at this only if no one was watching, so he left him with these thoughts, and instead turned back to see how Braq was doing.

Braq, in a trance working on his own drawing, had noticed nothing.

"After Benedict left him," said Bevol, "I watched, as discreetly as I could, in between watching Braq. Nollo gave some impression of trying to do what Benedict had explained. And his drawing immediately got better. But I had the feeling that Nollo was just humoring Benedict because, though he started building up shadows, he also kept reinforcing that horrible thick outline.

"But none of this even mattered very much because he soon got bored with the whole thing. His arm dropped into his lap and his shoulders slumped. He began craning his head around to see what everyone else was doing. Finally, he tossed his charcoal and pad down and stood up. He strolled off, working his way down the length of the studio, inspecting the drawings and paintings each student was working on. Sometimes he dawdled in front of one of the many pieces of art that littered the place. Nollo diddled away, peering at all of this. I paid him no more attention. Instead, I turned back to Braq who was still utterly absorbed in what he was doing.

"It was a bit later that I had the testy exchange with Gert which was interrupted by Nollo suddenly reappearing in a hurry, grabbing Braq with such urgency, and dragging him away to the far end of the studio. I followed them and, coming up behind, I saw them both stop abruptly, staring upwards, stock still. Nollo pointed at the statue. He kept jabbing his finger and saying, 'Look! Look!'

"I watched this with some interest for a minute or so, and then stepped up to the two of them.

" 'I see you're admiring the écorché.' They both turned their heads to me, but Nollo blurted out, 'No, it's ugly!'

" 'Thank you, Nollo,' I said. 'It's my own design. Thaddeus Derosch sculpted it. Would you like to know what it's all about? Then perhaps you'll think differently.'

"Nollo said nothing. He just kept the same unpleasant scowl on his face. But Braq nodded eagerly. He had no reaction other than astonishment.

"I explained. 'An écorché is a figure – it could be a human or an animal – represented with the skin removed. *Écorché* is a French word meaning flayed. It's been done since the Renaissance. It's a teaching and learning tool. We represent the figure with both the skin and the fat removed so you're left with nothing but muscles. And the point is this: you can only draw or sculpt such a thing if you understand completely the form of every muscle in the body. So it's a way of learning anatomy.'

"I was very proud of this particular statue. It was life size, and had been sculpted by Thaddeus – but I had done all of the preliminary drawings, and created the pose. The great Houdon had created full-scale écorchés of men in elegantly simple repose, and Chaudron had sculpted an écorchéd man in violent tension as if in a fight to the death. *I* wanted a runner. I wanted a figure showing the tension that comes from purposeful action but with the ease born of complete self-confidence.

"My drawings had depicted from several perspectives a runner in full stride, arms thrusting in contrary action to the legs, torso leaning into his stride, but head held confidently high. I emphasized the muscles slightly to show the tension, but I did not make them bulge tautly. They were more the muscles of a swimmer or a dancer than a weight lifter. At least this was my intention. I make no great claims as an artist – only as a teacher. But the drawings gave Thaddeus a clear idea of what I wanted. It required a master sculptor who could walk the tightrope between the two extremes of tension and relaxation for every muscle in the human body and maintain the balance between these two extremes without a single slip. Thaddeus had done it. I thought it was a tour de force. And, like all écorchés, it was a whole course in anatomy.

"Nollo's reaction got no sympathy from me. In fact I thought it was very strange. Most boys are fascinated by body parts, even if – sometimes *especially* if – they're gory. And this was not gory. True, I had seen some students react in this squeamish way, women more so than men. But most artists anyway had Braq's reactions – admiration for the artistry, fascination at the beauty of the natural design of the body, and endless curiosity about the intricacy with which the muscles create the forms we see every day, whether we're aware of them or not.

"But some people just seem to miss the point. They focus on the fact that the figure has no skin, that he has been flayed, as if he has been stripped not just of skin but of his humanness. At least, that's all I surmised at the time about Nollo's reaction. Looking back though it seemed there was more that I was missing. His reaction was more personal than most people's – as if the statue threatened him.

"But what is an artist, or a doctor for that matter, to do? A thing is what it is. A thing is – *all* of the things that it is. And a body is made up of bones and muscles. Why should we blanch to see a simple fact presented in the cool beauty of marble? It's not as if one has to deal with the gore and stench of a real cadaver in dissection class after all. And even the viscera an artist with a soul can represent as a matter of beauty. 'Viscera' – or 'guts.' Your core values will determine which way you look at it.

"Nollo turned away with a shudder; on the other hand it looked like Braq might want to stay there forever. Just as Nollo took some personal and malevolent meaning from the statue, Braq drew a personal and uplifting, even an inspiring message. I think it was the runner, and the stylized abstraction of the muscles that spoke to him. I tapped him on the shoulder and said, 'Let's get back to work.' To my surprise, he made no objection, but he turned his fresh face up to me with a grin, and then pointed with three crisp strokes to patches of shadow on the écorché and pronounced with didactic mimicry in his voice, 'Cast – change of plane – turning!'

"He was right! I snapped my thumb up to tell him he had it right, and I smiled to say it was good that he had made the identifications. We walked back to Braq's and Nollo's work stations. Braq had a spring in his step, but I noticed that Nollo gave another uneasy glance over his shoulder back down the hall toward the écorché as if he thought the flayed runner might be following him.

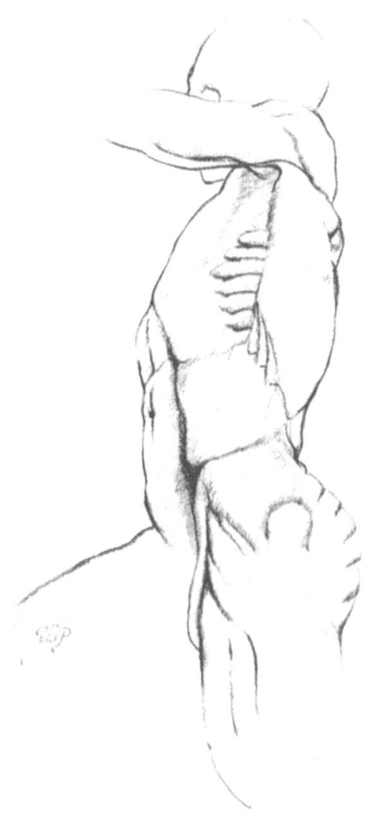

CHAPTER 38

Mentor and Pupil

Bevol Stagri's face lit with a special glow.

"I want to tell you about two lovers — "

The students pricked up their ears. With their attention intensified, he went on, "– Braq and the Atelier.

"If ever there were two beings made for each other, it was these two. The brilliant boy who lacked only guidance; the school created to guide just such a light that it might shine out in all its glory."

Benedict Skye and Bevol Stagri told Mrs. Derosch that first night how well Braq had done with his first cast drawing. The next night, La Maestra herself took over. She set Braq up, not with another of the face features such as the nose or ear or mouth. "You can do those on your own," she said. Instead, she gave him a large bust of Homer to render. This bust, a famous one, drawn by art students for countless years, was quite a step up in difficulty. Most students would labor at a drawing of this kind for many hours, perhaps even many three hour sessions to bring it to completion. At the end of an hour and a half, Braq had finished a superb rendering of Homer.

The students at the Atelier were mostly adults. They were, in some cases, experienced artists, many of them with a solid measure of achievement behind them. Braq was a nine and a half year old boy. Through that grapevine that branches remorselessly through any group of people, everyone in the studio during that evening's session repeated, "Go see what this kid has done."

Even before getting up close to the drawing, they saw what had made people buzz. Braq's drawing of Homer fairly leaped off the page even from quite a distance. It was accurate, even unquestionably so, but it also had the kind of individuality that said this was the creation of a very decided person. Though La Maestra had given him many pointers, it had his own imprint.

But no one laughed. What was there to laugh at? It was just a student exercise; there was no originality to the composition. They had all had to draw this same cast themselves. Two nights later they all laughed.

As each student arrived for evening class, they passed by Braq's corner and peered in to see what the kid might now have done. They were brought up short. There was a new drawing pinned on the wall. In this drawing, two objects stood erect. In the foreground a pedestal with that very bust of Homer ensconced on it; in the background Mount Olympus. On a broad plain, from the foot of the pedestal and scattered all the way to the foothills of the looming mountain were fragments and remnants of many Greek columns, strewn randomly, shattered to bits, and abandoned by the centuries. The compositional arrangement forced your eye to keep coming back to the two upright objects. At the top, in a dancing cursive script that was uniquely Braq's, was the title, "Still Standing."

"The kid" had gone to the Atelier's library and read up on Homer. He had found, with Bevol's help, some references for the many types of Greek columns he drew as ruins, and a picture of Mount Olympus. Even so, it could not have been easy – Mount Olympus is not a free standing peak such as Fujiyama or Rainier but part of the Olympus massif, so it took quite a bit of imagination to render it as a rising of its own and then visually to relate the pedestal and bust to this peak. He had created the whole composition and whipped it off – God knows when he had found the time. It is possible that he used some of the time that he should have been in the Schaal Chugrana. The truant!

So when the students, and even the faculty, got their first glimpse of this drawing, they began to laugh at the audacity of this child who had ventured to put Homer into a full-scale composition of his own devising; who had read and understood enough to know that this Homer was an eternal; who could make the connection to compare him to a mountain that stands throughout the ages; who was so bold as to recreate the mountain itself according to his own conception; who already had the skill to integrate all of the elements of his picture into a whole; and who had the skill to strike you full in the face with the originality of the whole blessed thing.

They laughed, and Braq laughed with them. To look at the world and make it his was Braq's joy. But having spied that joyful wonder, he took even more joy from showing others the window into his world.

Antigone Derosch saw that this was a fire to be stoked, not a little ember to be husbanded with chary caution. She wanted to goad this boy, to drive him on and up. She gave him more busts to draw, but quickly moved to having him draw whole figure statues of which the Atelier had scores. Since he was so clearly ready to attack more complex and sophisticated compositions, she added architectural elements as backgrounds for him to draw in order to learn about perspective. Voraciously, he soaked up concepts of horizon lines, observer's viewpoint, vanishing points, one-point perspective, two-point perspective, three-point perspective, and the role of visual measurement.

Braq was way ahead of the game when it came to the issue of light and dark – he had already discovered so much on his own. But he was tickled by La Maestra's slogan, "Get your darks darker and your lights lighter." It was a principle for producing more dramatic compositions. He loved it.

He watched with mesmerized attention as she showed him how to vary the thickness, intensity, and quality of a line, with hardly a flick of her wrist. Here too, his familiarity with pen and ink had set him well on the road to this skill. But she showed him how and where to create accents that made a viewer see just what she wanted them to see, accents that revealed and emphasized the architectural stresses and thrusts of a building or a body.

"Line can tell you *that* a thing is; it can tell you what a thing is. But until you add light and shade, your objects float in a spaceless world, ethereal and insubstantial. These two tools, line and value, work together, but each has its special job in making the world of objects real. Master these two and you're an artist."

She showed him tricks and tools of measuring, of sighting up, down, and across an object, and transposing those measurements onto his page. He loved doing the quick roughing in of a drawing. He would hold his palm up, as La Maestra had shown him, and find a handy unit of measure. For example, one of his thumb joints would just equal the width of the eye on a statue; so, he used his thumb to mark out the units on his paper. Altering the words and the meaning of Protagoras's ancient dictum, Braq decided that Man was the *Measurer* of All Things.

Antigone showed him how the eye measured but the mind judged, and might alter those measurements. How, respecting the truth in front of him, he could then create that innocent falsity which was a work of art – the world not as it was, but as it might be.

"Dr. Stagri says that this is what gives us the power to be artists," she explained to Braq. "An animal, whether fowl or fish, cannot measure, then choose either to omit measurements, or specify them – to look at the world as it is and as it is not – to compare the true and the not-true.

To say, 'It is not, but it *might be*!' This is what we artists do. And *your* 'might be' is what makes you Braq. Mine makes me Ann."

And Braq learned one more thing. When La Maestra drew, she might jump from one point in her drawing to some other part and add a stroke or two. When she did this, the picture would suddenly regain its focus, its balance, its unity. She kept integrating the whole composition so that one part did not overwhelm the rest. Braq could already do this but she pushed him ever further in the direction of integration.

"Composition," she told him, "is the most important thing of all because it unites all the other elements: placement and size of objects is only part of composition. How they all relate to the size of the paper or the canvas, how you balance the lights and darks, how you handle perspective are also part of composition. Even color. When you get to painting, you'll have to deal with color, with pure color versus grays, transparent versus opaque, warm versus cool. All of these elements must balance and unite to create a single whole.

"Color is especially treacherous to a composition," she said.

His eyes bugged out at this statement for reasons she had no inkling of.

"Draw the most perfect composition in the world in black and white, and if you put a small red dot in the corner, everyone's eyes will shoot right to that red dot. Color can rivet our eye, or confuse it. So mastery of color must be part of your skill at composition."

She finished up by saying, "Braq, as long as you're here at the Atelier, I will make many suggestions to you, other teachers will do the same. But only *you* can decide whether those suggestions are true to the whole conception you're creating."

It was good that Ann said this. On the other hand, it was unnecessary. Little Bratabraq did not need to be told to assert his own selfish vision of the world. No more than he needed to be told to breathe.

Night after night, La Maestra drove her charge up a steep defile of achievement. Only rarely did he falter, in starting a drawing with a poor conception. Then, remorselessly, but with utter and benevolent calm, she would take a chamois cloth and wipe down his pad removing most of the charcoal, leaving only a light grey remnant on the paper. Then she would start him again with a better idea.

Nollo was watching the first time she did this, and he gaped to see her obliterate Braq's drawing. But Braq laughed at the brazenness of his mentor. She obviously knew what she was doing; he was there to learn.

Why should he get in a huff? She was wiping his work out, but what replaced it would be even better. On the edge of his consciousness, he thought of a sand sculpture washed away by the waves, and of Zaq.

Braq and his new friend, Gideon Raeburn, compared stories about La Maestra's gruff admonitions and corrections. Gideon, Mrs. Derosch's great grandson, was the *enfant terrible* of the Atelier, recognized by all as being a prodigious talent. Now, he had competition in the person of Braq. The two became fast friends. Gideon had no sense of jealousy or insecurity about Braq. Rather, in the way of healthy boys, he saw an exciting challenge. The two boys taunted each other. They would ask Benedict to set up a still life composition for them in some manner or fashion that was new to them. They would then take a three minute egg timer and smack it down on a stool. This was the time each had to study it. When the egg timer ran out, they had to leave the room and draw the composition from memory. They would then compare drawings to see who had done better.

Gideon, having grown up in the Atelier, had an advantage over Braq, but Braq's uncanny skill kept Gideon on his mettle. The other students would study both of their drawings with admiration.

Nollo did not join in these jousts. He had not the skill, he could not stand to "lose," and he was not accustomed to being other than the leader of other boys. Besides, Gideon was three years younger. And Braq – well! He was just Little Bratabraq after all. Nollo could not put himself on the same level as Braq. With condescending acquiescence though, he did tag along when Gideon led Braq on treks through the buildings and grounds of the Atelier. It was an exploration, a reconnoitering, a scouting of the territory, and that seemed worthwhile to Nollo.

In the normal course of events, if Nollo had been a new student at the Atelier, on his own, he would have lasted for but the briefest time. Antigone Derosch would never have tolerated his surly defensiveness and his antagonistic cooperation with his teachers. Life was too short, she would have said, to suffer such unappreciative hostility. But as the price of having Braq there, she accepted Nollo into the bargain, and found the bargain cheap. It was the kind of concession she rarely made.

The family members who were part of the Atelier faculty were there at Ann's choosing because they were up to her demanding standards; she had added an occasional "outsider," such as Bevol Stagri, who owned unique teaching talents; and, when the bright young Gideon came long, she was as happy as any great grandmother could be, at his promise. She had around her, by her own devising, an extended family that enhanced the values of her life. But in Braq Churai she recognized the kind of talent a teacher may hope to have under her influence but once in a lifetime. Had it been necessary or possible she would have filed adoption papers. Failing that, she instead filed adoration papers. Antigone's adoration took the form of driving Braq relentlessly, remorselessly, unswervingly to become what he had in him to become.

And Braq?

By the end of the semester of night classes, Braq was in love with the Atelier's founder – though the shadow of the chasm of many decades fell between them. He was not so silly as to desire this woman sixty-five years his senior: he was no neurotic. In his waking hours at the Atelier, he felt boundless admiration for her, and affection. Her ruthlessness, far from terrifying him as it did so many, only incited greater eagerness. He wanted the same things that she did. But in that lawless realm that a person enters at night in sleep, when reason no longer keeps our thoughts in thrall to reality and truth, when images may meet and merge unsupervised, when senseless ideas may make their appeal, when volitional control no longer drives one's thoughts to their rational ends, then in that realm of dreams Braq saw two lovers. With the omnipotence of the dream world, they were both the same age, or – without age. Nor could he have told you what race either of them was, or if they were of any race at all. Braq did not dream in color.

They were only lovers.

And the more fervently austere she seemed, this ageless, raceless dream woman with the knife-like features, the more irresistible she seemed, and the more erotic his dreams.

CHAPTER 39

Decisions

Ann had to look at it again.

She got up from the bed quietly so as not to disturb Clark. She put on a robe and went downstairs. She and her husband had redesigned the old manor house with light in mind; above all, an artist needs illumination. On other nights Ann took pleasure in the shafts of moonlight which sliced through the many windows and skylights of this house. But the cool beams, creating a composition made up of bars, wedges and panels of alternating light and shade, tonight meant nothing to her. She crossed the entry hall, went through the peripatos and into the main studio.

In the vast open space, the bright luminance of the moon threw angular silhouettes against the floor and the walls. The solitary figure of Antigone Skye Derosch was another flung silhouette. She looked about her, taking in the large room. It was her domain, the world she had created…to what end?

She flipped on a reflector floodlight over Braq's workspace. In contrast to the spread of moonlight around her the cone of light was narrowly focused and warm. She took a large folder of drawings out of Braq's storage bin. Her hands arced and flashed inside the cone of light as she turned over one drawing after another.

She came to Braq's most recent drawing which he had called "The Captive Freed." She studied this amazing drawing by the ten-year old. It heightened her anxiety. This was why she had been unable to sleep. Some worm of an idea was making its way into consciousness. With a gasp she realized what it was. Only two more sessions of evening classes remained. Then summer. Braq would leave. Oh, no doubt he would return in the fall. But what a calamity that would be!

Seventy-five years old, Antigone had been an artist for seven decades. She had been a teacher of artists for five of those decades. She had seen every type of person pass into this realm of which she was master. She had seen the brilliant novices whose flame burned brightly and then, hissing, extinguished in unfulfilled promise. She had seen others with a spark of genius whose flint struck over and over but never quite flashed into a blaze of glory. She had also seen the steady perseverers who ignited but a few small coals of success, unnoticed after a generation or two, judged mercilessly by Time to be less than first-rate.

She had seen other things, too. She saw that there were frighteningly few people with the knowledge and skill and breadth of vision to equal the master achievements of the past – because the culture and era she lived in disparaged and depreciated the worth of what those artists had done – those who had so magnificently recreated reality in the image of their deepest values. Those who *now* set the values of the culture preferred, and encouraged, people who could only swab patches of color without meaning.

It was horrifying. To live submerged, looking up through an overhanging atmosphere at glories – of the past. To see no grand, heroic achievements in your own time. To know that there is nothing around you to admire. To feel that the human race is – used up. Not for lack of talent, but because people were indifferent to talent. Perhaps indifference was too charitable an explanation. Talent sets one above the rest. That there are individuals *above* – how wonderful she thought. Else how could one look up. To be moved to laughter, to joy, even to tears by the vision of a hero or a genius. How could one want anything but this? Yet she knew that the dominant reaction of her era was to look at heroes and geniuses – and yawn. To choose instead to contemplate the puniest of accomplishments, to pat some well-meaning mediocrity on the back – and yawn. To stare at the most vapid pablum of entertainment, and yawn. To mawkishly praise the "achievements" of untrained children, pathetic cripples, and pretentious charlatans – and yawn. And all of mankind reduced to a herd, a herd made up of smaller herds – with no expectations, no exaltation, no peaks, no Olympuses, no individuals standing alone and upright.

Within her Atelier refuge, itself engulfed inside this cultural paddock like some rare and exotic bird from the past, Ann preserved her values and her spirit. Now there came before her this Chugran boy, this Braq Churai. Almost out of nowhere. A present for her old age, a blessing, a treasure. She saw that he had gifts unlike any she had ever seen. And not just one gift – he had it all. He could put it all together.

He was only ten. What might he not do when he was twenty? Thirty? But between now and then there could be chasms. The worst would be for him to waste these early formative years, and for her to stand back and let him proceed by easy stages, until finally at the end, he had missed his chance for greatness.

Imagine a man picking up a stone from the beach. He looks at it with a simple untrained eye. He gives it a few rubs with a cloth. He remarks, "How pretty." Perhaps, he even takes it home where it gathers dust on a shelf. But a skilled stone cutter might have taken that same raw stone and by his exactions turned it into one of the world's most dazzling gems, for people to admire glistening in a museum for long centuries afterwards. Antigone Derosch was such a stone cutter; she saw that for Braq only to return in the fall to night classes would be merely to give the stone a few more rubs and nothing more.

How could she have let it go this far?! She had been so intent on working with him, challenging him, enjoying watching him night after night. In a way she had just taken his presence for granted, as if he, Braq, were the normal world, and everyone else who had sat in that studio in the past had been inconsequential ghosts. One doesn't question the normal. Now it hit her with such urgency that she felt sick to her stomach. She had to speak to Braq's aunt, Jule. Ann felt an almost irresistible desire to jump in the car that very minute and drive to the Churai house. But she knew so little about the family, about the people. Chugrans! What were they? What were they like?

She was in such a reverie of concentration that she heard nothing around her. That was what made the illusion so startling. A dark hand – how strange! – it seemed to be a Chugran hand – looking like the hand of God in Michelangelo's Creation, reached into the cone of light.

It pointed with one finger at Braq's drawing. A voice spoke. "You mustn't let go of him."

She looked over her shoulder. She saw Bevol standing beside her.

He too had been unable to sleep. He too had felt some nagging worry. He too had found himself walking in the moonlight from his cottage into the house, and around to the main studio.

He repeated, looking into Ann's eyes, "You mustn't let him go."

She nodded slowly and emphatically, "I have no intention of letting him go."

He felt a warm release of tension go through his body. It was electrifying. It occurred to him that they always thought so much alike…that it was late at night…that they were both wearing robes, standing next to each other alone in a shadow, just outside the cone of light. Then the whole field of what he knew flooded back into focus. She was thirty years his senior. She was happily married. He was happily in love with another woman. The moment passed.

One thing that had not occurred to him to think was "She is white; I am Chugran"; he did not think in those terms; nor had she ever referred to his racial identity. But suddenly Ann said to him, "Bevol, you're a Chugran. Is there anything I should know when I speak to his aunt to try to persuade her to let Braq come here full-time, to be a resident student?"

He thought for a few minutes. He shook his head. "From what I know of her, and of his family, from what I have learned from him and Nollo, I think they're like people everywhere – a mixture of many values." He explained to her the Chugran ban on image-making, a religious doctrine with which Ann had only passing familiarity. He added, "The fact that she sent him here in the first place is a good sign. But Chugrans can surprise you with the damnedest old viewpoints. I just don't know. Would you like me to be with you when you speak to her?"

Ann nodded vigorously. "Yes! I want all the artillery I can muster. I don't want it to come down to kidnapping if I can help it!" They laughed yet marveled that they could contemplate such a thing.

They looked at the drawing again. Bevol said, " 'The Captive Freed!' indeed. If only we can keep him captive!"

***

"How much do you know of art?"

That had been the woman's question to her. The woman was abrupt, even – by Chugran standards – curt to the point of rudeness. But Jule was familiar now with the range of American ways: the breezy assumption of instant familiarity, getting down to business quickly, the use of your first name without asking. In Chugrana, she would have expected more formality, more preliminary courtesies.

This man, Bevol Stagri, had spoken courteously, more in the manner Jule would have expected, but it was clear that he was an American born, not from Chugrana. Also clear that he, like Mrs. Derosch sitting across the table, had a look on his face indicative of some specific and significant purpose. Jule felt that she was under a spotlight, and that the spotlight would not leave her until something had been accomplished.

Jule said, simply and unapologetically, "I know very little."

Antigone Derosch nodded, and her eyes narrowed, studying Jule even more intently. Jule was not intimidated by this inspection, though it was a gaze more intensely personal and appraising than any she had ever felt – except from Braq when he was drawing her. And there was perhaps some similarity between Braq's gaze and that of this elderly woman who sat across the table from her. Jule, Antigone, and Bevol were in a section of the Chew Emporium which Jule had added as a delicatessen for customers to sit and have lunch. Mrs. Derosch had a coffee in front of her, untouched. Jule and Bevol were sipping frishy. Jule still did not know why they were here. All she knew was that she had received a call from Mrs. Derosch that morning asking if she and Bevol could come see her on a very, very important matter regarding Braq. Jule had said, "Of course. Do you mean today?"

Ann had said, "Yes."

Jule, noting the curtness, said "Can you come to the Emporium? We can have tea or coffee there. I would rather not be away from the store." It was not until she had hung up that it slipped across the back of her mind to wonder if there was some problem with Braq and the Atelier. It seemed so unlikely.

The first thing Ann took out of the portfolio she had brought with her was a large drawing pad. She said to Jule, "Please look at these." Jule opened the pad and began to turn each page. She was not sure what the point of this was, what she was supposed to be looking at – or looking for. What she saw was page after page of cast drawings. Charcoal drawings of an eye, an ear, a nose, a mouth. Of portrait busts of men and women – ancient and modern. Of statues of figures in a huge array of poses, many of them nudes.

Jule had been honest with Mrs. Derosch. She knew little of art. Still, how much knowledge does it take to see that a drawing recreates the world? That it reveals consummate craftsmanship. That skill had been harnessed to a vision. Jule saw all of this. At the bottom of each page, she also saw "Braq Churai," in the unmistakably effervescent calligraphy that made you think of laughter.

Jule closed the pad and said, "They're very good, aren't they?"

Ann shook her head. Her retort was quiet, almost a whisper. "No, not 'very good.' They are superb – far better than most talented adults who have been drawing for many years."

Bevol interjected, "And all completed in this one semester of night classes – four nights a week. Most people would take about three or four times as long to finish this much work."

Ann now produced another pad. Jule again looked at each sheet. These were not drawings of portrait busts, but portraits of living faces. They were not just faces, but expressions. They were not merely expressions of the moment, but of a lifetime. They captured a whole person in a particular moment. Though they were of strangers, Jule felt that she would have recognized each instantly if he or she had walked through her door and that in some uncanny way she would already know what kind of person he or she was, just from the drawing.

Jule looked up at Antigone. Her eyes crinkled as if she was beginning to suspect – what?...she didn't know. But Liz had said…that Braq was special. At the time, Jule had not doubted her, but neither had she put overly much significance on this observation. What mother did not think her child special?

Antigone withdrew another pad from the portfolio. She wanted to speak to Jule – no, she wanted to scream, she wanted to grasp Jule on either side of her head and squeeze into her the insight to appreciate what she was seeing.

She knew that one person could not think for another. She handed her the pad.

The first drawing Jule looked at showed a father and son, running. The boy was slightly in front, closer to the viewer, at a three quarter perspective. The young boy was running intently, seriously, focused on his purpose. He seemed oblivious to his surroundings, only aware of the fact of his running. He was single-minded. His father looked down toward him with an expression of tenderness and pride, and his left hand hovered behind the boy's shoulder in a gesture of affection.

Jule laughed softly, because she felt all of a sudden that Zaq was there in the room with her, running right off the page. Braq had used drawings of his father for this portrait. And the boy? Braq had not used his own face consciously, but it is said that every portrait a painter does is a self-portrait, and perhaps it was in some such way that the boy resembled Braq.

Jule turned the page. She laughed again. She turned over another sheet. She shook her head in amazement. Each drawing was different, surprising, even astonishing – and done with a technique so good that you scarcely noticed it – unless you wanted to. She went on through more and more drawings. Some were complex and grand, some simple. She saw that this boy could, on a flat piece of paper depict the nimble calligraphy of a squirrel's gambol along a tree branch, or autumn's despairing shed of last leaves – and make you feel the joy of one and the sadness of the other. She saw him depict a sculptor standing in front of his rough block of marble, about to begin, his face and posture making you want to see the finish, when the statue would stand forth in all its glory – and you thought that it *would be* glory.

How could one elicit such meaning from a piece of paper and some chalk?

She turned another page.

If Jule had known more about art she might have thought of Michelangelo's Unfinished Captives – sculptures only half finished, figures only half released from their marble encasements, in struggling gesture to free themselves from some stifling prison. Certainly this must have been part of the inspiration for Braq. But he had drawn a sculptured figure now all but released – the figure of a young girl, naked, running right out of a block of marble, almost bursting from it. Only her right ankle was still held fast and that seemingly not by the rude stone, but by a chain. Kneeling beside was the sculptor, chisel and hammer poised to strike through that chain for the final liberation from the stone, or from some greater shackle.

Jule laughed because she had never seen such a thing, because it had been done with such originality of vision and done so well, and because the girl was Kaki N'Tosh.

Braq had used as his model for the sculptor in the drawing Thaddeus Derosch, but for the girl he had consulted his older drawings of Kaki. Since he had never drawn his childhood playmate nude, he used statues at the Atelier as his resource.

Bevol asked Jule, "What do you think he calls this?"

Jule studied it again. "Something to do with 'Liberation?' "

"He calls it 'The Captive Freed,' " said Bevol.

The two people waited to see what Jule would say, what she thought.

Jule looked up at the two of them, then away into a distance. "His mother told me this…but I didn't know what she meant."

She looked back at them again. "But what is it that you want from me? Why are you here?"

Antigone Skye Derosch answered. "I want Braq."

Jule raised her eyebrows with a slight frown. She did not understand.

Antigone continued. "I want him to come to live at the Atelier as a resident, full-time student. From the time he gets up till the time he goes to bed, he'll be immersed in the world of art. He'll be exposed to the best. He'll soak it in to his marrow. He'll go through an apprenticeship. He'll become a great artist."

Bevol did not know if Jule Churai subscribed to the Chugran doctrine that spurned images. He said to her, "If you have the ability to write a symphony, the desire to write a symphony, the opportunity to write a symphony, you don't turn to writing pop tunes. Braq has the ability, he has the desire. We want him to have the opportunity."

He looked around at the humming business Jule had created out of nothing. "How," he thought to himself, "can I appeal to her?" Then, aloud, he said, "Jule, the human race moves forward by the grace of those few who have the talent and the courage to show us the way. To do this" – he gestured to the drawing pads – "may not seem like courage to you. And perhaps so far it has not been. But it will. Before too long, it *will* require courage. An artist lays his soul bare before the world in a way that no other person does.

"In every painting, or concerto, or poem, he has the freedom to recreate a whole world in his own soul's image. The scholar must show us the world as he finds it; but the artist shows us the world he *wants* to find. The scholar shows us the truth open to all – any intelligent historian could lay bare the rise and fall of empires. But the artist shows us the truth that only a single individual can know; only Hugo could have written Les Miserables, only Chopin the "Heroic Polonaise."

"Braq has this ability – and, I believe, this courage."

Seated at the table, the three figures made up a lopsided landscape: on one side the daunting crag of Antigone Derosch and the muscular eminence of Bevol Stagri; on the other the diminutive hillock of Jerule Churai. If it were a contest, the scales seemed out of balance.

Jule asked, "What about his education?"

Bevol replied, "With four Ph.D.'s in residence, I'm sure the Atelier can give him a first-rate education. Far better, by the way, than what I hear passes for an education at the Schaal Chugrana nowadays."

"What will this cost?" asked Jule.

"Scarcely more than the Schaal Chugrana," answered Bevol.

"And if it does," added Ann, "we have a modest scholarship fund. I can't think of anyone who has ever deserved it more."

The two artists were leaning forward, pressing their case as two promontories lowering over a lesser one. But the lesser did not cower.

"I must think about this," said Jule.

She stood up. Mrs. Derosch and Bevol saw that they could do no more at this time. Jule threw her palm out over the drawing pads lying on the table. "I would like to keep these for now."

Mrs. Derosch peered closely at Jule. "They will be ..."

"Safe, of course," said Jule.

Mrs. Derosch said, "It's just that... I know there is this thing about images." The head of the Atelier was not just thinking of the Chugran religion. She had not yet heard of any Taliban: she was remembering the Enfants Sauvages of the Chamberlain Institute. She felt uncertain.

Jule replied. "There is, for some Chugrans. But I am not a savage, Mrs. Derosch. I know something great when I see it. These drawings will be safe."

***

Through the remainder of that day only a portion of Jule's mind was on her work. She kept coming back to the visit of Ann and Bevol, to Braq, to his drawings, and to the decision she had to make.

Decisions are easy where there is no opposition. It might be asked what objections could have arisen to oppose the project. That evening, many snakes spat their venom.

Braq was "special"! You don't say! What about Ma'rik and Szu? Were they not special too? Were they not Jule's own blood? Was she not like mothers all over the world? Was it not "in this her honor dwells"? Surely, no she-wolf would do less than favor her own over some other's brat. Was anyone gushing over *her* children, making a fuss about *their* talents, offering *them* scholarships? It is undeniable that, loved as these two children were, neither of Jule's and Rodit's children had shown any aptitude for being anything other than average...still, they were blood of her blood. Surely that was what was important. And why should someone who was only a mixed breed get such priority over pure Chugrans like Ma'rik and Szu? Or even Nollo, son of Zaq and Semíra, for that matter. Why should a child of Liz be shown such favor? And why should he be yanked from the Schaal Chugrana? It was almost like an abduction – who were these white people to put themselves and their vaunted training and skills above the Schaal – above the lowly Chugers?! Even if that turncoat Bevol Stagri was part of the plot! What had been good enough for generations of Chugrans here in America should be good enough for Braq. What an astonishing insult this would be to the Schaal – to all Chugran-Americans, even to Chugrans in the homeland.

Did those people at the Atelier think that because he was half-white they had a right to him? Was he the property of their race? And this whole affront of art, of doing art *as a profession.* It was one thing – and bad enough – to dabble in private scribblings in a private sketch pad. But to parade those images before the world. When the whole of Chugran religion and culture forbade it! Anyway, who was to say that Braq was really so good? These two self-interested people from the Atelier? They probably just wanted the Churai's money. And even if Braq *was* good at it, individual skill should be submerged in the greater good of the race. If Braq was so intelligent, he should pay it back to the race that gave him that intelligence.

This whole venomous brood of rebuttals, and more, hissed and snarled at Jule's feet.

But they were not spawned by Jule.

Not one of these had occurred to *her.*

The vipers slithered not out of the mouth of the head of the Churai household; they issued from the old woman, Rodit. That evening, after dinner, and after she had driven Braq and Nollo to the Atelier for the next to the last class of the semester, Jule returned home instead of to the Emporium. She described to Rodit the meeting with Ann and Bevol. She and Rodit stood with Braq's drawings spread on the table between them. Rodit had barely glanced at them. He seemed offended by their even lying there on his own dining room table. One by one he dribbled out each of his mewling protests. At the end of the litany, Jule looked at this man she had married, protected, nursed, helped, bolstered, and buffered from the misfortunes which a poorly led life had brought upon him, and she realized that what she now felt for him was disgust. He was not the kind of man she wanted.

Rodit's objections seemed so irrelevant, so irrational. She resisted the urge to join combat with each of his whining complaints. Only one cut into her feelings, and that was the idea that she was being unfair to her own children. This particular she answered. "If Mark or Sue ever told me that they did not want to help at the Emporium, if they ever asked me for support in some other line, I would give it to them gladly. If they had ever shown any special aptitude I would've encouraged them in it. They haven't. They seem to enjoy going to school like ordinary American children and *with* other American children, they seem to like working at the Emporium, and they have never complained. By the way, I think –

if they choose to continue helping me as they become adults – they'll have much more commercial success than their father ever did."

This was true. Cruel, but quite true. And it crushed Rodit.

He could not understand how and why it had happened that his wife now stood in this relation to him. She was not acting by the rules. The family was...everything. It made you what you were. The tribe, too and the race also played a part, but it all started with the family. Without the family, you were nothing. But the family had to have leaders. You couldn't submit every little thing, or even every big thing, to a vote, for God's sake! All right, he understood, he accepted that he was not the best of leaders. He would be a follower. A family or a tribe needed followers too. He could just let someone else decide things for him. He would not have to make decisions, like that time…with Zaq and Jonni. Rodit gave a shudder of revulsion.

But now he was still having to make decisions. Why? How? It wasn't working. Jule was making the wrong decisions. This wasn't supposed to happen. Her decisions put the family in a clash with the tribe. Couldn't she see that? What was wrong with her? What did individuals' talents have to do with anything? What did individuals themselves have to do with anything?

He was willing for Jule to be the decision maker – but she was making the wrong decisions! She should defer to the larger group, to Chugrana. He wanted her to think for *him*, but he didn't want her to...think for herself.

And now she crushed him with this insult. She made him feel impotent. He sank his head. He would just submit.

But it still wasn't enough for her! Didn't she see that he would *just let* her be the leader of the family?! Why was she still going on this way? Why was she trying to *persuade* him? He didn't want to be persuaded. That still left it up to his mind. He just wanted *to let* someone else. Do what? Rodit did not even put it that way to himself; what he felt, with no words to name the feeling, was: let someone just do everything.

As this stew simmered in Rodit, Jule brought the discussion to an end by saying: "All this is beside the point. Braq doesn't belong to us. I promised Liz and Zaq – your brother – that I would care for him as they would have. I have a trust to keep. Do you really think they would want to deny Braq this opportunity?"

Rodit just kept his head down in a gloomy bow of sullen deference.

***

"Braq, get in the front seat; I want to talk to you."

Jule waited for Braq to climb into the front seat, while Nollo took the back. She put the car in gear and pulled out along the gravel drive from the front of the Atelier Derosch.

"I had a visit today from Mrs. Derosch and Mr. Stagri."

Braq turned and looked at his aunt. "Why did they do *that*?"

In the back seat, Nollo's ears pricked up instantly, and he said, "Yeah, *why* did they do that?"

Jule did not answer the question. Instead, as she pulled past the gatehouse out onto Old Rolling Road, the darkness of night closing around them, she said, "They brought a whole portfolio of your drawings. Braq, I had no idea just how good you are. The drawings are quite amazing."

Braq beamed. "Thank you, Aunt Jule." He added, "I love it."

She said, "You love doing the drawings, or love going to the Atelier?"

He gave a little shrug of surprise at the alternative she suggested. "Both," he said with enthusiasm.

After a minute or so, Jule said, "I especially liked your drawings of Zaq, and of Kaki."

In the back of the car, Nollo perching on the edge of the seat, his arms on the headrest just behind Braq's head, heard this and pursed his lips in a sullen pout. He had seen the drawing, "The Captive Freed," when everyone hovered around it at the Atelier. That old tartar, Mrs. Derosch, had given him a funny look, and said, "So, this is your girlfriend, Nollo?" He didn't like the fact that the whole world heard this remark (all right, so only three bystanders heard it, they would spread it all over the world quickly enough). And he resented Braq appropriating Kaki through this drawing anyway.

Braq looked at his aunt again and said, "I still don't understand why they came to see you."

After a pause, Jule said simply, "They want you."

Braq said, "What do you mean?"

In the darkness behind him, Nollo's eyes widened and his mouth froze in a strange grimace, cheeks sucked in.

Jule said, "They believe that your talent needs to have special attention…a really intensive influence…a sort of apprenticeship that will give you in depth-training…a total immersion."

She paused again. "They want you to come live at the Atelier as a full-time resident student, so they can work with you morning, noon and night. They are even offering you a scholarship to cover any extra cost."

Nollo could not help himself. Without thinking, his finger snapped out and he thumped his brother on the back of the head, and he spat out, "Smart ass!" He tried to make it sound like simple boyish badinage by adding a snickering chortle afterwards, but there was a vicious little edge to his tone that Jule noticed. So did Braq. And the thump had stung.

Jule screeched the car to a stop. There was, fortunately, little traffic late in the evening, else there might have been an accident. "Nollo, don't you ever use language like that in front of me again!" Nollo cowered and said, "Sorry, Aunt Jule. It just slipped out. I was just joking."

She accelerated again. "Where did you learn to talk that way?"

His aunt could not see him in the darkness of the rear seat, so he gave the back of Jule's head a nasty look, and he screwed his mouth up sarcastically. But he put a humble tone in his voice as he said, "Somewhere…I guess…I heard teachers say things like that…and worse." He thought for a moment and an idea flashed in his head. He added, "At the Atelier."

Jule gave a cough of disgust. "Braq, is that true?"

Braq said, "Not that I noticed."

Nollo said, "He wouldn't notice anything. He's always got his head buried in his drawing pad. People could be shouting the worst things in the world and he wouldn't notice."

But Braq said, "I do notice it at the Schaal. From people like Mister Ku."

Nollo let out a yawp at this slur on his mentor, and he tried to defend him. For the rest of the trip home, however, Braq's mind was not on this little spat between his aunt and Nollo. He was thinking about the Atelier.

The next morning, Jule did not go to work. Instead, she drove the two boys to the Schaal Chugrana. She took Braq's portfolio with her. When she arrived, she went straight to the office to see President Carroll. Braq went to class, but Nollo went in search of Pranti Ku.

Ku was not in class at the time. He was sitting in the cubbyhole of an office they gave him, munching on some sweet pastries and sipping coffee. His face brightened when he saw his favorite disciple. "Nollo, Nollo, come in, Oh Crown Prince!" he effused. Lately he had taken to calling Nollo things like this, even in front of the other students. Another boy might have been embarrassed, but it reminded Nollo of remarks his uncle Jonni used to make to him about royal blood and the like, and he felt warm and elevated when Ku used these honorifics publicly.

But this morning, he gave a sour grimace. He said, "It's not me who's the crown prince now."

Ku said, "Oh? Who is, then?"

Nollo said, "My little brother."

Ku raised a corner of his mouth with a touch of disdain. "Your Little Bratabraq?" He knew Nollo's nickname for Braq and used it with a tone of disparagement. "Why is he so honored today?"

Nollo said, "Those people at the Atelier want to crown him as a kind of artistic genius. They want to give him special treatment, even give him a scholarship so he can go live there as a full-time student. They want him to become their apprentice – or their slave!"

Now Ku's forehead creased and his eyelids would have raised also if the muscle fibers had allowed, but the several surgeries he had undergone made it difficult, so although his forehead crinkled, his lids still seemed droopy. He gave the extraordinary appearance of someone in a startled stupor.

"Oh, he really *is* giving us the slip, isn't he?" said Ku.

"That's right!" answered Nollo heatedly. "He's getting away…I mean he's getting away with…" He stammered trying to think what it really was that Braq was doing. "…going off and being selfish."

"It is selfish," said Ku. "And disloyal to the Schaal…and to the Race."

They both seemed to be groping for something, some common theme on which to attach their thoughts, and their whirling emotions.

Nollo said, "I don't know why he should be allowed to get his way, why he gets to go off on his own like this – just because they think he's so good."

Ku asked him, "You've been there…you've seen what they do at that place. Just how good is he?"

Nollo was silent for a minute. Then, he said, almost as if conceding defeat, "He's good."

Ku said, "I see."

He flapped his hands on his belly. "So he thinks his talent entitles him to desert his own people, to leave the Race to fend for itself. He is abandoning those to whom he belongs – his own family, his own tribe, his Race. It's almost as if he's saying that we're his enemies."

The word seemed to touch a chord in Nollo. "Yes! An enemy!" Nollo did not know when this feeling had started. Braq still called him "Big Brátano," though perhaps not quite as often. Sometimes Nollo felt that the childhood endearment now had something less wholly reverential about it. There was nothing distinct, concrete, tangible…but it just was not the same. Nollo could not have known – and in any event he would have been indifferent to the fact – that what he sensed came, at the very least, from the fact that Braq was now eight years older than when he had coined, out of his infant's prattle, the worshipful nickname. As a gear slipping one sprocket on its wheel, worship had now depreciated to great affection. Love still but somehow…less.

There had been a few other slippages of the wheel…whenever, for example, Nollo said or did something which by chance stood in clear contrast before Braq's eye to the exemplars of Liz and especially of Zaq. Though it had been almost three years since he had seen his parents, Braq still carried their image before his mind's eye – as he carried the drawings of his parents in his sketch pads. Perhaps, thanks to his extraordinary gift for rendering character with his piece of chalk, when he looked at those sketches they brought to him more than just a camera's image of a face, they brought the person himself. Thus, with his drawings he could refresh his soul's remembrance of his parents, a reviving draught from the well of memory.

And on occasion a word, an expression, an action of Nollo's would hit Braq in just some particular way as to make him stare in confusion at the fact that his Big Brátano was different from his father. At these times, the gear slipped another notch.

But now, with this prospect of Braq going to live at the Atelier, Nollo felt not just one slip of the wheel that had given him seemingly unconditional admiration, but a collapse of the whole mechanism. His brother, his pal, was rejecting him, leaving him. It was almost as if his whole family, his whole tribe was rejecting him. As if his family was saying that he was now an orphan...or an adult...alone...that he must stand on his own.

The prospect was terrifying. So terrifying that he had to keep the truth of it even from himself. In this he succeeded.

Yet more. This new development meant that Braq would now move even farther – very far – from the great Chugran "project" under way at the Schaal. Nollo could not have articulated what that "project" was, but he felt it. Felt that the atmosphere was fermenting – from the yeast thrown into the pot by people like Ku, and now also by Nollo himself. Felt that he was recreating not just the homeland of his birth but his spiritual homeland. He loved this ferment, and he felt the complete support and accord of Ku. Whatever the project was had nothing to do with Braq's stupid and incessant drawing. That was just something that involved Braq as a sole, solitary person with his own selfish desires. It was just about Braq as an individual. Who cared about that?

And with all this, and even in spite of his immersion, in spite of his almost lascivious surrender to the "project" at the Schaal, just this very immersion felt at times to Nollo like a trap, a commitment to a definite course that had its own identity, from which a person might not be able to escape. And so, even though he felt so "at home" at the Schaal, he felt that he did not want to be tied down to one place, or to – anything. He wanted to be able to – get out! And here was Braq doing just that.

"It's almost like getting away with murder" – the phrase made Nollo jump when Ku muttered it, just under his breath. "The murder of the Race. This Atelier Derosch…Tell me again." He and Nollo had discussed it many times, but he wanted to see what else there might be. He probed Nollo, but learned nothing that was helpful in their cause. Nollo confirmed that there were students of various ethnic backgrounds there, that everyone was treated well except that everyone was treated equally brutally and mercilessly in regard to their art. "Still," said Ku, "except for that bastard Uncle Tom Stagri, they have no other outside faculty, do they?"

Nollo hesitated. "I'm not sure. There may occasionally be one or two other outsiders."

Shaking his head, Ku said, "It's a reactionary enclave. It needs to be shut down…or taken over. Well, we'll find something."

There was a lull as they both sat in dudgeon. Then Ku sighed and asked, "When exactly is this coronation supposed to happen?"

Nollo said, "I'm not sure when he'll enroll full-time. Aunt Jule is here now talking to President Carroll."

Ku gave a start. "She is?! Oh, she's really moving quickly, isn't she? I had no idea… They mean business, don't they?" He thought for a moment. "I will have to go see Carroll."

Nollo was following his own line of thought. "Yes, she took him Braq's 'portfolio!' " He said the word sarcastically, but there was some other note also – was it vindictiveness – as if the portfolio was an injury to him personally. Ku, always alert to innuendo, wondered what this might be. But he couldn't stop to ponder it. There was something else floating about, some connection he wanted to make. The Schaal? The Atelier? Braq's portfolio? Something he needed to do? Oh well, perhaps he would think of it later.

When he got up to go, Nollo stopped and turned back to his mentor. Ku saw that there was something on his mind. "Yes, Young Blood, Nollopa?" Nollo hesitated for a second, then said, "It's just...when you talk to Carroll, don't tell him that I complained about this business."

Ku thought for a minute, and then agreed, "No, no, we might need to keep your good relations with everyone for later."

Nollo left, pleased that they saw things so much alike.

***

"I wish I had been there that night," said Bevol. "It must have been quite a row. What with Ku there."

Bevol, of course, was not at the Churai home that night. He only learned of it from Braq, and later from Jule. It started with the Churai doorbell ringing. When Mark Churai opened the door, he saw the large shape of Pranti Ku standing very close to the door as if he were already in the act of entering.

"May I speak to your parents?" he said, and not waiting for Mark to motion him into the entry hall, he shoved past him. From this hall he spied the whole family seated at their dinner in the next room. "I hope I'm not intruding," he called out uselessly, blatantly ignoring the ongoing meal. In fact he had timed his visit, with Nollo's precise information, exactly to arrive during the Churai dinner. Everyone gaped at this unlooked for and bizarre apparition leering through the doorway of the dining room at them, but Braq in particular stared at Ku with alert and wary attention as one might at an adversary. Ku did not look at Braq.

Jule and Rodit stood and offered Ku a seat at the table, but he flapped his arms from the elbows, demurring. "Thank you, thank you! It's so nice to see the old Chugran manners, the Chugran courtesy, 'even unto death.' But I have eaten. And I don't want to impose."

It was ridiculous for Ku to talk about "courtesy even unto death" since no one was dying, or even ill, but Rodit brightened at hearing the old expression. He insisted that Ku sit. Holding forth from smack in the middle of the table during the remainder of the dinner, Ku did manage to pack away quite a bit of food in spite of his protestations. Everyone resisted the temptation to ask what in hell he was doing there. It would have been rude to be so direct. But it made Ku feel good to know that they were all seething with curiosity.

And Nollo felt good about it too. He eagerly waited to see what Ku would do. He knew that Ku had paid a long visit to President Carroll after Jule departed the Schaal that morning. And Ku had had another brief discussion with Nollo during lunch. During this, Ku had let Nollo know that Ku would undertake some maneuver or stratagem or at least a rhetorical assault and that Nollo should lie low and not reveal himself in any obvious way as an opponent of this Atelier disaster. Now, as the meal ended and Jule brought out cups of frishy for everyone, Ku leaned both arms on the table and clasped his hands as if he were about to pray. He looked up and down the table and let out a sigh of satisfaction. "Ah, it's so nice to see the Chugran family unit – " he looked at Nollo and Braq – "the extended family unit, gathered about the hearth, at the feet " – he looked toward Rodit " – of the paterfamilial."

Rodit tried to look humble; he succeeded.

Jule had taken her seat again. Ordinarily, she would have been on her way back to the Emporium with Mark and Sue by now, but it was obvious that Ku was there for some purpose, which she had to learn, and in any event it would have been rude to jump up and leave her guest. She sensed that he was working his way around to his goal; she just wished he would get it over, and stop what she took to be this inane prattle.

"If only more of our Chugran families kept to the old ways, as you do, revering the old truths.

" 'The race before the tribe; the tribe before the family; the family before the individual.'

" 'Before I was, the Race was; after I am gone, the Race will be.' "

Jule, on the other hand, looking at Ku, thought, "After you are gone, relief will be," but she held her tongue. Ku's first statement was not an old "truth." It was something he had just made up, but it sounded vaguely like something they had heard before. The second statement was, of course, very well known to Chugrans, and again Rodit felt a warm reassurance at the familiar sentiment.

Ku kept on. "It is this spirit we are trying to cultivate at the Schaal – even against all the odds, against all the pressures and influences of this selfish, individualistic, materialistic culture we're suffocated by. To make our students proud of their Race, of the Racial achievements, the sacred Racial traditions. I can't begin to tell you how helpful Nollo has been – "

He broke off suddenly, and inhaled as if in a mystical ecstasy. He threw both his arms out across the table as if framing Nollo. "Look at this boy…this beautiful Chugran boy!" Nollo blushed, but he failed at that in which Rodit had succeeded. He could not look modest.

And indeed he was an utterly attractive young man. He was fourteen, but he seemed as if on the verge of manhood, with none of the blemishes or awkwardness of adolescence. Ku's voice took on a devotional tone. "Look at Chugrana!" His blotchy hands still waved at Nollo's face. "The very embodiment of our Race! And this young Chugran warrior is gathering about him the sons of the Race to do battle."

At this, Jule interrupted. She didn't have a thimble of an idea what Ku was talking about, but a memory of Jonni Churai shot into her head. She had no intention of allowing any such development in her household. "What battle are you talking about?" she demanded.

"Just a figure of speech, a mere metaphor," said Ku waving a hand breezily. "I'm just talking about our plantchi teams. My, we're being prickly Chugrans, aren't we? Well, that is our Chugran way too, heh, heh! isn't it? So I forgive you. I'm talking about how this wonderful young Chugran avatar is setting an example, organizing the boys into tribal teams, giving them old Chugran names and emblems, even chants…um, athletic chants…and showing them how to play the game. He's gotten just about every boy involved in one way or another, even those who are not athletic, or have no aptitude for the game…all except his younger brother…we hope *he* will join one of the teams next year."

As he said this, he leaned his face over and looked past Sue, who was sitting on his left, straight at Rodit at the end of the table and then at Braq who was between Sue and Rodit. At Ku's gestural urging, Rodit looked down at Braq and said, "Well, yes…er…Braq…I'm sure you would want…well, why haven't you joined up?...Of course, he will!" Then his eye quickly darted down the table at Jule. He seemed to display fear and defiance in the same cant of his head.

Jule was sitting bolt upright now. She looked straight at her husband. "Next year Braq will be at the Atelier," said Jule.

Rodit answered with some timidity, "Oh…well, I mean…that hasn't really been decided yet, has it?"

And, speaking almost at the same time, Ku's voice boomed over Rodit's, "Ah, I had heard a bit of a rumor to that effect, from President Carroll," he said with a slight emphasis on the last phrase. "I couldn't believe my ears! The son of Zaqqaq Churai deserting the Schaal Chugrana!"

Jule said, "He's not 'deserting' the Schaal. He is going to receive special training, the kind he needs to develop his unique talents."

Ku looked at Jule as if he were patiently giving a catechism to a rebellious child; but occasionally he included Rodit in his glance. "*His* 'special training'…'*he* needs'… '*his* unique talents.' Where does all this egotistical talk come from? Certainly not from our Chugran heritage. Doesn't it sound like a self-centered way to go about the duty of life? What about the needs of the Schaal? The needs of Chugrans? The needs of his family?" His arm encircled the table as he said this, suggesting in some way that Braq was leaving the Churai family in a foundering lifeboat.

There was a restlessness as several people shifted in their seats or scraped their chairs about. Suddenly Sue added her voice to the fray. "What's all this about Braq and special training at the Atelier? Do you mean more night classes?" Jule had had no opportunity yet to talk to Sue or Mark about any of this.

Before anyone could answer Sue's question, Ku threw his arms up and shrugged his shoulders. He also looked upwards as if he were in a pulpit. "You see! You see how even in this harmonious family, child will be set against child, cousin against cousin, brother against brother! Secrets will be kept from one another. The village will be split against itself. Plots will be hatched behind people's backs! All for solitary, anti-social selfishness!"

Now everyone really was in an uproar. And partially because Ku had lapsed into the unfortunate Chugran future tense, so they didn't know if he was speaking historically or making a prediction. Everyone spoke at once. "What plots?!" "What are you talking about?" "That's right – brother against brother!" "There aren't any secrets!" "I was just trying to find out what was going on!"

Finally, as the hubbub diminished, Jule's voice stood out from the rest. She spoke rather severely to Ku. "I don't know what gives you the right to come into our home and intrude in our family's private affairs."

But Ku was equal to this. "All Chugrans are your family. And, as a spiritual leader of the Chugran community, I think I have every right to advise members of that community. After all, a prester has *some* authority."

There was a blank silence at the table. Then Jule said, "A…prester?"

Ku tried to keep a serious face, but a hint of a smirk lifted the corner of his mouth. "Yes – you must have heard that I am a selected Prester of the Chugran fold. 'Prester Pranti Ku' is the title I am authorized to use, but I don't like to put myself forward as above people so I don't often insist on that mode of address."

Well! – they had all heard the title "Prester," or sometimes "Presbyter," but only in passing, as something from far in the past, or maybe as a term that only a few small sects still used, they weren't really sure. But it was news to the whole table that Ku possessed any such title. At the same time, it did not sound completely out of place.

And this was part of Ku's canniness – to know just what chord of ignorance or gullibility or lenience or deference he could pluck when he wanted to launch one of his lies. And to frame it in such a way that though it *was* a lie, still it had a thin patina of plausibility. There *was* such an old title floating about in Chugran cul-de-sacs. Some Chugrans *did* look up to Ku as a spokesman for them and their grievances. He *did* lapse, and frequently, into Chugran religious or rhetorical cadences, really the same thing. And he *did* seem to have the kind of learning one expected from a trained minister.

So, when he sprang "Prester Pranti Ku" on them, he tossed one of his usual outrageous bluffs on the table – and he won. No one could quickly collect the pieces of knowledge with which to challenge him. Except that Nollo almost guffawed. "Prester Pranti Ku!" Perfect! He too did not know whether it was true, or partially true, or almost completely false. He also knew that it didn't matter to Ku – or to him. Truth was fine – when it was needed. And so was falsehood. They were both just tools. And Ku's tool had worked. He had established his authority and his right to intrude. So that was what counted. Still, it was funny! To be able to stifle people that way! As he had on more than one occasion, Nollo discreetly nodded his head in approval and admiration of Ku.

"*Someone* has to speak for the community." Ku was going on. "Especially when outsiders, people of another race, another background, another culture, try to spirit away our children this way. And these people, these...Derosches...," he said it with scorn, "exhibit the worst of this kind of phoniness, this...individualism. I am always suspicious of people who have no ethnic pride. How can an individual be anything apart from his tribe? To put this young impressionable boy" – he gestured in Braq's direction without looking at him – "into such an environment would be genocidal."

Rodit was nodding now. How could he have been on the verge of assenting to Jule's traitorous proposal?!

Ku went on, sensing that things were moving his way. "How can we survive if we do not stick together? How can we hold our heads up as Chugrans if we do not proclaim our heritage to the world? Each of us must give back to the community what it has given to us – our precious identity. We must squash this sense of shame we all carry about with us." His harlequin face was becoming even blotchier with emotion.

Jule changed tacks. "Braq's parents are not here to decide for him. I'm acting on their behalf. I'm doing what they would want."

Ku answered, "You're very sure of yourself. How can you know what they would want?! They have not been able to see the boy for three years. How do you know they would choose to strike him from the honor roll of Chugrana, choose to cast him into the midst of a bunch of racial strangers this way? These Derosches may be as honorable as anyone," (his tone suggested that he thought otherwise) "but they know as little of our ways as any Dryruger. And the very fact of what they are doing – images! – trying to capture the mystical spirit of the world through representation! That itself shows how hateful they are to our own culture, to our way of life."

"Yes!" muttered Rodit vehemently, then again, his voice rising, "Yes!!"

Ku stood up, looming now over the table. "Braq Churai is a son of Chugrana. He must be for his own people. He cannot deny his blood. Blood must speak its mind! Let him show his gratitude to the Race for what it has given him, even this talent which he boasts of so arrogantly, and which he owes to the genetic genius of Chugrana. Let him not turn his back on his people, lest they turn their back on him. Let him not make his own into enemies.

"Let him be who he truly is!"

And at that moment, Mark, in tones that contrasted with Ku's florid manner of expression so Americanized was Mark already, said, "How come no one has asked Braq what *he* thinks?"

For a long moment, there was a stillness. They all seemed frozen figures in a photo. Then Braq stood up. Leaning behind Sue's chair, his lanky lance of a frame tilting toward Ku who drew back startled, he said, "I am enrolling in the Atelier."

He said it, and it was like a single metallic drop of sound in the pool of silence that continued on.

Then he walked out of the room.

***

"Do you think it strange that no one – not La Maestra, not me, not his Aunt Jule – no one had thought to ask the boy what he thought about the suggestion that he become a resident student at the Atelier?"

Bevol laughed in self-deprecation. "It seems lunatic when I look back at it. We were just all so focused on other priorities, and each with our own unquestioned assumptions: La Maestra and I on whether his aunt would approve, Jule herself on the thicket of objections from Rodit and Ku, and on what Zaq and Liz might think. Rodit was focused on the blow to his shaky self-esteem, so dependent on family cohesion. And Ku – well, I think Ku deliberately avoided asking Braq point blank because he knew what he would get from that quarter.

"Braq told me – this was long after, when he could look back at the moment – that he had been faintly amused to hear everyone marshalling arguments one way and another, to see Jule's serious, attentive reflection and deliberation – as if there were a decision to be made. He was amused because the decision had already been made – by him. It was as if it had been made in some other life, it seemed so irrevocable – like some searing cuneiform declaration that *he*, Creator, had annealed into the first stones fired on earth. He knew that he would go to the Atelier the way he knew he would take his next breath.

"And more. Braq had been recreating the visual world from that time, as an infant, that he had sculpted and drawn a 'Pfut' in the ochre Chugran sand, and then on through the years of his great discoveries of the wondrous powers of light and shade on a piece of paper. But I don't think he had ever seen a professional artist at work, or knew that there was such a thing as a 'profession' for artists – he just drew and was utterly, self-sufficiently happy in his drawing – until the day he saw Benedict Skye at the exhibition. Saw him as an adult engaged in this wonderful activity, *as an adult's occupation.*

"There, then, in that moment, Braq realized that he was going to be this also – an artist. It was not even what you might think of as a conscious decision, although a philosopher would probably identify it as such. The decision had already been all but assured by the countless choices he had *already* made – every time he had picked up chalk or pen and decided to draw, and again to draw, and again to draw – loving the act and loving the deciding.

"Now, it was more a realization or a discovery than a decision – as if a man placing his feet nimbly for a thousand artful steps along a slender rope suspended in air suddenly looked down, saw where he was, said to himself, 'Oh! I'm a tightrope walker! How exciting!' and then to the amazement of a watching throng continued his dance, high above their heads, oblivious of them and of the abyss below!"

CHAPTER 40

Maroons

Zaqqaq Churai rotted in a Chugran jail.

Liz Churai worked to free him.

She wrote to everyone in the world she could think of who might help. She spoke to Gyce Dooley. He had been powerless to change the minds of his fellow Quinqueviri. His influence only extended to a few other Dryrugers, in and out of the government. One such was Quint Pullili, Jr., son of one of the Quinqueviri. The senior Pullili, dead of a stroke, had left a son who worked in the Ministry of Justice. This son paid lip service to the regime, but in private discussions he was swayed by Gyce Dooley. The young Pullili thought the incarceration of Zaqqaq Churai was an outrage. He funneled such information as he could to Gyce and Liz. One lone functionary, he could do nothing to get Zaq released.

Liz had lost not just her husband, but her two children. Only rarely could she smuggle a letter out of the country to them, via Vasc Sulam's agents. By informal adoption, Liz had gained a daughter: Kaki N'Tosh. Kaki still lived with the neighbors she had first attached herself to, but she came every day to see Liz.

No information had ever surfaced as to Kaki's parents, nor would such information have helped Liz to understand Kaki any better. There was no special reason why Kaki's father and mother, Glenfield and Mighi N'Tosh, should have given birth to such a happy child. They were parents of no particular distinction; they had accomplished little in their lives save keeping their family, as the saying has it, "going." It is true that they loved their children with sincere affection, but else they possessed no other secrets of child-rearing. If you had asked them for advice on how to turn out such an effervescent infant, they would have shrugged and turned up their palms, and indeed their three other children, sons all, were, like the parents, unremarkable.

But there was something special about Kaki.

Until the age of five, this girl observed the blessings of which life is full. Only these blessings did she focus on. Sights and sounds and pleasures palpable. Smiles and the fulfilling of innocent desires. Curiosities satiated and the inexplicable made clear. She ran to meet these blessings, full-tilt. When there came one of those abuses life throws at a child – a bump, a scrape, a pang of hunger – she looked at it as one might at a bug that crawled across one's picnic plate. She waited for the bug to disappear off the edge, and then resumed the feast. She had no doubt that the feast was still there. She knew there were bugs in the world. She saw no reason to promote them.

In a single instant, when Kaki was five, something crawled across her plate that she could not dismiss. There was nothing special to single her family out, merely that her father and three brothers were in the wrong place at the wrong time – the wrong place being inside of improperly shaded skin. For this fault alone they were slaughtered as they stood frozen with alarm in front of the house, as the rioters poured into their street, fleeing through the yards and over the fences, followed by the torrent of bullets from the police. Her mother ran to the front door in time to see them fall. She started to scream "Why?!"

A simple word, "Why." It marks one as a scientist – or as a moral being. A simple sound consisting of two syllables eliding to a diphthong. Kaki's mother died with this word, "Why?" cut off in the "Wha-" of the diphthong. Kaki raced for the back door of their house, then for the woods behind, with that guillotined diphthong ringing in her ears.

This was no minor abuse but a horror, one which many children might not survive intact. Yet, a child may recover more easily than an adult. Hope may win out. The child, plastic and resilient, has not yet had years for the hardening off of despair.

A cork now stopped Kaki's effervescence. The cork was a question. The radiant love for life still shone out, and often, in her play with the Churai boys, or in her contemplation of the countless amazing things life puts in front of us. But after each spurt of enjoyment, inexorably, the cork was replaced. Then there came over her a calm, implacable seriousness, as that of a scientist.

Perhaps, after all, Kaki was an entomologist.

When Kaki running from the disaster that had destroyed her family came to the Churai's neighborhood, when she met Nollo and Braq, when she adopted the Churai, there was this change: she still saw life as a feast, but now she had to *know* where such vile things came from with their slimy, reeking trails to crawl across the plate of life. This image of the bug was her own. It was the way she saw the people who committed such acts. No matter how enormous their crimes, she saw them as puny and pathetic in stature, in worth, even in power. It seemed wrong to her, in some way she could not yet name, to grant these pathetic non-entities even the regard of fear. If only she could discover the secret of what made such vermin possible, she could stop them, squash them, or just step out of their way.

This was why she began attending Zaq's and Liz's Schaal. The things they spoke of seemed to touch the core of what she was seeking. Not every subject – Zaq or Liz might engage the three children in anything from zoology to mathematics to literature to mythology. But when Liz told the children that in America she had been able to publish whatever she wanted, whenever she wanted, without permission, and without fear of imprisonment whereas in Chugrana Zaq's writings had brought the truncheon of the state against him and might again at any moment, then Kaki stared at Zaq in wonder. She thought long about this afterwards. How could such vermin stop a man like *Zaq*, even if, as she noticed, he seemed so unsmirched by it?

Again, when she heard Zaq mention that in some of the tribal regions of Chugrana, weavers submissively plied their looms because the village told them to, and that a man who dared to challenge the commands of the village would be beaten, she frowned as if she had spied another crawling thing.

"You must study history," Zaq said.

"Learn what men have done, what they have been, what they have tried, what their reasons were, what succeeded, what failed. Or you will understand *nothing*. You'll never be able to judge what *should* be." Neighbors niggled at Zaq and Liz. The very pair of adults with whom Kaki made her home said to Zaq one day, "Why are you trying to teach a six year old about such things? You're going way over her head." But Zaq answered, "You are underestimating Kaki – and perhaps me. It is *she* who asks the questions, *she* who wants to know why such things happen, *she* who recognizes that injustice is wrong. Should I just shrug and tell her to accept? Or instead point her to the paths that can change the shackled way we live?"

Liz thought now of Zaq's advice to Kaki as she sat down to write to her husband. She was in Zaq's study. When she walked across the room a floorboard squeaked. It brought to her memory the sound of Zaq pacing this room. She smelled the remnants of his tobacco smoke —

even though it had now been almost three years since his arrest. She sat in his chair.

It was almost more than she could bear.

She wanted to feel *his* arms, not the arms of his chair, to sit in *his* lap, not the lap of his chair, to press against *him*, not this frame of wood and leather.

In two and a half years, she had seen him once – through the narrow slits of a fenced enclosure. The wide vertical planks were spaced only one half inch apart. This was part of the deliberate cruelty. If Zaq stood close enough to the fence to speak quietly through the slit to her, she could see only a sliver of his face. If he stood far enough back for her to see his whole face, the two of them had to speak up, which allowed the guard to hear what they said.

She could hold the privacy of his mind, or the vision of his person, but not both. She could not have the whole person of the man she loved.

And it was the same on his side of the fence.

They had to speak cryptically. The guards stood quite close on either side. The officials, in their generosity, had relented so far as to allow Zaq and Liz to speak of anything that was not politically sensitive, or that did not contravene the laws of Chugrana. This meant that the following topics, listed on a card for them, were forbidden:

Zaq's work.

Zaq's writings.

Zaq's newspaper.

His Society for the Rights of Man.

His brothers – one dead, one having betrayed Chugrana by emigrating.

Anything to do with his imprisonment or with his health, implying that he might have been mistreated.

Any efforts to bring pressure from outside to free him.

Their son, Braq – "bastard fruit of an illicit union."

Their love for each other – forbidden.

Their life together, past or future – proscribed.

Still, it was generous of those authorities to allow so many other topics.

Zaq and Liz alternated standing slightly away from the fence, so that the angle of aperture allowed each to see the other whole. They took each other in for a long moment. Then, Liz expressed this encyclopedic thought, this whole religion, this sum of everything she lived for. She said, "Zaq."

He responded lengthily with his own profound creed. He said, "Liz."

After a moment, she said, "You look well."

He answered, "I am," and with the barest pause, "now."

He stepped closer to the barrier. "Nollo?"

She too moved in. The guards could still hear them, but it allowed Zaq and Liz to lower their voices slightly in an illusion of privacy.

"Safe and well." She let a moment pass. Then she added with the barest emphasis on the first word, "*Any* son of yours could not be better."

He smiled with relief, grasping her amphibolous answer to the other half of his question.

Limited to so few topics and words, they spoke extraordinarily slowly, drawing out their exchanges as much as they could, to savor every word and moment...to make the experience last for a lifetime if need be.

After another pause, she stepped back from the slit to let him see her whole face. She said, looking at him significantly, "Minds are speaking to minds." He looked intently at her, to try indeed to read her mind. After a moment he nodded. "As *they should*."

The guards were uneasy about this last exchange, but it was so vague. Just that old Chugran saying. It didn't mean much, did it? Still, one of them, in fear that he might be punished if he allowed one of the forbidden topics to be broached, barked "Time's up!"

But Zaq said, authoritatively, "Just a minute." He pressed his eye to the slit, and said to Liz. "Step back." She did so, knowing that he wanted a full view of her figure, of her person. She stood, utterly upright, her arms at her sides. She turned her palms slightly toward him, as if she were offering herself to him.

After a long moment, she stepped up to the fence, and said, "You." Zaq stepped back now to allow her to see him complete.

The guard suddenly had a glimmer of understanding and yelled, "Stop that! Take them away!"

And this had been all.

A few sentences. A few glances. Yet each knew that each was still alive, and the same person that each had been. That their sons were alive and safe and well. That Liz was working to free Zaq. It seemed that they had spoken volumes to each other, past the barriers erected by those for whom race mattered.

Liz sat now at Zaq's desk. What should she say in her letter? Most of the ones she had written had been returned. One or two had not, but she had no idea if these had reached him. She knew that she had to be cryptic in her writing, as she had been in person, if there was to be any hope of getting them through the censor. She thought again of Kaki. The young girl was now her courier to the outside world, through intermediaries, in Vasc Sulam's network. They had to be as discreet as possible. Liz was working to organize Zaq's papers, editing a collection of his speeches and editorials. Someday, she hoped, this collection could be spirited out of the country, and then published abroad, to throw a light on Zaq from the free world.

Such endeavors had led to the release of political prisoners before, in other places. Liz had to hope that it might here too.

But Kaki was also her courier and her link to the world that *had been*, the world of Zaq and Braq and Nollo. Every day the little girl ran to Liz's house, where they would talk for hours. Liz held this remnant of the Schaal, for Kaki's benefit, and for her own. At one point she suggested that Kaki begin writing. She knew that writing had the enormous power to clarify thoughts, to make them objective. Kaki surprised her by saying, "I have been keeping a diary for several years."

She further surprised Liz by asking, "Would you like to read it?"

Liz said, "If you wouldn't mind, I would love to. But are you sure? A diary is so – *personal?*"

Kaki said, "There is nothing in it I would not want you to see."

Now, planning her letter to Zaq, Liz went back over some of the passages from Kaki's diary. They floated before her, snatches of visions of a young girls' mind.

Why did they do it?

They killed my father. They killed my mother. They killed my three brothers. By luck I escaped, or they would have killed me.

Why did they do it?

I loved my family. They all loved me. They are gone. They had harmed no one. They were not rioters. The rioters came – they burst into our street. There were men behind them – police – soldiers. They had guns, cannons, fire. They killed everyone, whoever moved they killed.

Why? Why us? Did they not see we were human beings? That we harmed no one, that we only loved each other.

They killed the wrong people.

I will never understand this.

I must understand this.

. . .

Nollo will help me. Nollo is the Churai's older son. Today he asked me about my beloved family. He said, "We'll pay them back." I asked him how, and he said, "We'll find them, we'll kill them, we'll bring justice to them."

Justice. That must be what I want. But I need to know why they did it.

I don't want to kill the wrong ones.

Who are they? What if we kill the wrong ones – like they did to us? We were not rioting but they killed us. What kind of man does this?

Maybe if I know why, I will know who.

Nollo is some kind of prince. A wonderful prince. I think Braq thinks so too. Braq is younger than Nollo. I think he's my age.

Is Braq a prince too? Why isn't he?

. . .

I like the Churai family. As – (she had struck out this word) – Almost as much as my own family. Zaq and Liz – if I were their daughter ? ? But then I would be Nollo's and Braq's sister. I don't want to be their sister. Why not??

Zaq has told me things about what happened. I still don't understand. What is this stupid thing about 'race,' about skin? Because of skin, they killed my family?!

But I think Zaq will help me to understand better than Nollo. Nollo wants revenge. Nollo said he wants justice. But when I ask justice against who, he says "Dryrugers." This is what I don't understand. Liz is light-skinned – she's not a Dryruger – but she is still a good person, she's his mother – well, Braq's real mother and Nollo's step-mother.

Zaq seems to know a lot about this.

. . .

I think I will adopt the Churai.

. . .

Braq's pupils get so big when he looks at me. When he draws me. Sometimes, just when he looks at me. His eyes are so brown, and they shine – not like Nollo's –

I don't know why they're different – maybe that's just the way they are.

But Nolly is beautiful. And strong!

Braq does such drawings! I've never seen anything like that before. I have no idea how he does it! What makes a person able to do things like that?

Zaq is helping me to understand more and more about these evil people who killed my family. I guess it's not just here in Chugrana. It's happened in a lot of places.

I admire Zaq. I think I would like to be like him.

...

Braq stood up to Nollo today. I was surprised. I never saw him do that before. Nollo gave in. We played the Dryrugers and conquered him. I think he let us win, he didn't try very hard. That was different.

It's just a game.

Except that the Dryrugers – the Quin- something – are coming to visit the Churai family today.

...

Last night I saw a hero! Nollo Churai. Those terrible people set fire to his Uncle Rodit's Museum, our Museum. The Museum for Chugrana. Nollo called in the alarm, and went into the fire, and tried to put it out, and tried to stop the Dryrugers!

It still burned to the ground, but he risked his life to stop them! He was covered with cuts and blood and soot and burns. Everyone – everyone! – sees now what a hero he is. I always knew it.

His bike was wrecked.

He stood up to the Dryrugers. "We're not your slaves," he yelled at them. If everyone stood up this way, I wonder what it would be like. Could we stop the evil?

Zaq calmed everyone down. He said this isn't the way. I mean the rioting.

What is the way?

The only thing is – why did Nollo get so mad at Braq?

...

They've gone. I had to say goodbye to my family again. My second family. There's only Liz left.

This is terrible. Again.

I guess I love them. Nollo and Braq. Nollo is my hero – Zaq is too. He's been arrested. His newspaper is destroyed.

And Braq – well, he's like me. It's like I was gone from myself.

I still don't understand why these people are doing this.

Liz looked at the past – at her two sons, at Kaki, at Zaq – and at the future – at the path to safety she was trying to steer. She thought that the letter she was writing had to have the succinctness of poetry; it had to condense vast ideas to a few simple images. But Liz did not have the facility of poetry.

She picked up her pen. She wrote to her husband, "Kaki follows the advice she received once from a wise man, to study history. So some great minds are speaking to her…"

She also included this piece of information: "Kaki has read that one of her favorite artists studied at a great Atelier in a foreign land. That he found a beneficent home there. It may have been Michelangelo…or some other young artist… I forget which…"

And one more thing Liz inserted. "Kaki has also read in one of her history books that not all battles can be won. There are times, she has read, that the only outcome of a particular battle may be self-destruction, with no victory for the right…"

Liz wrote this last and dropped her pen on Zaq's desk. She looked away, into some distance. "Will you hear this, my Beloved? Will you heed it?"

PART IV

A World Enlightened

CHAPTER 41

Interlude: The Last Painting - Revisions

It was too important.

This painting meant too much to the Painter. In some way that he did not yet fully understand, this painting would embody everything he had learned. That was why it was so important to get the composition right.

He had changed the composition again. It was still three figures, but now there was no white hind, no goddess in disguise: Artemis was only herself, a divine female. And Ephialtes had, in the Painter's new conception, succeeded in winning her. He, the man-god, and she, the goddess-woman he had conquered, together walk toward the viewer, leaving the wood behind them. To one side, Otos stands, bow hanging at his side, useless. He seems bereft.

The Painter could not understand why the drawing had evolved this way. It seemed to have some life of its own. But, at the same time, the composition was, he thought, an improvement over the last two attempts.

He had thrown out the needless complexity of the first conception. He had vitalized the deadening symmetry of the second one.

He compared his many sketches, searching to find what was eluding him. Otos was supposed to lust after Hera, but the Painter had eliminated this part of the myth completely. Was this a mistake? Should he have included her after all? Why? And what difference did it make, anyway? This was just a story about love and desire, nothing more. He shook his head. It seemed to him that it was about more than that.

Preparing his canvas, he had now finished the process of stretching and tacking, stretching and tacking, working outward from the center of each side. He had known not to make it tight as a drum; if you didn't know better, you would have thought the canvas was now impaled on the four stretcher bars too loosely to be of any use. But he knew what would happen as soon as the hot rabbit-skin glue splashed into the fibers: immediately, each linen thread that made up the weave of the fabric would start to shrink, and the canvas would begin to contract dramatically. He had seen canvases, strung too tight, shocked by the glue bath suddenly shrink, warp, and, with a frightening snap, crack the stretcher bars into pieces.

To know how tight required judgment, and judgment, he knew, required experience. One time a canvas he had stretched too tight, upon receiving the bath of hot glue, warped into a freakish geometry and, without his touching it, began to spin violently like a lunatic gyroscope, as the continuously shrinking canvas pulled the members out of position. Amused, he watched it whirl on the floor. Then he dismantled it and started all over again.

But he wanted no such amusements now – not with something as important as *this* painting. Not with the love between mortals and immortals.

CHAPTER 42

Braq Escapes

Braq eagerly carried his suitcase up to the second floor and along the corridor to his new quarters. It was the same suitcase with dusty leather straps he had brought with him in the flight from Chugrana. Mrs. Derosch showed his room to Jule, who had brought Braq to his new home and had trooped up the stairs to see for herself how he was to be housed. His was a small room at one end of a long hallway, at the opposite end of which were Ann's and Clark's rooms; the main staircase to the second floor dropped one off right by the door to their rooms, and since the wooden floors of the stairs and the hall itself creaked as they do in old houses Ann and Clark could always hear if someone was going up or down the stairs. Ann was at pains to point this out to Jule so that she would know that they would "keep an eye" on Braq's comings and goings. Not that either woman thought him likely to get into mischief. But Ann knew that Jule would be reassured by her watchfulness.

Braq felt his spirits lift the minute his last class at the Schaal ended and he knew that he was now about to move to the Atelier. Was this an escape? If so, from what, or whom? Certainly from the Schaal, where day by day the atmosphere was becoming more and more racially saturated. Ku was pushing new and increasingly inflammatory projects onto the students. Each student was being encouraged to research his genealogy, and to procure clothes reflective of the tribe he thought he was, or might be, descended from, and even to wear these clothes every day, almost as a uniform. The students were encouraged to dredge up, or even to make up, tribal slogans or chants: hoary old clan mottoes on moldering coats of arms, last heard in the croaking throats of ancestors three hundred years removed, now rang from the piping voices of uncomprehending children. But it was not just the tribal clustering and breast-beating that bothered Braq. Ku encouraged, and seemed to revel in snide racial epithets, directed at "whites" especially, but also at Jews, Latinos, and "A-rabs". He spat his venom at black Africans, at brown people, at yellow, at any group of the moment whom he felt was not "respectful" of Chugrans. Braq could hardly believe what he was seeing – that Nollo seemed not only to enjoy this, and that – how could this be possible?! – Ku seemed to look toward Nollo for approval and support in his diatribes and in his proposals for new racial activities.

One day Braq asked his brother, "Why are you going along with all of this stuff of Ku's…what do you think father would say?"

Nollo thought to himself, contemptuously, "He thinks it's coming from Ku!" He was about to make a resentful, angry reply to his little brother's naïve interference, but the mention of Zaq stopped him. Instead, he said, "Oh, it's just a bunch of fun, finding out who our ancestors were, seeing the tribe emblems and mottoes…you know…it's just for entertainment. Don't get so uptight about it, Little Brata-braq...Don't you remember when I made my chart of The House of Jolofer? Father didn't mind *that*."

Braq only vaguely recalled the chart; at the time he had been preoccupied with drawing his brother's hands instead. But Braq could still hear his father's voice saying, one starry night, that one should not pay attention to racial markers, that these were not what was important about people. And he remembered a bitter explosion from his father on another occasion: "Interesting shapes, colors and sounds – and not one damn thing more" about the paraphernalia of the tribes. Now, Braq wanted to get as far away from all of this as he could. He did not want to get away from his Big Brátano, he thought…except that Nollo seemed to enjoy just that which their father hated. This was very puzzling to Braq, even though he still looked up to his brother. As it turned out, Braq did not have to worry about leaving Nollo, because his brother had, surprisingly, arranged to continue as Braq's "chaperone" at the Atelier. The idea was that Nollo would drop in whenever he wanted to see how his little brother was doing.

Perhaps, if Braq had put his feeling into words, he would have said that he was just escaping from the "world of race" to some other world, a world where people were just individuals.

Now, exulting in his new world, he followed La Maestra and his Aunt Jule downstairs and out to the front. He heard La Maestra tell his aunt that Bevol Stagri or she would give her monthly reports, by phone or mail, on Braq's progress and well being. Now it was time to part. Jule said, "You know we're not that far away if you need us."

Braq nodded. Impulsively, he launched himself at Jule, flinging both arms around her. Though only ten, he was already sprouting into his lanky frame, and Jule was tiny. His lunge caught her off guard, and they fell against the car.

"Braq!" she said laughing.

"I'm sorry, Aunt Jule, it's just that I'm really happy to be here…and I wanted to thank you for it" he said as they got their balance again. He kissed her, and she held him at arm's length to look into his face. She had never seen him be so affectionate to her. "It was *your* decision," she said, and added, "I couldn't have stopped you if I'd tried – could I?"

He shook his head, grinning. "No." Then he said, more seriously, "But you didn't try, did you?"

She answered, "No, Braq. I'm sure this is what your mother and father would want for you…what I would want if you were my own son. It's what you need…what you deserve."

Jule got into her car. As she drove away she saw in the rearview mirror a skinny boy bounding eagerly up the steps into the house that was the Atelier Derosch.

***

"By now we had that one semester of night school behind us so we knew all about his brilliant talent in drawing and composition," said Bevol. "As yet we knew nothing about what he would do with *color*…but why should there be any difference there? La Maestra had asked him if he had ever painted in color before, and he had said something about a watercolor he had once done…said it was unsuccessful, but he could not explain why. No matter, we thought. We'll start him at the bottom, as with everyone, and let him rise…let him rise.

"You all know what 'the bottom' is here." Bevol's students nodded knowingly, some groaned, some raised their eyebrows as if they had gone through the most sadistic boot camp in the world. "So we set him to doing master copies of still lifes, as we do with all of you. I hope you understand why we do that – you know how complex oil painting is – one red pigment is opaque, one is translucent, one blue dries fast, one slowly, one yellow goes on thick, one thin, some blacks are cool, some warm. Not to mention all of the problems of composition, of handling the brushes and the medium, of whether or when to use turpentine – you've all dealt with the thicket. So we have you do copies of easy still lifes by great masters – they've already solved half of those problems for you – all you have to do is learn how to manipulate your pigments and your brushes. When you're ready…" – he raised an eyebrow pointedly – "…we let you create your own masterpieces."

"So Braq polished off the first few still life copies with dispatch. Yes, he lived up to our expectations...there…without question. Then he tackled a couple of landscape copies. Here too, his drawing skills were phenomenal, although he chafed at merely copying the compositions, even of masters. He changed them here and there – for the better I would say.

"And the issue of color with these copies seemed to hold no terror for him. There is so much to know, but each of us gave him our knowledge, which he seemed to soak up as if the well he poured his knowledge into had no bottom. He marshaled the pigments on his palette as if he were a seasoned campaigner putting his troops through familiar maneuvers.

"Portraiture has its own set of difficulties, so – although Braq had already shown that he was crackerjack at depicting faces in chalk, charcoal, pencil, and pen and ink – La Maestra at first had him render his oil portraits only in one pigment, the typical monochromes such as burnt umber, or raw umber, or perhaps raw sienna. Then she had him do several portraits in grisaille – some of you haven't tried that yet – it's just like doing a charcoal drawing with all the shades of gray, but using oil pigments instead of charcoal. With all of these techniques, he was brilliant.

"Yes, those first few weeks, I was tickled pink, I was ecstatic, and so was Mrs. Derosch. She didn't often get such a glow, but you could tell just by seeing how she lingered in the background, watching this boy work – letting him make mistakes, but occasionally stepping up and telling him, "Get up," then taking his palette and brush and showing him how to create a form with a few miraculous strokes.

"Everyone who comes through here admired La Maestra, but I don't think any student ever looked up to her the way Braq did. She was a heroine to him. Her uncompromising respect for the reality she was dealing with, her knowledge of how each pigment and brush would behave, how they would bring a world to life on a two-dimensional canvas, her refusal to let him off with less than he could achieve – she was just the kind of person he wanted in his world.

"When La Maestra and I spoke with each other about Braq and his training, it was as if we were speaking of our own child – I think all of the teachers here felt that way. He was so open to us all. We had there in our hands what every teacher dreams of – precious, supple, responsive, clay to mold as our minds and hearts desired. What more could we ask? What, we thought, could possibly go wrong?

"Braq began his apprenticeship with us in the summer session that year after his last class at the Schaal. My own anatomy classes were abbreviated in the summer months, as usual; I started them several weeks later. I was so eager to have Braq in my class. I couldn't wait to start pouring that knowledge into him, knowing how it could help his figure drawing. I was not thrilled to have Nollo there too, but he still had some vague and ill-defined status as Braq's chaperone, and he would drop in and out of classes whenever he felt like it. So he too was there that first day of anatomy class. This also happened to be the day that Braq was going to try his first color portrait in the afternoon session.

"I wheeled my skeleton out" – he put his hand fondly on the skeleton's head – "this very one. I began my lecture. And when I got to the point in my introduction, which some of you have heard many times, the part when I say that for all the differences between each human being still there are certain essential similarities, just at that point I touched the skeleton on the head, and – he collapsed in a heap of bones at my feet with a horrible clatter. It startled me so much that I jumped back and knocked over my flagon of frishy that was sitting on the table behind me. It broke. The fragments went sailing everywhere, and there was frothy frishy leaking along the floor under people's chairs.

"You can guess that I blurted out a 'Damn!' It was my beautiful skeleton – and my favorite frishy cup. I swear to this day I just gave that damned skeleton a little tap. Why that screw was loose I don't know. Maybe I hadn't tightened it properly the last time I made an adjustment. I wondered if someone had fiddled with it on purpose.

"The class was in an uproar, half of them laughing, the others gasping. I noticed that Nollo was snickering in a way that seemed to mock me. Several of them helped to straighten things up. I sent Gideon to the tool cabinet to get a new bolt and nut to secure the skeleton to its hanger because the old fasteners had rolled off into oblivion.

"Finally I was able to resume. I picked up the thread and went on with my point – how the basic skeletal and muscular features of everyone on earth are strikingly similar, whereas the differences in proportion are usually a matter of fractions of a millimeter. And that this applies between men and women, young and old, and among races. I mentioned the silliness of the older anthropologists who ran about measuring skulls to prove differences of intelligence but only ended by proving their own stupidity. I quoted one such imbecile who said that the shape of the pelvis of 'the darker races' showed 'their animal character,' and I refuted this astonishing piece of 'science' by pointing out that anatomical studies showed no such differentiation – either of shape or of moral stature – among pelvises or races.

"During this whole presentation, I noticed that Nollo now seemed ill at ease. Whenever I made eye contact with him, he returned a tight-lipped stony face, or he did that trick of his of staring away at nothing. He was not my concern, and I didn't want him in the class anyway, so I ignored him as much as I could, and I was happy when the class was over and he left.

"The afternoon session was portrait class, as usual, and as often happened, the model hadn't shown up. Someone suggested that I sit for the class, and I agreed, although I was dying to see how Braq would do with his first color portrait. In my eagerness I'm sure I would've hovered behind him, as I caught myself doing frequently then. Instead, by posing in front of the class, I would be able to look at his work only during the ten minute breaks. Still, I'm egotistical enough to enjoy having my portrait done, although with twenty artists you'll get twenty different images of yourself…not all flattering either...but it's fascinating to compare how they all see you.

"So I sat. Ann took up her usual position of honor in the middle, and she had Braq sit next to her so she could easily see how he was proceeding. I struck what I thought would be an interesting pose, my index finger alongside my cheek, gazing reflectively over their heads. Occasionally, my eyes would drift down to look in their direction. Each time I did this, I felt suddenly naked – because two pairs of eyes were looking at my face as if they would strip the skin off my bones, and the bones off my soul. You would not strip your soul bare for just anyone, would you? But for those two people I was willing. So I felt the pleasure I was experiencing flood into my face, and I didn't mind who else saw it.

"At the first break, I strolled around the room, looking at each person's canvas. This was interesting, as I say, but I was really champing to see what Braq, and La Maestra, had done. Finally, I arrived behind their chairs. For this first twenty minute session, Braq had started with an umber underpainting – a common, if conservative approach. Ann, in the meantime, was already into full use of color, with the confidence and authority of seventy-five years of mastery behind her.

"Even though they were sitting next to each other, there was still a slight difference of perspective. And the fact that one painting was as yet only a monochromatic rendering while the other was in color made a big difference too. So there was really no comparing them, if I had wanted to. But you could see that each artist had gone deep into his subject and pulled out some essential features – as each one judged the essence. I can't tell you what Ann or Braq saw in my face, or how they might have put it into words – their medium after all was the visual, the world in two dimensions, not literature – but I liked whatever it was that each saw in my face.

"I heard Ann say to Braq, 'After the break, go into color,' and I thought, 'Yes! Braq, take the plunge – let's see what you can do!' I was impatient. I cut the break short. I sat again. Again the eyes looking intently at me, perhaps even more so than before. I think I no longer had the same glow in my face…at least it felt different now, more like a flush, burning sensation. I was so impatient. *Why* was it so important to me to see his first venture rendering humans in color? Did I feel that I was there at the Beginning when God was creating Man?

"Finally, the buzzer went off indicating the end of the twenty minutes, and I think I leaped out of the chair I was so eager. I tried to control myself; I forced myself to walk slowly around, and again I arrived behind his chair. I looked at the painting.

"I must have blinked ten times.

"It was wrong. His painting was wrong.

"I looked over at Ann's painting, but there was no point in that. I looked back again. What was it? Had he suddenly lost his drawing skill? No, the brush strokes were fluid, incisive, accurate, purposeful. Were the values wrong? No, darks were dark, and lights were light, even dramatically so, as one would've expected from Braq.

"Were the colors wrong? Well, no two painters will approach the use of color in the same way. We all know that. But there was *something* about the color…it was…off.

"After the break I went back and resumed my pose. Well, how silly I was! So it wasn't perfect yet, it wasn't the work of a genius this time. It was his first attempt. What was I thinking?! He would get it right, sooner or later. And he had the greatest teacher in the world sitting right next to him to guide him. I felt my confidence grow as I placed my finger next to my cheek to resume the pose. All the same I no longer felt the glow or the heat. I felt something else.

"At the next break, I walked directly over to Braq's chair. I looked at his painting. It was still there. I mean the problem. He was further along in the rendering. He had worked in some background, and hinted at the shoulders, so the spatial context was established. He had the tilt of my head, the gesture of my hand against my face. Yes, everything seemed accurate, and well integrated, full of character – you might say 'artistic'! But it was that damned color!

"I tapped La Maestra on the shoulder covertly, and gestured toward Braq's painting with my eyebrows raised as if to say, "What's going on? She patted the air behind her with her palm, meaning 'Cool it!' Her expression seemed calm and unconcerned. As if she saw nothing to worry about.

"During the next period I heard her murmur a few things to him...leaning over and pointing to his canvas and toward my face. Finally, she took his chair, and I saw her talking to him, and then she grasped his palette and brushes and must have made a few strokes to show him what she wanted. He sat down again and continued.

"Ah! now he would be on the right track!

"At the next break I walked over expectantly. I looked a bit better on the canvas, but it was only because of certain brush strokes that I recognized as La Maestra's. In those areas, the skin color was richer, more vibrant, more…human?

"The remainder of the session went on that way. At the end, I trudged over for a last look. Yes, he had made some small improvements. But it was still not right. He had captured me all right. It was a striking portrait, full of character. But the skin, the skin…. The face was mine; the skin was not.

"La Maestra studied it. She said, 'The drawing is good, the values are good, the color…' She hesitated. Then, stating a plain fact, '…the color is not right.'

"She continued to look at it. Then she said, 'Wipe it out.'

"She said it calmly, matter of factly, as she always uttered that dreaded phrase to a student who had worked for hours, or perhaps much longer on something that was fundamentally ill-conceived.

"I was shocked to hear her say this – after all her great principle was, 'It's not the color, it's the value that's important.' Now here she was telling Braq to wipe it out because the color was just – all wrong.

"I winced, but Braq seemed accepting of the impartial judgment. He looked up at La Maestra's calm face, a face that said 'You can rebuild if you have to, and the next thing you build may be as good as or even better than the last. Don't be afraid to let go of what is hopeless, but carry your hopes and dreams and your vision to a new place, and start again.' His young benevolent face, his mouth relaxed and his eyes clear, held the gaze of his stern mistress. He picked up his paint rag and dipped it in his turpentine cup. He began wiping my face off the canvas."

CHAPTER 43

Progress

Nollo wiped some sweat off his forehead with irritation. Why were there no cars just then when he was trying to hitchhike from the Atelier to the Schaal? It was noontime, there should have been lots of cars, but Old Rolling Road was never predictable and sometimes even quite deserted. Wouldn't you know it would be so just when he needed help. But at least he was out of that damned Atelier, with that phony Chuke, Bevol Stagri, acting like a white man. He with his stupid pretense of behaving like a Chugran just because he drank out of a frishy cup....Well at least that was broken! That was a small bonus. In the whole six months or so that Nollo had been at the Atelier, Bevol never once had referred to anything about Chugrana, or Chugrans, had never even acknowledged that he and Braq and Nollo were all of the same race. For that matter, no one at the Atelier had. It made Nollo feel very out of place, almost invisible. Why did no one ever speak of Nollo's race...or their own race for that matter? It was true that one or two had asked him some questions about Chugrana, but that was more historical curiosity than racial.

Ah, here was a car, finally. Nollo stuck out his thumb. It was a small pickup truck, and it roared close by him, spewing gravel and dust in his face. The driver leaned out and brandished a fist, then made an obscene gesture, and bellowed, "*Chu*ker!"

Nollo coughed with disgust and shook his own fist at the disappearing truck. He had been told that hitchhiking might be dangerous, but that simply egged him on. When he finally got a ride, he became even more irritated. It was a student from the Atelier, on her way to get some supplies. She saw Nollo by the side of the road and pulled over. "Nollo! Get in...don't you think you shouldn't be hitchhiking? It's not safe for a boy like you." She meant that he was young; that was how she perceived him.

"You mean it's not safe for a *Chu*ker?" he asked belligerently.

"No," she said, ignoring his tone, "I meant for a young boy. You don't know who might pick you up. Someone might kidnap you or hurt you."

"I'm *not young*," said Nollo heatedly. "I'm fourteen."

"Well, all right," she conceded to avoid a fight. "A young man, then." She glanced at him. It was true; he was on the cusp of manhood. She took in his clear complexion and perfectly modeled features. "I'll bet you have all the young ladies interested in you."

He turned his head and ran his eyes over her figure. After a moment he said, with a faint expression of contempt, "Yes...they are."

He wanted to slap the smile off her face.

Before they came to the turn for the Schaal, they passed the street that led to Rodit's and Jule's house. He asked her to let him off there. He walked quickly to the house. He was anxious to get to the Schaal to talk to Ku, but first he had to check something. Only Rodit was at home. Nollo always made a point of being polite to his uncle; Rodit doted on Nollo. "Hello, Uncle Rodit, just stopped off on my way to the Schaal," said Nollo. Then he ran downstairs to his room, the space in the basement that was his alone now that Braq was gone. He stripped off his clothes and examined himself in the mirror. He didn't know how you could tell about a pelvis without dissecting the person. He felt vaguely that he wanted to peel his skin off in order to see. Peel the skin off...he thought of the écorché statue. He shuddered, but at the same time he couldn't get rid of the idea of peeling his own skin. He wanted to see if it was true about the pelvises of "the darker races," as that man had said, the one Stagri had quoted. Nollo was inclined to discount what Stagri had said in refutation of the man; it was obvious to anyone with eyes that there were significant differences, only the anthropologist had gotten it backwards; it was the white races who showed "animal character." Still, he wasn't sure just what differences he was trying to find in his pelvis. He wondered what his "Jolofer bones" looked like.

He thought exactly this: "I have Jolofer bones, not Churai bones."

He shrugged, and put his clothes back on. He went up, grabbed a quick bite, said goodbye to his uncle, and then took the shortcut to the Schaal. He quickly arrived at the grotto. He lingered only for a moment, taking in its dank smell, and then climbed the hill to the plantchi field. It was still lunchtime, and the plantchi teams were on the field practicing. Nollo surveyed them with pride. They were his creation; they looked to him for guidance; they were almost his...subjects.

A figure separated itself from one of the groups and approached Nollo. Wearing his "clan colors" you could not have told him from any of his teammates, but as he came across the field, Nollo instantly knew it was Fempy. A salamander exhibits its amphibian character in part by its writhing locomotion. Carrying the moist slime of its primordial past with it, it seems to swim – on land. Planting each of its four feet in alternation, it drags its form across the ground in a writhing S-curve. A two legged, upright creature – say, a man – could scarcely duplicate this style of movement. Fempy managed it. Walking on two feet, his body yet seemed to undulate through the air. And it did not matter whether you saw him from the front, back or either side; he undulated from every aspect.

Fempy Lobbel slithered up to Nollo. He stopped and gave a little duck of his head. "Hi, Pal Nollo."

Nollo had waited for this almost negligible act of deference. When he got it, he gave Fempy two little strange pats on the back of his head. "Hi, Pal Fempy." His acolyte was wearing the colors of Nollo's team – or was it his clan? The difference had become blurred.

What had bloomed two years earlier was now something more than a mere sport. Each team had its own identity, based on tribal markers. Whence came these markers? The naïve thought they came from Chugrana, from its old traditions. But Ku and Nollo knew that this was only part true. They knew because they had created the other parts themselves. Nollo could not say who had originated the idea, or the method they followed. He supposed it was Ku. But the two of them were pals of the soul.

The whole thing began when Nollo told his mentor about the tribal gathering, when each tribe had marched resplendent in their regalia accompanied by raucous drums and rattles into the sunblasted sunken plantchi field in the uplands of Chugrana. Ku had listened with rapt attention and running his tongue over his lips, said, "Oh! I can just see it! I wish I could have been there. If only we could have something like that here!"

He grilled Nollo on the tribal names, colors, patterns, and chants. Nollo dredged a wealth of information out of his adhesive memory. Without this, their little scheme (not so little any more) would never have gotten off the ground because few Chugrans in America these days set any store by or even held onto any of these moribund traditions. They knew the names and uniforms of America's baseball teams: they did not know old tribal designations. And all but the newest students owned baseball uniforms, until recently worn at the Schaal, but since the arrival of Nollo packed away in cupboards and closets. The Schaal had on a time competed against nearby schools in the national pastime. But Nollo and Ku told them that baseball was an *American* game, a white man's game, a game of colonial oppression designed to wipe out the true genius of Chugran plantchi. Now, plantchi supplanting baseball, the students of the Schaal competed only against each other. They turned inwards.

No matter, thought many parents and teachers. The children will still get the benefits of sports even this way. The first year that Nollo and Ku organized the games, they held tryouts and assigned the team members by ability. Only halfway through that year they abandoned this scheme. Several parents complained that their children, who were indeed untalented, had been assigned to teams which were hopelessly outclassed by the two or three top teams. This was undeniable. Ku and Nollo heard these complaints with sympathy. Nollo especially was dissatisfied. Though most of the kids looked up to him as an expert on the playing of plantchi – he had taught them to play after all – the best athletes had quickly surpassed him. One of these, Jonatan Gee, the captain of the top team, told Nollo to get lost when Nollo officiously handed some advice to his team that Gee thought was stupid.

"I think we should try a different way of choosing teams," Nollo told Ku. "There are too many unhappy people." Ku did not ask how many this description encompassed; he didn't care. He trusted Nollo. No, it was more than trust; it was some affinity of spirit. Nollo was his "beautiful Chugran boy." He *was* Chugrana. Almost out of nowhere, it seemed, he had come as a present for Ku, a blessing, a treasure. He saw that Nollo had gifts unlike anyone else. Ku felt that it was his special destiny to promote this boy and his goals, whatever those might be. He felt no need to identify what Nollo's gifts were, no need to inquire into his goals; he felt that those goals were his too, by virtue of what he thought of as his racial instinct. It was not his way to inquire explicitly about motives, least of all his own.

The two of them reassigned the teams on a more egalitarian basis. They distributed the best players among all the teams. "And Pranti Ku will level the plantchi playing field," he announced to them all on the day of this reorganization, in his annoyingly ambiguous Chugran speechway, by which he meant, "I have already done it."

But by the end of that year, Nollo was still dissatisfied. In spite of the reassignments, talent will out. Certain teams had emerged as consistently the best, even though the teams were all supposed to have the same number of good and bad players. No doubt it was because some of the best people can also bring out the best in the worst. So it happened that the second best player in the school, Bill Brown, turned out to be the best captain: he inspired every one of his fellow team members, even the most awkward, to realize every drop of skill they possessed.

It seems that the goal of leveling excellence down can never quite be achieved. "Ah, well...one can keep trying," thought Ku.

There were more complaints about the composition of the teams – there always are such. Some parents cannot accept the reality of their children's limitations; so they put limits on the rest. Again, Nollo was receptive. It was not primarily, however, because he shared the motive of the envious: hatred of ability that it was able. Ability or lack thereof was not his main concern. He was playing a different kind of game

Ku and Nollo next tried to create teams based strictly on family, clan, or tribal relations. This idea quickly fell apart. The small student body of the Schaal had scores of family names, with only a few who could claim to have any relation. But Ku persevered in the idea, and under the guise of encouraging the children to "discover their roots," he got every one of them to create, over the summer, a family tree – however scant the number of branches.

Scarcely a person in the world does not take an interest in his family lineage, given the right opportunity, so Ku's project seemed the most innocent thing in the world. There was a time when many Americans took the issue of ethnicity as a harmless diversion. At county fairs, one could sample Italian sausages, Polish kielbasa, or Scottish scones; one could hear Philippine or Irish singers, and instruments from the steppes of Asia or the Swiss Alps. In movies and on television one could hear and enjoy quaint and curious accents and customs of thirty different peoples. And commonly, an American child might say, "I'm one quarter English, one quarter German, one eighth Irish, one eighth Italian, one sixteenth Lithuanian, and one sixteenth Choctaw." And having pronounced this earth-shaking piece of information, he would then go about his life with no further notice of his own ethnicity because on the scale of his values, ethnic lineage ranked somewhere around number two thousand in importance. It is true that there were other Americans with different priorities – priorities which put the tribe and all its artifacts first in importance so that every day, and throughout the day, such people were tribally aware.

The parents of the students at the Schaal, as benevolent as any Americans, innocently supplied their children with all of the information they could assemble to build a family tree. Unsuspectingly they sent their children off to Schaal with sheets of paper mapping those trees with neatly printed names of ancestors. The children turned the sheets in to Pranti Ku. He and Nollo pored over them as if they were archaeologists studying ancient hieroglyphs. By scouring the array of generations of ancestors, they were able to patch together, though still arbitrarily, clusters of "relations." Thus, they plucked out a number of Balews, Vehoés, and Mings. They winnowed some Odhnans, Smythes, and Greaves. The problem with the tribal teams from the first, as Pranti complained, was all of the intermarriages. If only every Balew had married only Balews. Then there would be pure families, pure clans, pure tribes – best of all, a Pure Chugran Race. But it had never been that way. As Zaqqaq Churai had pointed out to the tribal chiefs on that day several years before (and Nollo had remembered this, and even regurgitated it to Ku), the restrictions on intermarriage were enforced until – they weren't. Until it was convenient to ignore them. Zaq, of course, had disparaged the whole idea of racial purity, a fact which Ku was well aware of. "I don't agree with your celebrated father on everything," he said to Nollo, almost with a tinge of an apology. But Nollo was not his father's defender. He just shrugged.

"They won't behave," said Ku morosely as he pondered the problem. "They just won't behave. The groups will not remain pure. If only we could reverse history and purify them."

And this was the moment when Nollo, staring at a spot on the floor between his feet, said, "We could purify them if we created them ourselves."

Ku looked at Nollo, not entirely blankly. Some idea was stirring, almost in the atmosphere between them, almost as if they were not responsible for it. Ku knew he had been right to trust this boy. "Create them?" he queried.

Nollo looked straight at his mentor. It would have been hard to say who was inspiring whom.

"Ourselves."

He explained his idea about the family lineages; the explanation was not too specific. It did not need to be. Ku grasped enough to understand. *Fiat gens*; let there be a family. By mere act of subjective will. All that was needed was someone with the will to pronounce the fiat. By mutual but unstated consent Nollo assumed this godlike power.

And as the exact composition of each clan, or tribe (neither Nollo or Ku could ever decide whether to call these collectives "clans," "tribes," "families" – they just said whatever came to them at the moment) was not important, only that there *be* such collectives, so it was not important that there be any historical accuracy in regard to the fabric patterns of their uniforms, or the clan "mottoes," or the "battle cries," and so forth. Before Nollo ever arrived at the Schaal, Ku had been encouraging the students to wear tunics, but this had been a random, haphazard thing. Now, Nollo made each tunic a badge of recognition for each "family." The identity of such racial embellishments was not important, only that there be *something* to mark off the groups.

Nollo suggested that there be a Kuro clan, out of respect for Pranti, but Ku set this aside. When Nollo tried to probe about Pranti's own origins, Ku was evasive and said, "I am just a humble plebeian; my tribe is that of all Chugrana."

There were no Churai at the Schaal save Nollo, and in any event he seemed not to favor "Churai" as a tribal designation in spite of his father's fame and the long line of Churai who had figured in Chugrana's history. Instead, he created the "Jolofers," after his mother. There was only one such name among the students – a ten year old girl, Mary Jolofer. ("God!" thought Nollo. "How ordinary! *Mary* Jolofer!"). This made no difference – Ku and Nollo created the Jolofer tribe, of which Nollo became the head. To the Jolofer tribe, they assigned a number of children, each of whom Nollo personally selected, by some criteria of his own.

The members of Nollo's "team," the Jolofers, were not the best plantchi players. But they were team players nonetheless. They were adept at going along with…something…or someone. They were especially pleased to be part of "Nollo's team." Nollo did not seem to care that his team rarely did well in the plantchi games. In their practicing, he seemed not to focus on the physical requirements of the game. He focused on other, Chugran things. He focused on the uniforms, the patterns, the names; he devised chants. His method of practicing struck some people as if it were all just rituals. Moreover, he and his fellow team members, by example, and by subtle hints, inveigled the other teams into similar tribalism.

Thus, without the parents knowing how it was done, Nollo and Pranti Ku, by the alchemy of their arbitrary assignments transformed the base slag of the Schaal's children – only loosely related from a time centuries ago – into precious metals which were "major tribes," and although Nollo's new tribe was near the bottom in the rankings from the actual games played, everyone looked up to the newly ordained members of Nollo's clan, "the Jolofers."

Fempy Lobbel was one of those who – suddenly – found that he was one of these admired Jolofers. Ku and Nollo had had to pore over the genealogical charts for hours to come up with this particular christening. If anyone had scrutinized closely they would have been baffled at how the surname Lobbel became associated with the clan Jolofer. Ku himself could not have explained it. But it did not matter to him. It did not matter to Nollo. Nollo seemed insistent on Fempy's inclusion. Evidently master and serf are equally in need of their correlatives. Ergo, it was done.

There was something of a flap when Bill Brown, after this third team reassignment, quit the Schaal, along with several other students, saying, "What's the point of killing ourselves to be the best at a game of skill when skill is penalized and being a phony is rewarded!" But it was summertime, and most of the parents pushed the issue aside; came the fall and they sent their children, as usual, to the Schaal.

When anyone objected to the racializing of the atmosphere at the Schaal, Ku and Nollo would scurry behind the excuse that "It's just a game – it's just for the plantchi teams. It builds team spirit. You're not opposed to team spirit, are you?"

Of course they weren't.

And some of the children had no objection at all. Before the new tribal entities, a student like Fempy was shunned by everyone, even ridiculed. Now, he was someone, without effort. He was Nollo's right hand man, almost acting as a second in command of the most important clan, the clan everyone looked up to. You could see it in the way everyone turned to watch as Fempy, having received the two little pats of recognition, followed Nollo across the field to find Ku.

They found him on the far side of the field where he was trying to resolve a dispute within one of the teams, the Greaves. Half the team wanted as their captain Jonatan Gee, who was the best plantchi player in the Schaal. But the others, some of whom were friends of Nollo, were pushing one Chompy Screws on the ground that he had more "Greaves blood." This was not true – or at least no more true than any of the familial linkages forged out of thin air by the Creators, but lineage was, more and more, becoming the way to decide all kinds of issues.

Chompy was an emaciated boy, whose rib cage through some quirk of congenital deformity was collapsed, and whose little potbelly pitifully protruded like that of a child who had been malnourished. Chompy was not malnourished. He was just a scrawny little kid. He worshipped the more robust boys, and especially his god, Nollo. He was pleasantly baffled that Nollo's friends should now be pushing him forward as their candidate for team captain. The absurdity of anyone looking to the frail creature who was Chompy Screws as captain only made him revere Nollo more.

Ku, trying to sort out the dispute, was just amazed at what happened next. He explained the situation to Nollo. The whole time Nollo listened as if he were a learned judge hearing a case. When he finished, Nollo allowed a few moments to pass. He did not frown; he gave no hint that this might be a difficult decision. He acted calm and confident, master of the situation. He looked into each of the faces in the throng. He stood with his head up, even arrogant, as if he were a commander and they his troops, or, thought Ku, as if he were a divine pronouncing his mystical insight to his disciples. Then, he walked up to Chompy. He patted him on the back of the head twice, in a peculiar way. He said, "Anyone with an eye for the true Chugran, anyone born to Chugrana, can see that the blood of the Greaves runs strong in Chompy. If you have any sense of loyalty to your own kind, if you do not want to disrespect your own blood, if you're a true Chugran pal, you have no choice. Your blood has made the choice for you. Chompy is your captain."

He turned to Jonatan Gee, who was crestfallen, even slightly angry. He put his hand on Jonatan's shoulder. "The individual is nothing in comparison to the family; the family is nothing in comparison to the tribe; the tribe nothing in comparison to the Race. A good man knows how to sacrifice his own pride, his own vanity, to the common good."

Jonatan lowered his head. He submitted.

To Ku's wonder, the children began to murmur, "Chompy, Chompy!" The issue was settled. Ku saw, moreover, that while they all now accepted Screws as their captain, they looked at Nollo as a god. Chompy especially glowed when he received Nollo's peculiar pats.

It was almost laughable; but Ku didn't laugh. He beamed with pride at Nollo. With this boy, he thought, anything was possible.

CHAPTER 44

Novitiates

"I can do anything," thought Nollo. "They're all falling in line. I can get them to do whatever I want." But it was not just "them" he had in mind with this "whatever." He luxuriated in a certain feeling, then he actually let the feeling coagulate into words. "*I* can do whatever *I* want."

It was a liberating feeling. The thought actually flitted by his mind that *this* was what true liberation really meant – to be able to do whatever you wanted, whenever you wanted to do it. But, he thought, it was not everyone who could feel such a thing. Ku had implied as much when he said, "It is not given to everyone to be as you are, Nollo. You have no barriers before you."

"If I can do anything..." Nollo allowed himself to slip into pleasant fantasies. He did not know why, almost instantly, he was picturing the grotto, with its dank walls, and Nollo, in the grotto, with someone...darkness surrounding...he was smashing...soundless...the other...young...thin arms reaching out to Nollo for protection....even as he smashed....

Nollo jerked his head with a shudder to bring himself out of the reverie. He smirked to himself. "I'm off in a trance just like Little Bratabraq." He looked, once, back at the fascinating, horrifying vision. Could he even do that? Was even that possible? Wasn't there some wall that Ku had overlooked, some Barrier to stop him from such a thing? Well, why *should* there be such a Barrier?

Nollo let himself slip, again, with fine reluctance, into his reverie.

***

Braq clambered over the rocks ahead of Nollo. They had left Rodit's and Jule's house, where Braq was spending this Sunday in October on a visit, and had set out to explore. Braq followed Nollo down to the bank of the Severn River. Nollo gave no sign of any purpose, but when Braq turned left at the river's edge, Nollo instead strolled to the right, following the river's southeasterly course.

By chance, he found an item of interest. If it was not this, it would have been something else. He yelled to Braq and waved him over. It was a deer carcass, the bones almost completely denuded by carrion and time. Braq, as Nollo expected, was fascinated. He revealed his growing knowledge of comparative anatomy, identifying mandible and scapula and femur and tibia, which were some of the few remnants still recognizable. There were also a few tufts of hair clinging to patches of skin scattered about.

Nollo began to get queasy. He continued on his way along the bank. After a bit, he let Braq overtake him. He was nearing the pathway that led to the grotto. Nollo watched him. A magician asking you to "take a card" knows ways to "force" the selection of the card he intends. Having inveigled Braq to explore in this direction, he did not, as it happens, need to do anything else. It had been many months since Braq was here, and so he followed familiar paths over large boulders and then through a tree covered defile, up the slope. Nollo followed. Then he saw his brother stop.

Braq loved the way the arcade of beech trees mimicked a cathedral in a long curved vault – a translucent vault of yellow, yellow-green, and orange leaves as if nature had created a ceiling of stained glass with occasional branches for ribs. He was trying to figure out which pigments he would use to capture this, and how he would go about it, and exactly how he would make the brush strokes. He was entranced.

Nollo watched him. He felt a smug, complacent contempt. Braq was so vulnerable. He wasn't even *watching out* for himself. Anything could happen to a person who was so "out of this world," thought Nollo. It did not occur to Nollo to question this feeling. He did not, for example, ask himself why Braq Churai, standing with his trusted big brother in a peaceful Maryland woods on the banks of the broad Severn River of a Sunday afternoon under the domestic tranquility guaranteed by the United States of America ought to look around him, fearful, apprehensive, watchful. This was not bear country; there were no mountain lions rampant; few poisonous snakes made this their home. Why *should* this boy guard himself against predators when he knew none?

This was not, after all, Chugrana.

Braq resumed the climb. Finally, he rounded the corner of the pile of rocks. His nostrils contracted as he smelled the dank rotten odor of the grotto.

In the gloom of the cave, he saw two figures. He recognized Fempy Lobbel and Chompy Screws. As Nollo came up to join them, Fempy squiggled out of the deepest gloom and said, "Well, well, if it isn't Little Bratabraq. How is the 'boy wonder' who's too good for his fellow Chukes at the Schaal Chugrana?"

"Hey!" said Nollo, "Don't pick on my little brother!" His words sounded like he was coming to Braq's defense, but his tone said that they were all pals, and that he saw nothing really wrong with Fempy's remarks. Braq observed Nollo's words; he noted Fempy's tone. He wondered why the two boys and Nollo did not exchange greetings. It was almost as if they had arranged to meet here, as if they expected each other.

"Well, he hasn't been back to see us since he left," Fempy went on. "He doesn't play plantchi with us anymore, he doesn't belong to any of our clans…I mean our teams."

Chompy piped in. The youngest and smallest of the four boys there, unsure of himself, and at the same time brazen, he squeaked, "Isn't Little Bratabraq a Jolofer, like Nollo?" He had taken it for granted that a brother of Nollo's would automatically be a member of the same clan.

Fempy was going to answer, but before he could a "No" snapped out, sharply reverberating back and forth across the grotto's jagged walls. This syllable shot from Nollo almost before he could think; the stone walls amplified it. It startled even Nollo. He softened his tone. "We had different mothers. My mother was Smíra Jolofer."

He did not name Braq's mother.

"Oh," said little Chompy.

Fempy chimed back in, looking back and forth between Nollo and Braq. "Prester Pranti Ku says our blood is spilling out of our veins into every other race." He did not quote his mentor so far as to make any mention of "Chugroids" or "Sinusoids." Nollo interrupted him with a correction. "It's not scientific to say 'blood.' It's our genes that are being squandered…and weakened."

"Right!" answered Fempy, grateful for the correction from his superior. He resumed as if he was in the middle of a catechism of lament. "And soon the Chugran Race will be wiped off the earth!"

"Do you mean like the Vikings?" asked Braq.

"Hunh?" said Fempy. They all looked at Braq dumbfounded. He explained. "Dr. Stagri says that the Vikings invaded northern Europe from Scandinavia, but that by 1400 they had all blended into the native populations. In places like England, France, and the Kievan Rus. There were no more Vikings! There were just people who were the children of other people. "

At first the boys could not get their minds around this fact. They could not respond. Braq added fuel to the fire. "There are also no Hittites…or Maya…or Etruscans…or Picts…or Phoenicians. What difference does it make?"

"It makes a big difference," said Fempy, his voice rising. Chompy nodded his head in violent agreement. He was horrified by this racial parlor trick Braq had pulled, this putative disappearing act of ancient tribes.

"Yes! A big difference!" said Chompy.

"To whom?" asked Braq.

This stumped them. As they gave no answer, after a moment Nollo came to his lieutenants' aid. "Maybe to all of those who came before."

The lieutenants sighed in relief; Nollo was saving their cause. They crowded in a bit closer to Braq. But Braq stood his ground. "How can it matter to dead people?"

Nollo said, "It *would* have mattered to them when they were alive, to know that their Race was being swallowed up."

Braq said, "Well, it didn't matter to the ones who intermarried, did it?"

He was met with three stony faces. "No," said Nollo, "but it did to all those who opposed it."

Fempy and Chompy glowered with an expression of belligerent self-righteousness. For the first time Braq realized that he was alone in this grotto with the three boys, and even if one of them was his Big Brátano, he felt not fear but a threat. Unconsciously, his stomach tightened, as if readying himself for an assault, and he felt his feet grip the damp stones. Braq faced Nollo more squarely, ignoring the other two. He could not believe what his stomach was telling him. He could not be in any danger when his Big Brátano was here. He said to Nollo, "But that's just what father argued against! Are you saying he should not have married Mother?!" There was a second's pause. Braq drove the point deeper: "Are you saying I should not have been born?"

The thrust was too deep, too telling: it caught Nollo off guard. It frightened him. He gave a comradely scoff, and clapped Braq on the back. "You fool! Of course, not! Don't be an ass. God, what a touchy Chugran! We just want you to be a part of the clans…the teams. We miss you. And we want you to show solidarity with Chugrans."

"Yeah, solidarity," piped Chompy. Braq noticed that the other two boys had not joined Nollo in disclaiming the implication Braq had named – that it was better in the interest of racial purity that he not have been born.

Chompy went on. "Prester Pranti Ku says we Chugrans all have to stick together now especially, since we're trying to get all the political prisoners released, including your father."

Braq was dumbfounded. He looked at Nollo. "Is this true? What's he talking about?"

Nollo nodded. He said, "If you were around more, you might know about this."

This was an unfair crack as Nollo himself had just found out the previous day from Ku that several Chugran groups and other civil rights organizations in and around Washington, D.C. were planning a protest at the Chugran embassy. Now, he briefly told Braq their plans.

Without a moment's thought, Braq said, "I want to be a part of it. How can I participate?"

Nollo looked at him with some skepticism. "Are you sure?"

"Yes," said Braq.

"We're going to have buses here at the Schaal two weeks from Friday to drive us into D.C. If you're there at nine, you can go."

"Great!" said Braq. He and Nollo discussed the coming protest for a while longer. During this discussion Braq noticed that the two other boys still seemed to be standing as if on guard duty, or as if they were not finished with whatever business had brought them there. At length, he looked at Nollo, and said, "I think I'll go home now."

"Fine," said Nollo, and as Braq went back around the corner of the entry to the grotto to head down the hill, Nollo turned to the two boys and gave them a peculiar sign. Then he followed Braq. After he left, Chompy squeaked to his pal, "Why do you think he let that half-breed brother of his off so easily? I thought he wanted us here to help teach him a lesson."

But Fempy shook his head. Repeating the ideas he had ingested from Ku, he said, "Do you think you can understand the thinking of a much purer Chugran than you are?" Chompy shrank back humbly. "Don't try to figure out your leader's plans. You have to trust him. Prester Pranti Ku says we've only begun to see his genius." After a minute or two he added, "And Prester says we need strong Chugrans. To follow the leader and give him support."

In the moist darkness of the grotto little Chompy shivered. For some reason he didn't feel strong enough.

Walking down the hill, with Braq ahead of him, Nollo felt something gnawing in his stomach. It was not hunger for food, but a sense of an opportunity missed, lost, gone. Was it too late? He felt the answer: it *was* too late. He had let it slip. Why? Perhaps everything was *not* possible to him after all. Why had that Barrier proven so impervious? He knew just when the Barrier had loomed. It was when his brother asked, point-blank, "Are you saying I should not have been born?" As Nollo watched Braq pass under the glowing cathedral of leaves and branches ahead of him he asked himself, "Why didn't I tell him what I really felt? Is it because we're still brothers? Still Chugran…pals? Maybe our blood is that strong." He felt it as some mystically incomprehensible dogma, as some last restriction preventing him from…dealing…with his brother. He resented this last Barrier; it meant that *not* everything was possible.

***

When Braq had demonstrated anatomical knowledge about the deer skeleton and displayed his erudition regarding Vikings, he had not been showing off. He had been testing and reaffirming his own knowledge. To give something such as a scapula or mandible its name is to keep in order the fleet of thousands of concepts which are asea inside one's head. Names keep the ideas in reach, ready for use, each one distinct and clear. Moreover, to recapitulate newly acquired knowledge is to fortify your grasp. And Braq needed such order and such fortification. These days at the Atelier he sometimes felt that his brain might explode.

Antigone Skye Derosch, Benedict Skye, Thaddeus Derosch, and Bevol Stagri had constituted themselves into their own *universitas magistrorum* for the purpose of designing a curriculum for Braq. He was ten at the start: they did not know when he would graduate. Antigone served as the rector of this concise university, settling any disputes.

The quadrivium they set for their scholar was this: mathematics, science, history, and literature. They had grasped that Braq, and his brother too, had both received an unusually good education already, from their parents it seemed. Thus, they had but to build on top of this foundation.

Their distinctive method was to interweave the next layer of Braq's education with the other curriculum he was imbibing – art. When, for example, they instructed him in how to cut and stretch a canvas, they required him to perform exacting measurements. These measurements he then had to use to solve algebraic equations pertaining to the canvas dimensions. When he learned about perspective, he also learned plane, and then solid geometry. At every opportunity they built mathematics into his work. As for the sciences, he had this: in biology he had to capture from the Atelier's environs, and dissect, such victims as frogs, rabbits and squirrels, make detailed pen and ink drawings, and then compare these observations with those he was undertaking in his human anatomy classes with Bevol. For chemistry, Antigone used Braq's newly germinating acquaintance with pigments to introduce him to simple concepts of elements and compounds, and had him assist her in some of her researches in her laboratory in the plantation's old smokehouse. Since light is of such indispensable importance to an artist, Braq's exposure to physics consisted of optics, revealed through experiments Benedict Skye set him using prisms and other devices. Also, Thaddeus Derosch taught him about weight, mass, force and leverage through the problems a sculptor of large works faces in manipulating and hefting his work by means of winches and pulleys. His literature burden was lighter – he received a list of two hundred classics, sixty of which he had to read by the time he graduated. A simple matter for an intelligent boy, except that he also had to make pen and ink drawings of the main characters and of the single most important event in each story, justifying his decision before the assembled faculty. His masters had him tackle history thusly: in painting composition class, Benedict Skye with Braq in mind might compare the compositions of two paintings such as David's "Death of Marat" and Trumbull's "Signing of the Declaration of Independence." But then it was Braq's task to research the history of these two great revolutions, the French and the American, the one leading to tyranny, the other to freedom, and write a résumé of his conclusions. Or, Braq would be given prints of portrait masterpieces such as "The Doge Loredan of Venice" or "Pope Leo X", both by Raphael, "Don Carlos" by Velazquez, "Marie de Medici" by Rubens, "King Charles I" of England" by Van Dyck, and after studying each of these artist's delineations of character, he was required to research the subject portrayed and write a one page monograph of the historical context for the painting.

For his research, reading, and writing, Braq could use the Atelier's bulging library, but he had to accomplish all this in the evenings and on weekends because his days were largely spent in the Atelier's intensive art classes. Classes in anatomy, figure drawing, still life, landscape, genre, portraiture, and imaginative works. Classes in drawing, composition, oil, watercolor, and sculpture. Classes on materials – on how to prepare and paint on linen canvas, on boards, on copper, on paper; how to cook the black oil used to carry the pigments, and the medium which when applied by a master serves not only to facilitate the application of paint and to amplify the effects possible but also to bind the whole matrix of paint so integrally that it will not crack or disintegrate over time, but will retain its jewel-like luster and translucence for centuries. Classes in methods of grinding and mixing those very pigments. How to create the special effects of trompe l'oeil painting which so fool the eye that the viewer thinks he is seeing not a painting but the real thing.

Braq loved learning the "ways of artists," immersing himself in the *special skills*, intelligently worked out, of a profession, explained to him by people who knew what they were doing. His Draconian regime might have ground down a lesser man than Braq. In his case, it stoked him up. Upon opening his eyes at sunup, he might from his bed spy a drawing he had been working on the previous night. Studying it, and seeing some needed corrections, he would leap out of bed in his pajamas. An hour later he would still be engrossed in the drawing before realizing that he had not yet showered and dressed. Invigorated at having started the day so productively, he would trot downstairs to the Derosch dining table for breakfast.

It must be said against the Atelier Derosch that its meals were a matter of happenstance. Not the timing of them – that was necessarily at regular intervals due to the class schedule – but the food itself (not a negligible part of the meal, one must admit), and the chefs, who were unpredictable. One day Hara Derosch might prepare a delicious dinner for the whole clan and any resident students, but the next night, without notice, no one prepared a thing, so everyone would be found jostling each other while peering into the refrigerator or pantry for an impromptu repast. On a random morning Tressa might prepare a huge English breakfast for everyone, only to find that most of the intended stomachs were out in the grounds painting plein air in the early morning light; she could not persuade the stomachs to come in for the delicious breakfast.

In the midst of this chaos, Ann made sure that Braq had regular healthy meals.

Before or after breakfast, Braq might go outside and run, or he might prepare some materials for the day's classes – prime a canvas, tint some paper, sharpen chalks, or grind pigments.

Then, from nine to four, with a break for lunch, he participated in the classes, with his usual complete concentration. "The Braq trances" became legendary. One day, Braq finished up a morning session of working on a still life painting. He had spent three uninterrupted hours at his work station, but far away in another world. He set his palette and brushes down, stood up, stretched, and turned to leave only to find himself staring at an impenetrable barricade of chairs, easels and stools erected so as to enclose his work area. Several pranksters during the morning had erected the barricade without his hearing them, so deep had been his spell.

Braq laughed, and so did everyone in the room. But the others also wished they could have those same powers of concentration.

Between four o'clock and the dinner that Ann ensured, Braq typically worked on projects of his own, or, if he chose, he went outside and roamed the extensive grounds or beyond, often in the company of his new companion in arms, Gideon Raeburn.

Until recently, Antigone's great grandson had been enrolled in the local public school. Disgusted by the dismal academic performance considered acceptable there, his father, Fritz Raeburn, finally yanked him out and subjected him to the same home schooling regimen designed for Braq. Thus, the academic chain gang at the Atelier had two wretches in its grip. After dinner, these two fellow sufferers were invariably found in the library reading or writing, and sometimes even engaged in arguments. The political altercations of eleven-year olds bear some scrutiny, especially when they come from such different races and cultures. Once Ann, passing by the library, heard from within the following heated exchange.

"It says here in the dictionary that a 'cavalier' is 'a gentleman skilled in the use of arms.' *This guy* doesn't look like he could fight anyone. Especially not in *those* clothes, and with that ruff around his neck....I'll bet he *had* to fight a lot, when the other soldiers saw him in *that*." The voice who pronounced this considered judgment was Braq's.

To which she heard Gideon reply, "You dope! They all dressed that way. Anyway, I looked it up: 'cavalier' is someone who supported the royalist cause of Charles the First....hmm, so I wonder why Hals painted him with that jovial smile."

Ann looked round the corner for a moment, enough to see the two scholars with their legs crooked underneath them kneeling on their chairs, bent forward over the library table, their heads almost touching, poring over a print of Frans Hals's portrait, "The Laughing Cavalier."

"He's probably smiling because that mustache tickles," said Braq. "Hals probably told him to sit still and he's trying not to laugh."

Gideon conceded his opponent's point graciously. "Yeah – and he's trying not to let that cavalier hat fall off his head."

After another moment, she heard Braq yell, "Hey! Stop it!"

Again Ann peered round into the room. Gideon said to Braq, "Hold still." He was trying to draw the cavalier's mustache on Braq's face with his pencil. When he finished they both ran to a mirror to admire the result. When they came back to the table Braq said, "Anyway, I don't think he could have been the kind of cavalier who supported Charles the First. In the first place, Hals was Dutch, not English."

"Maybe he took a vacation in England to paint this picture," ventured Gideon.

"No, it says here he lived his whole life in Haarlem. And besides, the painting is marked 1624 and Charles I was beheaded in 1649. So you're nuts!"

Bowing before this elegantly expressed scholarly opinion, Gideon switched tacks. He consulted the huge dictionary beside them. "OK, it also says a cavalier is 'a lady's companion or dancing partner.' "

"That's it! That's it!" yelled Braq. "Hoo hoo! A dancing partner!" they hooted to each other.

Then silence. The debate seemed to be over. Ann peered once more around the corner. She saw two heads buried in their books.

Finally, after a typical day, tired but happy, Braq went to bed.

Perhaps "happy" is an inadequate description.

As a self-starting, self-sufficient person, Braq Churai had always carried his own benevolent sense of life with him, even when he was immersed in the fetid atmosphere of the Rolling Road Schaal. But with no guidance or challenge from without, and even pursuing his drawings assiduously on his own, his mind had been, as it were, swimming easily through a placid pond. Now he had chosen to go over a spillway in that pond, plunging into a strong current that was carrying him, powerfully, out to a great sea. He could have stepped out of the current at any time. He did not choose to. And so long as he held on his way, he had to work to stay afloat. This was no gentle beck but a tidal tributary. This torrent, and the sea it led to, Braq knew to be the element his soul was made for.

If the regime at the Atelier seemed harsh, Braq would not have asked for anything less.

A final part of the program was to visit museums. La Maestra remembered the words of her old master, Isaac Choate, who had said that nothing could substitute for getting your face into the actual canvas, to see how a painter accomplished his work, and that reproductions were of little value for this purpose. Now fifty years later, she still thought the same, no matter how superb the modern techniques of color photography. She included Braq in the Atelier's trips to museums in D. C., Baltimore, Wilmington, Philadelphia, New York, even as far as Boston. And she awoke in Braq a passionate desire to see the three fourths of the world's great art treasures outside of the U. S. "Save your money," she said, and though he was but eleven, and had no income except a tiny allowance doled out by Jule from Liz's reserve, he began to think even then about how he could finance his dreamed-of European trip.

Weekends were a special treat for Braq because they gave him time to work on his own creations. But sometimes, missing Nollo, or Jule, Mark, or Sue, he would arrange to spend a day or two with them.

In all of this there were only two clouds in Braq's sky, one so low on the horizon he scarcely saw it. The negligible cloud was Braq's painting problem. The fact that he was having trouble rendering skin tones gave him not a single minute's anxiety. In fact, the only person anxious at this time was Bevol. Braq was too busy learning and accomplishing to notice this seemingly slight obstacle.

No, if you had asked him he would have said that the only cloud in his sky was his parents. Might it be said that Antigone Derosch, "La Maestra," – or even the Atelier Derosch itself – was taking the place of Braq's parents? In one sense, perhaps. But sometimes Braq, looking through his sketchbook and, coming to a page with a drawing of his father or mother, would stop. His breathing would stop too, just like that. He had not seen them since he was seven, but seeing the drawing it was as if they had just stepped out of the room a minute ago. At such times, he might look at the door, wondering why they were not walking through it. He would, all of a sudden, press the pad against his chest, crushing it against him with both arms, and stare...at nothing...bleak, helpless, forlorn.

At such times, he would run. He would go outside and run, steadily, relentlessly, eyes focused far into the distance at some goal only he could see. At the end, he was no longer unhappy. He did not dwell on what he could not change or solve.

But when Nollo proposed something, such as this trip to the embassy, that offered a chance to do something for Zaq, Braq leapt at it without a moment's hesitation.

CHAPTER 45

Opaqueness

Braq returned from his excursion with Nollo and his visit to Jule's early that evening. Dusk muted the fall colors around him as he stepped out of the car by the old gatehouse. He waved as his cousin Mark sped away into the twilight darkening the road. A phrase from somewhere popped into his head: "When candles be out, all cats be gray." He looked at the gray cats of leaves above him that in the sunlight had been ablaze with color. Though the light was dwindling, he felt safe here, at the Atelier. As safe as he had felt, years earlier, with Zaq and Liz. But his family had *not* been safe. His father had wished for an impregnable wall to keep some...enemy...away. What was the enemy? Braq was uncertain. "I'm impregnable here though," he thought. "They can't get at me." He didn't know who "they" were, or why the thought clicked unbidden into his mind.

He walked quickly up the drive toward the main house. Bevol Stagri was coming down the front steps on his way to his cottage. He greeted Braq and asked him how his visit had gone. Braq, falling in with Bevol, told him excitedly about the planned trip and protest in Washington, on behalf of his father and other political prisoners.

Bevol peered closely at Braq in the gathering darkness. "Who has organized this?"

Braq said, "Several groups who are working to liberate Chugrana."

"Do you know their names?"

Braq told him everything he had learned from his brother. Then, "Is there some problem?" he asked Bevol.

Bevol sighed. "Braq, it's never wrong to protest injustice. It's never wrong to keep injustice in people's eyes and minds, they'll forget about it all too easily, they'll become complacent. And Chugrana is so obscure and remote a place that most people think it's mythical, much less know how bad conditions there are. But you must always be careful whom you ally yourself with. Keep your eyes open. Not everyone who protests slavery aims at freedom."

They were, as it happens, now walking past those grounds where the converted slave cabins, residences now, were situated. Braq, as if for the first time, looked at the dark silhouettes, from each of which glowed a rectangular yellow chip, a skylight, each of which now at nighttime threw light out into the darkness, saying that an artist was at work inside. Braq pictured to himself a man or a woman in each cabin bent over a canvas. The picture in his mind changed. He saw a man working not from choice, but from compulsion.

When Braq had first gone on the Grand Tour of the grounds of the Atelier with Gideon, he heard the boy refer to "the slave cabins." He had seen the rude exteriors of log with plaster fill in the interstices, preserved even in the renovations. Gideon had shown him through one of the temporarily empty ones, and he had thus seen the now comfortable – some might even call it cozy – interior. For artists – considering the tatterdemalion squalor many of that tribe live in – it might even have been thought luxurious, especially with the cleanly furnished interiors and the light-flooding skylights. Only the most privileged students were given the option of living in these individual studios.

Braq had not thought much more about the original function of these cabins. He knew that slavery had ceased in America some century and a half ago, and that a great war had been fought to end it. Now, walking past the former slave cabins, Braq asked, "Dr. Stagri, who were these slaves?"

"Do you mean, by name? Do we know who they were?"

"Yes."

Bevol said, "As a matter of fact, we do know some of them. Clark Derosch has a collection of books on local Maryland history – one of the descendants of the slaves compiled it. It discusses the old Cockey plantation, "Cockey's Delight," which this used to be. It's called Slaves along the Severn."

He paused. "You do know that there were very few Chugrans imported as slaves into America, don't you?"

"Yes," said Braq.

After a moment, Bevol asked, "Braq how much do you know about the American experience of slavery and the Civil War?"

Braq told him. The knowledge he revealed was accurate but scant. In other words, he knew far more than most American children of his age. Bevol gave a slight "Hmp" of disdain to indicate that that would not do. He gave Braq his next history assignment. He added, "That will teach you to divulge what you don't know."

Over the next two weeks, Braq began studying the sources to which Bevol referred him in order to deepen his knowledge of the history of slavery in the United States, of the Civil war, of Jim Crow and its demise. He and Bevol discussed the tangential track of Chugran immigration to the States, and compared slavery in the Americas with slavery in Chugrana.

In the meantime, Bevol did some research on a matter of his own. He placed a call to President Carroll of the Schaal Chugrana, and asked for a list of the organizers of the protest. Then he investigated each of these to find out what they stood for, and what their primary goal was. He called the head of the group organizing the protest and spoke to him at some length. The result of his researches was that he believed this would be a peaceful march, that they would picket the embassy for most of the day, and that there would be speeches. He then called President Carroll back and informed him, to his surprise, that he would be accompanying Braq on the bus trip as his chaperone, and to join in the protest.

Explaining his actions, years later, Bevol said, "You must act on the basis of your knowledge. Based on my investigations, to the best of my knowledge this was to be a peaceful protest. And it was worth doing. As I told Braq, Chugrana had slipped off the radar screen of the world's consciousness, and conscience. Occasionally, it registered a faint blip. An ambitious reporter would return from that land with a story of the calamity, he would publish it, obtaining five minutes of notoriety, and then – silence.

"The protest was worth it, if only in the hope that brave souls in Chugrana might hear of it – know that we knew – and take heart. And worth it to keep the rulers there aware, always, that those in the world of free men condemned them.

"But remember – a group of men is only: individual men. The group is not some separate entity, or organism, with superior metaphysical status. In the end, the National Society for the Protection of blah-blah-blah is only the men and women who make it up, even though these organizations often try to act as if they're more than that, and will try to speak for all of their members even on matters for which it has no such right.

"I determined that the organizers had as their stated goal to demand the release of the political prisoners in Chugrana. That and nothing more. That goal I could support whole-heartedly. Beyond that I knew that the major groups supporting this protest all had established records of being peaceful, trying to use moral suasion to advance their causes. And they were by no means only Chugran groups. Some had worked for the cause of human rights all over the world. It *should* have been peaceful. If I had had a whiff...but I didn't.

"In the days leading up to it, I tried to explain all this to Braq. How the people who were 'against' the situation in Chugrana were yet 'for' all sorts of things – some for a restoration of the ancient tribal monarchy, some for a socialist dictatorship, some for a European welfare state, and a few (too few I thought) like his father for a limited constitutional republic dedicated to protecting individual rights. I tried to explain to him that if the protest had been just to 'end the Dryruger rule,' I would never have participated; that to be only *against* is to invite anarchy, which means nihilism. And I explained that nihilism and annihilation are cognates – in every sense.

"Oh, he was bright, more than bright, but still he was only around ten or eleven. He was joining with everyone to help free his beloved father. I think he took my warnings as academic. And he was joining with his Big Brátano too, his hero, the two of them as of old, but this time not in imaginative play, this time real Chugran warriors finally going shoulder to shoulder to do battle – what more worthy cause?!"

The day started peacefully enough. Bevol and Braq pulled into the Schaal parking lot, where there were already six buses. Students were swarming, and most of them wore their "clan" uniforms. Festive bands of children boarded the buses. Faculty and parents joined in too. On the drive into D. C., there was much singing and chanting, all of it in seeming good spirits. But Bevol did notice that the group surrounding Nollo, this "Jolofer family" or team, or whatever it was, in their bright red shirts with cobalt blue slashes, really almost tunics, in some intangible way kept Braq on the outside. Of course, Braq was not a Jolofer. Nor did he think of himself in any such way. (That hardly any of the members were really Jolofers was also irrelevant, to them). But Bevol thought to himself that if what united them all on these buses was a common goal of freeing prisoners, then everyone should have been welcomed as an ally in that goal. Yet it was clear that "the Jolofers" regarded themselves as something separate.

"I don't think Braq noticed this," said Bevol. "He credited people with good motives unless he had evidence to the contrary. And I think he thought they were all there for Zaq, and so he was even grateful to them all. But I was under no such naïve trust. I watched them. It wasn't that Nollo was in the least rude or dismissive of his brother. But 'his people' all seemed to take their cue from Nollo. No...that's not it...It's this...You know how a school of fish all respond the same way, all darting in unison, all pointing the same direction, all acting as if governed by a single will...well, I know it sounds weird, but that was the way they struck me, all looking and moving and darting to some ineffable end indicated somehow by Nollo. And as only the school of fish matters, or even exists, for the school, so I felt that no one outside of their own clique, or clan, or tribe, or family, or team had any meaning to them. As if Braq did not exist. As if I did not exist.

"I noticed too that some of the other students on the bus, who belonged to other groups, also held Nollo in a kind of awe.

"We got to the rendezvous and unloaded. In a broad public park people made inspiring speeches. It was well organized by someone with a sense of tidiness, everyone knew where to go, and the whole thing went on schedule. Everyone seemed in a benevolent mood. I found all this reassuring. We marched down the street in the direction of the embassy. Only a few policemen and reporters with their cameramen accompanied us.

"We arrived and set up our several picket lines. It was one of those Indian summer days that are almost hot without being unpleasant. The whole atmosphere was that of a festival. On occasional breaks for rest, or a meal, or a snack, one could take in the whole panoply. There were placards that said, 'Free the Prisoners,' and 'Free Chugrana,' and 'Let Our People Go,' and 'Emancipation Now.' Some signs named the individuals who were in jail, saying, 'Free Yoris Inigosh-Li,' 'Free the Tamas Brothers,' and 'Free Zaq Churai.' Braq carried one of these signs that named his father. He was solemn, serious, dignified. I was very proud of him.

"But as the day went on, I began to notice some other placards, I don't know where they came from. They appeared, as if by magic, one by one, from nowhere. They said things like, 'Down with Dryrugers!' 'Chugrans Revolt!' and then, 'White Tyranny, Black Vengeance!' and 'Death to Dryrugers!'

"Whatever one thinks of such sentiments – and I will concede that people oppressed so long are justified in an anger that is not always fastidious in the slogans it slaps on placards – I was not there for the purpose of supporting these particular ideas. I began to feel a distinct wariness. That feeling only increased when I noticed that some of the people bearing these particular placards in the later afternoon were ones I had not seen earlier in the day. They were, for the most part, young men who had a thuggish air about them, with hooded lids and a sulky glower on their faces. I had no idea who they were, what organization they were part of, what their goals were, or who was responsible for bringing them there.

"It was right at that time that I became aware of the bloated figure of Pranti Ku. I had regarded it as fortunate that Ku had been on a different bus that morning and that our paths had seldom crossed. I wanted as little to do with that charlatan as possible. Now, out of the blue, he was moving nervously up and down the lines, flapping his arms from the elbow, exhorting, 'Stay calm, everyone, stay calm! Our cause is just! There's no reason to get excited.'

"This made me *very* nervous because until then no one *had* been excited, it had all been as calm as the occasional yellow leaf dropping through the warm, still air, so why was he saying that?! And why did he suddenly and for no reason tell us 'our cause was just' as if we were in the middle of a dangerous and violent émeute in Fulon about to be charged by the bayonets of the police? But we weren't. His entire behavior was ridiculous.

"I am always alarmed by the irrational. I looked around for Braq. I couldn't find him. Suddenly, there was a crash as a whole mass of people surged without warning against the gates of the Chugran Embassy. There were shouts and moans from the crowd (what had happened to the neat lines that had been there a minute ago?!) that was now roiling as if in a cauldron.

"Just then I saw Braq. He was still holding his placard that said, 'Free Zaq Churai!' He was staring at me with a frown as though puzzled to realize that he was in danger, but calm as if he was merely deciding what action to take. God! Even in that terrible instant, he gave me confidence. I pushed past the intervening people and grabbed him by the hand and began pulling him away from the gate, as far and as fast away as I could. We passed a cohort of policemen rushing in the direction of the Embassy. We got out of danger. I saw to that!"

Bevol was not completely accurate in his explanation of Braq's frown. Braq was puzzled, but not for the reason that Bevol stated. Some minutes before the outbreak, Braq had been looking for Nollo. His brother shouldn't be so terribly hard to find, he had been so conspicuous all through the day, but just now he seemed to have gone underground. Braq was just starting to notice that the crowd had become more active and noisy, even rude, when a clutch of several people suddenly separated in two in front of him, only for a moment, and he saw, some thirty feet away, three patches of red. A large broad patch was the Jolofers gathered together in a kind of huddle. In front of them was a single patch that was Nollo, who was waving his arms at them, as a coach would in explaining a maneuver to his team. Slightly apart was a small patch of red that was Chompy Screws, also looking at Nollo. Then the crowd closed in again in front of Braq. A moment later, when it reopened, the patches of red had vanished, as if stagehands at a theater had quickly changed the scenery while the curtain was down.

It was only a few minutes later that Braq heard the violent crash as the bodies jolted against the gate. And then he experienced what he never had before – and hoped he never would again – that moment when a crowd turns into a mob.

It was then that he saw Bevol.

Hand in hand they ran in the midst of a growing crowd, all fleeing they knew not what. But all the time, there was still a remnant of a frown on Braq's brow. He did not understand something.

They arrived at last at the rendezvous and boarded the buses, as did everyone, without any attention to which bus they had arrived in or who their companions were. President Carroll was there, looking very shaken, but clipboard in hand, he was checking everyone in. After a bit, Braq saw Nollo leading his group up the street. They boarded a different bus. Out the window, he heard Pranti Ku say to President Carroll, "I'll stay with Chompy, and make sure he's OK. Then I'll take him home in a taxi."

Braq had no idea what this meant. Rumors were flying all over the bus. "The police attacked us!" "A boy was killed!" "No!" "Yes, it was Fempy Lobbel!" "No, it was Chompy!" "We did nothing! Why did it happen?" "When can we leave?"

They did leave, the mood of the morning shattered, and at last reached the Schaal. It was only that night on the television and radio news, and in the next day's newspapers that a little more light was shed.

But only a little more. The evening newscasts variously described it as a "riot," or "a protest," or a "demonstration." No two reporters gave the same story as to how things went awry. They all gave tremendous attention to the little boy named Chompy at the hospital, leg in a splint and bandages, being escorted out by the man they all respectfully called "Prester Pranti Kuro."

Ku was in his element. He would have held forth for the cameras for hours if they had let him. As it was, the editors at the stations had to work overtime to reduce his endless stream of bombast to some presentable length.

But it was a newspaper description several days later that caught Braq's eye. The description quoted one of the police officers. He said that he and his men had been rushing to the gate of the Embassy because they heard the violent clang. Suddenly they realized that they were right on top of a whole group of children who seemed to be dashing back and forth unpredictably in front of them, but all so close to each other that there was very little space between them. To have stayed on their course, the police cohort would have crushed these boys. They swerved to avoid them, but the boys – all of whom were wearing red shirts – swerved too. "I felt we were cattle being herded by a clever quarter horse," said the officer. "We were just about past them, but just then one of them, this little squirt, was under our feet. We couldn't help it! I'm really sorry, of course, but it just couldn't be avoided! We ran right over him!"

Braq took this article to Bevol. He watched as his teacher read it. Bevol finally looked up and said, "Well?"

Braq waited for a minute, and then said, "It's just that that is a good description of a special play we use in plantchi to confuse the other team. You train your team to 'swarm' just like that – it's closely packed, it's unpredictable. The swarm makes your opponent move in a certain direction. Then, one of your team runs the plamball past them, to its goal."

"Well," said Bevol, slightly confused, "but what was the goal here? Certainly not to have Chompy run right under their feet?! Who would play such a stupid trick on a little boy?" He thought for a minute. Then he said, "You say it describes a plantchi strategy, but it's also a description of what can happen in a mob of people." His voice lacked conviction.

Braq did not answer. He turned and walked away, still frowning. He was thinking about the last sentence of the article. The police officer had added that, as they tried to help the trampled boy, they heard a lot of screaming around them, and one strong young voice yelling above the rest, crying, "We are not your slaves!"

For a reason he could not have explained, Braq could not stop a disturbing image from flashing in his head: a boy riding a bicycle into a stream.

CHAPTER 46

Sanguine

Braq threw the book down in his excitement, and leaped off the bed. He grabbed his sketch pad and found a pencil. His hand flew over the page. In only a few minutes, he had a thumbnail sketch of his idea, a drawing approximately three inches by five inches. There were figures sketched in, three of them sitting at a table, one standing.

He drove his pencil back and forth again over the pad, darkening areas of the thumbnail, the first sketch. He studied it for a few minutes. He was satisfied. Again, he shot over to the corner of his room where he kept his supplies. He came back with his pen and bottle of ink. Taking a fresh page, he recreated his idea, but larger this time. His steady hand indicated lines of perspective and points of accent. Again, his hand slashed diagonally across the page in a rain of hatches darkening more areas with the deep sepia ink.

Once more he studied the result. He made a few amendments. He was not satisfied with the layout of the figures. He started again. He redrew the entire drawing on a new page.

He compared the thumbnail with the two pen and ink drawings. Now he had a better idea of what he wanted. He was ready. Once more to the supplies, this time coming back with a larger pad, and his box of chalks. He opened it and studied the inventory of sanguine pencils. None were sharp enough. He sighed. He took a bunch of the sanguine pencils and his sanding block over to a small trash can and began sanding each one to a fine point, leaning over the trash can to catch the dust.

He knew that to achieve what he wanted he had to respect the reality of his tools. In this case he needed sharp pencils and there was no point in pretending otherwise. He whistled a little march to go with the steady strokes of his hand. Before long he had a pile of sharpened pencils. Arranging his large pad on his drawing board, he began. He drew boldly and confidently; he was methodical and not quite as brusque as he had been with the pencil or with the pen and ink. This was to be a much more finished drawing.

Yet he loved them all, these media were his friends. He loved that one could use any of them – no matter how light or dark – to draw a person of any race. This was because each tool, in the hand of a skilled artist, could give you a range of values, and because every person exhibited a range in their skin tones. People loved to talk about the "white race" and the "black race," but the lightest skin still showed very dark shadows, and the darkest skin had areas of very light value, including bright white highlights. What each drawing tool allowed you to do was to recreate on a two-dimensional piece of paper a physical body, three dimensional, massive, complex, active, and to endow it with a soul, a personality. In the process, you could delineate certain racial features of the face. You could suggest the value – the shade of light or dark – of the skin.

What you could *not* do, because each medium was essentially monochromatic, was to represent the true skin color. Even the true color of a bright red apple cannot be shown with a single red pencil. The apple defies such a simplistic approach. The reddest apple, though it sits at first glance with seeming innocence – simple – in the light of examination flaunts a brazen range of color. Crimson to red to orange to light pink and even as you look again, complementary greens, not to mention blues or purples and even grays, all these disport themselves right in front of you if you but study this hussy, this apple. On the other hand, if you swab away unthinkingly at your canvas with a single red monotone, your apple will look as if you dunked it in a paint can.

So much more so with a human being.

"What color was the suspect?" asks the police detective, and the witness, respectful of the truth, duly answers, "White" or, again, "Black." Of course, this witness is not so silly as to think he saw someone the color of a flake in driven snow, or of night in a coal mine. But even if he is particular enough to differentiate "lighter" or "darker" skin tones, even so he little realizes that the artist, to achieve a true color rendering of this person, may end with thirty different puddles of color blended alongside each other on his palette, in order to recreate the colors of the bridge of the nose, in contrast to the side of the nose, or the wings of the nostrils, or the highlighted cheekbone or the shadowy hollow beneath it, or the taut skin stretched over the zygomatic bone leading to the gray as temple turns toward forehead which itself exhibits an array of different hues.

Braq loved that his monochromatic tools – pencil, ink, charcoal, chalk – removed the issue of color from the picture: he *wanted* it that way.

Although his drawing was about an issue of race, and explicitly so, yet he did not think it was about color. At least, that is what he said to himself. The book he had thrown down in excitement, Slaves Along the Severn, the latest of his readings about the history of that terrible institution, had caused a ferment in his mind. More than anything it made him think of his father.

Separated from his father at four years remove, and having to reach back to an age of five or six or seven to recapture his father's words, it is scarcely remarkable that he could scroll down the screen of his memory only a few snatches of phrases, and some tones of voice and facial expressions to go with them.

"It is an insult to make a person's skin color important!" This memory seemed to go with his father's clenched jaw. "It's ridiculous to make skin color important!" This remark was linked with a trace recollection of a hot, jagged tone of voice. "Everyone is human…" Is that what his father had said? Perhaps not exactly. "Ignore their skin color!" A severe tone, a violent swish of a bpangash frond. "The kind of men we want are…" What had his father said about that? If only he could recall his exact words. He felt that something very important was slipping just past him. These people Braq had been reading about – the slave masters – they thought skin color important, they thought race important, that it mattered, that the slaves were not even human. Wasn't that something like what his father had said?

"Who was the not-human," thought Braq. "The slave or the slave master?" Was it not the one who enslaved another man that was lowering himself to a level less than human?...An idea suddenly flashed into his brain. That was when he grabbed his tools and began the drawing. Several days now passed during which he worked on it steadily in every spare moment. Then, one morning, he went downstairs to look for Mrs. Derosch. He found her sitting in her usual place at breakfast. He sat down next to her. He said, "Maestra, will you have a chance to look at a drawing today?"

She saw from his expression that it was important. "Of course," she said. "How about later this morning?"

Braq thanked her and then ate his breakfast. At mid-morning he excused himself from class, went up to his room, picked up his drawing, and walked down the hall to La Maestra's quarters. Hearing a "Come in" to his knock, he entered. He passed through the bedroom and on into her studio, her private sanctuary. La Maestra was sitting with her back to the north light, the gently waxing light of March. She peered around the side of her easel at Braq. "So, what have you brought me?"

He approached and handed her the drawing. She removed her canvas from the easel and stood his drawing in its place.

Five minutes later, Antigone was still studying the drawing, having said nothing. Occasionally she looked up from her chair at this boy who stood beside her waiting for her appraisal and critique. Finally, she spoke. "What do you call it?"

He answered, " 'The Master Race.' "

"Ah," said Antigone, nodding.

After a few more minutes, she stood up. She turned square to Braq and said, "Well, what are you waiting for. Paint it. In color."

He grinned, and then nodded, once, with an abrupt little shake of his head.

She made one or two minor suggestions regarding the composition. Braq thanked her and left.

He selected a canvas from those he had already stretched and primed. He painted a light ochre tone over this canvas, a tone that would glow through the shadows and act as a unifying, integrating atmosphere. After this was dry, to start the transfer process he put a large piece of tracing paper over his drawing. He carefully traced the major outlines of his figures and the various objects. Turning the tracing paper over, he dusted it lightly with a dry umber pigment. Then he turned it over again and placed it carefully over his canvas. Using a sharp point, but not so sharp that it would puncture the tracing paper, he impressed that outline onto his canvas. When he lifted the tracing paper, the outline in umber was on his canvas. He had successfully transferred his drawing. Now he could begin the painting. Using greenish umber pigment over the traced image he recreated the drawing as an underpainting. This stage allowed him to check the composition on the canvas itself. He verified proportions, lines of sight, vanishing points, and a host of other details. When this had dried, he was ready for color. For several days, he worked in the late afternoon after class, taking only a short break for dinner. He worked over the weekend. He was indefatigable. He was quick, but not slapdash. He could paint for hours without tiring or losing his concentration. He did not neglect his studies. He simply got less sleep. He finished the painting that Sunday night.

Monday morning happened to be one of the days that Nollo dropped in, "carrying his letters patent," as Bevol put it. "He had two of these letters, you know, one from the Atelier and one from the Schaal. Oh, I don't mean that he had actual documents, but it annoyed the hell out of me! It seemed that he could just come and go the way he did with his permission from the Atelier as Braq's 'chaperone' – that was one of his letters patent. The other was the fact that from the Schaal he had secured 'independent study' status (whatever that meant!) via Ku's intercession so he was free to leave that place whenever he wanted. The result was that he always walked around as if he had special privileges from life. Sometimes I used to wonder if I was being unfair. I couldn't help it, though. It struck me that he not only carried two letters of patent, but also a letter of marque – you know, those authorizations from your monarch to wage war. And yet I can't say that he had done anything blatantly bellicose at the Atelier. It was more like an air that he brought in with him."

That Monday morning Braq set up an easel within his space, placed the painting on it, and brought La Maestra in to see it. Word ricocheted around the huge studio, and before long everyone had trooped over to see what "the Chalk" had done now.

The painting was approximately four feet wide by about two thirds of that high, a rectangular composition based on a golden ratio, showing an interior scene. A dark-haired man of obvious wealth sits at the right hand end of a luxuriously appointed dinner table. Thus, we see him from his left side, though he is turned slightly toward the viewer. The man is clearly white. Behind him and to his right, dressed in rude clothes with a slave collar round his neck, stands a young Chugran man. The back of the master's right hand waves dismissively toward the Chugran, and the master looks with contemptuous condescension over his right shoulder. At the left, at the opposite end of the table sits his lighter-haired wife, holding a teacup to her mouth, genteelly. She is attractive in a well-groomed sort of way, but her expression is utterly superficial. Perhaps most striking for a young artist's psychological perceptiveness, much less his ability to render it in paint, is the master's adolescent daughter. We see her sitting on the longer side of the table, between her parents, looking upward from under her blonde bangs toward the young Chugran man. She looks at him with an expression of concupiscence. These three whites are portrayed as stupid, cretinous, even slightly inhuman in their features and expressions, while the Chugran is idealized, handsome, intelligent. (Some of the observers wondered if Braq had not used his brother Nollo as a model for this figure. He hadn't…not literally.)

"The concept of the painting," said Bevol, "was far from sophisticated. On the contrary, it was pretty obvious. The master race, putatively superior, Braq portrayed as grotesquely *inferior*; the Chugran, allegedly inferior, he showed as *noble.* I don't think he had thought much about the fact that he was displaying this idea in a venue – the Atelier – that many people took to be a bastion of 'whites.' I don't believe he ever thought of the Atelier that way – nor did I. No, he was thinking about the history of Chugrana and about the institution of slavery. Anyway, however historically broad his vision was, I'm sure there were at least a few people there who took it as directed at 'the white race,' and, therefore, at themselves, and they became somewhat cool to him for a while, at least until they realized in time that he meant no such thing, even though, when they asked him what the title was, he said, simply and without concern, 'The Master Race.'

"But most of the hubbub was due to the fact that this boy just entering his teens had pulled this off. And yet…

"Well, as usual, the strength of his composition and his portrayal of people in the very moment of expressing their values was so on the mark sapient that it made everyone chuckle to witness it. As artists they were a generous lot – both the students and the faculty.

"And yet…"

He stopped for a second. "I think what struck everyone most was the recognition that here, in front of them, take it or leave it, on a simple canvas, was an individual's soul – on display.

"And yet…"

Again he hesitated. "Of course, Gert Derosch couldn't see what was in front of her face. At one point, seeing how everyone was admiring the painting, and pretending to erudition, she said to someone standing next to her, 'Braq's painting looks like Hals' in its freshness and immediacy...it's like Caravaggio in its strong composition of light and dark...and like Chardin in its deft handling of still life elements…and Rockwell in its expression of facial character.' Whereupon Mrs. Derosch turned and said brusquely, 'No Gert – it's only like Braq Churai!'

"And yet…!

"Why do I keep saying that? Why did I keep thinking it? Why did I have these reservations, even though it was flabbergasting to think that a boy had painted this?

"Of course, it was those skin tones. They were still wrong. Both the white people and the Chugran. Nor was I the only one to notice it. I heard one or two of the students trying to figure out what 'the Chalk' meant by it. They apparently thought he was trying to make some racial statement – as if he was one of those modern artists who deliberately paint people with lurid skin. I wanted to correct them but I decided it was neither the time nor the place. However, I felt that I had to discuss it with Mrs. Derosch so I grabbed her, and we went outside."

***

Nollo did not know what to think. When his brother unveiled his painting, when he set it on the easel, and people began to congregate in his space to look at it, Nollo too went over. He pushed around in front somewhat rudely. He saw the figures in the painting, he took in their expressions and gestures, especially the daughter's lascivious glance, and then he heard Braq say in answer to someone's query, "The Master Race."

Nollo looked again at the painting. Yes, Braq seemed to be glorifying the Chugran and condemning the whites. Well, well! And he did it here, he displayed it here brazenly, right in front of them all…a bunch of white hypocrites…except for Bevol, he wasn't white, but he was a hypocrite too, he shared none of the values of a Chugran, it really wasn't necessary to even consider him, he wasn't a proper Chugran at all…It was pretty brave of his little brother...Why are those two students looking at my brother so suspiciously, with their stink of ill will...Yes, who would've thought Braq would be such an incendiary…Although he might have warned Nollo he was going to do this, so he could be prepared, just in case…well, he didn't know what these people might do...

He felt very self-conscious. He felt they were all aware of him, the Chugran. Especially because the Chugran in the painting "looks like me" thought Nollo. "Well, not really…does it...?" He heard a vague speculation from someone. He suddenly felt that his own skin was glowing with paint, attracting attention.

He noticed people come up to look at the painting, suck in their breaths; saw them chuckle; saw them let out a whistle of air in amazement, or a "Whew!" or a "Phooff!" or a profane compliment. He heard one say, "He didn't do that by himself, did he? He must have had Maestra's help." But another answered, "No! I know her brush strokes – this isn't her." Another said, "Is this an original, or did he copy it?", but then saw Braq's sanguine drawing and preliminary sketches lying on his drawing board nearby; he and a couple of others went over to study these and confirmed that it was an original. They came back shaking their heads.

Nollo also heard, and it was not the first time, a word popping up in the hubbub swelling around him. The word was "genius."

And still another question from someone – "Who *are* these Churai anyway? Chugrana is just some cultural backwater. I've never heard of any Chugran artists before. How could they produce such an accomplished artist?"

It was his own brother they were talking about. Little Bratabraq. The little squirt that had always looked up to him…well not so little any more. He felt a mixture of pride and offense – "Who are these Churai," indeed!! Braq was showing them "Who!" As Nollo would too…and would have shown them already…he too had artistic ability…and other abilities…and would no doubt have revealed his genius if he had cared to spend the time….All the while, something else inside said that he *hadn't* spent the time. Were they all looking at him critically, thinking that his little brother had outshone him, had even shamed him? Anyway, it was just a damned painting. Why were they carrying on so? It was like some holy religion to them...Braq included…maybe even Braq most of all. Nollo felt a kind of nausea, he felt like kicking someone…. And wasn't this whole brouhaha disrespectful to Chugrans? As if only whites could do these things.

Nollo noticed that during all of this – for quite a long time it seemed – that old woman, Mrs. Derosch, stood next to Braq with her venerable hand on his shoulder, as if she was very proud of him.

Lurking about in the hubbub he caught another set of words in the form of a question – "What's wrong with it?" He pricked up his ears. "Damn!" He wished some of these stupid people would shut up so he could hear just what he wanted out of the swirl of sounds. He could hardly go stick his face into the middle of someone's conversation, even though that is just what he wanted to do! He heard the person who said "wrong" say something else about "skin tones."

Nollo looked back at the painting again. "Yes!" He saw it too. There *was* something wrong. Of course! Why hadn't he noticed it right away? So his little brother wasn't such a genius after all.

A bit later, he saw that Mrs. Derosch was standing next to Bevol Stagri, and that Stagri had a frown on his face. Always alert to such emotional cues, Nollo studied Bevol as unobtrusively as he could. He saw him squint at the painting, then saw him frown again. He did this several times. Nollo saw him rub his chin and shake his head as if in admiration, but then a moment later there was the frown again pushing through the skin on his brow. Finally, he saw him take Mrs. Derosch's elbow. The two of them left. They walked through the peripatos and out the front door into the gardens. No one watching him, Nollo also slipped out, by a side door.

***

"Now, Bevol, my friend, I think you have a bee in your bonnet."

She had waited till they were out of earshot of the house. They were walking side by side on the lawn approaching a high yew hedge that skirted one of the perennial gardens. It was a mild day in early spring, but she had slipped a sweater on. Bevol was in his shirt sleeves and slacks, but he was feeling very warm.

"I do, I do!" he nodded vigorously. "I know I shouldn't, but I can't help it."

She said, "It's the skin color isn't it? The flesh tones."

He said, "Yes! What is the *problem*?!"

"I could be perverse," she answered, "and ask you 'What problem?' "

He looked at her dubiously. He said, "I know you must see it. I don't have to tell you. Yes, I know every artist is different, every painter will handle skin tones differently…but if you take the way Bellini handled skin – so radiant it makes you want to sing or to cry with joy – or Rubens' ruddy, glowing, healthy flesh (not to modern tastes, perhaps, but *he* obviously reveled in it!) – or the deep bronze luster of his 'Moors' – or the luminous skin of a Bouguereau with its shimmering pearly pallor – or a dozen others – all of them different, but every one making you want to walk right into their canvases and touch that lovely skin!"

He stopped beside the hedge. La Maestra waited. "And?" she said at last.

"I want to walk into his paintings," he said. "But I want to give those people vitamins! They seem…unwell!"

He thought he heard a twig snap somewhere nearby inside the hedge. He started to peer in, but just then a covey of small birds flittered out of the hedge past his head. He pulled back with a start.

Ann laughed. "I think you're exaggerating. It's not nearly that bad."

Bevol expelled a breath of tension he had not even known he was holding in. "Yes, you're right. It's just that I want him to succeed…and

I know he will…but I'm in a hurry for his glory." After a moment, he added, "And I can't see why he's painting the way he is."

She replied, "I come back to my question: 'What problem?' "

He looked at her in puzzlement. "But I just told you!"

She shook her head. "No, you told me what's wrong with the way he paints skin tones. But you didn't identify a Problem."

They rounded the hedge. Their eyes flew open in surprise. Yesterday, the flowers had been sheathed. Now, masses of color from spring bulbs impatiently and prodigally thrusting up their tumid heads covered the sward in front of them. Bevol looked down the alley along this side of the hedge. There was no one there. He turned back to Antigone. "Explain yourself, Maestra."

"OK, you just said that every great painter handles skin tones differently. Every one is individual. But do you know *how* individual an individual is? How unique? How different from every other person? Bevol, I know *you* don't do this, but there are many teachers who try to teach by making everyone perform in lockstep. They treat learning like one of those old polio braces: – all muscles and all bones must fit into one torturous type of brace. Or like that traction machine they hooked me up to a few years ago when I had that back problem. Dreadful piece of machinery, supposedly fitting every body! How ridiculous! I could say that teaching should be tailor made – and tailor made clothing is wonderful. But tailor made teaching is even *still too rough*, too *approximate.* Each person must take the instruction he receives, retrace its origins, integrate it with his own stock of ideas – try it on for size *himself!* It's not just that you can't do his thinking and learning for him, you can't force him to absorb an idea *now* on *your* schedule. You have to let *his* mind work *as it does.*

"I know you know all this. But I still say to you 'What problem?' It is not a 'Problem' that he's painting as he is, even though you and I know there is something wrong with the skin. He is a brilliant artist – already. And his brilliance includes the fact that he's already able to paint what is inside of him. Most people, even talented ones, take many years before they can translate an idea into a uniquely evocative work of art. I'm not saying that he won't grow – of course, he will! He will grow beyond what I can see – given time and the kind of opportunity we are offering him — "

She added, "If no one stops him — "

She looked back down the lane of yews toward the Atelier. "And who can stop him?"

She went on. "But there is no wall, Bevol, between what is inside of him and what he puts on the canvas. He is so honest! He knows no fear of what anyone thinks, he doesn't fear them, or himself! If he paints the skin that way it's because something in him tells him to. God only knows why!"

Bevol interrupted her. "I'll bet you anything it comes from that damned Schaal – and from Pranti bloody Ku!"

She shook her head again. "You don't know that. It could be something else entirely. And I don't really care. If he's painting that way in twenty years, then maybe we can ask him why.

"As for now…" She gave a flip of the back of her hand over her shoulder dismissively. She pulled her sweater around her, took Bevol's arm, and said, "Let's go back inside. I'm getting a chill." They walked back along the hedge. Antigone found the blaze of pastels from the bulbs exhilarating, but Bevol thought their smell was cloying. Ahead of them, he thought he heard the faint snick of a door closing.

CHAPTER 47

Shards and Skyscrapers

He had waited for the warmth of the studio to flood back into his skin, taking the spring chill off of him. Then he approached Braq's space with a new lilt in his step. Everyone had returned to their own work now, and Braq was alone, working on a new drawing. His painting, "The Master Race" was standing off to the side on an easel. Leaning his arm against a piece of molding projecting out from the wall, Nollo studied the painting, as if he were a connoisseur. In spite of Braq's concentration, it was hard for him not to see Nollo intruding partially into his line of vision. "Hi, Big Brátano. Where have you been?"

Nollo answered breezily, "Oh, nowhere special."

Then, before he lost Braq to a trance again, seeing his brother start to bend his head to his work, he said, gesturing toward the painting, "It's really good, Brakis."

Braq smiled at the compliment and at hearing the archaic name. He had not heard that in a long time. "Thanks, Nolly," he said.

But then Nollo got a contemplative and slightly concerned look on his face as he seemed to study the painting. "It's only..." He left the sentence dangling. He waited for his brother to ask him what he meant, but the damned kid didn't. He was just staring at Nollo.

Nollo shrugged. He pretended to look at the painting more closely. He screwed his eyes up. Then he screwed his mouth. Finally, he gave a tiny chirp of dismay with his tongue against the roof of his mouth, and said, as if he were not sure of himself, "N-no...no, it's fine." His brother still wouldn't take the bait; he just kept staring at Nollo.

Finally, Nollo turned away from the painting and passing by Braq gave him a punch on the shoulder, saying, "Good job, *genius*!"

To compress these thoughts into one –

"There is no such thing as a genius."
"*You* certainly cannot claim to be one of them."
"If there *are* geniuses, they are freaks."
"You and I are on the same level (which is not that of geniuses),
so don't give yourself airs."

"Aw, I don't mean any of it, we're still pals,"

– would seem a difficult job. Without the least tone of sarcasm, Nollo managed to convey all of the above in three words, although the performance required a tone of voice, the facial expression, and the punch.

Nollo walked away.

Braq was, simply, baffled by his brother's behavior. He shrugged and returned to his work.

Nollo spent the rest of the morning strolling about the Atelier, peering over people's shoulders, flipping the pages of art books, and even sketching a bit. He was in an unusually cordial mood with everyone. He felt as if a load had been lifted, he felt vindicated. He felt just fine.

The afternoon class was sculpture. After lunch Nollo, deciding to stay, went into the studio and set up a sculpture stand. He prepared an armature to hold the clay, and took some bags of damp terra cotta to work with. He took a lump and smacked it onto the armature confidently. He threw another, then another. When he had a mass accumulated, he began, quickly, to mold it into a torso, a writhing figure emerging from a shapeless chunk at the base. He looked at it. It was good, as a start, and Nollo knew that it was. He exulted to himself, "You're not bad, Nollifer...this looks like Michelangelo had been working here!" He added, "Well, maybe not *that* good," but he did not believe his own demurrer.

Fingers still working, he paused in his mind for a moment still less modest. "Maybe I *could* be a Michelangelo…this will show Braq…he's not the only one, Mr. High and Mighty…yes, Nolly, this is damned good." He went on mentally stroking himself.

Although no one was paying much attention to him, in the back of his mind as he worked he pictured a crowd of people, not too well defined, but perhaps – he vaguely saw them – his parents, a teacher or two, maybe some unspecified but great sculptors of the present or the past – or even the future, it didn't matter – all murmuring their approval, eyes glowing with admiration. He hardly took in the one or two words of advice that Thaddeus Derosch gave him from time to time, when he stopped by Nollo's sculpture stand. Nollo thought the advice was unnecessary, but he felt generous and pretended to listen to what this officious teacher was telling him. He smiled at Thaddeus with more affability than anyone had ever seen.

Occasionally, he stood back, as if to make a critical appraisal, but he saw only good in his work. Finally, as four o'clock, the end of the class, approached, he draped a barely wet cloth carelessly over the clay and walked away, snapping his fingers and whistling. It was the longest he had ever worked on anything. Now for the unfinished business.

People were packing up to leave. Nollo strolled over to Braq's space. Braq in the afternoon's sculpture session had been copying in clay a female nude statue he had been drawing in the morning. His clay copy was not exact, but rather had been pushed to a state of greater dynamic tension. Thaddeus Derosch had worked with him, explaining that the statue had to be self-supporting, and that if he was not careful his statue – transposed into plaster or marble – might easily crack at the ankles. The beautiful figure might come crashing down to the floor.

Now Braq was sitting on his stool with his knuckles against his chin, deep in thought, looking at his clay statue.

Nollo decided not to wait on Braq's damned concentration; he was tired of playing that game, always having to stand in attendance until Braq deigned to notice him…as though Braq had the right to keep him waiting. He said, somewhat too loudly, in order to cut through Braq's spell, and as if they were still carrying right on with the morning's conversation, "I think it's the skin tones."

Braq looked up at his brother in some surprise. He saw him gesturing to his painting, "The Master Race," and following the line of his arm and finger, looked at the figure of the slave.

There was a note of diffidence in Nollo's voice, yet curiously he seemed at the same time to suggest that he knew just what he was getting at.

"What are you talking about?" asked Braq.

"Well…it's just that…it doesn't really look like a Chugran."

Braq studied Nollo. After a moment he said, with a smile, "Do you think I'm going to say, "What's a Chugran?"

Nollo did not find it funny.

Seeing that Nollo was not going to respond, Braq said, "Just what is your problem with the skin tone?"

Nollo said, with an edge of umbrage, "*My* problem? *I'm* not the one with the *problem.*"

He gave the last word a very special tone and emphasis. "I'm not the one who's ashamed of his own skin. I'm not the one who doesn't even know his own color…the one who has no pride in his own race. Of course, I'm not a painter – I'm not saying I could *paint* it." He said this to forestall an objection that Braq was in no way about to make. He finished this unlooked for blitzkrieg with, "But *you're* the great painter, you *should* be able to."

Braq was dumbstruck. There had been hints in the past and furtive innuendos, there had been what he took, in his innocence, to be brotherly jokes. This was different. It was as if some emotion burbling stinkily beneath the surface had just burst through the skin, through a dishonest integument Nollo had pasted over his soul.

"What do you mean 'ashamed of my own skin?' "

"Well why else would you have this problem?" Nollo said.

Braq answered, "Nollo, I *love* my painting. I know I have a lot to learn, but I think my painting is *good.* La Maestra is helping me to get better. I'm not ashamed of anything."

Now Nollo struck in earnest. "That's not what *she* thinks. She and Bevol Stagri had to have a special conference about you. I happened to overhear it. They both think you're not painting the way you should, that you're not living up to your 'great' potential." A tone of sarcasm had definitely seeped into his voice now, when he used the word 'great.'

Braq said, in amazement, "They did what?"

"That's right. They honestly don't know why you're painting the way you are. Oh, they're not going to throw you out, don't worry...they think you can be fixed…that you'll eventually be able to do a painting about" – he gestured to Braq's painting – "skin color and get it right."

"But I wasn't painting skin color!" said Braq. "That's *not* what this painting is about."

Nollo was bewildered. "It's not? Then what is it about?"

Braq said, "It's about slavery, about slaves and masters, about those who think they're superior to other people. Color is just…" He couldn't find the word. "…a side thing. This painting's about people who think color matters. It's important in the painting only as one of the things that helps show the main point." After a moment he added, "And I don't think you're right about La Maestra and Professor Stagri. I'm going to ask them."

"Oh, Christ!" thought Nollo. Aloud, he said, "Well, don't tell them I told you this – they probably want to tell you in their own way…and I'm sure they didn't want anyone to hear them, I just happened to be passing by when they were talking. OK?"

Braq did not answer his brother.

A spy having spied may be spied upon in turn. Lurking by the entry just around the corner where the studio and peripatos joined, Gert Derosch stood, listening around the ajar door as closely as she could to Nollo's remarks. And this second spy observing spy may yet have her own role reflected back again. At the opposite end of the peripatos standing halfway in the door from the main house, stood Bevol Stagri watching Gert. There were no more secret agents in the tableau: the series was complete.

The tragedy of Gert Derosch's life was in longing to be a member of a tribe. To have to function as an individual was, she felt, a fundamental injustice. She deeply resented that the Derosches took no particular notice of their German-Alsatian heritage, or of any other ethnic strains in their background. Once, she asked a new student, one Will Buchan, "What nationality is that name?" "Scottish, I think," he replied indifferently. She asked, "What sorts of things do you do?" He was baffled. "What do you mean?" Gert said, "You know, what foods do you eat, what Scottish holidays do you celebrate, what events do you go to, what clothes do you wear?" He shrugged without concern; he said, "Nothing." To his mystification, Gert's shoulders slumped, as she turned away, saying, "Me neither."

Eavesdropping now on Braq and Nollo, and hearing nothing for a moment or two, Gert walked on into the space, and feigned surprise at seeing the two boys. She thought to begin with a compliment, but in the words, "Quite a painting, Braq!" there was already an edge in her voice. The two boys looked up at this sudden intrusion. Even though her voice did not sound terribly enthusiastic, Braq politely said, "Thank you, Gert."

She gave the painting a malign look and then tossing two loose fingers toward it she said, "So…does this mean you think you're part of the superior race?"

Braq's eyes widened. Nollo's hackles rose. Braq started to say, "Of course not!" Nollo wanted to shout, "Yes!!" at Gert. But before either one could do this, she went on, "Because it's ridiculous! The white race is now and always has been superior to the dark races."

Braq was so outraged by her misunderstanding of his painting and by her last statement – so blatant that he was amazed she had made it – that he stood up abruptly. Not to confront her though: he found her so offensive and so irrational that he wanted nothing to do with her. It is also true that, intelligent as he was, he was not sure how to go about directly refuting her inflammatory charge. But he did not even care to argue with her. Instead, he wanted to leave. He was about to turn and begin putting away his things.

Nollo, on the other hand, looked as if he was about to leap at Gert.

Gert, meeting no response, was encouraged to say what she really thought. "Name one Chugran who has accomplished anything."

Braq couldn't help himself. He stopped in mid-motion and shot back instantly, "My father!"

"OK," conceded Gert, unfazed and with a sneer. "That's *one*!"

"And Professor Stagri," Braq added.

She held up two fingers, and stared at him with exaggerated sarcasm.

Braq thought his two examples were sufficient to refute her. He stopped. But now Nollo threw fresh troops into the assault. He started with Pranti Kuro's name, then President Carroll, and then, from his memory of the pamphlet cataloguing great Chugrans, the one printed for Rodit's Chugran Ethno-Folkloric Museum, he began rattling off a list of names – which of course Gert had never heard of – and their accomplishments. As he spewed out the names of mathematicians, composers, teachers, entrepreneurs (he included Vasc Sulam), an astronomer, and even philosophers (names such as Aima, and A'veri) – Gert, placidly smug, kept count with her fingers. When Nollo had named some twenty-five, he stopped. It was not an unimpressive list, especially since Gert, of all people, knew only the names of Zaq and Bevol.

But Gert responded, "Are you through? It took you all of three minutes, and I have used twenty-five fingers. Now, if I wanted to name the achievements of the white race, it would take many days and I would need thousands and thousands of fingers."

Braq had returned to packing up his things. Nollo was going to answer Gert: his answer was going to be a profanity. But a resonant voice cut in. "That was an estimable recitation, Nollo." It was Bevol Stagri. Standing just outside the space, as she had before, he had heard Gert's thesis. Now he stepped into the workspace. "There were names in your list even I didn't know."

Nollo glowered at Stagri. He didn't need him butting in. He was also nervous that Braq might mention Nollo's spying. Further, it did not endear Dr. Stagri to him that he admitted not knowing all of these names of eminent Chugrans. "Of *course* you didn't know them all, you traitor!" he thought, but he said nothing.

Seeing Braq putting away his things with an air that said he was leaving, Bevol said, "Braq, I'd like you to stay." Then he turned to Gert.

"You mentioned 'the achievements of the white race,' and something about thousands of fingers. But, of course, it only takes one finger to enumerate 'the white race.' If you claim to need thousands of fingers then you must be enumerating thousands of *individuals*, aren't you?"

Gert said, "*Yes*," with a nastily rising inflection, and she flopped her head from side to side with rude sarcasm to imply "So what?"

"Now, this 'white race' you referred to – you yourself are a Christian, I believe?"

She said, "Yes," suspiciously, not knowing where he was heading, especially since she suspected that Stagri was an atheist.

"Your Christ, he would be one of those great men, I suppose?"

"*Of course* he would," she said.

"But he was a Semite, right…a Jew?"

Gert grudgingly assented. But she tried to stand her ground. "OK, OK, the white rac*es* then."

Bevol nodded. "I suppose you would include Thomas Jefferson on one of your thousands of fingers?"

"Yes," she said.

"The man who said 'All men are created equal.' So even though he and many of the greatest of your whites proclaimed this truth, you pit yourself *against* your own great men and deny it?"

"We're just talking about *achievement*, not their equal rights," Gert said.

"Good!" said Bevol. "Let's just talk about achievement. It's your contention that the lighter the skin the greater the achievement?"

She nodded.

"So albinos have contributed the most?"

"No, no, no," she said scornfully, "just normal light skin."

"Well, what about Danish skin versus Jewish skin? Which of those skins has accomplished more in science, art, mathematics, music, etc?" She looked confused. He continued, patting the air with his palms. "Never mind the Danes, that's not important, but just where do you draw the line in your classification? After all, India had quite a sophisticated mathematics, and lots of them are very dark skinned – yes, yes, I know – all those fingers again, though I think you might do a little research on the accomplishments of *that* dark-skinned group. But just how light or dark or medium were the epidermal coverings of Aristotle, or Charlemagne, or Marco Polo?"

"I don't know," she said, "but they were all Europeans."

"Still," he answered, "you don't know what the lineages were of each of them, and of all the other thousands on your fingers, do you? You don't know if any particular one came from some so-called pure stock or from some *tainted* line, do you?"

He turned to Braq. "What about it, Braq, do you think you'd be better off if you came from undiluted white stock?"

Braq said in disbelief, "You mean if Mother and Father hadn't met…and married? That's a rotten thought! I think it's great that they married and had me. So I'm mixed – so what?"

Bevol turned back to Gert. "Well, there you are, Gert. The poor unwitting victim doesn't even want to be saved...he has no shame. Do you think Braq would be better off having two white parents?"

Gert shook her head in frustration. "Of course not! Exceptions are just that though. They prove nothing. What we *do* know is that if more than a handful of the great achievers *had* been black Africans – or Chugrans – we would've heard of it by now."

"Fine, fine," said Bevol, still in perfectly good humor. "Let me grant your premise. So: more accomplishments have come from lighter skinned people than darker. These thousands of fingers on your anatomically strange white hand – these are out of a population of countless billions, aren't they?"

"Yes," she said.

"So, holding everything we know in focus, and in context – a relatively *small* number of people from time to time hurl mankind forward, a *small* number create a civilization wherein *anyone* can flourish."

She objected heatedly. "But the numbers are still impressive!"

Bevol continued to advance his argument. "We at the Atelier – as artists – we're free here, are we not? Could we – as creative artists – function under tyranny and slavery?"

"No," she conceded, unsure again where he was heading.

"You wouldn't say, generally, would you, that the mind can function very well, if at all, under tyranny?

She hesitated, but finally conceded the point.

"So, if that is the case, do you think it's fair, so long as a population is held in subjection, whether foreign or domestic, whether subjugated by political control or a stifling religion or oppressive customs, to judge the scantness of their achievements, especially compared to the achievements of a *free* people?"

"So?" said Gert.

"Is the history of what you're calling 'the white races' an unbroken swath of freedom and achievement?"

She thought for a moment. "No."

"No!" said Bevol. "It has been a long struggle, through Dark Ages, through savage tyrannies, theocratic dictatorships, various reigns of terror, through the totalitarian charnel houses of communism and Nazism. Tell me, are places like Cuba, or North Korea, in the last few decades, glowing repositories of achievement, of science and art – or tombs where intelligence rots? And doesn't each halting step of greater freedom depend upon unusual discoveries and linkages of crucial ideas which support liberty – such as the sanctity of the individual, the freedom of the mind to reason, of reason itself? And these greatest discoveries, the ones that make all the others possible – don't they come from a *handful* of discoverers – from some of the men on your list?"

"Yes – *on my list*," she said.

Nodding, but unfazed, he went on, "So, looking at the whole of history – not just one strand – instead of saying, 'the white race is superior,' wouldn't it be more accurate to say that *mankind* – white, black, brown, *all* of them – achieved next to *nothing* of its potential, for countless thousands of years until, *finally*, a few giants, standing *above their own races*, emerged and lifted us all out of the muck of oppression, of ignorance, of suffering, and degradation? And most of those few giants, those great benefactors, happened to be lighter-skinned."

"*Exactly*!" said Gert.

"*Happened* to be," said Bevol. "Maybe they were also between the heights of five feet four inches and five feet eleven inches...You look to be about five feet one inch yourself. Is that fact important?"

"I don't see why it should be," she said defensively, frowning in confusion.

"So you think you can feel pride for being a 'whitey' but you have to feel shame then for being a 'shorty.' Doesn't that sound just a little absurd?"

He went on. "What if I told you that all of the high achievers were people with long muscles?"

"What's that got to do with it?" Gert yelled, in exasperation.

"Exactly!" he said. "And maybe they had predominantly brown hair. Yours is kind of dirty blonde. Where does that put you...? So do you think skin color matters, but hair color doesn't? And since you're so scornful of non-Europeans, what about your mother's namesake – her grandmother Hara – who, I believe, was from Japan. That means you're a mongrel. Where do mongrels fit in? Are they high-achievers or low achievers?"

Gert finally reassembled a thought. "Well, Japanese are still lighter-skinned, and they have a high culture – and what about the fact that black Africans achieved little, over all that time you're talking about? You *still* can't get around that."

Nollo interrupted in a tone as belligerent as Gert's. "What about the Chugrans? Why are you lumping them with Africans? What about all of the achievements I just told you about?"

But before Gert could answer, Bevol cut in.

To Nollo he said this one word: "Shards."

Nollo looked at him in bewilderment. Bevol went on, with a sad little smile. "As far as Africa is concerned, if you subtract the Arab-Muslim, the Egyptian and the Mediterranean-European contributions from African history, you're left with shards."

"What??"

"Shards – pots and broken pots. And I have to tell you, Nollo, that Chugran history is not that much more illustrious. You'll never be able to compare a clay pot with a rocket ship that takes man to the moon; or a bronze fertility doll with the Sistine Chapel ceiling; or a tribal wedding dance with a Romantic symphony. No, you'll never be able to answer someone like Gert here by denying or belittling the achievements of Western civilization. Look – in the list of accomplishments, *someone* had to be least. You can't make them *all* equal by wishing or pretending. Face facts.

"To you, Gert, I say this, for thousands of years blacks achieved what just about *every* culture, including whites, did: in tool-making, agriculture, cattle-raising, metalworking, pottery, primitive arts, and trade. Every culture was about the same. *Then* – because of the *few* men, the few *individuals* we have just discussed – great advances were made. But *somebody* had to happen – that's right *happen* – first. Or, do you think that suddenly every race and ethnic group and sub-group – however you define them – suddenly, *suddenly* – on cue from above – should have produced the same, identical world geniuses at precisely the same time, with the same history-changing ideas, the same level of insight – in fact the very *same* insight, all over the world?! That not only a Greek Archimedes, but a Nigerian one, and an Olmec, and a Chinese should each have sat in their identical bathtubs and each uttered a 'Eureka' in unison – not even taking into account the different time zones in these various points of the globe where each bathtub was situated?"

Braq laughed out loud.

Nollo was reluctantly impressed.

Gert said nothing.

"That not only a Greek Aristotle but an aborigine, a Gupta, and a Celt should each have pointed his genetically pristine finger at his consanguineous students and enunciated the Law of Non-Contradiction, bingo!, at precisely the same moment in history!

"*One* of them, I say, had to happen first. That doesn't mean it was blind chance, in the personal sense. Aristotle and Archimedes thought their brilliant thoughts out of their own volitional minds. But racially it was chance. Oh, not that Aristotle could have sprung from nowhere in some random backwater of the world. But his predecessor, a man like Thales, could have – a man who asked himself, 'What one thing is all the world made of?' And once such a simple but staggering question is asked, all who follow that man, in *his* culture, are lifted above the rest of the world which has not *yet* asked it."

Bevol continued with more fervor in his voice. "Gert, you agreed with me earlier that a people without freedom to think can hardly achieve much of value. Blacks have had intellectual and political freedom for only a *short span* of years – a short span here in America, and far *less* in their original lands – and even then, their liberation was less than a fully healthy, a fully life-affirming, mind-enabling situation since it was 'colored' by the legacies of slavery and the resulting inferiority – "

Nollo started to frown, but Bevol forestalled him by saying, "If you're ashamed to acknowledge this fact, Nollo, you'll never overcome it."

Then he returned to Gert " – the resulting inferiority, dumbing down, self-doubt, humiliation. Give them – or any people – a hundred years of pure intellectual freedom and self-respect and see what wonders they'll produce – as many *already have done*, even in this short time. Achievements come not from skin and races, but from the *minds* of individual men who look out at the world with the light of reason, confident, curious and un-coerced, believing the world a wonderful place in which to exercise their powers. Minds encrusted with the fungal rot of tribal mysticism and barnacled to a race will achieve nothing!"

***

On her way up the stairs to the untidy den she lived in on the third floor, Gert said smugly to herself, "Good! I got His Highness Stagri to admit that blacks – including Chugrans – have accomplished nothing compared to whites!"

***

Out on Old Rolling Road, hitching a ride, three things mingled as pustules of thought and emotion in Nollo's mind. The first was expressed in words, aloud: "God damn that Bevol Stagri! How dare he admit that darker skinned people have not accomplished what whites have! It would have been blasphemous enough to admit that even among ourselves, but never – never! – in front of a white! It was treason!"

The second was just an image, an intriguing image that embossed his mind from Bevol's discourse: "A few giants, standing above their own races." He ignored the context that Bevol had established for this description; he thought instead of a phrase uttered by Pranti Ku which was similar – something about "the very embodiment of our Race." Well, maybe it wasn't the same...yet there was some idea there that captivated him, an old idea...and of course, it was natural and fitting that he should think of it...he, a prince of the blood, a royal Chugran. The image he saw was that of a large statue of...a figure that resembled himself...standing well above and dwarfing a throng of pygmy people.

The third was a sound, more like a growl, so faintly muttered that it could hardly be thought that he actually enunciated it to himself. It was more like a tribal call and response echoing from deep in a primordial forest, guttural and feral. No, even that was too explicit, too articulate; he did not even let himself know the meaning of the chants. It was more like the distant clang of a bell, muffled and indistinct, tolling from an unknown spot in a fog, the first stroke of the knell saying, "If no one stops him," and the dismal answering stroke saying, "And who can stop him?"

CHAPTER 48

The Color of His Skin, The Value of His Skin

Gert and Nollo had gone, and Bevol too was about to leave, but Braq stopped him. "Dr. Stagri, may I talk to you about something?"

Bevol always enjoyed his talks with Braq, but something in his tone was different from anything he had ever heard in Braq. Had Bevol touched some unsuspected nerve by the salvo he had just thrown at Gert? But it was not that. Braq had picked up his sculpture tools again, and as he cleaned the clay off of them, he flicked his hand, holding one of the tools as a pointer, in the direction of his painting. "Their skin."

Bevol looked at the figures in the painting and then at Braq. "What about their skin?" A feeling of misgiving flashed into Bevol's mind – had Braq somehow heard what La Maestra and he had discussed that morning?

"Am I a problem for you…and Maestra? Am I letting you down with my painting?" He looked at the painting. "Those values seem right to me – isn't that what you teach us here – get the value of light and dark correct and the color will take care of itself? 'Get your lights lighter and your darks darker,' isn't that one of the Atelier's slogans? And the colors – they look right to me also…except they're not even important anyway…I'm not ashamed of my own skin. I know what color my skin is, and I don't care. But I'm not ashamed. I know what a Chugro is, or a Chugran…whatever name you want to use. I still can't understand why people think it's important. It isn't."

He finished this outpouring, which he had spoken passionately, but quietly, while examining his painting, and he turned and tilted his face up to Bevol, and repeated, "Am I a problem? I would hate to let Maestra down…and you, too."

Bevol felt his knees go weak, and he felt a chasm suddenly gape inside his stomach. He grabbed Braq by the shoulders, and stared into the boy's eyes as if he would peer right inside of him. "No, Braq, no! You're not a problem…you're…the opposite! Good God! How…why…what brought this on? Just because of something in your painting that's not really even that important, as you just said! A problem for me?! For Maestra?!" He laughed, but it came out as a bitter moan. "We love you – you're, you're, Oh good God! You're already three times the artist that most people who come through here are even after they graduate. What if there is some little problem, some infinitesimal flaw, with the skin" – he caught himself, he backtracked jaggedly – "no, it's *not* a problem! It's not! Your painting is…almost…perfect!"

The poor man. He was choking. Choking because he had not yet digested what Antigone Derosch had said to him that morning, and he knew that he did not want to make the mistake she had underlined of trying to make Braq paint according to someone else's timetable and values. Choking because he was appalled to think that something he had said might have come back to Braq's ears in God knows what distorted way so as to undermine the boy's confidence in himself. Choking because he did not know how to strangle this snake coming out of Braq's mouth.

Bevol suddenly rushed over to "The Master Race." He grabbed the canvas and without thinking – foolishly, because the paint might still have been wet and some paints are toxic – he kissed Braq's painting, and exclaimed, "Keep painting just this way! Don't question yourself! Do it exactly as you have! Don't let anyone say this skin looks sickly…I mean…it's not…I mean…Oh, Braq, what am I saying?! I'm an idiot – where is Maestra, she'll set me straight, she loves your painting…I'm just an impatient old fool who wants you to be the world's greatest painter. Pay no attention to me!"

Braq looked at his painting, still in Bevol's hands. He said, " 'Sickly'…is that the problem?" Then he laughed. "Well, they don't look sickly to me…Hmmm…Why didn't you say something?"

Bevol answered, "Because, Braq, I teach artistic anatomy, not painting. It is not my place to critique or advise you about how you paint when Maestra, who knows one hundred times more than I do, is here to help you. And she is, I repeat, completely – *completely!* – happy with you and your work. You said you're not ashamed of your skin, and you should no more so be ashamed of your painting. They are both *who you are*. You should feel the greatest pride in your painting – that's something *you have achieved*. Not," he held up an admonitory finger, "not that you should feel pride in your skin, or your race. Those are *not* things you ever did to feel proud of."

Braq nodded. "That's what Father always said. Race is irrelevant – for everything."

Bevol rushed ahead, not really hearing Braq's last phrase. "I would expect him to say just that! My guess is that he would have told you – 'Don't be ashamed of yourself for being who you are – including a person of a certain race – or mixture of races. Like all of the things in the world you may ever take notice of, you too are – all of the things that you are. Every single attribute is part of your identity.

"But don't be like those who confuse 'pride' and 'value.' It would be silly to feel *pride* for having five toes, or a helical ear, or for breathing with lungs instead of gills, or for having twenty-eight or twenty-nine vertebrae, if you happen to have a spare, as some people do – or for having dark skin. But every detail is *part* of yourself and it's the healthiest thing in the world to *value* yourself – in every one of your details. But valuing is not the same thing as feeling pride".

He hesitated for a moment, then added, "But if it's a mistake to demean what you are, it's also a mistake to make the wrong things *important.* Your five toes are not who you are, most essentially. Your *mind*" – he looked intently into the boy's eyes – "and your *character are.* What you think and what you do – that's the core. Thought and action. The thinking you do, or don't do, and the way you translate those thoughts into action – two sides of the same coin. Those are the most important parts that make you up. That make you the kind of person you are."

" 'The kind of man we want,' " said Braq.

"What?" asked Bevol.

"It's something Father used to say. I'm not sure what he meant."

But then he repeated Bevol's phrase, almost to himself, "Thought...and...action."

Braq's face lit up in surprise at a sudden thought of his own.

"That's why," continued Bevol, "when those people a few years ago started shouting, 'Black is beautiful,' (not that they ever had Chugrans in mind of course), even with their good and perfectly understandable intentions – Oh, I forgot, you weren't here then – they were trying to make up for years of people saying that dark skin was ugly and inferior, even so, I wanted to say, 'No! *Human* is beautiful! The human body and the human mind!'

"The kind of man you are – that's what human pride should be all about. Those people who talk about animals, like lions, or dogs, or whatever, acting 'proudly.' They're just confusing the healthy *self-assertion*

– the self-value that any living creature feels – with *pride*, which is a distinctly human emotion. It's just rank fantasizing when they call an animal proud. Probably from watching too much Walt Disney. Have you heard the word, 'anthropomorphic'? Go look it up.

"No, Braq, what I always felt was this – if someone threw my dark heritage at me as an insult, I would say, 'Yes, I *am* that, and I am proud – not of the darkness itself – but of *my*self.' Just as, by the way, if someone threw your dark, or your light, or your mixed heritage at you as an insult, you should say, 'Yes, I am that, I am who I am, and I value who I am...I am proud of my character...I am a living *man* who is *not guilty*...I need feel shame about *nothing*...And whatever I am is part of me, so I feel good about it.' "

Braq nodded. Bevol's accent and manner of speech, even of gesture were different from Braq's father, but the ideas – he felt as if it was Zaq speaking to him now.

Bevol said uncertainly, "Still…what was it…there was something you said that was very important…something I wanted to come back to…I wish I could think of it."

Braq said, with a smile at the corner of his mouth, "About the sick skin?"

Bevol gave a rueful, half-apologetic laugh. "I called it 'sickly.' Not 'sick.' No, it wasn't that. But as for that, you just listen to Maestra. Ignore me or anyone who tries to throw you off track, OK?"

Braq nodded.

It seemed like a good opportunity to end the conversation. Braq really did not enjoy this whole topic of race. It had been pleasant enough with Bevol, unlike the conversation with Nollo and Gert. It just was not something he wanted to talk about. Especially not now.

He set his sculpture tools aside. Then he looked up at Bevol and said, "Excuse me, Dr. Stagri, I've enjoyed our talk, but may I go now? I have an idea for a drawing I'd like to get started on." His face was clear and unclouded. Stagri saw no anxiety, no doubt, no uncertainty. He breathed more easily. He even laughed. As he watched Braq striding away, down the corridor of the peripatos, he shook his head. Why had he been so worried for Braq?...

But what was it that Braq had said that bothered him? He could not for the life of him remember.

***

Chompy Screws was sweating. It was a clammy sweat. Not like the warm invigorating moisture that their plantchi calisthenics had brought forth earlier that day. This was the sweat of fear.

He had felt *so* good half an hour ago. He and all of his pals had coagulated on the field to perform their accustomed exercises that were almost a ritual. Nollo, the leader he worshipped, had taken them through the movements. Chompy didn't know just why it was so important to get the sequence perfect, he only knew that he did not want to appear unworthy in Nollo's eyes. They all felt that way. Through these exercises, and other signs and tokens, they bonded together, as any animal does with its pride, or herd, or pack.

And then Chompy had seen their other great mentor, Prester Pranti Ku, heave his great bulk into view and sink with a spreading motion onto a wooden bench from which throne he watched the boys. Nollo left them to continue their calisthenics and went over to confer with Ku. Over some minutes the group dissolved one by one, as first Fempy Lobbel, then another boy, and then another left the group and gravitated to the clutch, in the center of which were Nollo and Ku. Finally, sensing that it was now all right to leave off, the last two, Chompy and another recent disciple, stopped also and hurried over so as not to miss anything.

Seeing the whole pack in attendance, Pranti Ku effused, "How absolutely fitting that you have all come together through sport – through the gut, instinctual, muscular energy of your blood and bowels – not through the arid, anemic intellect, through that desiccated 'Mind speaks to mind.' " This from a man who had trouble walking without wheezing.

Probably only Nollo knew what "desiccated" meant, but they all murmured their warm approval. Nollo smiled over them, benign and complacent. He felt that he and Ku occupied a different plane from the rest of these Chukes. That was how he thought of them. As they drifted one by one off the field, he thought. "Oh, here come the Chukes!"

Still, he welcomed, even craved, their presence, and their admiration. It was, he felt, what he was entitled to. Certainly it was what Ku kept telling him he deserved by virtue of his, Nollo's, "special qualities," the qualities which made him "a quintessential Chugran," and "a Chugran avatar," and other terms that were somewhat vague to Nollo, but flattering nonetheless.

When Ku had first waddled up to the bench and Nollo had joined him, Nollo had related the events from three days before at the Atelier, in particular his brother's stunning success with the painting, "The Master

Race." He also told Ku about "the Problem" Braq was having with skin tones. Just as he had with Braq, he gave Ku a rather distorted report on the conversation he had overheard between Antigone Derosch and Bevol Stagri. To Ku he made no bones about having sneaked outside deliberately to eavesdrop, and Ku chuckled approvingly to hear it. For many months now he had become accustomed to Nollo giving him detailed reconnaissance reports on the Atelier; he had even encouraged Nollo in this, asking him very pointed questions about the Atelier, its faculty, how they did things there, what motivated them. Now, Ku laid beside him on the bench a book he had brought with him and said, "Well, it isn't surprising that a mixed breed like Braq would have trouble painting Chugrans – *or* whites for that matter. He is a freak, after all…not a pure human being belonging to a *definite* race."

"*He* seems content enough," said Nollo. "Except that he got very defensive when I confronted him with it…said he was perfectly happy with what he was doing."

Ku replied, "Well, he would, you see, because he can't step out of his own mixed skin, or his own racially mixed brain. He can only see the world through the distorted lens of that mongrel mind."

Nollo said, "*Stagri* sees it, all right! He's beside himself. I think he wants a magic wand to wave over the painting, over all of Braq's bad paintings, to transform them into what he wants."

Ku sighed, "Yes, my young prince, so would I, if I were Stagri. At least in that way we're both Chugrans. We remember our tribal magical days, when we had power over things. Power over the wind and the waves and the trees. I always did think that Xerxes lashing the Hellespont because it destroyed his fleet and Canute commanding the waves to stand still were my kind of people – sometimes I wonder if they weren't really Chugrans instead of a Persian and a Dane!"

Ku, by the way, had never met Bevol Stagri; he merely made his assertion as if he knew the man – or knew the race, which he took to be the same thing. Nollo, picking up Ku's thought, said, "I think Stagri is in agreement with you on another point, too."

Ku tried, unsuccessfully, to raise his eyebrows.

Nollo said, "He told us that every so often, maybe not too often…well, pretty rarely…a race throws up a Great Man who stands above his own Race…he said that this Man lifts them all up. Even lifts up the whole world. That the Race suddenly throws up this man, who puts that Race on a new plateau, above the others."

Was this corruption of what Stagri had said deliberate, or had Nollo simply misunderstood? It would not have mattered. He preferred the idea the way he had just stated it to Ku.

"He said that, did he?" said Ku. "Hmmm…I wouldn't have thought it of him." He gave Nollo an uncertain look out of the corner of his eye. After a moment he asked, "Tell me, was he looking at you when he said it, when he mentioned this Great Man?" He wondered if he should become jealous of Stagri's attention to Nollo, assuming that Nollo was telling him the truth, an assumption of which Ku was by no means confident.

"Well… part of the time," said Nollo.

Ku said, "I mean, do you think he was speaking to you, *of you*, with this idea?"

Nollo got a smug caricature of modesty on his puss, but it came out as a kind of smirk. God! How contemptuous he was of Ku in times like these, that he could fall so gullibly into such a line of thought. And at the same time Nollo relished it, he felt a sensual pleasure at the adoration implied in Ku's manner.

"I won't say he named me specifically," he said, "but he did keep looking at me."

Fempy Lobbel had just slithered up to them, but Ku went right on. "No doubt, no doubt," he effused. "Of *course*, he would keep looking at you. You are the physical embodiment of Chugran beauty. The one in the many. Just as it says in our book."

He held up the volume he had brought out with him, a book he and Nollo had been poring over recently, at Ku's suggestion. It was an abstruse work, by one Manoel Slovomir, Professor of Philosophy and Esthetics at Chamberlain University. Its title was The Submerging of the One in the Many: Readings in Collectivism.

"You are one of the divine ones they all talk about, one of those who will lift us up, who will arouse us, who will show us the glory of the Race. 'Ad majorem Chugranae gloriam' – 'to the greater glory of Chugrana!' " he said, showing uncharacteristic accuracy of expression. But then he followed it with, "...who will show us that Chugranness is next to Godliness!"

As more boys came over, Fempy asked in regard to this last eruption, "What was that phrase you used?"

Ku said, somewhat dismissively, "It's nothing you need to worry about. Maybe someday you'll be ready for it. Let's just say it means what

I've maintained all along – that Nollifer Churai here," he put his hand on Nollo's shoulder, "is Chugrana in the flesh, an ideal type of Chugran. Nothing will stand in his way! When his blood is up, nothing will stop him. He will lift the rest of us up – as he has lifted all of you up already!"

He gestured to encompass the plantchi field, the students, even the whole Schaal.

Nollo swelled under the praise. But he wished Ku wouldn't put his hand on him that way. He really didn't like people touching him. It was presumptuous of them.

As more of the pals came up, Ku went on. "Everything has its ideal. Nollo is an ideal Chugran. Plantchi is an ideal sport. The floumiix is an ideal instrument. And each one shows us what the others of its type should be."

"Is there an ideal teacher?" asked Fempy. He was shamelessly looking up at Pranti Ku when he asked this. Ku did not have the self-restraint not to blush. Harlequin blotches suffused his face. "No doubt there is," he said. He patted Fempy's head. Then, looking around vaguely, he said, "And somewhere there's an ideal tree. And an ideal school."

By now Chompy had arrived. The little boy thought he was chiming in with everyone, he wanted to chime in, he didn't want to be left out. "And an ideal plantchi stick?"

Ku gave him a contemptuous look, and said, scornfully, "Yes, Chompy, a perfect plantchi stick too. But don't trouble yourself about it. It's not given to everyone to be able to see these ideal types. It takes a certain level of innate superiority to be able to recognize the ideal."

All of them strained to lift themselves to that rarefied level. Some of them thought they could just about do it.

Chompy strained too, looking around him to see how the others might be doing it. The attention he had garnered from his injury in the D. C. riot had now waned. He had sunk back once again to being just "little Chompy." He looked about him at the other boys. He was still terribly confused about something. And he so wanted to get it right, to be part of the group. He raised his hand. Ku sighed in a mock display of patient longsuffering. "Yes, Chompy, what now?"

Chompy took his meager courage in his hands and said, "Er…I know that Nollo is the ideal." He blushed. "But…when I look around at everyone else…well…how do I know who is second most ideal? I mean…everyone's skin shade is different." Just then he happened to look at Ku, with his leprous skin, and now the poor boy blushed ferociously. He hurried on. "Everyone's nose is not the same, everyone's ears and lips are different too." He studiously avoided looking at Ku's eyelids. "So which thing is the most important? Which feature determines second place? Or do they all mix together? How do you keep all of these things straight, to know how to rank everyone?"

They were all looking at him as if he were an idiot, "or not even human," he thought. They were looking at him, he thought, as if he were a bug. In truth they were all merely trying not to disclose the fact that they had no idea how to answer Chompy. He hurried on. "I know I'm the least." He thought this might placate them, and he did in fact feel "the least."

Still no one said anything. "And I know I could never be an ideal, I just want to know what I should be looking for…after Nollo…how do I know?"

Ku looked at Nollo with an expression and a gesture that seemed to say, "What can one do with such material as this?" And then he actually went ahead and said exactly that. It was offensive, and its meaning seemed to spill over from Chompy to others, perhaps even to the whole group. "This Chuker material" found its way into one of Ku's sentences. Ku didn't care that he said this in front of them. And, strangely, *no one* cared. They took it as right that he should speak that way to Nollo about them, in front of them.

"One thing is for sure," said Ku. "It's only a person from a degraded stock who could ask such an idiotic question."

Nollo nodded. Then he twisted the knife (and it occurred to him that something about twisting this knife in Chompy gave him pleasure, so much so that he almost felt that he might just let loose and kick the little boy), saying, "I may have made a mistake about the purity of the blood that runs in Chompy."

This was when Chompy began to sweat.

"Oh, please, Nollo," he thought, "don't shut me out this way."

Nollo's fingers were loosely touching the book lying on the armrest of the bench. He said, looking around the group and finally back at Chompy, "I have decided to reorganize the teams." Everyone gave a slight shudder. "Really, they're not *just* teams anyway, and we should stop referring to them that way. They are akin to families, but families which represent each noble strain of Chugran blood. We are going to call them 'Familisteries.' I'll let you know who the members of each will be...after I've re-evaluated."

A minute ago they had all been members of the Jolofer clan. Now they all trembled to think they might be excluded from Nollo's new "Familistery." They wondered if *this* one would also be called "Jolofer." Chompy shook so much that one of his legs went into a kind of jerking spasm. He couldn't control it, and that made him even more terrified. What must they all think of him?!

Ku, marveling once again at Nollo's mastery of people, his seemingly instinctive knack for which buttons to push, supported Nollo, in tones of a stentor, almost as if he were reciting a heroic ballad. At the same time, he lapsed into the Chugran future tense, and once again he confused the hell out of everyone because the Chugran future was supposed to be used to describe events that had already happened.

"The lot of a Great Man will not be an easy one! He must be prepared to sacrifice the one for the many. And yet he will himself *be* the One for that many. He must become the Personification of the Race! He must use his special insight to see into the Race. And then the many will sacrifice themselves for this One. This many will be prepared to be the servants of the Race, to be the drops losing themselves in the ocean of the Race, each one must become a blank slate on which the Racial Mind will write, even will become grubs to be devoured for the sustenance of the Race!"

"Oh Yes!" thought Chompy, "Let me be a grub!"

The boys looked in awe at Nollo. He felt that he was in the center of a kind of aura. He felt that he belonged there.

CHAPTER 49

Lord Bacon's Straightjacket

The next day Nollo returned to the Atelier. He was still euphoric, still carrying a sense of what a special individual he was. When he walked into the main studio he almost felt that everyone would notice his arrival, that their busy murmurs would drop to a reverent stillness.

For some reason, this did not happen.

They were all engrossed in their work. This morning's class was watercolor. Each student in his workspace set up a new still life to paint. Tressa Raeburn gave a few instructions and words of advice. Then they all bent to their work.

Nollo watched several of the students. This looked easy. You splashed some water in the little cube of pigment sitting in its well, mixed it with another on the white tray, and then began dabbing. It seemed much easier than the laborious process of oil painting. This, he thought, would be something that would make these people see that he too was talented, perhaps more than any of them thought. After all, he had seen Braq do this stuff when he was a little child in Chugrana...oh, yes, that stupid painting Little Bratabraq had done of Nollo himself...that had been a watercolor. His euphoria was still bearing him along on that rarefied level above all others.

Nollo went over to Tressa and said, "I'd like to try this." He said it with utter self-assurance, his fingers fluttering in the direction of several of the students who were working nearby.

Tressa hesitated. She foresaw a disaster, but then she recalled Nollo's fractiousness and belligerence. She thought, "What the hell!" She assigned him an empty space, and gave him some of her own materials, paper, a palette, several brushes. "Do you have an idea of what you'd like to paint?"

"Yeah," said Nollo. He had heard one of the teachers say recently that ovals were particularly difficult to draw, even harder than circles. This struck Nollo as ridiculous. What could be hard about it? It is possible that he had seen some of the artists at the Atelier draw these geometric shapes with seeming ease. It may even be that they had some special tricks that made the task easier. But, seeing the facile sleight of hand in several simple flicks of the wrist, one does not realize how many thousands of times that artist may have executed that particular trick to reach the day when it seems so easy.

But Nollo knew he could prove how easy it was, and the watercolor too. He went in search of some objects for his still life. He did not go to the "prop room," where he would have found a wealth of objects to choose from. Instead, he went over to the main house, to the dining room. There he removed from a large glass cabinet a beautiful plate, a cup and saucer, and a goblet. He went into the kitchen and opened the refrigerator from which he extracted an egg. With these he returned to the studio and to his work space, where he began setting these objects into what he thought was an interesting arrangement. He cracked the egg into the saucer, and laid the two shell halves artfully alongside.

Seen from Nollo's vantage point these objects presented themselves as ovals: the egg yolk, the egg white, the plate, the top and bottom planes of the cup, the saucer, and the multi-layered planes of the ornate goblet.

Nollo picked up a brush to begin painting, but Tressa, who had been watching, quickly stepped over and said, "You're going to do a drawing first, aren't you?" He looked up at her with annoyance, but she didn't wait for his answer. "Yes, you are!" She handed him a pencil, an eraser, and a pad, and said, "Do a sketch first, to establish what you want to do. Copy it on the watercolor paper. Then you can start the painting."

His mouth pouty, Nollo took the materials from Tressa. He looked resentfully at the setup and then quickly began to draw. After a few minutes he had a number of ovals impressive for their inaccuracy. Out of the corner of his eye he saw that Tressa was watching him. He used his eraser and tried to make some corrections. Was it a bit better? He sat and stared at it. He knew that it was still an amateurish thing, but he had no idea what to do about it. His jaw clenched. Tressa stepped up again and pointed out that the planes of each oval in his drawing did not make sense; the objects seemed as if viewed from different perspectives at the same time – as a human eye cannot do. It was, therefore, not possible to integrate these contradictions in a single act of vision.

Nollo made a few more attempts at correcting the perspective. Tressa, thinking to encourage him, said, with gentle patience, "Once you understand this, it really frees you up!"

"Frees you up?!" said Nollo peevishly. "It's like being in a straight-jacket!"

Tressa refrained from saying that the straightjacket was reality. She just persisted. "Once you get it, you can do any still life you want. You can draw something from any perspective. It becomes objective. You understand it. You know how to do it, you have acquired the skill of judging spatial relationships, so it really does free you. Do you know the saying, 'Nature to be commanded – "

Nollo interrupted her, hostile at what he took to be condescension on her part. "Yes! Do you think I'm ignorant? 'Nature to be commanded must be obeyed.' He said, raising his voice slightly, "OK, OK, I'll obey! I'll fix it. But not with you watching me all the time."

"All right, Nollo," said Tressa. She gave him a look. She walked away.

Nollo turned back to his drawing. He squirmed a bit in his seat. He glanced around to see if everyone was watching his discomfiture. No one was paying any attention. He felt relief and at the same time, at a far deeper level, the beginning of a massive depression. He looked back at the still life. He looked back at his drawing. Something had changed. Had someone touched it? That was absurd. Yet the relationships of the plate to the cup, and the cup to the goblet, seemed different now.

He tried to make some changes to his drawing. But the objects were still floating in a chaotic space of conflicting planes. He felt like smashing the whole thing to pieces.

It did not occur to him that countless other people, in similar circumstances, had run into exactly the same problem; in any event he was not like other people. It did not occur to him that the perspective on an object viewed from a short distance will change significantly if the viewer moves even a little to one side or the other, or slumps in his chair; in any event an object, he felt, should not have a mind of its own; it should obey *him*.

Other people might solve their problem by fixing their viewpoint carefully until the main structure of perspective was secured.

And still another solution might be to practice.

None of these occurred to Nollo. He tried a solution of his own. If his drawing did not conform to the objects….

He began moving the cup and saucer and goblet to try to make them fit his drawing. Now, some errors of drawing might be correctable this way. But objects sitting on the same plane are – on the same plane. Tressa, still observing from a distance, shook her head. She would have let him stew, but she also noticed that in his frustration he was petulantly banging the dishes about with a clatter. This was good china which he had no business using. She went to the prop room and got some other less precious objects similar to the ones he was using. She brought these back and without asking his permission began replacing the objects. "The things from the main house are only to be used by special permission and only with the greatest care. Except," she said, pouring the raw, slippery egg from the nice plate to the common one, "for the egg. That you're welcome to."

Humiliated, and with suppressed fury, Nollo sneered, "Oh, don't let the little Chigger boy put his dirty hands on your good china!"

Tressa gathered the good dishes and without a further word walked away. She did not return to Nollo for the rest of the session.

Nollo worked desultorily for about another half hour. His drawing did not get any better. The raw egg pooling on the plate began to sicken him. He gave up. He was uninterested now. He had even forgotten what he was going to "show everyone." He never touched the watercolors. As the morning class drew to a close Nollo walked over to Braq's station. He was glad that Tressa had seated him far away from his brother, so that Braq had seen nothing of what had transpired. He gave Braq a fretful little smack on the back and said, "Let's go have lunch." He was tempted just to get out of there altogether, but he had one more card to play, one more chance to re-pump his ego.

Braq said, "Oh! Good, Nollo. I want to talk to you. By the way, how did it go today? I've been so busy I didn't come see what you were doing."

Nollo answered blithely, "Oh, no problem. I just played with some drawings. Until Tressa Derosch let me know I wasn't good enough to touch her china."

Braq frowned, but decided not to get into this with his brother. They made a couple of sandwiches in the kitchen and took them out into the warm spring sunshine.

Now, Braq asked his brother this surprising question: "We're not rich are we?"

Braq was eleven, Nollo fifteen. Up to this time neither boy had bumped into the problem of money. In advance of their flight from Chugrana, their parents had transferred a large portion of their modest savings to America under the care of Jule and Rodit. Though frugal, Jule had always given Braq the funds he needed to replenish his art supplies. But now, as a full-time art student, Braq used things up at a much more prodigious rate than ever before. Even more importantly, he had a new goal. Inspired by La Maestra he dreamt of joining one of the Atelier's summer European tours. He learned that it would cost a substantial sum of money.

It would have been an easy thing for Braq to go to his aunt and ask her for the money. Perhaps it was the sum involved, perhaps it was something else. But at this time Braq decided that it was his responsibility to pay his way. If he wanted to grasp some value, it was, he decided, up to him to bring it to fruition.

Could it be that the process he was learning of bringing a work of art to completion was teaching him this lesson: that from the first conception in his brain through the many steps to the reality at the end he was responsible for each step? No doubt it *must* have had some bearing. These are the ways one learns life. Yet – some artists recognize, or at least bow to, such iron laws in the creation of their work and then run to sponge shamelessly from their fellows. One may know a truth and not grant it. One may know it in this place and deny it in another.

Now, when Nollo heard his brother ask, "We're not rich are we?" he looked at him with mock dismay. "No," he said emphatically. "Why?"

Braq explained why he needed the sum of money. "I don't want to ask Aunt Jule, and I don't know how much money there is from Mother and Father. Anyway, I thought *they* might need it someday. What if Mother needs money to get Father out, to bribe the jailers, or something like that?"

The idea had never occurred to Nollo, but he conceded the point. "Why don't you just ask Aunt Jule for the money? What's the problem? What is she there for?"

But Braq shook his head. It was too hard to explain. "I just don't want to."

In thinking about his parents, he had flipped open an old sketch book he had brought with him. He longed to see his parents, and he thought Nollo would enjoy seeing the sketches as much as he did. He opened the book to two facing pages of drawings of Zaq and Liz. Nollo stared at them blankly. He gave no reaction.

It had been some four years now since he had seen them. During that span, not once had he ventured to look at any of the numerous sketches Braq had made. Such a look would have freshened his memory of these parents. He had never sought to do so.

After a bit, seeing that his brother was not interested, Braq closed the drawing book.

He said, "I have an idea. Gideon earns money around here doing chores. Maybe I can too. I'm going to talk to Clark Derosch."

Nollo was going to object, but he saw that Braq had already decided. He said, "I think I'll come along with you. I'm still your chaperone you know."

"OK," said Braq, "Let's go." They found the general manager of the Atelier Derosch in the cubbyhole that served as the Atelier's business office. Braq stated his business. Clark mused for a moment and then, stroking his chin, he said, "Chores, eh? Well, there's no end of *them*. Yes, I think Gideon could use reinforcements. The faculty always needs canvases stretched and primed, brushes cleaned, pigments ground, pencils sharpened. Then there's gardening, cleaning, repairing, grounds keeping. Take your pick."

Braq said, "Wherever you need me. Where I can earn the most money." He was thrilled at the prospect.

"What are you going to pay him?" asked Nollo. His voice carried the faintest tinge of belligerence.

Clark looked at Braq appraisingly. He scanned him up and down as if he was evaluating a horse he was about to buy. Nollo thought this insulting, but Braq wanted to laugh. After a moment, Clark answered, "I'll pay him the same amount I pay Gideon." He named the wage, which was a combination of hourly rate and piecework rate. This seemed perfect to Braq. He prepared to leave, but Clark stopped him. "I have another idea. Braq, you're very young, but from what I've seen, and what Mrs. Derosch tells me, I think some of your artworks might already find buyers. I think you should select some pieces for the gallery and also for the year-end show. You can earn more money that way."

This was a splendid idea. Why had Braq not thought of it himself?! He thanked Mr. Derosch, but again Nollo interjected. "What sort of price would he get for his paintings?"

Clark said, "That depends on how good they are, how large, what the medium is, and how people evaluate them. The market decides."

Nollo contracted one side of his nose. "Why can't he just set the price he wants?"

Clark laughed. "He can. He can also find no buyers."

Braq added, "Besides, Nollo, no one knows who I am, or anything about me, yet. Maybe eventually I can set my own price." He looked up at Clark, "Right, Mr. Derosch?"

Clark raised his eyebrows at the confidence of this boy; then he said, thoughtfully, "Yes, Braq, maybe you *will.*"

Nollo turned to leave; over his shoulder he grumbled, "It seems unfair. People should have to pay what it's worth."

But Braq just shrugged.

Outside, Nollo said scornfully, "They're making you into their little slave boy. Guess they can't get the slavery out of this place after all."

Braq looked at his brother in disbelief. "Nollo! *I asked* to work for them. That was the idea!"

Nollo was disgusted. The whole idea of working for someone repulsed him. Especially for "whites."

Contemptuously he asked, "When are you going to start saying 'Yes, master!' and bobbing your head?"

Braq looked his brother gravely in the face. He said, "On a day that will never come, Nollo."

The lunch break was over now, and the afternoon sculpture class was getting under way. It had been several days since the last sculpture session, and Nollo wanted to resume work on the terra cotta he had been so pleased with, his "masterpiece." He had to vindicate himself after what had happened that morning. Surely now people would notice how wonderful his achievement was – how striking, how original, how unique!

He brought the draped figure out from its storage shelf and set it on a stand. He removed the drape, and then stepped back a number of paces to observe it from a distance, as he had seen others do. Yes, it was a fine piece of work. He stepped up to it. He began smoothing down some of the surfaces. He was not changing its form in any way but merely, so to speak, polishing it. Another student, Seth Pule, stepped over and said sententiously, "What's important, you know, are the forms, the masses, not the surface. When you come into a room" – it sounded like he was quoting a lesson – "and look at a statue from a distance, you see the forms, not the surface texture."

Several other people, including Braq and Thaddeus Derosch, had come over. "Wouldn't you know they would come over *now*," thought Nollo resentfully.

Pule went on. "Skin is not important. Not to a sculptor. And it shouldn't be important to any of us anyway."

He said this, not looking at Nollo; he was not thinking of Chugrans, or whites or anything of the kind; he had heard things like this before, and he was merely regurgitating unquestioned truths.

"Think of a flayed figure," he said. "An écorché. What more do you need to know about a person?"

Nollo said, belligerently, "*My skin* is important! Chugran skin is beautiful!"

Thaddeus Derosch joined the conversation. "Yes, Nollo, but unlike painting, where you can go from blocking in the main shapes to presenting the surface appearance in almost the same process, in sculpture you'll alter the surface many times before you get to the final forms you want, so there is no point in polishing away to achieve a mirror-like sheen only to have to remold the whole form, perhaps even to add or remove whole chunks of clay. As you work to refine the form, stage after stage, you'll finally arrive, at the *end*, at the surface texture. I think Seth here has stated as an alternative – a false alternative – what is only a matter of sequence, of the order in which you do things.

Nollo was in no mood for distinctions. He looked across the sculpture stand at his brother. Braq was watching and listening. Tilting his head sarcastically, Nollo said to him, "So, if the racists can't enslave us through the color of our skin, they'll just strip it off. They'll flay our skin off of us altogether!"

Braq frowned. He did not know why Nollo was so angry. He thought Thaddeus Derosch's words had been clear. Mr. Derosch was just trying to identify the error Pule had made. What was Nollo's problem, anyway?

Thaddeus went on. "In any event, Nollo, it's a good beginning of 'The Heroic Captive.' "

"Hunh?" Nollo had no idea was he was talking about.

" 'The Heroic Captive.' The statue in the Louvre, by Michelangelo. Looks just like this. Or, I should say, yours looks just like his…I assumed you were trying to do a master copy."

Nollo clenched his teeth. He was furious. "This is my own idea! I don't know anything about your damned Heroic Michelangelo, or your Louvre!"

Thaddeus was completely unfazed by Nollo's anger. He just stared at him calmly and implacably. "How extraordinary coincidental that you just happened to come up with exactly the same twist of the trunk and precisely the same angle of the head and the very gesture of the arms that the other statue has. I take my hat off to you."

It was in fact the case that one of the books Nollo had perused several days ago, on the morning of Braq's presentation of "The Master Race," was a selection of works from the Louvre, including "The Heroic Captive," and that Nollo had been struck by this photograph. It was also the case that he had no recollection whatsoever of this perusal. Why should he recall such a thing? To give credit to someone else? To acknowledge the authority of someone else's achievement? What for? Nollo could say with total honesty that he had no memory of the photo or the sculpture.

It did not assuage him in the least when Thaddeus said, "There's nothing wrong with doing a copy, to learn from it, so long as you credit the original and identify your work as a copy so people don't think you're palming it off as your own."

He left Nollo's side and circled the statue, coming closer to it as he did. Suddenly he walked right up to it, from the back, and peered closely. Then he looked up and said, "Nollo, I *told* you that you have to keep terra cotta moist. It's cracked – in three places."

Nollo ran up to the other side of his statue and saw to his dismay three jagged fissures severing the statue into separate pieces. His face fell and his nostrils became pinched.

Thaddeus added, "And I also told you to keep turning your statue, keep walking around it, to look at every perspective, to work in the round…sculpture is *three* dimensional!...If you had, you would've seen these cracks!"

He had no patience with Nollo – with any student who did not listen. And he had by now had just about enough of this boy's belligerence. But he was a teacher. Lifelong habits of encouragement reasserted themselves. He said, "Don't worry, we can fix it. The pieces can be rejoined. There's always a way."

The sentence was hardly finished when Nollo, with an angry, vindictive lurching of his whole body, sent the statue crashing to the floor. Pieces of the ruddy terra cotta went flying everywhere.

The whole school looked up. They saw Nollo bump into Seth Pule and then push past Thaddeus and Braq. He stormed down the length of the studio and through the double doors. Braq cried out, "Nollo!" but his brother ignored him. Braq looked back at the empty sculpture stand. He saw Thaddeus gravely shaking his head.

Braq ran after Nollo, through the peripatos, out the front door and down the drive. He caught up with him just as Nollo was passing the old gate house. "Nollo! Stop! What is it?"

"Why wouldn't you back me up?!" snarled Nollo.

"Back you up?"

"Take my side!...Just because I'm your brother!"

Braq shrugged. "I was thinking about what Mr. Derosch said about the surface and the form. I was trying to understand…And your statue does…did…look like the Michelangelo."

Nollo spat back at him, "You sanctimonious little jerk! What difference does it make? It was *us* against *them*!"

Braq said, "I don't agree. It was just you and Thaddeus and Seth Pule having a discussion. Nollo, I admired you for standing up to Pule – he's really a peculiar person – and speaking your mind about Chugrans being beautiful, but I still need to think about the mistake Thaddeus said Pule was making."

Nollo said, "Well, don't think forever. The time is coming when you'll have to act!"

He turned to leave and took two steps away. Suddenly he whirled around and walked straight back to Braq. His face was livid. He leaned right into him. His voice lashed out, chin shaking with fury, "You and your precious Atelier can go to hell! I don't know why I ever came here. You obviously don't need, don't *want* a chaperone. You don't listen to anything I say anyway. And I think it was a mistake for me to let you talk me into trying these stupid things. Talking me into going against the Chugran religion, the Chugran traditions. Into making images! I think…you're…not even a Chugro!"

He whirled about. As he hurried down Old Rolling Road, away from Braq and the Atelier Derosch, he positively stamped his feet into the ground as if he were mad at the earth itself.

CHAPTER 50
Human See, Human Do

The Seth Pule that Nollo bumped into, who had spoken so sententiously to Nollo, was a boy of thirty-three, average in height, but very narrow in appearance: a narrow torso and a narrow head, as if whoever had designed him had gotten the width and the depth of his body mixed up. He gave the strange impression of being at once nervous and wooden. Upon meeting someone for the first time, he would shoot out his hand mechanically and abruptly, as if to say that this is what courteous people do, but his eyes shunted off to the edges, never making contact with the other person's eyes. On more than one occasion, he missed the other person's hand altogether, but instead of looking down to find it, he just withdrew it, also abruptly, and stuffed it in his pocket. At the Atelier, he would walk hurriedly with many small steps straight to his space, his arms not swinging but held down by his sides, head forward, as though he noticed no one, but his eyes flicked as if with some astigmatism from side to side to take in any human presence that might be there. If the Atelier was quiet, he could concentrate intently on his work for awhile, but suddenly, his focus would break, and, as if not just his attention but his whole person had been shattered, he would dart his eyes round the room, as though he was afraid everyone had deserted him. When he saw that each person still existed, and was still in his or her place working calmly and quietly, he would return to his own work.

His painting was invariably at some extraordinarily high level of execution – but devoid of every shred of originality. He had done hundreds of copies, which in themselves were superb reproductions, long after his first year, long after he had achieved a unique mastery of his tools. His "originals" turned out to be facile reworkings of some master's work, with a little change here or there.

But the objects within his paintings were also copies – copies of some stereotyped way of painting that object. If it happened to be a pear, it was identical to every other pear he had ever painted, almost as if he saw a photograph of it in his mind and just pasted that same photograph in place. Every grape was identical and every rose too. He seemed to have a formula that fit each object and no variation of measurement ever crept into that formula.

And it was beyond him to get a likeness of a person. His fabulous drawing skills failed him when he had to look into a face, or even *at* a face. He had racial formulas as well as fruit formulas. If he saw dark skin, he automatically painted thick lips, a broad nose, and a sloping facial angle. If he saw light skin, he painted a skinny nose, thin lips, and a vertical facial angle. He spent most of his time, head down to his canvas, rarely looking at the model. When a teacher asked, "Why did you paint this nose this way?" Seth would say without defensiveness or any other emotion whatsoever, "Well – he's black." If the teacher asked, "Did you look at him? Did you *study* him?" Seth would say, unconvincingly, "Unh hunh."

In accordance with his formulas, he would probably also have painted a degraded intellect to go with the black skin, and an elevated intellect to go with the white skin, but he was incapable of depicting any intellect at all, for any racial type. The faces he painted were masks. Even the skin adhered to a formula for its texture, but it was the same formula as his fruits, as though all "skins," all coverings were the same – all fruitish. So he produced in one portrait the skin of a Caucasian apple, and in the next an Oriental apple, and in the next a Negro apple.

More than one person found it revolting.

One day in portrait class, La Maestra sat, painting the model, a Philippine elf who happened to be Bevol Stagri's fiancé – Mila Merani. During the breaks Mrs. Derosch walked the room, giving an occasional word of advice. On this day, Seth Pule had positioned himself so that he could easily see La Maestra's canvas. He was working at his easel, all the while glancing frequently at her painting. After an hour or so, she strolled about the room. When she came around behind Seth and saw his canvas, she gave a start; her breath suddenly hissed inward.

"Wipe it out." This was said quietly but curtly.

Seth looked up at her, his eyebrows hoisted into his forehead in disbelief, his jaw open. "But…but… it's just like yours," he stammered.

This was quite true, in a sickening way. In fact, placing the two paintings side by side and glancing very quickly, it would have been hard to say who had painted which. But if you more than glanced, and you had a human soul, you would have said that the first was painted by looking at a real person, and the second was painted by a machine.

Ann said, "I am not some god or priest to be slavishly imitated. I made those brush strokes, *looking* at this person – *at Mila* – to show a viewer what *I wanted* them to see in her, to see this person through *my eyes.* You are supposed to be training your own eyes to see the world, and your hands to paint what your own eyes see. We train people here, *at first,* through copying the great masters, not in order to *see* through those other painters' eyes, but to learn how to mix the pigments, to handle the brushes. You've been here for four years, don't you have eyes of your own to see with? When I'm 200 years in the grave, you can copy me.

"Wipe it out."

She went back to her easel. Students standing near her saw her glance once more at Seth, and heard her mutter, "Damned chimpanzee!" When Seth had finished wiping out his work, one of the students looking on yelped out, with a wicked grin, "Clean slate, Maestra!" Antigone looked over at Seth and said, with asperity, "Now start over – and look at the model, not me."

That evening some of the faculty were relaxing in the drawing room, a large room chock full of art by generations of Derosches, including paintings, sculpture and furniture. Several beautiful oriental carpets created a sense of order within the room.

Ann related her story about Seth from that afternoon, to the amused dismay of the others. They each threw in their personal anecdotes about Pule's paintings, methods, and behavior. Benedict said, with cool contempt, "He paints nothing but stale archetypes…disembodied abstractions…nothing real!"

Bevol took issue with him. "Painting an abstraction is not really the problem. No, it's the *nature* of Seth's abstractions where the problem lies. Abstractions – concepts, really – are little packets of labor-saving thought. Probably space-savers, too – space inside our brains, that is. Instead of naming every one of the earth's five billion human inhabitants, I just say, 'humans.' Presto! Immediate condensation of a huge amount of information.

"But first I have to do the hard work of molding that concept the right way. I have to note the essential similarities the five billion share, and leave out the whole range of measurements in which they differ, or I end up with a mess. The abstractions let me keep order in the billions of bits of data I take in through my senses every day – if I know how to create the abstractions in the first place.

"All of this was spelled out brilliantly by a philosophical Maestra, named Rand, a few years ago."

"So," asked Benedict, "what is it that Seth does?"

Bevol said, "I think to some extent it's laziness. A stereotype can be a lazy man's way of avoiding work and effort. It's much simpler to say 'All pears are identical in *every* respect,' than to discover how they're similar and then to note the differences that allow you to give each one its individuality. So he evades work in creating the concept in the first place, and he evades it again when he paints an individual pear.

Ann chimed in, "And when it comes to race – poor Seth! – it gets a hundred times worse. A person like Seth assumes that everyone can be put into one distinct race or another – preferably three or four."

Bevol nodded, and said, "It's true you could have three concepts of *skin color* – light, medium, and dark – if that's all you wanted. Like this: 'Where is that doctor we asked for?' 'He's the dark skinned man over there.' 'Whom should I ask for the roll book?' 'Ask the light-skinned girl in the front row for it.' That's all fine when your purpose is identification...and when your definitions are clear. Just as you could have categories of nose width, lip thickness, facial angle. The problem is they don't all go together...or rather, only *sometimes.* But what about the four billion people who don't fit the categories of combined characteristics? My lips are slightly thicker and my skin is dark, but I don't have the ear shape of African descent. My nose is thin but I don't have the skin color of a Swede. The world is populated with such freaks as me. Derosches have thick lips, but no lineage that says African; Skyes have the facial angle of an East Asian, but not their eye shape.

"When you sculpt concepts in the studio of your mind, you need to be very accurate in your use of 'all,' 'none,' or 'some,' especially when you're categorizing humans. 'All doctors are this;' 'all children are that;' 'no tall people can do this.' Because most of what we want to say about people day in and out has nothing to do with their genetic heritage and everything to do with their choices and actions, with their character."

"You mean *volition*?" asked Benedict.

"I do," said Bevol. "Volition. How you choose to use your mind. And that brings us back to those abstractions. Seth needs other people to do his abstracting for him – which can't be done. So he freezes the measurements. He copies. Because one person can't think for another – can't abstract for another. Nor can an artist."

Tressa joined the conversation. "Bevol, what do you think brought Seth to this way of thinking?"

Bevol smiled ironically. "I think you're being a little disingenuous, Tressa. What 'brought' him? What 'made' him? Are you looking for some traumatic event that stamped him forever, never to be changed, never to be questioned by himself? Maybe he has trouble with portraiture because his parents told him not to stare at people. Who knows?! I've known many people, for example, who have perceptual problems because of religious prohibitions: they're taught that music and dance are evil, therefore, they grow up shunning music. Later, a person like this decides to learn music, but he has to fight his psyche even in trying to *hear what music is.* Music is expressive; to hear music is to hear what it's expressing; but this is just what the religious injunction forbade. A person can't instantly reprogram his subconscious. So – the difficulty."

He added: "*Any* prohibition can accomplish the same thing.

" 'Don't listen to this!' 'Don't sculpt that!' 'Don't paint such and such!' Or even, 'Don't paint things in a certain way.'

"These *don'ts* have a terrible life of their own."

Stagri looked at Tressa and said, "What brought Seth to this way of thinking? I have no idea. But I know that every time one of us says to him, 'Seth, not all pears are alike,' he *could* stop and think. But he doesn't."

"What about the Churai boy? What insight do you have on how *he* thinks?"

Stagri asked, "Which one – Braq or Nollo?"

Tressa said, "Oh, Nollo, of course. Not Braq, he's fine, isn't he? No, I meant the other one – what's Nollo's method of abstraction?"

Bevol looked down at an intricate Persian carpet spread beneath his feet. He stared at an alizarin arabesque that seemed to writhe out from under one of his shoes, its deep red coiling through the carpet insidiously, without beginning or end. Finally, he looked up, but he did not see Tressa, or any of them – his eyes were intent, his expression harrowing. He seemed to be staring at some horror inside of his own vision. Ann touched him on the arm. "Bevol?" she said with concern.

He came back. His face relaxed. He said to Tressa, "I don't know Nollo's method. But it's something far worse, and far less innocuous than Seth Pule's."

It was some thirty minutes later: everyone had gone except Ann and Bevol. She looked at him again with concern. "Something's bothering you, isn't it Bevol?"

He smiled with appreciation. "You know me, don't you Maestra?...It's Nollo and Braq. Not Nollo really. I could care less about him. But I think, I *know* they were *very, very* close – at least Braq saw it that way. He worshipped him – can't you just see it? Nollo! And here we all want to just jump down the little s.o.b.'s throat, he's so…impossible! I finally let loose the other day to Braq – I said that Nollo was irrational and we didn't care if he never showed his face around here again!

"Oh, I know I shouldn't have said it to him.

"Braq just flew at me! Braq! The boy I love like a son! Well…I guess we all do. Anyway, he didn't exactly raise his voice, he just tensed his whole body and looked at me fiercely, and said – very hot, but controlled – 'Why don't you all just leave him alone?!' Then, he turned and walked away from me. This was outside by that yew hedge that needs pruning. He didn't get to the end but he turned and came back. He looked up at me. He seemed so forlorn. I felt just awful. He said, 'I'm sorry, Dr. Stagri.' Then he added, 'It's just that…he's my…' He didn't finish, but I think I knew what he meant.

"I put my hand on his shoulder and said, 'It's OK, Braq.' "

"I think we're friends again. But I know that I never felt like that in my whole life...and I hope I never do again."

Ann laughed gently. "I'm sure you're friends again. Braq couldn't hold onto that feeling for long. Unlike his brother."

She added, "You said we all regard him as a son. You're right. But I think I see him as even more than that. I see him as the future. He's the best that can come out of the – human – race."

There was a little lull. Then she asked, "Or do you see him as a son in part because he's a Chugran, like you?"

Bevol considered. "You might be right. You know, in some ways this place – the Derosches – are more of a family to me than my own was…Ann, do you love your whole family?"

Thinking of Gert, she shook her head decidedly.

Bevol said, "Of course, there is no such blob as 'family,' only the individuals, existing in certain relations. If you didn't know that you might fall into the trap of 'the member of my family, right or wrong.'

"But all of this affection, this connection, comes from the *actions* of the family members, the single most important one being their bringing you into the world...That's why it's wonderful that Braq kept his sketch pads with all those drawings of his parents. He can *see* his parents whenever he chooses, but even more, he can see his own memory of them. No! – he can see his evaluation of them – he can almost touch the emotion whenever he wants."

Ann said, "You seem to have strong ties of affection to *your* parents, Bevol. I've seen you with them at several of our parties, and you seem quite close."

"We are," he said. "Even though there's lots that we don't share."

He paused, then added, "The events that accompanied you as you traveled from infancy to adulthood were nurturing, if your family was a good one. This is one of the most important reasons why you feel the tie in the first place. But, even if the events were not all pleasant, or even if they were unpleasant, up to a point, you will still feel a tie, because those events constitute your personal *history*. They are *where you came from*, the landscape through which you traveled in life, they are the very life you led. They are your roots and your branches.

"Like a stupid song that you disliked, that was popular when you were growing up – and if you hear this silly song later in life, it may arouse a kind of nostalgia – 'that was part of my childhood' is what you might feel. You might also feel: 'How unfortunate!' because it really is a ridiculous song, but the nostalgia and the association exist right alongside of one's *present* evaluation of the music.

"So, in the same way, your sister might feel, 'This guy is my brother; I used to admire him; I grew up with him; we played, we had all those good times, and perhaps some bad times; they were all *part* of my growing up. *Now*, I wonder if I care for him very much, but he's still part of *my* history.'

"That's how your family becomes a part of your sense of your self."

Antigone nodded. Then she asked, "This personal identity, this 'self,' does it extend beyond family? What about race? Is that any part of it?"

Bevol said, "Of course, but the tie based on nurturing there is far less. Race is usually just an accident of birth. As to your history and roots, there *may* be a natural tie, as with your family. One can look at another person of the same race and recognize him or her as coming from the same background, perhaps – in the distant past – or from the same place.

"In looking at such a person, I may feel – that's what *I* look like. That's a part of who I am, at least physically, but perhaps historically also.

This stranger walking down the street might be *my* cousin, *my* aunt, *my* nephew. If my grandfather was a slave, this stranger's grandfather may have been tethered next to him, may have shared his shackles. Was my great uncle killed in a pogrom? This stranger's great uncle perhaps felt the same fusillade. Did my ancestor champion the freedom of his – my own – people? Perhaps this stranger's ancestor laid his shoulder alongside that same struggle.

"In this way, one's race can become a part of one's identity. *Only* a part, and certainly not the most important one – rather minor perhaps. Surely, the fundamental problems of day-to-day which face anyone are a much more important part of one's identity. Still, to deny *any* part of yourself can be treacherous."

He paused again.

"Oh! how I wanted to say all this to Braq. But I had already put my foot in it, so I shut my mouth.

"Ann," he said, staring at the pattern at his feet, "what will a person do...a very good person...who is an individualist...what will such a person do when he comes to realize that his dearest pal of a brother is a thoroughly rotten person, perhaps even someone who bears him all the ill in the world?"

Antigone Derosch too looked down at the alizarin trail in the carpet. "Find out."

Bevol looked at her in bewilderment.

She said, "We'll have to wait and find out."

But Bevol said, "Why am I so afraid for Braq?"

CHAPTER 51

The Three Humors of Torquemada

"This seems quite charming," said Jerule. Standing in the middle of Braq's new quarters, she looked about her. Mark looked at Braq behind his mother's back and raised his eyebrows; he and Braq exchanged a look, grimacing at the word "charming." It was not the word Mark would have used – "cool" was his correction of his mother's description. In the end, did it come down to the same thing? Perhaps not.

Over the summer Braq had learned that he was to be awarded one of the newly vacated "slave cottages." This privilege, coveted by all of the students, Mrs. Derosch had insisted on. She knew that Braq's upstairs room, cramped and having only a single, small, east-facing window, was less than ideal for an artist. And she wanted him to have an ideal space. She thought he was mature enough to live in this cottage by himself. In any event, he was close to the main house and to Bevol's quarters, if he needed anyone.

Gideon had expressed his admiring jealousy. Gideon himself, as a resident Derosch, already had the run of the entire Atelier establishment, and could go, draw, paint, or sculpt wherever he wanted. Still, there was something enviable about having "your own place." Hence the following remark made by Gideon as he looked about him on his first visit to his newly ensconced friend – "the Chalk has *arrived*."

The cottage's single room served as living quarters, bedroom, and a compact kitchen. A few pieces of modest furniture, sturdy and of simple design, were complemented by a capacious drawing table and an easel. Above, a loft or half-attic reached by a small staircase and lit by a generous skylight facing north. A small bathroom was attached to one side of the cottage.

Withal, the space was tidy and thoughtfully designed, hence Jule's "charming"; rustic and free-standing, hence Mark's "cool"; and a functional artist's studio, hence Gideon's "the Chalk has arrived."

Mrs. Derosch had not wanted to risk any misgivings from Jule Churai so she had invited her and her husband to come inspect Braq's new living and working arrangements. Rodit declined to go. He had withdrawn more and more into a nostalgic world, pottering about his home, the neighborhood – "the Village" as he called it – and the Schaal, only those places where he could mingle and converse with other Chugrans. He ventured beyond this circumscribed milieu rarely, and when he did so, it was with alarm. Even to go to the Emporium with Jule or Mark or Sue made him anxious. He would sit far in the back, inconspicuously, and look with suspicion at the customers who continued to make Jule's enterprise a success. Immigrants sometimes find a new culture incomprehensible, particularly because they can understand scarcely a word that is being said. But Rodit did not have this excuse.

These customers were – due to Jule's great success – only occasionally Chugran. That meant, to Rodit, they were alien.

He could not understand why Braq, his nephew, his ward, should have abandoned their home and the Schaal and – as it stood in his mind – Chugrana, to go to this wretched art place run by foreigners. It did not matter that it was not that far away. It did not matter that Bevol Stagri was there. It certainly did not matter that the place was to any objective observer the Eden for which Braq was created and which was created for him.

To Rodit, Braq was a deserter from values far, far more important. Hence, his refusal to visit the Atelier to see Braq's new dwelling.

His children had no such qualms. Mark and Sue were curious so they tagged along. And with this Churai embassy went also Nollo. He had pretty much given up visiting the Atelier, whether in the guise of "chaperone" or student or anything at all. Since the day he had stormed out, he had dropped by only a few times. Now, with the rest of the family, he entered Braq's prized residence through the low doorway, craned his neck about with what seemed a suspicious and at the same time condescending gaze, and after only a minute or two, went outside to wander about in what appeared to be a restless and aimless manner. But as he walked by the yew hedge, he looked back and forth from the main house to the row of slave cottages, and to the other buildings with some sense of consideration or appraisal.

He had the same look of appraisal when they all emerged from the cottage. As they departed, he looked at his little brother, thinking to himself, "He couldn't even stay attached to *this* family, these Derosches…he had to try to escape them too…to get away…by himself." He felt – and the very image angered and depressed him – almost as if Braq was not just moving from the big house to "this little hut" but moving further away from him, Nollo – almost as if Braq was moving into some – career. It was ridiculous! He was still just a kid. What right did Little Bratabraq have to be 'out on his own?' "

After his family left, Braq went into the main house. He went into the dining room and over to the sideboard, an elegant piece of furniture designed by a Derosch from a previous century. On top of this sideboard was a silver vessel, designed by the same Derosch, a covered tureen resting on a separate silver stand. Some years ago Ann had bequeathed it to her daughter as a wedding present. By rights it should have been called a brazier since that was its intended use, but wickedly everyone insisted on calling it "Tressa's brassiere." Wicked, because this vessel was used day in and out not for heating comestibles but as a receptacle for mail, receipts, bills, and notes: the inhabitants of the Atelier would frequently urge people in search of, or in possession of, some piece of paper, to "look in Tressa's brassiere," or to "put it in Tressa's brassiere."

Sharing in the Atelier's frivolous badinage, Braq now took the lid off the vessel and searched for his latest list of chores from Clark Derosch "in Tressa's brassiere." He found the list soon enough, sandwiched into the paper compost. He studied it and then went away to attack his tasks.

As to the compost, Clark turned it – as any good gardener should – periodically. Perhaps not as often as he should have. The result of such neglect is the germination of certain unwanted weeds, sometimes noxious.

Bills he removed and paid promptly. Incoming mail to others he distributed as the Atelier's personal postman. Mail identified as "junk," which arrived by the cartloads, this being the modern world, he winnowed, threshed, discarded, or tossed back into "Tressa's brassiere" to be looked over at some later time. Some of this junk was from the bureaus – also of the modern world: the bureaus which levied taxes; the bureaus which announced inspections; the bureaus which tried to make sure that the incompetent were not put at a disadvantage by the able; the bureaus which tried to protect people from – life.

One such missive had arrived during the last year from a local school board newly reconstituted, the Home Schooling Oversight and Review Panel, demanding that the Atelier prepare an accounting of its entire program of "home schooling" for "your two enrolled students, Braq Churai and Gideon Derosch Raeburn."

Clark gave this particular piece of dirty work to Bevol with an ironic face. "One of the duties of a parent," he said.

Bevol prepared a detailed description of the curriculum the Atelier was inflicting on the two boys. He showed it to Ann and Clark for their approval, and sent it off.

As is annoyingly common with such bureaus, one month later the Panel sent a copy of the very same letter they had sent originally, stamped, "Second Request." It was doubly annoying because the Atelier had already been required to go through the same rigmarole the year before. Clark and Bevol stared at the letter in disgust. "What makes it worse," said Clark, "is not only that the left hand of these incompetents doesn't know what the right hand is doing, but that they can call their police power demands a 'request.' "

Bevol mailed a copy of his original report, with a superscript in colored ink, "Second Reply." Those who have to deal with such bureaus will not be surprised to learn that still a third request came, this time five weeks later. Again Bevol sent a copy of his report, not quite as promptly as the second time.

When the fourth envelope arrived from the same people, Clark muttered to himself, "Oh, good God! These people are hopeless," and tossed the unopened envelope into the compost in "Tressa's brassiere."

It was several weeks after, around the time that Braq gave the inspection tour of his new residence to Jule and her family that Clark performed another culling of the brazier's contents. Clamping a sheaf of letters, envelopes, and notices under an arm, he impatiently ripped open the envelope from the Oversight Panel. He scanned the letter. The entire heap of papers rained as a sudden cataract straight down from under his elbow onto the floor. He read the single sheet again.

Within three minutes he had assembled Antigone and Bevol in the drawing room. They huddled over the letter.

"Those bastards," said Bevol.

"Those bastards," said Clark.

"Those goddamned bastards," said Antigone.

The letter directed, curtly, that "the principal" of the institution "known as the Atelier Derosch" present himself or herself at a special hearing, first, to show cause why the students, Braq Churai and Gideon Derosch Raeburn, should not be returned to "the appropriate school setting from which each was taken"; second, to answer pending charges that each child was being given "inadequate instruction in the standards and materials commonly accepted by school boards in Anne Arundel County, and in the State of Maryland, and in the United States"; third, to answer charges that each child was being abused as "child labor," and fourth, in particular, to answer charges that the child known as Braq Churai was being "disrespected" and even "humiliated in ways insulting to his racial and ethnic heritage."

Antigone tossed the letter onto a table in disgust. She looked at Clark. "You realize this hearing is in three days," she said flatly. He nodded. "That's my fault. I thought it was just another of their bureaucratic bunglings. I'm sorry."

"It doesn't matter. It would've made no difference," she said.

Bevol, his face ashen, said, "To return Braq to the Schaal??? To return Gideon to his third-rate school with its juvenile delinquents?"

Clark immediately said, "What can we do to prevent this?" He felt that he was a captain seeking a strategy from his general in the face of an imminent assault by a horde of savages.

Antigone said, decisively, "We will go to this hearing. We will answer their questions. Their stupidity is so obvious they can't succeed."

Thus, her confidence in the ultimate goodness of the world and in the ultimate victory of reason over irrationality.

After a pause, Bevol added, "And as a last resort, if they try to take them, there is always murder."

They were not sure if he meant it.

***

The hearing was set for a day late in August. It arrived with a hot, wet haze that made people squint to ward off the oppressive glare. A little caravan from the Atelier pulled into the parking area, and some dozen or so people emerged from the cars into the humid blanket. Arriving, Bevol noticed two persons standing off to the side of the building. One of them had a camera with which he was taking lots of quick shots of their whole group. The other seemed to be taking notes. Bevol assumed they were reporters, though he had no idea why they had been summoned to this event.

They walked quickly into the little building only to find that there was no air conditioning, only a lone ceiling fan slowly failing to stir the torpid air.

The building they entered was just inside the city of Annapolis. It was a "one-room schoolhouse" from the nineteenth century, designated a Place of National History by the Federal government. But the county also used it to hold hearings for the Home Schooling Oversight and Review

Panel. The county thought there was something antique about home schooling and that it was, therefore, appropriate to hold their hearings in this quaint setting. The entourage from the Atelier walked through the front door to find themselves in a tiny space, with a small number of desks in rows. They were ancient desks, with attached wooden seats, scrolled iron sides and legs, and broad wooden tops with inkwell holes. A narrow aisle up the middle led to a teacher's desk squeezed into a space at the front of the room. At each of the back corners of this desk an extra chair had been added, so that three people could sit behind the desk, but with no room to spare. Only one of these was occupied when they arrived.

Sitting in the corner chair at the right hand side as they all faced him while walking up the constricted aisle was a wan, morbid-faced man, whose eyes sloped down despondently toward their outer corners. He was blowing his nose into a tissue when they filed in, and he continued to do so throughout the morning, though there seemed to be no reason as the tissue never became damp and was never discarded. He had thin scraps of hair about his narrow head, and a very scrawny nose that seemed to have a wet drop of something on the end of it, but it was really just the tiny little tip of his nose. As more and more of the group from the Atelier came in, he eyed them with a hopeless and forlorn shaking of his head, as if there was just no point to this whole affair, as if he felt they had all come to the wrong place. He kept shaking his head this way at unpredictable times during the whole proceeding.

His nameplate read "Horace Bittar."

Since there seemed to be no place to sit other than in these ancient student desks, everyone began to take seats on one side, to the right of the aisle, as if they were members of a wedding party. "Are we for the bride or the groom?" asked Tressa. When Mrs. Derosch sat down, she found the desk intolerably uncomfortable for her bad back. Therefore, she stood up again, and over everyone's concern and protests, insisted on standing. This was not any kind of self-pity or huffiness on her part; she actually preferred standing unless she was in one of her favorite chairs at the Atelier.

The result was that the Atelier contingent was arranged in this way: in the front row of desks, glowering at the gloomy little man behind the desk, were Bevol, Clark and Thaddeus Derosch. In the second row Braq, Gideon, and Gideon's father, Fritz Raeburn. Next were Tressa, and Thaddeus's wife, Hara. Behind these, several who knew about the hearing and wanted to show their support. Mrs. Derosch continued to stand in the aisle, just behind Bevol's shoulder, as if she were a bulwark, with Braq seated on the aisle just behind her.

Soon another person arrived, President Carroll, wearing a brand new suit. He walked up the aisle, stopped and nodded at Braq with a tentative smile, and then squeezed by Mrs. Derosch. As he did so, he turned and gave a bit of a bow to her. He said, "President Pakker Carroll, of the Schaal Chugrana." Mrs. Derosch looked straight into his eyes with an unsmiling glance and said, "Antigone Skye Derosch." She did not extend her hand. He looked around him at a loss, and then took one of the desks in the front row on the left hand side.

Next, Rodit and Jule Churai entered the little room. Nollo had come with them, but for some reason he stayed outside for a bit, and only came in when the hearing was about to begin. Rodit and Jule walked up the crowded aisle and took seats behind President Carroll. Rodit did not look at anyone on the right hand side, even at Braq. But Jule, before sitting, looked up at Mrs. Derosch, a sparrow gazing at an eagle. There was a momentary softening of Antigone's glance and as the two women looked at each other, they each gave a single slight nod, as if they shared some kind of communion. But no one took this in. Then Jule sat down beside her husband.

Three more people came, or rather marched in, in a cadenced procession. Fempy Lobbel, Jonatan Gee, and Chompy Screws, wearing tunics, trooped in and took seats behind Mr. and Mrs. Churai.

Another person walked in, rather slowly and methodically. He was slightly chubby, with ham fists, a bulbous nose, and large earlobes. He was wearing a short-sleeved shirt and tie and he alone of everyone in the room seemed unfazed by the stifling heat. He took his time squeezing past Mrs. Derosch, saying nothing, and took the other corner seat on the left of the front desk barely nodding to Mr. Bittar who gave him a lugubrious nod and then followed it with another regretful shake of his head. This second member of the Board was Mr. A. B. Guddud.

Finally, two more people arrived. A middle-aged woman came rushing in wearing, in spite of the weather, a light cloak. She immediately bumped into two of the desks, first one on the right, and then in a kind of ricochet, one on the left just ahead of the first. She stopped and glared about her at everyone as if they had all committed some *act*. Then she resumed her rush up the aisle. But the cloak, caftan, or whatever the garment she wore caught on the scrollwork of one of the desks and she had to stop again. She gave a vicious tug to free her garment and then swirled past Mrs.

Derosch, glaring at her over her shoulder as she did so. She petulantly squeezed past Mr. Bittar on the right of the desk and took her place in the chair at the center.

She was thin in a stringy sort of way, and her long hair fell in thin damp serpentine coils past her shoulders. From time to time she would irritably toss the pasta of hair from one shoulder to the other as if it were an annoyance caused by someone, somewhere. When she was not tossing it, she was peering from behind one curtained side or the other with a single baleful and pale reddish eye.

With a high-pitched peremptory voice she introduced herself as Ms. Tacy Backett-Snee, the Chairwoman of the Oversight Panel. As she was saying this, and preparing to introduce the other Panel members, Messrs. Guddud and Bittar, she was interrupted by the other person who had come in with her.

This man, very neat, even prim, in his three piece suit and bow tie, was extraordinarily short, and had been scarcely noticed by anyone because he was more or less swallowed up in Ms. Backett-Snee's caftan. He had blown in, so to speak, in her wake, and now he was trying to squash behind her to the other side of the desk, so she had to stand up again to let him by. He immediately, out of nowhere, produced a low stool on which he sat down somewhere between Ms. Backett-Snee and Mr. Guddud. When he did this, he almost completely disappeared from view, in which state of near complete concealment he remained for the duration. Except that, at intervals, he would produce a document, or a file, or sometimes just a small slip of paper. A hand would appear from behind, over the back edge of the desk, with the paper, or the file, and crisply deposit it before Ms. Backett-Snee. Then the hand, clad in jacket sleeve and cuff, would disappear again behind the desk. Just the barest suggestion of the top of his head, in a very close flat cut, could occasionally be seen moving about, right before some new paper materialized. He was Othmar Swart, the Staff Assistant to the Panel.

The chairwoman tried again to perform her introductions, but just then there was another interruption. With a disturbing amount of noise – why are some people so noisy, even in the very way they move, as if they are shattering the air itself in their vicinity – Pranti Ku came through the door. He wheezed up the aisle, and this time Mrs. Derosch had to step completely out of the aisle by squeezing in between two desks, because his girth was such that he could not have gotten by her. After he had oozed through, he turned to the Panel and said, bowing with immense formality, as if he were an ambassador from some court or other, "Prester Pranti Ku! Prester Pranti Ku!"

Then, he took a seat next to President Carroll. It was almost impossible. The whole room gaped to see him try to squeeze his whole self into one of the desks. It took some time.

No one noticed exactly when Nollo had come in. When they happened to turn their heads around, by chance, now and again, they saw him sitting at the back, on "the Atelier side." No one knew just why he sat on that side instead of with his pals from the Schaal, who also did not seem to mind this slight from their leader.

Ms. Backett-Snee was finally able to proceed. Her first comment, annoyed, was almost to herself, but she did not lower her voice, so everyone heard her. "Who *are* all these people?"

Mrs. Derosch said, "I am Antigone Skye Derosch, head of the Atelier Derosch, and," she gestured to the right hand side of the room, "this is most of the faculty and several of the student body, including the two whom you're trying to take away from us."

Ms. Backett-Snee replied with slight irritation, "We're not trying to take anyone away. This is just a hearing. Nothing has been decided." Without stopping or taking a breath, she added, "Why don't you sit down?"

Mrs. Derosch, as erect and immoveable as an obelisk, said, "Your desks hurt my back; I prefer to stand."

The result of this brief exchange was that the Panel felt the towering figure of Antigone Derosch ensconced front and center as a reproach to them and to the entire proceeding. This was perhaps not unintentional. If asked Antigone might have said that her primary feeling as to her role in that moment was as a human battlement over whose dead body they would have to storm to get at Braq and Gideon.

Recoiling from this rebuff, Ms. Backett-Snee looked vaguely at the other side of the room. President Carroll introduced himself, and Ku reintroduced himself, unnecessarily. He continued, waving his hand grandly behind him, "The guardians of Braq Churai – and, I may say, guardians, that is…all of us…guardians of the Chugran heritage…spokesmen for Chugrana in America, Chugrana in exile…" He would have gone on this way, but Backett-Snee flared up. Tossing her hair to the other shoulder, she said, "Well, I hope everyone will observe good order, and wait to be recognized by the Chair."

She turned her attention now to President Carroll, who under her questioning gave a fulsome account of the Schaal Chugrana and its educational merits. He did not omit to refer to "the age-old Chugran tradition of 'Let mind speak to mind,' " which seemed to impress the Panel, who had never heard this saying before. Not that they knew much at all of Chugran ways. Carroll, of course, eschewed any mention of the disrepute the old Chugran motto had fallen into lately at the Schaal. He concluded by saying that he was "baffled, surprised, and hurt" when he had learned that Braq was going to be leaving the Schaal to enroll at the Atelier.

President Carroll was taken up rather short by a sudden cross-examination by Panel Member Bittar. Bittar subscribed to the idea that there was only one legitimate educational standard to which any and all questions should be referred, and that was whatever was ordained by the State and its educational boards and officials. There could not, therefore, be anything worthwhile emanating from this group of immigrants, neither from any Chugran individually, nor from the Chugran people as a whole as they might be represented in this Schaal Chugrana.

Member Bittar, wiping his nose gloomily, asked President Carroll, "What are your test scores?" The words were scarcely out of his mouth when a detached hand and arm shot across the front of Backett-Snee with a piece of paper. Bittar took the proffered sheet from the invisible Swart and scanned it as Carroll was trying to put as good a light as he could on the matter. Bittar rejoined, "Your test scores are among the lowest in our whole district." He said it hopelessly, as if no ingenuity in the world could ever cure such a state of affairs.

Predictably, Ku leaped to counter this disparagement. Or rather he tried to leap, but he was so wedged into his desk that when he tried to stand up the desk came up with him. Realizing how ridiculous this was – even he finally realized how ridiculous he looked – he sat back down. This turned out to be a blessing for he remained seated for the rest of the session.

Anyway, it didn't stop him from talking; he roared to the defense of the Schaal. This "great world-historical Lyceum of the Chugrans…abandoned by the racist society in which they found themselves entrapped…forced to rely upon donations from the financially crushed Chugran community…languishing now in its separate, unequal, but still proud and even splendid isolation…not a whited sepulcher, sanitized on the outside while foul within, but a blackened sepulcher – seeming to be sullied in its reputation while pure in its inner Spirit…preserving for all time the Chugran values and the Chugran

Race...What matter these white test scores when the Schaal is more interested in the inner child, the true Chugran, as only we can know him...I myself always had the greatest admiration and fondness for this boy when he was at the Schaal – he was so polite, the old 'Chugran courtesy unto death' " (they hadn't the least idea what he was talking about), "until he went to the Atelier and as soon as he started taking classes there his whole manner changed and he became a different person – distant, aloof, even rude to me."

Ms. Backett-Snee finally got her high-pitched voice wedged into this verbal flood to ask, "Well, who authorized this anyway? I mean, if this Schaal is so wonderful why did you let the child go?"

Ku answered, "We were given to understand that the boy's parents would have approved of his removal. I, for one, never believed it. I took it as one more Removal by the white power structure of tribal peoples from their rightful place and homes to an approved Reservation – in this case, the Atelier Derosch Reservation."

"Where are his father and mother? Are they here?"

Ku took it upon himself to answer. "The great Zaqqaq Churai, who I'm sure you have heard of, (she had, vaguely) is in prison in Chugrana, a defender of Chugran values, a prisoner of consciousness, a great symbol to us all. His wife is also there, fulfilling her connubious duty, and remaining by her husband's side, well, not exactly by his side, but...er...*there*. But Braq's uncle and guardian is here – Mr. Rodit Churai."

Unable to turn, he gestured over his shoulder.

"Mr. Churai?" queried Ms. Backett-Snee.

Rodit stood. Something about his manner suggested defiant timidity. His head was sunk into his shoulders, but he had a sullen set to his mouth.

"Why did you authorize this transfer of the boy?" asked Backett-Snee.

"Well...really...I never was in favor of it," said Rodit. "I would much rather have written to my brother for his advice. I think Braq should have stayed at the Schaal with other Chugran boys, as his brother Nollo did. Braq should have followed in his brother's footsteps, and been a good Chugran. Respectful, not moving off on his own. He should have respected our ways, and not defied the prohibition which we have had forever against making images. I can't believe my brother, who was a champion" (more than one person noted the use of the past tense) "of Chugran values would have approved of this."

At this point the rather leaden voice of Mr. Guddud was heard intoning "Quite right!" Mr. Guddud believed that each group – ethnic or religious or national, any group whatsoever – determined the best educational environment for its own members. He believed it self-evident that every child should be kept strictly within the confines of its own group. Now, with approval, he stolidly intoned, "To each his own."

Rodit, encouraged by this, nodded and said, "I would never have approved this if it had been my decision."

The Chairwoman was about to ask whose decision it had been when she heard a small but clear voice saying, "May I speak?" It was the diminutive but resolute figure of Jule, now standing beside her husband.

"Who are you?" asked Ms. Backett-Snee with annoyance.

"I am Jerule Churai, Braq's aunt. This," she gestured with a spare movement of her hand, "is my husband."

"Yes?" said Backett-Snee brusquely.

"I whole-heartedly approved Braq's going to the Atelier. He was obviously a child with brilliant talents to paint, to draw, to do art, and the Atelier trains people to do that. They have a national reputation in the field...in case you didn't know. He was one hundred percent eager to go. I inspected the place and was sure he would be treated well – in fact, would get everything he could possibly need. I have found that to be the case since then. I have no cause for complaint.

"And as to writing my brother-in-law, there is no way to be sure of getting correspondence in or out of Chugrana. Rodit knows that!"

Her husband turned his head away, and down toward the floor, even more sullen. He did not argue.

"And another thing! My brother-in-law, Zaq, is not a champion of 'Chugran values.' He is a defender of liberty. And, Braq's mother, Zaq's wife, Liz specifically asked me to make sure Braq got the education his talents deserved. Sending him back to this *Schaal* (her voice was scornful) would be disastrous for him."

There was a lot of commotion, but Ku managed to boom over everyone else. His hands were flapping spastically as he shouted, "Your honor," and there was so much uproar at this point that no one took the trouble to point out to him that Ms. Backett-Snee was not entitled to any such mode of address, "Your honor, this whole statement is irrelevant and you should have your man there (he gestured in the direction of the hidden Swart) strike it from the record. Chugrana is a strictly patriarchal society and neither Ms. Churai, Rodit's wife, nor Liz Churai, Zaqqaq Churai's wife – and she's an American by the way, not a Chugran of any kind, so she really doesn't enter into this – has any standing to give authority to any of these decisions!"

The cat was now rampaging through the pigeons. Three more people leapt to their feet: President Carroll, Bevol Stagri, and Fempy Lobbel, though no one paid any attention to Fempy. Ms. Backett-Snee slapped her palm on the desk and got some order for the moment. "Who are you?" she asked Bevol.

"Dr. Bevol Stagri, Professor of Artistic Anatomy at the Atelier Derosch. I'm a Chugran American, and know as much about Chugran traditions as that person." He pointed disdainfully at a sputtering Ku. "On the contrary, if anything, Chugran culture was always *matriarchal.* There are numerous examples of women taking the lead. The whole idea of 'Let mind speak to mind' even came from a woman, Ara Redtree.

"And another thing, by the way, Mr. Rodit Churai mentioned the prohibition against image-making. That's also not universally held in Chugrana. Only the most conservative, traditional religious sects maintain that ban. There are plenty of other people in Chugrana who hold no such thing. Zaqqaq Churai himself encouraged his son in this activity. And finally, I just want to say that I'm a Chugran in America, as much as Mister, or Mister Prester, or whatever he calls himself, Ku is – and I'm not 'entrapped,' I'm not 'languishing,' and I'm not in any kind of 'sepulcher,' *white or black*!"

There erupted a cacophony. The rest of the room saw the entire Chugran population within the four walls yelling at each other. Ku, Carroll, Stagri, Rodit, Jule, and the three boys from behind, also Nollo – they were all on their feet, except for the entrapped Ku, throwing claims and counterclaims at each other about who had more authority in Chugran life – men or women – and about images, sacrilege, and, above all, about Respect! The Panel Members eyes were goggled. So were the others from the Atelier. Only Braq laughed. It reminded him of some of the disputes he had heard in Chugrana.

Ms. Backett-Snee at last restored order. Everyone except Mrs. Derosch sat down. The Chairwoman and her fellow Panelists were dismayed. How could they decide what was a "Chugran value" with so much disagreement from the Chugrans themselves? Who could decide for them? What was wrong with these people, anyway? Why was there no unanimity, no unity, no consensus, no gentle flowing into a "mainstream" of opinion where everyone knew what was what? Why couldn't they be – like white people?

Ms. Backett-Snee received help from her aide-de-camp. The ghostly hand thrust another scrap of paper around in front of her bosom. She looked at it, and then addressed Mrs. Derosch. "Let's move on for a minute to something else. We have been told that you're using this boy as your own personal slave labor and have even put him out of your house where you first agreed to house him, and now have him in some kind of old slave shack or kennel. Can this outrage really be true?"

Antigone Derosch's venerable face was a mask of cold fury. She swiveled it from Backett-Snee to the other two Panel Members, and then around the room to Ku and Carroll, then to Rodit, and she even arced her glance round to aim her face directly at Nollo. She stared at him for a long moment. She had no way of being sure who was the source of this outrageous smear. And for a moment she was just speechless. Her husband stood up, perhaps afraid of what Antigone might do if left to herself. He said, "I'm Clark Derosch, Antigone's husband and co-founder of the Atelier. Braq is not 'slave labor.' Whoever told you that is a bare-faced, shameful liar. Braq came to me on his own and asked if he could do anything to earn some money to pay for a trip to European museums he wants to take with other members of the Atelier. My great grandson, Gideon, whom you've also hauled in here, is doing similar chores. These chores are not physically onerous – no more than the chores boys have been doing since the dawn of time." He described their work, the pay each boy received, and the savings account each had established. He turned at this point and asked each of the boys how much money he had accumulated, and each was proud to announce to the penny the balance they had saved.

Clark went on. "I spoke to Jule Churai, Braq's guardian, about this, and she told me that Braq's parents secured a sum of money to pay for whatever his education required, but Braq did not want to touch that in case his father ever needs it to get out of Chugrana – a motive which says volumes for this boy's sense of responsibility and maturity.

"As to the 'slave shack' – I won't even repeat the other degrading slur you used – once again your dirty little liar has fed you poison. The cabins that used to be slave quarters are now the most prized living places for the senior students at the Atelier. They battle each other to get to the top of the list in order to live there.

"I noticed, when we came in, a photograph on the wall there," he pointed to the far wall by the door, "of a class of students here in your historical building at the turn of the century. They're all white children.

This was a segregated school, wasn't it? How would you feel, Mrs. Backett-Snee, if someone accused you of holding a segregated hearing today with whites on one side and blacks on the other, in an old segregated school house, in order to humiliate the participants?"

Backett-Snee choked and then rasped out, "That's ridiculous!"

"Yes," he said calmly. "*Just* as ridiculous."

Backett-Snee turned her attention back to Mrs. Derosch. "But why would you want to take this boy away from his own culture?"

"His culture," Ann shot back, "is the riches of civilization. It is the great achievements of art over the centuries. It is the glories of the mind. Even in Chugrana, they don't say, 'Let *Chugran* mind speak to *Chugran* mind!' This boy has the most precious thing in the whole world, a fertile, active mind. It was being wasted compared to what he could do."

The disembodied arm behind the table performed a trick again with a scrap of paper.

The Chairwoman looked at it, and then she said, "Is that the same rationale – some alleged educational inferiority – for removing the other boy, Gideon Raeburn, from *his* school?"

Several of the people from the Atelier thought that Ann was going to launch herself at this woman because they saw her step forward, level now with the front row of desks, and she leaned toward the front table. The three Panel Members flinched.

"It was not anything *I* said about the inferiority of that place, the Schaal – your own records" she flipped her wrist sharply at the papers on the desk, "have already demonstrated that. But I would've wanted to take Braq away even from the best school in the country to give him the art training he's getting from us."

"You seem improperly confident of the superiority of your Atelier, even arrogant," said Ms. Backett-Snee accusingly.

" 'Arrogant' means to claim something you don't deserve. The Atelier Derosch deserves every ounce of praise she gets," said Antigone.

At this moment, Fritz Raeburn stood up. "*I* took my son, Gideon, out of the local school when I found that they were teaching him no facts or principles of any consequence, and instead were indoctrinating him in the latest cultural bromides, and training him to *adapt* to the other little hoodlums which their educational methods were creating by the dozen."

The Chairwoman's head shot up like an irritated wasp.

Ms. Backett-Snee had always been opposed to what she, and many others, called "stuffing little heads with facts," that is, with knowledge.

She was equally opposed to teaching principles, in any field, as this was "overly analytical." It brought the "the cold, dead hand of rationality into what should be the warm, loving cocoon of acculturation." She was particularly hostile to anything that suggested individualism (of which, she was beginning to see, the Atelier reeked). Or anything that encouraged thinking for oneself, or using one's own judgment, or challenging accepted mores, views, or the values of the group. She particularly bridled if anyone, in discussing educational goals, referred to "objective standards," which sounded to her like some incomprehensible term from a dead language.

Now she shrilled, "We're very proud of our public school system!"

"That's right!" "Yes!" chimed in Guddud and Bittar.

Raeburn was undeterred. "Your Mr. Bittar criticized the Schaal Chugrana for having the lowest scores in the district. He didn't mention that your *district* has the lowest scores in the State, and that, while the State of Maryland's scores are not too disreputable compared to the country, the scores of *the country* are pathetically, shamefully low compared to the other literate countries of the *world*. And getting worse. The education my son and Braq are receiving at the Atelier on the other hand is superb!"

"And just what does this education consist of?" asked Mr. Bittar with a sadly detached expression, looking at the floor under Raeburn's feet.

It fell to Bevol to describe the curriculum they had devised, and how it tied in with everything else they taught at the Atelier. "The basis of it," he concluded, after some minutes, "is the principle that if we train either of these boys in how to use their minds they'll be free of us forever, because they'll be sovereign, independent persons. They'll be able to function wherever and whenever they want in order to achieve their values."

Ms. Backett-Snee said now, somewhat dismissively, "I think we've heard enough from all of the adults here, it's time we heard from the little boys themselves. May we speak to Braq Churai himself now?"

Braq stood up and walked around Mrs. Derosch, who gave him a pat on the back as he went by, to stand in front of the desk. The anonymous arm thrust a packet of papers upwards at Backett-Snee. She ignored them momentarily. She looked at Braq. He returned her gaze calmly, with an open face. This seemed somewhat brazen to her, but she pasted a smile on her face and said, "Now, Braq, how are they treating you, really, at this place?"

He answered, "Mrs. Backett-Snee, I *love* it there. I was fine at Aunt Jule's and Uncle Rodit's, but the Atelier is wonderful. I wouldn't want to be anywhere else, except maybe with my parents."

"*Maybe*?" she asked.

"Well, ma'am…I think it's pretty bad in Chugrana, and they sent my brother and me out of there because if we had stayed the government would've taken us away from my mother and put us in an orphanage."

She asked, suggestively, "Do you really like living in some old slave hut, considering what it represents?"

Braq practically shouted, with a glee that was specially his, "It's great!!"

She asked, "Why wouldn't you want to be at the Schaal with all your own people?"

He made a face that was eloquent. "It was boring there! I wasn't learning anything at all!"

Backett-Snee sat up smartly now. "Well, be that as it may, we need to know that your education is up to our standards, both local and national. Much as I hate the mere recitation of facts, can we ask you a few simple questions?"

"Yes, ma'am," he answered.

She suddenly gave him a little snippy rebuke, along with a toss of the hair. "It's not necessary to keep saying 'ma'am,' you know. Do they make you do that at the Atelier?"

As a rule, Braq allowed the strange behavior of adults to roll off of, or around him, without reacting personally, however much he might wonder about it. But this truly offended him. Quietly, he said, "No, ma'am. My *parents* taught me that. And that's the way everyone in Chugrana speaks."

"Well…well…whatever you want," she hurried on. "Now, don't be nervous about these questions. We won't be *too* hard on you." Her expression became suddenly severe.

"What is the capital of Maryland?"

"Annapolis."

"How many states are there?"

"In the United States, fifty, and in the continental U. S. one subordinate district, the District of Columbia which is the seat of government of the United States."

"It isn't necessary to show off," she said testily. "What is the capital of – " she ran her finger carefully down a list, " – Oregon?"

"Salem."

"And of Nevada," she continued, leaving her finger carefully on her crib sheet.

"Carson City."

"Very well, very well..." She skipped to the next page of her notes. "Who was called 'the Father of his Country'?"

"George Washington."

"And who freed the slaves?"

"Thomas Jefferson."

"No, you're wrong there," she said with a little note of self-satisfaction, as though she had, finally, some grist for her mill. "It was Abraham Lincoln." She shook her head sternly at Braq: "Jefferson was a slave *owner*."

But Braq answered, "Lincoln freed the slaves *in fact* with the Emancipation Proclamation in 1863, saying all former slaves are 'forever free.' But Jefferson freed them all *in principle*, in 1776, when he said, 'All men are created equal,' and that 'all men are endowed by their Creator with certain unalienable rights.' That's what made Emancipation possible."

"Is that what they teach you at the Atelier?" asked Backett-Snee accusingly.

"Yes, Dr. Stagri discussed that with me. But Father had already said it before that."

In the back of the room, Nollo got a sickening feeling in his stomach. He thought, "Oh, Christ, he's going to tell that story!"

Backett-Snee asked, "He did?"

"Yes. Nollo and I were studying a book on American history with Father in our Schaal, and there was a picture of Jefferson, and a discussion of slavery. After we read it, Father looked at us and said, 'A man who would enslave his fellow men must be a kind of monster.' "

Braq paused. Backett-Snee stared at him with petulant incomprehension. "*Yes*?"

"Then he kissed the picture of Jefferson."

She rasped, "He did *what*?"

"He kissed it. My brother Nollo said, 'Why did you do that, Father? After what you just said...?'

"Father said, 'Do you think Chugrans should be slaves?' We both answered, 'Of course, not!' Then he said, 'Do you think Chugrans should enslave others?' We said, 'No!' Then he asked us, 'Who taught you that? Where did you get that idea?'

"We both said, 'From *you*, Father!' but he shook his head and said, 'No, you got it from Thomas Jefferson. Every time you think of yourself as a free man, as the equal of any other man, as entitled to the rights which all men possess, you're thinking the ideas *Jefferson* gave you, and taught you, and glorified for all time.' "

Backett-Snee cleared her throat. She said, "Umm...why don't we get off the subject of history. Let's go on to something different, mathematics."

She consulted her packet of papers. "Hmmm... What is four times twenty-five?"

"One hundred."

"And one-third of fifteen?"

"Five."

"All right, all right...it seems that you're a bright boy," she said perfunctorily.

"Is that all?" Braq was genuinely disappointed.

"Why, yes," said Ms. Backett-Snee. She seemed eager to move on. She saw no reason to interrogate Braq any further, and was, for some reason, ill at ease at what might come out of his mouth if she continued. "Now we can examine the other boy."

But Stagri was on his feet again. "One moment, Madame Chairwoman. May I ask a question or two?"

"All right," she said grudgingly.

He came up alongside his pupil. "Braq, if you were going to do a painting on canvas to cover that wall behind these people, how much canvas would you need?"

Braq looked at the wall. He screwed his mouth up. "The ceiling seems about ten feet high, and the wall fifteen feet wide, so...a little over seventeen square yards."

Stagri said, "Isn't it a little *under* seventeen?"

Braq said, "No, Dr. Stagri. You probably forgot to add in a couple of inches on each side to stretch over the stretcher bars."

"Oh, right!" said Bevol, accepting the correction.

"And," added Braq, "you'd need to special order the linen because it doesn't come in this large a width."

"Thanks, Braq, for telling me that. Now, what if it were a *circular* painting to go on that same wall. A circle inscribed within the rectangle. How much canvas?"

Braq said, "Well...about eight and three quarters square yards."

"How did you figure?"

"The radius, five feet at the most, times pi, squared, and then converted into square yards."

"Did you work that formula out yourself?"

"No, Dr. Stagri," said Braq, shocked. "The Greeks did."

"I see. Did we get all of our math from them?"

Braq said, "No, the Indians discovered zero, and gave it to the Arabs who gave it to us."

"And calculus?"

"Oh, that wasn't till after the Renaissance when Newton and Leibniz discovered it. Unless it was Archimedes first."

"OK, Braq, you see that tool that Mr. Bittar is checking your calculations with? What's it made of?"

"If you mean the pencil, it's wood and graphite. If you mean his hand it's made of eight carpal bones, five metacarpals, and fourteen phalanges, plus a bunch of muscles, tendons, and ligaments. Do you want me to name them?"

"I don't think it will be necessary. What about that member of the genus *Rana* you dissected last month?"

"You mean that bullfrog?"

"Yes, the bullfrog. What about *his* hand?"

"He still had similar carpals, metacarpals, and phalanges, but not the same number and the lengths were different. Plus his radius and ulna were fused into a single bone for greater strength in jumping." He flexed his legs and arms and gave an uncanny simulation of a jumping frog.

Ms. Backett-Snee bridled at the indignity being introduced into the proceedings. "This really isn't necessary, is it? We can see the boy's bright." She did not say it now as a compliment. It might even have had a slight tone of an insult.

Sharp as a hatchet came Antigone Derosch's voice. "Since your letter accused us of 'inadequate instruction' and ordered us to appear here to show cause,' I think it damn well *is* necessary. Dr. Stagri, Braq, *continue*."

No one said a word to contradict her.

Bevol changed course. "Braq, you mentioned the Renaissance – how about telling us something about that period. Try to make it brief."

Some twenty minutes later Braq had emerged from the long night of the Dark Ages, passed through the first building blocks of the late Middle Ages, arrived at the explosive rediscovery of the glories of ancient Greece, and was now well into the early Renaissance with its discovery of perspective, of science, of anatomy, of literature, of music, and of man.

Bevol placed a hand on Braq's shoulder. Braq stopped.

Bevol Stagri turned to the stupefied Panel and said, gently, "Do you have any more questions?"

Mr. Bittar decided to inject his two cents. He addressed Braq. "You seem to approach everything in an extremely *rational* way." The word "rational" came out as a brassy honk, with a blaring emphasis on "rash."

Braq said, "Yes?"

Bittar continued, "Well don't you ever just let your feelings go?"

Braq asked, "What feelings?"

Bittar said, "Anything under the sun – your anger, your rage, your fear, your frustration."

Braq said, "I'm not angry at anyone – or anything." He paused. "When I get frustrated, I go outside and run and then I feel better and I can get back to work."

Bevol asked the panel, "Should we examine Gideon now?"

Ms. Backett-Snee's voice was a bit shaky as she said, "I don't think we need to follow this line of inquiry any further."

But Gideon yelled from the second row of desks, "But Dr. Stagri, I wanted to dispute one or two things Braq said about who was responsible for discovering the medium and the black oil we use – the Van Eyck brothers, or Titian, or da Messina."

Bevol said, "Later, Gideon, later."

Bevol turned again to the Panel. "And now I have a question for this panel: just *who* lodged this complaint in the first place?"

There was a nervous silence in the room. Ms. Backett-Snee said, curtly, "Our sources are strictly confidential."

"I thought so," said Bevol with contempt. He walked back to his desk in the front row.

But Gideon wasn't finished. He had handed something to Mrs. Derosch. It was Braq's drawing pad which he had left on his desk when he went up to be questioned. Mrs. Derosch looked at it. She just shook her head. Over and over. She handed it to Bevol, and he, Clark, Thaddeus, and Fritz all peered over each other's shoulders at the drawing. Their laughter rocked the room. They were looking at a chalk drawing Braq had made during the whole first part of the hearing.

Now, Bevol looked at Ann, then toward the Panel. "Should I?" he asked her. She too looked at them, then nodded grimly, as a judge affirming a criminal's sentence. Bevol walked to the desk and said, "If you like we can call the local newspaper and submit this with an article on today's hearing for their op-ed page. Or just call in your stooges from the press who are lurking outside."

Backett-Snee, Bittar, and Guddud, as well as Swart who finally stood up for this, looked at Braq's drawing. Braq had given it a title, "The Three Humors of Torquemada." It showed the Panel Members as priests torturing a victim: the victim tied to a rack and on whom they were administering their atrocities was Braq himself. The three figures, who were the size of pygmies, were not caricatures but succinct renderings of the faces and personalities of the Board-inquisitors. Braq's figure was of normal size, his face studying them in amused disbelief. Legends appeared thusly: over the head of Backett-Snee, "Choler," over Bittar, "Black Bile," and over Guddud, "Phlegm."

The three persons pilloried by Braq's chalk stared at the drawing stupefied. Then the heads of Backett-Snee, Bittar, and Guddud drew close together, as they held a hasty and subdued parley. The head of Swart disappeared. Braq wondered if he might have time to start another drawing – this time a three-headed hydra. Everyone else in the room could hear only sibilant murmurs and buzzes, which lasted only a short time. Could they have gleaned one sentence from the sub rosa conference to know the thrust of the discussion, perhaps this one from Backett-Snee would have summed it up: "I'm not going to make a further fool of myself in front of the press."

They concluded their little conference. Ms. Backett-Snee looked up. She pushed the drawing to the edge of the desk with a gesture of distaste. "In spite of this disrespectful and nasty little drawing, and the implication that we are somehow persecuting anyone, we stated from the outset that this was just an exploratory hearing. It seems that the boys are receiving an adequate" – her tone dropped disparagingly – "education, eccentric as it may be. One must have grave reservations about the degree to which these boys will be properly socialized, and able to relate to other people, whether of their own age and culture or otherwise. However, in the interest of leaving well enough alone, and not upsetting any apple carts…the boys may stay at the Atelier."

***

On their way home, in the car, Gideon punched his friend Braq on the arm and said, "Boy, were they stupid. They didn't even say anything about the fact that there were four humors, not three."

Braq said, "Yeah, but I couldn't work out the fourth. Othmar Swart" – he and Gideon roared in recollection, both of them imitating a disembodied arm – "sure wasn't the fourth humor."

Bevol, in the front seat, over his shoulder said, "No, Braq, but the fourth humor *was* in your drawing, although you didn't label him. It was you – 'Sanguine.' "

A few moments later, thinking about the "strictly confidential sources" that had produced the complaint, he turned and looked directly at Braq. "I know you love your brother – your Big Brátano. But is he your friend?"

Braq asked, "Do you mean my pal?"

"No," said Bevol, "I mean your friend...."

Back home, he said to the rest of the faculty, gathered in the drawing room to discuss the events of the day, "So the organ-grinder – Stagri – played his hurdy-gurdy and the monkey – Braq – performed his tricks. But it's a disgrace that such people have the power to command us to perform...Braq should have told us *this* today in his account of the Renaissance: Cosimo de Medici tried to coerce the truculent painter Lippo Lippi to his will, found that he couldn't, and *gave up* the attempt to do so. He justified his patience, saying: 'Geniuses are celestial beings and not pack asses'.

"Then came the American Revolution to say, '*No* human should be treated as a pack ass.'

"Finally, along came the modern world, to say to our children: 'No one should aspire to be any higher than a pack ass.' "

CHAPTER 52
Sense of Life

You gazed from a cool, shadowy, half-dappled glade through an aperture framed by columns of birch and sprays of maple into a sunrise just bursting beyond a deep blue mountain. You longed to follow the path that led from that glade into the sunrise, over the mountain and even into the sun itself. Your attention traversed the translucent leaves, it penetrated beyond them, past the figure striding away from you into the distance. Your gaze penetrated the haze that shrouded the foothills, and through this very haze on up to the gilded crown of the mountain. Every time your eye wandered to the foreground you found that eye's meander beguiled again up to the mountain and the light. You felt that something, or someone, commanded you to rise to the mountain and the light, you felt that on such a day, from that very glade, from its benevolent shadow, on such a path, nothing but good could come to you, and you – if you chose to enter that world – could come to nothing but good.

"Do you recall that I told you," said Bevol Stagri, "that Braq just about always put figures into his landscapes, even from his earliest days. He told me that he greatly admired the world's superb landscape artists and loved to contemplate their work, but – to spend his time on nature, without man – that was not him.

"So in this painting the figure is not dwarfed by nature, he seems a part of it – and almost as if trees, mountain, and the very sky lie but as the framework for this figure.

"He called it 'Zaq's World.' "

The students he was speaking to studied the copy of the painting carefully. They were surprised to learn the actual size of the painting, which was unexpectedly modest. Seeing a print of it in a book, one would have thought that the original must cover a vast wall such grandeur did it evoke, but it was in reality no more than of average size. Which did not stop people in the gallery when it was first shown from standing in front of it, and staring mesmerized for unmeasured lengths of time, as if it were a whole world unto itself. They entered and dwelt in Braq's miraculous world.

A student of Bevol raised his hand. "One of my professors called this type of art 'escapism.' "

"And I," replied Bevol, "would call that a particularly brainless cliché. He thinks it's an escape from 'the harsh world of reality', he thinks the 'realists' face up to 'the truth' – of grim and grisly defeat. Such platitudes I call 'brainless' because it never occurs to him that facing up to defeat is another way of saying – surrender. It never occurs to him that the battle of life *is* won – by some – by those who face it with the joy that comes from the belief that the contest not only can be won but is *worth winning.*

"Such joyous ones are not blind to hardship, to difficulty, to risk, to the possibility even of failure. They only realize that they don't *have* to make *these* the focus of their work. We 'escapists' believe that contemplating the good is very practical."

He paused and took a deep breath. "But even Braq could have a foul mood now and again. These moods very occasionally made their way into his art...but don't be too quick to draw a conclusion about an artist's sense of life. We say that your artistic creations show us who you are, and so they do. But not all *forms* of art have the *same* revelatory power. A novelist who takes ten years to write her magnum opus shows you the foundation pillars of her soul. A sculptor who takes six months to create a figure no doubt shows you *something* very important about his deepest values. A skilled painter who renders a completed canvas in only three hours may show you the impermanent mood he experiences during just that afternoon. And a skilled musician or poet can work quickly, throwing together a waltz or a sonnet, in less than an hour, transfiguring what is a fleeting sentiment into a work of art in a single sitting – as we say, 'alla prima.' So, you must be careful about judging an artist's core values from a single work.

"In such a fleeting mood, Braq painted a withered leaf caught in its fall by a single shivered strand of spider's web. Against an obscure gray wooded backdrop, you saw but a few iridescent glints of color, whose connection to the pendent leaf you felt but could not see. The faint flickering shimmers of the strand came from a cold, painfully bright, fall light, shattering through the limbs and leaves off to the left. The fragility of leaf and silky thread against the stark panels of light and dark made you feel with alarm the approach of a daunting winter; you felt how fragile a living being's security might be.

"He later called it 'Hanging by a Thread.' He painted it on a day when his hopes of ever seeing his father again were at low ebb. He was seldom subject to such spells of blackness, and having painted it he immediately wanted to wipe it out, but La Maestra and Benedict and I stopped him. It took all three of us because he was – so young! – already nearly perfect in his stubbornness, but it was our good fortune that he was young enough and tractable enough for us to gang up on him and get him to swear to leave it alone.

"But he 'paid us back,' as he put it, by painting 'Zaq's World.' It took him several weeks, not like 'Hanging by a Thread. The fact that it took him longer to create that one than the other illustrates Maestra's point – that the creation of beauty is hard work. Easier by far is the creation of a negative – even when it's an artistic, esthetically valuable negative, like 'Hanging by a Thread.' And this is another reason why beauty is not an 'escape.' *Negation* is the easy way out, the way of less effort. *Negation* is really the *escape.* To create beauty you must understand so much, you must *face up* to so much.

"I'm telling you about two of his landscapes. You can study them in the "Braq Catalog," which has photos of many of the works he did while he was a student here. Most of these are now in private collections. Extraordinary! For such a young artist to have such a book already published about his work! You should also study his figurative works. You know the drawing I told you about that made Jule laugh – the one of the father and son running – well, he turned that into a painting, equally successful…er…except for the skin color…oh, never mind that, don't get me started…It was still a father in benediction of his son, and you loved both of these people because he made you feel the nobility of the boy's serious purpose and the benevolence of the father's proud and loving glance. He called it 'His Sanction.'

"One of my favorites was another runner he did, this time a sculpture. It's about two feet tall, a typical height for a smaller work. It shows a young man running through a rocky landscape, uphill, swathed in a cloth, or robe, or cape, which swirls violently around him. He is purposeful, relentless, indomitable, charged with energy, an unstoppable force. It seems that a normal man would be overcome by this wind or these elements or whatever the unnamed force surging around the figure – that's where the cloth comes in – it lets him show you that – but this figure, this wonderful man, is unfazed, undaunted.

"Its title is 'The Unforgiving Minute.' That comes from a poem he read, a great poem, with this line in it: '…If you can fill the unforgiving minute with sixty seconds worth of distance run…'

"When he read this for the first time, he told me, he felt an electrical shock, a jolt, as if someone had just reached inside his head and grabbed his brain and shook it. He felt as if someone had looked into his innermost soul and seen just what he was at his deepest part. The phrase cemented itself in his mind and germinated there until the day when the vision of the sculpture exploded and he ran to get a sculpture stand and an armature and began throwing clay onto it.

"When he was finished, he cast it in bronze – umber shot with verdigris. I think Vasc Sulam bought it.

"Then there was a pair of drawings he turned out, drawings which he intended as designs for a pair of sculptures, though they ended up as paintings: 'Thought' and 'Action,' or 'Action and 'Thought,' whichever you want first; his point was that they're a pair – and he didn't want you to favor one at the expense of the other. That's why he wanted them to be sculptures on a rotating pedestal. I can take a tiny bit of credit for having contributed a kernel of the idea, but he ran away on his own tack with it.

"Take first the one, called 'Action' – really you might call it 'Action Intelligent' – the thought that is manifest in human action – intelligent, goal-directed, purposeful action. It shows a figure who is engaged in strong, even violent action. But every aspect of gesture is utterly controlled by an inner sense of unity – the unity that comes from an intelligent purpose. It is mind informing body.

"The companion is 'Thought,' but that really means 'Thought Active.' He meant it as a contrast, or even a rebuke, to Rodin's 'The Thinker.' Yes, it shows, like Rodin, a seated figure, who is obviously engaged in thinking, deeply concentrated thinking. But – far from being passive and immobile and turned in on itself – Braq's figure is charged with energy. He is tensed forward, about to explode from his seat – you almost want to jump out of the way. His hands and arms are not touching his body or his head or his chin, but rather they seem to be grasping the idea he concentrates on. It is Thought as the prelude to Action.

"An idea sparked the pair of drawings, the drawings sparked a pair of paintings, and the paintings in turn sparked another idea…Kaki…but that's a story for another day…Did 'Thought' and 'Action' ever get cast as statues?...To my knowledge, no…Will they?…I…can't say.

"There was another 'work in progress' that he started in those days. It was a follow-up of 'The Master Race,' and again it dealt with slavery.

But it shows once more how you can't get away from who you are. Oh, I know what he said he *wanted* to do. He wanted to depict the tragedy, the misery, the degradation, the stunting, stifling despair of slavery. The composition, of course, was the strongest aspect. It is filled with figures, a writhing mass of roiling bodies in a terrible throng. The slave masters seem caught in the same vortex of movement as the slaves. Some of the slaves are working with sledgehammers, but recoiling and wincing, or again working with a frenzied urgency. Other slaves are pulling frantically at their chains. Intertwined with this mass are the slave overseers with whips and clubs.

"What Braq wanted to achieve was the fact of slavery as a catastrophe not just for the slaves, but also for the enslavers. To show *the masters* as also enslaved to a great evil of their own making. To show them as tainted and degraded, and as unforgiven.

"What he ended up showing was, first, his growth as an artist from the earlier 'Master Race' to this painting. His stunning command of anatomy, of contraposto, of rhythm and movement. Second, he showed the nobility of his own soul. He couldn't help himself. He *could not* paint things that were gross, or crude, or obscene, even if he thought that he wanted to do such a thing. He forgot, when he planned this painting of 'Enslavement,' and he forgot when he was explaining his intention to me, that it had been his lifelong practice to throw out, or tear up, drawings, sketches, renderings if they were lacking in one critical feature – the ennoblement of the individual. If they had *that* quality, he kept them, even if they were deficient in some other aspect of drawing.

"I saw it happen time and again, even when he was so unaware of it himself. If he tried to draw a villain, as an illustration for a story he had read, the villain still came out as having some strong redeeming character. If he was assigned to copy a grotesque by Leonardo, the copy was not faithful – Oh, it was still a grotesque in *some* way or other – but it had a beautiful soul within.

"And he could not stand to look at art works that portrayed evil souls and ugly bodies – well, that eliminated ninety-eight percent of the moderns, didn't it?

"When you saw a figure drawn by Braq you wanted to stand up, you wanted to sing, you had the reaction many people have to sculpture – you wanted to go into the painting and *touch* the figure, it was so full of life. You were glad that *you* were of the same species as that figure. Even in his paintings…the eccentric skin tones notwithstanding. His paintings said that it was a blessing to be a man and to live inside a human body.

"You wanted to stay standing in front of the canvas forever, to let the vision be your world endlessly. When you left you felt you had had a spiritual shower. You wondered why so few artists wanted to give you this feeling, and why so many wanted to produce in you the opposite feeling – those 'realists.'

"When you look through the 'Braq Binder,' you'll find many drawings and paintings of nudes, a theme as it were. From the drawing of his imaginary Kaki, 'The Captive Freed,' through the hundreds of life drawings, and other imaginative works, to the…later…Laisa drawings and paintings…you don't know about Laisa?…well, I'll have to open that whole chapter for you…in time….

"In spite of the so-called 'sexual revolution' of the latter part of the twentieth century in America, people here are still bothered by nudity, even still prudish. They call a man who paints nude women, or who collects such paintings, a lecher. And, in case you hadn't noticed, 'lasciviousness,' yes, even 'lechery,' *are* found in adolescent boys. If you would avoid prodigious, assertive, selfish sexual desire, go live among inert elements – but not among living things.

"But the man who goes to the other extreme and *avoids* painting 'these Venuses wherein we see the fancy outwork nature,' may find himself accused of being a barren, blank misogynist, or queer. And this too may be as unfair a charge as the other; it may simply be that his interests, as a painter, run to other things. No objective law stipulates what subjects one *must* or must *not* paint.

"And Braq drew and painted lots of naked men too. Beautiful, strong men. So the great wise-alls of our age smirk and say, 'These are homoerotic,' but if he had drawn and painted them not nearly so gleaming, if he had endowed them with less, if he had given them not just feet but whole bodies of clay, or again, if he avoided these ignudi – robust or otherwise – altogether, these same pundits would say 'he must be a repressed homophobic.'

"Let them bleat.

"I will tell you that a person who chooses to paint the figure – and it's really irrelevant whether clothed or not – tells you something even deeper than his or her sexual desires or proclivities. He tells you about his *human* evaluations. One such painter says that it is wonderful to be man – another says it's terrible – still others (ones who lost their last spark of life) say it's meaningless, that man is a creature 'full of sound and fury signifying nothing.'

"But there was no question for or about Braq.

"You know that *every* portrait is in some way a *self*-portrait. Sages also observe that if you're deeply in love, something of your love appears in all of your portraits too. With Braq, what appeared in all of his male figures was either Zaqqaq, or Nollo (well, Big Brátano), or some blend of the two.

"It was not that they were literal renderings of his father, or brother. And after that first watercolor of long ago with its complex aftermath, he never put Nollo's face as such into a painting again, not even in 'The Master Race.' But no matter how Braq varied the pose, the stature, the action, or the setting, you saw in the figure he created a man *that a boy could look up to*, a man of indomitable self-assurance and strength. You saw a man who could; a man who would; a man who did.

"Braq did not know that the age of heroes had been declared officially over. He was too young when in Chugrana to understand such a thing, had there been anyone so corrupt as to say that to him. It would not have mattered – he reinvented his own world of heroes. In *this* respect he was not precocious. Every boy reinvents such a concept of heroism, looking at his father, or an older brother. It is pitiable that some of them allow the vision to fade.

"Later, when Braq did lift a rock one day and this slug of an idea, the idea of a world without heroes, oozed out and glared malevolently at him and at the sunlight, it was, thank God, too late. The mold of Braq's hero worship had already been broken. He was already a philanthropist – a lover of man. And *I* loved *him*. As my glowing son. As my glowing sun."

Bevol took a deep breath, put down his cup of frishy, and gazed away reflectively.

"A painter strips himself naked – strips his soul – when he paints, but it doesn't matter whether he's painting naked bodies or naked grapes."

One of the students said, "What about Caravaggio with his rotten fruit?"

Bevol said, "One of the first to paint the degradation of fruit – and of man. His apologists – the 'realists' – say: 'But fruit *rots*; it really does. And Caravaggio lived in an era and a culture that included sordid, bestial, brutal thuggery that would make you faint to read about. So, *of course*, he *had* to paint men that way, didn't he?' But I answer: an even greater painter, *Raphael,* lived in times with features as bad or worse, yet he *glorified* the human race – he *elevated* men and women. As an artist you have the whole world of possibilities to choose from. You may paint people the way *you want.* You choose from your own file of images, that *you* have created. This is part of what it means to be an individual. ”

Bevol had said the same thing to many of his classes. At one of those classes, one day, Braq and Nollo were both present. “Visualize your favorite art works,” Bevol had said. As the students volunteered their favorites, Nollo told no one what he was thinking, which was too bad as it illustrated Bevol's point perfectly. He had seen a print by one of the world's greatest artists, a Biblical subject in which work the artist included a dog defecating. It was precisely this revolting corner of that Rembrandt etching that Nollo returned to with interest and affection. He came out of his cloddish reverie to hear Bevol saying, “ – rotten fruit.”

“What,” thought Nollo, “is he talking about now?”

“You may say to me” (and here Nollo resented the fact that Bevol's glance just happened to light on him as he said this) “that decay is part of life, that we all have to face death. I reply, ‘You must accept the *fact* of mortality, but you don't have to *paint* that. You can choose to paint fruit which is just off the vine, glowing with new luminescent health. This is your choice. You may paint whatever your heart desires.’ ”

Nollo suddenly felt a surge of anger at Bevol. At all of these people. He felt they were trying to pin him down, to pigeonhole him, to make things be *only one way.* His glare shot right back at Bevol so pointedly that Bevol asked Nollo if he had some objection to what had been said. Nollo tried to answer in the tone of a classroom discussion but what he really felt was that he wanted to just smash…something.

“You say, ‘Paint whatever your heart desires,’ but your tone of voice says that we will all be condemned in your eyes *if* we don't choose to paint something *you* favor.”

Bevol thought for a minute – no matter the provocation, Bevol as always was respectful – and then answered. “In essence, Nollo, you *can* only show us three visions: healthy fruit, rotten fruit, or fruit in the back of the fruit picker's basket, identical to any other batch of fruit, uninteresting, undifferentiated, fruit that no one would look at twice – the scumbled background of a bunch of grapes behind the ones your paintbrush picks out as individual grapes to feature as worthy of attention. For the most part, in today's culture, whether in painting, or movies, or television, or sculpture, or literature, we get scumbled grapes and rotten pears. Today's artists show us no glowing fruit. Only here at the Atelier, and a few other lonely outposts.

"And yes, I will condemn, not the artistry which reveals the soul, but the soul revealed – if that soul deserves to be condemned. Or are you trying to do away with morality altogether? If a monster chooses to show himself through art, are we all supposed to ignore the fact that we are seeing a monster's soul? If a tawdry little amoralist writes a sonnet, do we blink at what he reveals about his soul just because he made cynicism rhyme?"

Nollo said nothing more that day, though he did not storm out either.

"Yes," said Bevol now to his class as he thought about that day years before, "Nollo was definitely of the sewer school...except in one way." He picked up his frishy once more. He looked at the students as if inspecting them. "Its...the ticklish issue...of the way people dress."

There was a nervous shifting in the chairs. One or two persons looked down at their clothes. Bevol went on. "It was the one thing Braq found so disagreeable here in America. You see, Chugrans were somewhat European in their dress. Their clothes gave a sense of style to the wearer, to their bodies, emphasizing the good features, stylizing them, flattering their anatomy; Chugrans endowed themselves with grace. Features *not* so attractive they disguised or de-emphasized. Chugran clothes were colorful, elegant, and uplifting. What Braq saw *here* were clothes that made people look lumpy, ungainly, and uninteresting. Some of this style was either deliberate – the fashionable 'grunge' look we've endured for several decades, which flaunts trashiness; some of it came from indifference. This was the one reason why Braq liked to go back and mingle among the Chugrans over in the community. He enjoyed seeing the ladies in their dresses swirling around their legs, their subtle makeup, and the men in loose slacks and shirts. No slobs.

"And you would think that Nollo might've gone the *opposite* way given his attraction to the sewer subjects in art, but you would've been wrong. Nollo dressed as thoughtfully and attractively as any of the Chugrans, if anything more so. For one thing, it was a Chugran tradition. And whereas I said that grunginess was the one thing Braq did not like about America, for Nollo it was merely one on a long list. He disliked just about everything here. Clothes were just one more way for him to show how he was not an American.

"He hated our familiarity. For example, the first name basis on which most Americans operate is very old. I think it comes from our dislike of aristocratic ranks and titles. If I'm right, that in turn comes from the doctrine that all men are created equal. But, of course, it also has a flavor of casualness about it, it's informal. So you might think that casualness in wearing grungy clothing and casualness in using first names go together. But Americans were familiar in their use of first names long ago, before grunge ever reared its ugly head.

"Anyway, Nollo hated this familiarity, and heaven help anyone who dared to call him "Noll," or any other such nickname. He would practically spit at them. And he was just contemptuous of 'Braq the Chalk,' even though the students used that as an affectionate, an endearing, even an admiring moniker. Nollo took enormous offense whenever he heard someone use that with Braq.

"The two brothers came at these issues from opposite poles. Braq respected himself – why not wear attractive clothes? And, he respected other people, so he assumed that others did likewise. Nicknames were affectionate and benevolent, as a rule. If they were demeaning, he would never have used them. That's why he cared less and less for 'Little Bratabraq.' It had mainly been Nollo's personal nickname for Braq anyway – no one else used it...maybe just Ku. And Braq was no longer smaller in height than Nollo. Besides, in some intangible way, things had changed. He no longer felt that his 'Big Brátano' – always more than a nickname, rather a title of reverence and enormous affection – was some superior being to whom he, Braq, was truly 'Little Bratabraq.' He was no longer little Bratabraq to Nollo's Big Brátano. The gear had slipped another notch.

"For Nollo, the issue was not one of respect – as Braq would have meant it. Instead, nicknames used by other people were impudent familiarities, to which they were not entitled. No…names were important tribal markers; they were not to be tampered with lightly. The same with the clothes – to Nollo it was not a matter of showing respect for yourself – but respect for tribal and ethnic customs, to which one owed mystical devotion.

"So Nollo tended, if anything, to *greater* formality, to rituals. I think he would've been happy to have everyone go back to the days of bowing – to him."

In this, Bevol Stagri was right – and wrong.

CHAPTER 53

More Progress

One day Nollo noticed an aged Chugran at the Schaal shuffling along a walkway, sweeping, and occasionally bending over to pick up a scrap of paper. Nollo suddenly realized that he had seen this man frequently over the years at the Schaal but had paid as much attention to him as to the negligible noise made by the withered branch of a scraggly shrub against one of the school buildings; for Nollo he was just an object that was part of a background. What finally struck Nollo was the habit this man had of touching his head, as if to tip a hat to Nollo. He wore no hat though.

The first time Nollo actually noticed this act of deference (which was far from being the first time it occurred) he presumed it was some unexplainable recognition by the ancient of Nollo's worth and stature. He felt, on the first occasion, that it was appropriate that people should do such a thing. But, over time, as the old man did this repeatedly, the fact occurred to him that no one but this wizened old man did so. Then Nollo noticed that he did it to other people too.

Finally, on this particular day, it irritated him. It suddenly struck him as obsequious, even degrading to both of them.

Nollo stopped alongside of him, and said, with a slight note of irritation, "Why are you doing that?"

The old man kept his gaze lowered, not making eye contact. "Doing what?"

Nollo practically shouted, "*This*," and gave an irritable imitation of the old man's gesture.

"Only to show my respect, sir," said the old man. He said this with an apology in his voice, and even some fear at Nollo's tone. As he spoke he kept dipping his head in a reflexive and abashed way. It made Nollo angrier.

"Well, stop it," he shouted. "I'm not your 'sir!' "

"Yessir" said the old man, helplessly, and again touching his forehead with his knuckle.

This was getting nowhere, so Nollo forced himself to calm down for a moment. He said, "What's your name?"

"Henry Crow, sir." He said "Henry Crow," but it sounded like "Henry K'row," and something about his pronunciation caused Nollo to make the connection. He asked, in disbelief, "Henry Kuro?"

By now, the old man had worked his bowing dance around Nollo, and was backing away from him, as if anxious to get on with his work. Also, he was intimidated by Nollo's manner.

Nollo was dumbfounded. "Kuro? Ku? Ku? Related to Pranti Ku?"

The old man stopped, beamed with a look of extraordinary pride, and for the first time his nod had nothing to do with deference. Instead, it signaled an affirmation of a fact of reality. "Yessir, that's my son."

But his head kept on nodding, and Nollo no longer knew whether or not it was back to kowtowing to him or still expressing a father's pride.

Nollo whirled and stalked away, irate. He suddenly recognized something about this behavior of the old man. Though it was more extreme in this decrepit man's behavior, it was very similar to mannerisms Nollo had seen in…whom? Oh, of course! – his uncle Rodit. It suggested a state of mind that was perpetually, humbly, deferential to the whole world. As if one's very survival required this deference. Slaves used to carry this bowing, humbling habit with them through their whole lives, even after they were freed. Sometimes it was even transmitted for generations. Nollo thought it was detestable. It did not occur to him to ask – as his father had certainly done – what ideas such a habit implied, and what ideas would constitute the antidote. For Nollo, nothing more was called for than – to get angry.

Not long afterwards, around noontime on a Sunday, Nollo convened at the grotto below the Schaal plantchi field a meeting of the Confraternity of the Familisteries.

This extraordinary thing was a child sired by both Nollo and Ku, and yet Nollo arranged to exclude Ku in a certain way from the actual birth. Nollo felt that the awe with which the pals looked up to him was divided: part going to him, part to Ku. Oh, he was the undisputed leader all right, but there was an equality in the pals' esteem that niggled at him. He felt that he needed to cut Ku out. And yet, all the same, he wanted Ku to be *part* of what he was doing. He was not ready to…go on his own. He wanted someone he respected and who knew his worth to give him…approval. So he told Ku that he had called a special meeting. He said to Ku, "Yes, it's to be a secret meeting – I don't want outsiders there, it's to cement us together in a new way, so it's just the pals and me."

He saw that Ku took this in. But before Ku could be offended at "outsiders," or draw any conclusions, Nollo went on. "It's to be at the grotto." He gestured in the direction of the path down the hill. "I hope it's secure enough." He got a slightly doubtful look on his face. "It's a funny thing about that grotto. There's a small seam in the rock, that's open right down into the back of the cave. If someone were to come along after we're all inside," he glanced at Ku, "say, just after noon, and exactly at the back of the ledge, get down on his hands and knees and put his ear to the seam, he would be able to hear every word from inside. It's some funny trick of resonance that magnifies the sounds right up to the crack at the top."

He looked down at the ground. "Of course, no one knows that but you and I."

He wished Ku were more subtle. Nollo had tried to be as indirect as possible, but when he looked up he found Ku grinning at him. At least the buffoon didn't wink. Instead, he said, "Oh, I think your grotto will be secure."

By noon on the appointed day, Nollo and his pals were all there, inside the grotto. At a certain moment, Nollo held his palm up to them to signify that they should stay there. "Let me check," he said conspiratorially. He left the grotto and scrambled up to the margin of the rocky outcrop. When he popped his head up, he saw a recognizable, blimplike shape darting behind a nearby bush. Nollo smiled to himself. He went back down to the grotto.

He called the Confraternity of the Familisteries to order.

This is what he was calling it at this particular time. It truly was.

He had assimilated quite a lot of jargon, much of it very pompous stuff, from Slovomir's book. Nollo and Ku kept wringing noxious intellectual spores from this anthology of musty ideas. So at this exact moment in the onrush of history, they had taken to calling the teams "Familisteries." Except for Nollo's own team, which was really no longer a team at all. It was just "Nollo's group," which he originally wanted to be called "Nollo's Familistery," but now had promoted to still another level. The lucky members of this group didn't even participate in the plantchi contests anymore. They acted as an order of higher beings; they set the rules; they assigned the membership in each of the Familisteries. And they now called themselves "the Confraternity," the distillation and embodiment of the other Familisteries. This is the kind of language they used. And the others accepted it.

They accepted it, in part – the smaller part – as a child's game. The larger reason was that Ku had convinced them – and perhaps "convinced" should be questioned – that one should not rely on the distortions of one's own mind, which are self-interested, but should defer humbly to those who spoke from an impenetrable wellspring of racial knowledge, of intuition, of insight into the truths for the Race – those rare individuals – one of whom was pre-eminently Nollo Churai. The unstated implication that Ku *also* was such a racial spokesman never rose to the level of inspection – not once! Authorities are just that, and just as it becomes a habit for slaves and ex-slaves to keep on bowing their heads, even after they are freed, so it becomes a habit, if one allows it, to bow one's mind to someone else's mind, and to keep on bowing.

The children who might have questioned such an implication had long since dropped out of these teams-clans-tribes-Familisteries, or even left the Schaal for good.

And though, at the earliest stage of this great progress at the Schaal, both Ku and Nollo had seen, instinctively, the value of vagueness, so now they moved toward more precision – of a kind. It was Nollo who took the lead, and, as usual, Ku both marveled at his insight and gave his immediate consent to this next step.

The "teams" Nollo had distilled from his own whim – plus one grain of genealogical compounding. The names for the teams he had assigned by drawing on old known Chugran tribal or family names, with Ku's learned assistance. But running through all of this mumbo jumbo were two rather contradictory ideas. On the one hand, Nollo seemed to say that there was something objective: the Chugran families, after all, *had* existed; they were real; their names were real. But, at the same time, he was the arbiter, the judge, the decider, the authority, the alchemist who alone could discern the true membership in each group, and even in the Race (the group which really mattered) itself.

And, as it happened, the same children who would have questioned the imposition of an intellectual Authority, the ones who had left the Schaal, were just by the sheerest chance the same ones who would have questioned the clash of contradictory ideas, such as objectivity and subjectivity.

So the remainder, the kids who *fit in*, did not give it even a fleeting thought. They were ready now to have their subjectively created racial membership objectified. Nollo said they needed new names. He told his elite group this startling fact, and let them know that they were learning it before any of the others at the Schaal. And he let them know how special they were to be privy to the latest development, how special they were to his eye – his racially sensitive eye. He had chosen the members of the Confraternity because of the special qualities he had discerned in them, he said, but it was now necessary to fix their identity with a name, and with a formal recognition by their fellow members, without which they could not attain to full racial participation.

And he himself was to be the first of these newly baptized Chugrans. Being a Chugran born, and of "aristocratic heritage," and being deeply steeped in the source waters of Chugrana, etcetera, etcetera, he – with the assistance of wise Prester Pranti Ku (who owned, as Nollo now knew, an undistinguished heritage – but no matter, Nollo kept it to himself) – he, Nollo, had thought deeply about the many manifestations of his name, and even of how his name should express his essential nature. His names: Nollopa, Noloran, Nollifer, Nolli, Nolpa (he was especially tempted, though he didn't tell them this, just by "No," but he finally decided such a name might be seen as *too negative*). And also Churai, Chu, Cheu, Churrana, Chiuglana, Chiughalana.

He rolled this miasma of phrases and names out of his mouth before them like incantations chanted over a mystic brew. They were fascinated and waited to see what the whirling cauldron would produce. It produced "Nollifer Chiughalana." This was Nollo's official "Race Name." This name was not, he explained, to be sullied by public use. Especially not to be used before "those other races…those lesser peoples." No, this was to be a name recognized only by the elect, *his* elect. As *he* would recognize *their* essential names. Which names he one by one doled out to them. And each one waited in a kind of blessed, enraptured expectation, as for a kind of climax, when they would find out who they really were. Which they had not known till now.

Fempy Lobbel came up to Nollo. He bowed his head, even stooped over a bit (as Nollo had instructed him beforehand when he had given him a "special" inkling as to the new rituals.) Nollo cupped the back of Fempy's head with three little prehensile pats, each one seeming to push Fempy's head slightly lower. When he released him Fempy walked away Fehempu Laul. Jonatan Gee submitted himself to this obsequy and was rewarded with "Yoh-Natan Gee-i." Little Mary Jolofer was now not so little. Having reached adolescence she was proving physically precocious, and when Nollo placed his hand on the back of *her* head for the three tugs, there was something especially possessive, or even predatory, in his gesture. Mary, now Marja, Jolofer felt a warm flush slither downward from her spine at Nollo's touch. She felt that she would have done anything he wanted.

On he went through the rest of his group. They all felt that there was now a new bond tying each to the others, and especially to Nollo...er...to Nollifer Chiughalana. (Only Nollo himself felt that this bond was not yet strong enough, that it needed something else, some *act* before it would become a bond that could be depended on.) By the end, without their consciously reflecting on it, Nollo seemed to them to be on an even higher plane than before because of his self-endowed power of christening – the power to *give* them their own racial identity.

Now, Nollo brought up a new matter. They had thought he had given them the whole story, the whole business – what else could there be? Except...just...Chompy. He was the only one left. They could all see that. It was, of course, obvious that this little insignificant boy should be left for last. He too felt that this was only just. He expected no better. Since the embassy protest, he had sunk ever lower in Nollo's esteem, judging by Nollo's behavior. But Nollo was going on now to something else. Had he overlooked Chompy? Forgotten him? The boy, cautiously, and trying to be unobtrusive, at the same time stood so as to be right in Nollo's line of sight, to jog his attention.

But Nollo seemed to look right through him, almost rudely it seemed to Chompy, and eventually to others too. But this, too, Chompy was prepared to swallow. He could not question Nollo's wisdom.

The persons assembled here now, Nollo was going on to explain, were becoming more and more aware of who they were – and such ceremonies as today's helped them on that road. But equally, they were becoming more and more aware of who was *not* of their blood, of their race. Not just the obvious ones – the Dryrugers and all other whites whose degraded physical features made them stand out as metaphysical grotesques, those whose stink revealed them for what they were – but also those who posed within the race as true Chugrans, but whose "inner spirit" was "altogether lacking" in that which makes a Chugran what he or she is. "Because you are not *born* a Chugran – you must *become* one. You must be *worthy* to be a Chugran, to be approved and accepted and recognized by your fellows – and by their representatives!"

How you could be the very essence of a Chugran "from your blood," and at the same time "have to become one" was another of those contradictions that someone outside of the little group present that day might have questioned. No one in the grotto did.

Nollo went on, and they felt that he was lashing them on to some higher purpose. They were not sure what it was. He still ignored Chompy, though he made eye contact with every other person. "And when the Race discovers such an interloper, a false Chugran, one who stands in the way of the progress of the Race, it will expel it, as an organism expels some foreign body. From deep in our history – so Prester Pranti Ku has learned – the Chugran Race has always *tried* to keep itself pure. At least in the golden era of the past it *used* to. It expelled these maggots; it pronounced the 'nifasta': the curse of expulsion."

Chugrans had, needless to say, never done any such thing. Ku and Nollo had invented it. Rather, Nollo invented the idea of expulsion – he wanted it, it seemed obviously crucial to him in some way – and Ku supplied the name from his usual fantastic expropriation of archaic English, Chugran, and other linguistic sources.

Nollo went on; he felt that his blood was up. "The Race will *nifar* such a spurious person – really not a person at all, he doesn't even deserve such an honorable description as 'person'. He's just a thing. A *nifanto*. And such a nifanto, once the nifasta is pronounced, will be *outside* the Race, and will suffer the fate of anything that tries to live apart from its own kind.

"And when the Race pronounces the nifasta" – they were beginning to recognize this new phrase just by its tone as he said it: to "pronounce the nifasta" – "it will use this person's Chugran name for the last time, to strip his name away from him, to strip his identity away from him. Forever."

Little Chompy was biting his lips now. His eyes were burning and the muscles around his eyelids were tight with fear and anxiety. Was this all about *him*? What had he done? He had always been so obedient, so enthusiastic, so submissive to Nollo. Why hadn't he received his own rebaptism? What was this horrifying talk about 'nifasta,' and 'nifar' and 'nifanto'? Did it have something to do with him? Why wouldn't his idol, Nollo, look at him? He was too frightened to raise his hand and ask, too frightened of what the answer might be.

Chompy had no new "essential Chugran" name. But he had not been "nifar-ed" either. Where did this leave him? He had no idea. His metaphysical status was utterly in doubt. *He did not know what he was.*

Nollo left the little boy this way. He said the word, "Forever," looking right over little Chompy's head. He turned his back to him; he walked out of the grotto. One by one, the other children melted away too. No one spoke to Chompy.

CHAPTER 54
Profiles

Some time later that afternoon, Nollo emerged again from the grotto. He brushed some musty leaves off of his pants. Even as he pulled the pants back on, he knew that he was still not satisfied. The intense flicker of pleasure was gone as quickly as it had come, and there had been nothing else to do but look down with negligent contempt at "Marja" Jolofer. He left her to put her clothes back on and went outside. She had served her purpose.

He had impregnated her – with a High Purpose.

He need not have done so. A virile and attractive seventeen year old boy and a promiscuous, budding thirteen year old girl servile to him need no grandiose philosophical motivation to do what they did. It might have sufficed merely to be unthinking, and to hold life – one's own life – as of little value and one's actions, therefore, as of little consequence. It is probable that most people with such a low sense of self are satisfied to justify it with some fig leaf of higher exculpatory rationale and then to let it go at that.

On the other hand, it is certain that Nollo could never accept such an unambitious, such a *common* appraisal of anything he did. Mary, or "Marja," Jolofer was, as he told her, serving the Race in myriad ways. The two of them were reviving the old, the original, and therefore, the sanctified tradition of Chugrans in which sexual selection of young girls was quite normal, was in fact "just what they all did," Nollo said.

This was not something completely fabricated. It had been a practice of old, bound up with selection and approval by both sets of parents and the tribes as part of the institution of marriage. Nonetheless Nollo evaded the fact that in those ancient times it possessed what then seemed the reasonable justification that women had a short life span, and needed to make maximum use of their fertile years. It was of no account to Nollo either, one way or another, that these women might have lived much longer had they foregone child-bearing. The end of producing children was the farthest thing from Nollo's mind, no matter what he said.

"To keep the Race strong and alive, to increase, and multiply the Chugran blood – that's why they did it! And even if there are no children, just having sex is the right of the strong Chugran men and women – to satisfy their biological needs and impulses. The stronger and nobler the racial type the more do they express it in sex. To refuse it is to deny the Race."

Another line he spun Marja was this: "The great men of the Race have to make their way above the common herd, even if they have to trample over the herd. Such men choose what they want and select the people who can be a help to them. That includes choosing their women."

These ideas were old and musty – certainly not original with Nollo. Still they were of service. No, Nollo did not have to engage in all of this prattle. He and Mary could have just done what they did, and that would have been that. But the prattle helped Mary accept the fact that he was degrading and contemptuous with her. It was her fig leaf. And it helped Nollo to *be* degrading and contemptuous. It helped him to be himself. Thus, the most cynical person in the world, contemptuous of such a thing as morality, still clings to some scrap of pathetic reasoning to cleanse himself of some tawdry little act. Evidently, he cannot escape the need to make himself feel that, in spite of it all, he is *all right.*

But now, it was over, and he was still unsatisfied. What did he want? He stared through the bleak branches down toward the Severn River. He began to walk quickly down the path. The walk became a run as he made his way along the "shortcut" back to the house.

He ran not from joy – which he did not feel – or in pursuit of a steadfast purpose – which he did not possess. Neither was he running away from what had happened in the grotto. He felt no shame, or guilt. Such emotions would have required an evaluation of wrongdoing. In the deepest mindshafts of Nollo's soul, he would have discovered no such evaluations.

Had he ventured into such shafts.

Which he did not.

Ever.

An evaluation of oneself requires at least this very minimal recognition of a truth: there *are* moral standards which one can be measured by.

To measure, to recognize, to evaluate, one must – *stand still.*

Nollo ran, not to accomplish a thing so clean as a purpose. He ran so as not to see what he was running at.

Arriving home, he asked his aunt if he could take the car. It was Sunday, Jule's day off. It was not unusual for Nollo to take the car on such days. Receiving the expected permission, he took the keys off their latch by the kitchen door, and a minute later was pelting down Old Rolling Road in the direction of Annapolis.

He pushed the car above eighty miles an hour on a straight stretch of road and barely slowed enough to avoid careening over on the next curve. The car tilted onto two wheels. Nollo snickered, and then slammed his foot down again on the accelerator as he came out of the curve. But then he had to slow down. He knew the lairs where the traffic cops lay. He drove easily past one such and confirmed smugly that there was a police car tucked neatly behind a dense edifice of azaleas, just before the road joined the main highway. Nollo gave a malicious little sniff looking over his shoulder, his eyelids half closed in contempt. Then he eased onto the highway, and smoothly accelerated into the traffic. He changed lanes abruptly several times. He took the car up to some frightening speeds, but only for a short space. It was nothing to do with respect for the car as his aunt's property, or with respect for the safety of the other drivers, but only because he knew that if he wrecked this car, he would be without a source of fun and liberty. Now, if only he had his own car....

A middle-aged man driving a black sedan pulled into a large shopping mall. He parked quickly, and ran into the mall. He seemed to have an urgent errand. Nearby, a young man sat behind the wheel of his car, waiting. He knew what he was looking for. It had worked before. He had been waiting with some impatience. Finally he was rewarded. He saw the man in the black car pull into the parking space and stop with a jerk. He saw him slam the car door shut and race into the mall. The noteworthy fact was what had not happened. He did *not* see the man drop any keys into his pocket. It was only a matter of fifteen seconds for the young man to walk quickly over to the car and look through the window to confirm that the keys were still there. Another five seconds to get in and put his hands on the keys. In another thirty seconds he was pulling out of the lot onto the highway. All done in under one minute. He bobbed his head with a contemptuous chuckle of satisfaction and vindication.

Now, he let *this* car loose. Several miles later, in the vanguard of a wake of very frightened drivers, he exited the highway again, still traveling at a dangerous speed. He had chosen a back road which he knew the police usually absented. There was always a chance of being detected, but that just gave it more spice. He shrieked around curves, several times putting the car into a sickening slide.

Neither the living nor the inanimate was safe. Hard by the edge of the country road was ensconced a stone house of aged vintage. Its owner had recently installed, right by the corner of the house, a white marble statue of a heron, from the beak of which the man had suspended his mailbox. It was cute, quaint, or kitsch according to the critic of the moment. The driver of the stolen car supplanted all of those verdicts with his own. He aimed the car straight at the heron. A thousand pieces of marble thrashed the air and the side of the house. The car squealed along the margin and back onto the road.

As to the living – it is probably true that it had not much longer to live anyway. The dog was old – so old that it could not move fast as it crossed the road – even if it had seen the car coming, which it didn't. Its greyed, watery eyes were straining to focus on the patch of road in front of it, and its flopped ears had long since belied their natural function. Its pale pink tongue sagged out of the corner of its mouth.

The driver saw the dog.

He made the car go faster.

Eventually, he ditched the car. He found an abandoned work area. State road crews at one time had used it to store their vehicles and supplies. It was now just a large concrete pad covered with gravel, and a dilapidated shed. The young man spent his last rage tearing back and forth across the gravel, putting the car into vicious skids. Finally, and intentionally, he sheared it into the shed. It jolted him, but not seriously. As to the car, its black sheen was now a crumple of dents, scratches, and blotches of muddy film.

The young man took off his shirt and used it to wipe any possible fingerprints from the steering wheel, gearshift, and door handles. Then he left the car as it was and walked away.

At last he was satisfied.

An hour and a half later, a security guard noticed a dark-skinned youth strolling through the mall. He watched him stop at several stores. He purchased nothing. He gave no evidence of shoplifting either, but the guard watched him nonetheless. After a bit, the youth walked outside. As he approached his car, he suddenly saw two police cars veer around a corner and speed right up to him. A policeman stepped out of each car and came at him from either side. Jaw clenched sullenly, the youth froze. They ordered him to lean against the car while they frisked him.

Sitting calmly in one's living room reading a newspaper account of this incident, one – being a normal, sensible citizen – might produce two hypotheses: that this seventeen year old boy with the surly pout was angry at being caught out at some crime, or, on the other hand, that he was angry at being unjustly arrested – that he was either resentfully outraged at having his wicked deed foiled, or perhaps justifiably outraged at being singled out because of his race.

Neither of these alternatives was true. The youth was surly because that was how he thought of the police generally. He would have behaved like that in any case. He did not feel that they were treating him unfairly as a human being, he felt that they were treating him unfairly *as the special person he was*, a person to whom no principles of morality applied. It was not an injustice to him that one race should be hostile to another: it was the world as he *wanted* it. The sensible citizen would have been surprised to find, could he have looked inside the youth's mind at that moment, not anger at all – none. Only calculation.

Which did not stop the youth from looking very angry nonetheless.

Instead of answering the policemen's questions, the youth struck an attitude. He knew this would only irritate them – and it suited him to do so. He even exaggerated his evasiveness. The police took him in "for further questioning." Getting into the police car, he asked the policeman what he was supposed to have done. The arresting officer, Sergeant Tommy Booge, said to his caged prisoner in the back seat, "Sticky fingers for the cars – eh, boy?"

The youth stared back at him in the rearview mirror. He said, "I don't know what you're talking about." The youth had made his denial with an air of utmost sincerity and conviction. He seemed to have turned a switch within himself and changed his entire demeanor from bellicose insolence to chaste innocence. It made Sergeant Booge think twice.

When they arrived at the station, Booge walked his prisoner to the holding pen. Then he went to fill out some papers.

Booge was in his mid-thirties. Other than the fact that he kept himself physically fit and that his eyes were set rather close together, he had no particularly distinctive features, or attributes. He asked the desk sergeant if "the new Chief" was in. When he learned that he was not, he breathed a little sigh of relief. If he had had to say why, he would have shrugged and said, "He'd make things harder, that's all."

When he went back to the holding pen, his prisoner demanded to make a phone call. After that Booge took him over to a desk to be fingerprinted, then into an interrogation room. His technique of questioning was maladroit at best. The youth either gave no answer or denied knowledge of any auto theft. He denied that he had "ever touched any car," especially "some white man's car." Booge had so far said nothing about any race of any car owner, but it seemed that the youth was just acting as a provocateur.

The door opened and another policeman came in. It was Chief Cutby. He shut the door behind him. Booge became rather self-conscious. "Hi, Chief. I'm just interrogating this guy about the car–"

Cutby interrupted him. "I know – I looked at your report. Go ahead."

But Booge was flustered. He had already decided that he was getting nowhere. Aimlessly, he asked some of the same questions again. After a few minutes, Cutby jerked his head over his shoulder as he said to Booge, "Let's talk."

They went to Cutby's office. Bill Cutby was the new Chief of Police for Anne Arundel County. He was forty, with a hard, lean body, gray eyes, and a creased face that would have suited a Ranger doggedly hunting down bushwhackers in the Texas Hill country. Except that his birthplace was Connecticut, and he had never been west of Pittsburgh. He had, however, been in the army for several terms of enlistment. As this had been during the period of fretful peace after Vietnam, he saw little action. Mustering out, he considered his choice of two fields: science or police work. He loved the process of trudging from tangled mystery to lucid order in the laboratory until the moment when one could say, "*This* is what *it is*." But he loved even more the process of sifting facts to determine innocence or guilt, leading up to the moment when one could say, "He did not do it!" or "He did it!" and then clap hands over the guilty party's shoulders. He chose police work.

Not that he saw any difference in method between these two choices. They both required well crafted generalizations from the data – induction – and rigorously logical application of principles to the specific case at hand – deduction. The two pincers of reasoning that together gripped the truth in confident grasp. Cutby had always tried to instill in his peers and subordinates – even at times in his superiors – his own unbreachable allegiance to facts and logic – which he called *justice* – in every part of his police work. He was not always successful: he felt now that he had met a great challenge in Sergeant Booge.

Cutby sat upright behind his desk, as a judge at a hearing. His tone of voice was not conversational, merely factual. "Why did you bring that kid in?"

Booge during the whole ensuing ordeal in Cutby's office was uncomfortable and resentful. It all came down to the first word Cutby had uttered – the word, "Why?" Booge was, after all, an experienced officer, and this new Chief had no business grilling him this way, questioning his judgment. Why did he have to do that?

"He was acting suspicious," he answered.

"How?" asked Cutby.

"Well, he was looking around, like he was trying to see if anyone was watching him," he answered.

Cutby noticed that Booge's glance wavered as he gave this answer; the Sergeant spoke in a manner that suggested not that he was seeing on his mind's screen something that actually happened but instead was concocting something to support his actions. His voice lacked conviction.

Cutby said, "He was walking from the mall to the car?"

Booge nodded.

"Straight toward it?"

Again Booge nodded.

"From the east side of the mall?"

"Yes."

"And the car was stolen from the west side?"

Booge shrugged. "That makes no difference."

"This stolen car – what was it?"

"A red Gracelle."

"And you've found it?"

"Yes, up the road, abandoned."

"Damaged?"

"No."

"Prints?"

"Yes, they're processing them now to compare with this boy's."

"When he was looking around, how do you know it was 'to see if anyone was watching him?' Was he skulking? Dodging?…meandering?

"Not exactly," said Booge defensively.

"You just said he walked straight toward his car, so I would say 'Not at all,' wouldn't you?"

Booge shrugged again. "I know a suspicious person when I see one. So did the security guard. He alerted us to this kid."

"Why was the security guard suspicious?"

Booge shrugged. Then he said, "The witness described him, you know."

Cutby was unimpressed by this detail. "Who is your witness?"

"A woman who was pushing her shopping cart along near the place where the car was stolen."

"How old?"

"I'm not sure. She mentioned that she was a retiree."

"And she saw the theft take place?"

"N-no, not exactly…but she saw a guy skulking around the car just before it went missing."

"Skulking?" The question hung in the air. Cutby went on. "So your witness, this retiree, also is an expert in 'suspicious persons' and 'skulking?' "

Booge did not answer.

"And how did this expert criminologist describe the perpetrator?"

"Said he was young, black, and…strange looking."

"Strange?"

"Yes…I asked her about that," said Booge with an air of efficiency. "She said he looked different from our blacks. Kind of foreign."

"*Our blacks*?" Cutby's voice rose slightly.

"Well, you know, the blacks around here. American blacks. Negroes. Afro's…whatever."

Cutby didn't let him go on. "When she said, 'black,' did you ask her to describe that? Was he light, medium, dark – brownish, bluish, grayish, what?"

Booge shook his head. "Just – black. It was getting on toward evening and the parking lot is covered, it's not lit up…so…just black."

Cutby shook his head too, in exasperation. "So, the light was lousy, and an elderly white lady says, 'black,' and 'skulking,' and you let it go at that, and arrest the first young 'black' male you find? Even though 'black' can mean anything from a tanned German to an African to an Indian to an aborigine?! It can also mean *nothing* about skin – some people call a person 'black' if they have thick lips regardless of the skin color on the assumption that they must have 'black blood' somewhere 'in there!' "

Booge did not reply. Cutby went on. "And also because of the 'one-drop rule' which means that one drop of assumed 'black blood' thirty-five generations ago makes you 'black.' Which – by the way – many blacks will embrace too: – 'You have one drop of 'black blood,' therefore, you're *one of us*, brother!' They've bought the same load of bilge – but it's not a description of objective physical facts – it's a *moral* judgment – 'you're one of them, you're one of us.' 'You're *different*!' "

He pressed the point further. "But, Officer Booge, what's it got to do with police work? What's it got to do with facts?"

His voice was steely.

"And what do 'strange,' 'foreign,' and 'different from our blacks' mean?"

"Well…don't you think he's...odd looking?" asked Booge.

Cutby looked reflective. "He looks like that movie star…um…" Cutby thought for a minute and then named the young idol who was the current throb of the teenage girls. "Is that what you mean by 'odd'?"

"No…I think this kid's not an American. His English is a little strange…something about…I don't know…I think maybe he's an African."

Cutby said, "But your witness never spoke to him, or heard him speak, did she?"

Booge grunted.

Cutby added, "I think if you ask him you'll find that he's a Chugran."

"What?"

"A Chugran."

"What's that? A country in Africa? What's a Chugern?"

"It's not African at all."

"Well…from India, then?"

"No, not from India. From Chugrana. Go get an atlas and look it up, Officer. There's a whole community of them right here in our county."

"Oh," said Booge. "Well, they're all…" His sentence dribbled off.

"Alike?" Cutby finished his sentence for him.

Booge looked at a corner of the room. Finally, he said, "How do you know this guy's a…Chugern?"

"His name." Cutby looked at the report. " 'Churai' is a well-known name in their community," said Cutby. "He may even be related to one of their heroes. So – you have 'odd' or 'foreign' and 'black' – none of which are defined. And 'young.' How old was this retiree?"

Booge said, "Maybe seventy…er…or so."

"Mmhmm," said Cutby. "So, to *her*, anyone under forty is 'young.' And you call this police work."

"But," Booge protested, "Statistics! If you're so big on science, you have to accept statistics! Statistics show they commit more crimes, proportionately!"

"*They*??"

Booge stuck to his guns. "Anyone who *most* people would call black."

"Well, then," answered Cutby, "why don't we just arrest them *all* and call all our cases closed? Or – since you want to use statistics – if we have a hundred open cases, let's just arrest any thirty-five blacks, if thirty-five percent of crimes are committed by them, if that's the number your 'statistics' call for, and be done with it. Sure would make our job easier, wouldn't it? Is that what this is all about, Sergeant – making your job – your job of *thinking* – easier? And what about justice?"

He went on. "Do you base arrests on these iron statistics? Or do you do *police* work – which means getting *evidence*!"

Booge finally rallied for one attempt at a defense. "So, are you saying we have to drop race altogether – are you some liberal who thinks we should close our eyes to facts?"

Cutby relished the chance to explain to Booge – hoping he might make a dent. Men who are committed to reason are like this – they can't help themselves. They will try to persuade the most irrational brutes – a sometimes unwise stubbornness.

Cutby said, "That's like a patient who runs from a quack who prescribes cyanide to another quack who prescribes strychnine.

"*Your* approach – cyanide – is to rely on dogmatic generalities – 'Suspect all blacks,' 'Suspect only blacks,' or maybe, 'Suspect blacks first,' or 'Whites are unlikely suspects,' or 'Suspect whites last.' It would be bad enough if you did it with shoddy generalizations about comparatively clear cut terms like 'Irish immigrants,' or 'New Yorkers,' or 'people with big noses' – and even those terms are not razor sharp, not when you're talking about guilt or innocence – when you're talking about jail time. But – 'blacks'?? Don't make me laugh.

"So you build 'blackness' into the person, and then you build 'crime' and 'guilt' into 'blackness'. It's all part of his nature. It's *intrinsic* to him. If you know his color, you know his guilt or innocence.

"Well, as I said, that certainly makes your life easy, doesn't it, Sergeant?

"So – the only other alternative you can think of, your second choice – is *strychnine:* namely, there are no principles, no rules, no facts, no guides, no probabilities, no reason, no logic. If twenty-five honest witnesses, sober, rational, of all races and types, swear that they saw the murderer in broad illuminating daylight – and his skin was the color of coffee – the modern 'fair-minded' liberal thinks we have to *ignore* that identifying fact and throw our brains overboard while we run looking for some *other* kind of evidence that will not offend – which by now will be of no use to us since we will have no brains left to evaluate this other evidence with.

"And since this type of liberal denies the reality of certain facts he doesn't like – such as that a black man may have committed this crime, or even that a disproportionate number of 'blacks' – assuming an intelligible definition – commit certain types of crimes, he builds guilt *out* of the person. He makes guilt and innocence *subjective.*

"Sergeant, you just have to face it: judgment is a difficult process; reasoning is not automatic. But you can neither guarantee the result by arbitrary rules, nor by subjective fiat – both of which are really just running away from the necessity of judging at all. It's not right to say, 'Strict racial profiling,' nor to say, 'No profiling whatsoever, however rational.' "

Cutby put his palm down firmly on the desk. "Judgment is neither intrinsic nor subjective, neither a mystic dogma nor a roulette wheel. It is *objective.* But to be discriminating without being discriminatory requires that you learn how to *think.* No, Sergeant Booge, no, we should close our eyes to nothing. Race is a perfectly good tool of identification – *if* you define it carefully. And if you ask questions. If a witness says, 'The suspect had light brown skin,' that's fine – assuming he knows how to make such a judgment. *You yourself*, Sergeant, know from your experience that there are people who couldn't do that if you held a color wheel in front of their face. If the witness says he had a skinny nose, or a broad nose, that's fine. Says he had wooly hair or straight hair – fine! But if he says, 'He was black; therefore, the same color as all blacks, therefore, the same nose, and the same lips, and the same hair – *and the same moral character* – therefore, he's a suspect,' then he has – quite truly – lost his mind, if he ever had it. He has never learned how to reason."

Cutby shook his head in disgust. "The modern intellectual," he thought, "would sacrifice his very power to reason in order not to offend. The squeamishness of today's liberal that forbids racial characterization would rather poke out its own eyes than remember that *stereotype* came from an old printing practice which produced *identical copies* of text or picture – *all* the same. Its purpose was to make every copy *automatically identical.*

"So avoiding a stereotype still allows us to *generalize*...providing we back it up with evidence. We can even go out on a limb and say, 'I have no specific evidence for this – it's a hunch, a guess, a surmise.' But we'd better be prepared to be instantly spurned by a healthy skepticism.

"*All*, *none*, and *some* – these, according to some philosophers, the terms of impotent and idle reasoning. But the syllogisms and their premises were *not* idle; these *all's*, *none's*, and *some's* could mean life or death."

To Booge, he now said, "In my book the truly inferior human beings are not members of some race, they are those who have never learned how to use their minds – how to go about thinking. It takes a lot of evidence and a long chain of reasoning to prove that '*All* A is B.' Anything less than 'All' and you've got to be *extra* careful. I won't have you using 'All so and so's are suspect' as the basis of your police work. Without a shred of evidence or reason.

"I won't have it, Sergeant! Not in *my* Department!"

There was suddenly a noise from outside, then a knock, sparing Booge more humiliation. Another policeman stuck his head in the door. He said, "There's someone here to get that kid released."

Cutby walked out to the front, with Booge following. He beheld the sight of Pranti Ku, blowing up like a great speckled toad in front of the reception desk. When Ku spied Cutby, who appeared to him a person of some rank or authority, his voice rose even more.

"A racial outrage! One of our finest students! One of our finest *young men*! Do you know who he is? Whose son he is? This is the worst kind of racial profiling! What is your evidence? We will sue you for your last penny!"

All this and more.

Cutby withstood it all impassively. He said, "Excuse me," and walked back to another area, taking Booge with him. He studied the fingerprint reports. He showed them to Booge, whose face fell. Cutby said, "Release him."

Booge brought Nollo out to the front. Cutby was waiting. He said to Nollo, "Thank you for helping us with our inquiries."

The wings of Nollo's nostrils raised in contempt. " 'Inquiries?' No results? No proof? Just 'inquiries?' "

He snickered and stalked out. Ku ushered Nollo out the door, covering his rear, so to speak, with all of his bulk, as if he were some cosmic guardian. He shot over his shoulder, "You haven't heard the end of this!"

Outside, he was still fulminating. "Just disgusting! Outrageous!"

Finally he noticed that Nollo was not disgusted at all. In fact he was laughing. They came up to Ku's little car. They got in. Ku drove away from the station. He started again. "How can they think you – *you* – would steal some idiot's car?!"

Nollo said with a snide little lilt in his voice, "Yeah, how could they *think* that?"

Ku looked over at him, but in the dark he couldn't see Nollo's face very well. Why was he behaving this way?...What did that sarcasm imply? Was his brilliant young man, his great Chugran pursuing some purpose of his own, some purpose Ku could not divine?

Ku spoke. "They obviously just assumed a person of color must have done it…?"

His inflection rose querulously and his voice trailed off. He looked over at Nollo again. Nollo was just staring at him. Was that a smirk on his face? At last, Nollo looked away. He didn't speak for the rest of the trip.

Ku decided they should…perhaps not pursue the lawsuit as he had threatened.

Back at the police station, Chief Cutby spoke once more to Booge. "Sergeant, I'm sorry the prints didn't confirm. We have to go only by evidence, not just blind hunches. And certainly not hunches that are just based on race. If it's any consolation, there was something…something about that kid…he didn't act…honest. But that's only a *feeling.* Not a piece of evidence, not a *fact* for an arrest. And it may be that he had a guilty conscience about something else altogether. Some private matter…Were there any burglaries at the mall…any other crimes?"

Booge shook his head.

"Any purse snatchings?"

"No…there was another car theft earlier, on the other side…where we picked him up in fact…a black sedan. Some guy ran into the mall. 'Just for a minute,' he said, and when he came out, his car was gone."

"Have you found it yet?"

"No."

"Well, let it go. We have more important crimes on the log. Facts – we can only go by facts."

In his mind, Cutby thought back to the interrogation room. In his judgment, it *was* a fact that this Nollo Churai had not displayed the demeanor of a person accustomed to looking at the world truthfully.

CHAPTER 55

A Falcon Takes Flight

Liz opened her journal and turned to a fresh page. She took a deep breath.

A journal.... Why do people do such things? It seems incomprehensible. Living in a tyrannical land, where rights are not recognized, privacy least of all, where thugs of the state may enter at any time and seize everything, including your notes, journals, and diaries – even in spite of all this, a person builds a written record in which day by day she strips her mind bare and lays it out in phrases which would mean her doom if the thugs burst in and read those scribed thoughts.

There must be a very powerful need to make one's thoughts objective – even in the face of such a risk, such a danger. For Liz was not the first and she will not be the last to keep such a self-incriminating journal. Even though the crime be only living and thinking.

Now, she read back through some of her entries, looking for certain passages.

I carry on the Schaal, just with Kaki. She is so young. How can I discuss everything that matters so much to me with this little girl. I can't put my burden on her. But "sending her to Schaal" here with me makes me feel that the boys are still here. And Zaq.

Thank God the girl is bright!

...

Kaki spends hours going through our library. She reads voraciously. Then she makes me explain whatever she does not understand. I try to fill in the blanks from my own knowledge of history and politics – how I wish, now, I had absorbed more! Sometimes I have to search through Zaq's books (how did he acquire them all, here in Chugrana?) to find answers. Sometimes, I can't find the answer.

She sends me on such philosophical scavenger hunts! "Why do people in America have the right to say and do what Zaq did without being imprisoned?" she asks of me. "How did they get these rights?" "Why are such rights 'unalienable?' " "Why doesn't it matter, there, what group you belong to?" "Why can't the government in America stop you from working just because you belong to the wrong race, the way they can here?" "Do people in America know how fortunate they are, how blessed??" She asks all of these questions with a tone of disbelief, but I don't think it's disbelief in America. Oh, no! America is the place Kaki was born for. To her, as to many, here, it is the Atlantis. I think her disbelief is in the irrationality of Chugrana.

I try my best to answer her. She is relentless. I think she must learn how and why the catastrophe befell her family – and ours – or perish. It is life and death to her. To me. To us.

...

Today Kaki asked another one of her questions. She had asked me about the history of slavery, so I gave her some of Zaq's speeches and editorials to read. She had read one or two of them before. But now, for some reason – perhaps because she is eleven and her knowledge has grown so much – she just began devouring everything he wrote. It's quite a body of work – so many years of speaking, writing, arguing, exhorting, persuading. All in the cause of being an individual. Trying to persuade his fellow individuals to let him exist by the power of his own judgment instead of theirs. And to persuade them to exist for themselves on their own judgment too. Not to sacrifice their minds to the tribe.

Kaki read for days. She would come out of the study, eyes bright, her face glowing. She looked into my eyes on one of those days, fiercely into my eyes. "You're married to a wonderful man!" she said.

I couldn't speak. For a moment I almost lost it all. Then – it felt like a moment that lasted years – I let my breath out. Finally, I just nodded.

Then she asked, "Do the people out there (she flung her arm out as if to take in the world) know about him? Do they know there is this wonderful man?! That he's in prison? Do they know how great a human being can be?! Don't they care? Why aren't they setting the world on fire to get him free? How can we tell them about Zaq?"

She asked me this so urgently. As if she wanted to pick up some intercontinental telephone right then and shout to the world – "He's here! This unique man! Do something!"

I am amazed, and almost slightly ashamed, that I had not pushed this particular ball further along. It's true that I had, slowly, been organizing Zaq's papers with the idea that someday they could be published.

But Kaki said, "Now!" She said, "We have to get these writings out now!"

We talked. I had never discussed this with anyone. It was such a release to be able to discuss it as a real project, to be able to do something positive and productive, now. We talked about the network for getting the manuscript out. Kaki left, in a fever, and I stayed, in a fever.

Also, – when Kaki said, "You're married to a wonderful man!" there was one other thing – She said, "I hope I'm married to one just as wonderful" It's that childish game, or whatever they thought it was. But can she really take it seriously...about the moon?

...

Kaki is relentless. She pesters me every day. She is driving me crazy. On the one hand, she wants to get the book out immediately. At times she almost seems manic to have the world get these writings. But then, when she goes over my edited copy, she questions every single mark I have made. She makes me justify every single amendment. I had to explain to her that Zaq sometimes spoke extemporaneously, sometimes he spoke having prepared three or four drafts, but then spoke without notes, that he sometimes dashed his editorials off quickly. To put all of this down in a book for the ages requires painstaking exactitude.

But her questions are always pertinent and searching. They are more and more sophisticated. I have been fearful for Kaki. Afraid that she might say something in the heat of the moment to the wrong person. Kaki is so passionate. She has the spirit of a revolutionary, because she is a moralist. But I am seeing a different side of her now that she is acting as my supervising editor. She will either become a bomb-thrower – or a philosopher.

...

Today Kaki resurrected an old idea. I had long thought to use some of Ander Churai's old pen and ink drawings for the front and back covers of my own book – <u>Freedom's</u> <u>Courage</u> – the book that first brought me here – that first brought me to Zaq!

But Kaki brazenly suggested we use it for "her" book, Zaq's book. I think it's a great idea.

I've also now completed the first draft of a concise biography of Zaq to serve as the reader's introduction to him. Also a concise history of Chugrana for those who don't know.

Kaki seems to want to be in charge of every aspect of the book. It's become her obsession, her passion. I'm very proud of her. She has learned so much for a thirteen year old. I have tried to tell her that I think of her as my own daughter, and that I'm sure Zaq would too, but she puts her slender palm up and says, "If I'm Zaq's and your daughter, I can't be married to Nollo, can I?"

We both laugh.

Later...I wonder if she still holds to that childish ritual. I wonder if she thinks they – she, Nollo, Braq – are all the same – all as they used to be.

Are they? Are my sons the same?

...

Now, Liz let her breath out and began the latest entry in her journal.

I don't know if this is the right decision or not. Time will tell. It's going to make things very lonely for me.

Kaki is going to hand carry the manuscript to America. To the publisher in Boston, Integra Press. V.S. has arranged everything. Through the network. He's given my instructions to the publisher. He will see that she gets the manuscript there, and that she is looked after – while she is attending to the publishing. She will probably even be able to go spend some time with the boys in Maryland.

She wants to do this. She will not rest until she sees that everything is done the way we want. She and I see eye to eye on everything. Hard to believe for a fourteen year old girl, but she just about knows every line of the book by heart. Knows each editing decision. Knows what we have put into it. What Zaq put into it.

Also, I think it is good for her to get out of here. She swears that she will return – book in hand. But I know the overwhelming seductiveness of freedom. Once she tastes America she may never return.

And she will see Braq and Nollo. It's a good time for her to do this. They are both about to graduate, Nollo from the Schaal, and Braq from the Atelier. My darling sons. Well, I hope Nollo has gotten over his earlier temper, and surliness – and – whatever made him so – what was it? – it's been so long – is it seven years? I can't really picture his moods any more.

I could have been the one to go, to take the book, but I know that if I go and return, I will be arrested. The Dryrugers are trying to hold back a dam that's about to burst. They daren't relax for a minute. And I can't go live somewhere where Zaq isn't!

Good luck! my darling Kaki.

***

Kaki walked off the plane from Boston down the passageway to the terminal into the throng of people all staring at the doorway looking for relatives or friends. She scanned the faces. Almost immediately she saw two Chugrans.

She knew them instantly. In seven years, children can change a lot, but it didn't matter. Braq was much taller, lankier – but he had the same open, alert eager face. Kaki took him in instantly. And Nollo? He was the same too, she thought…perfectly…beautiful…face and body. His face. *Was* it the same? She ran to the two boys' arms at once. One does not, in such a moment, stand back and inspect clinically. But she wanted to, and it's true that after the rapturous hug they held each other somewhat at arm's length to take stock anew.

The young girl, in her vermilion dress, had fairly flown into their arms to greet the boys with a voice that had the same sparkling delight they remembered, although – and it seemed a strange accompaniment – there was also an intensity, even a maturity, of focus they had only seen a hint of when they were all together in Chugrana. Braq and Nollo looked at her with a kind of intensity she had rarely experienced.

All this happened in a matter of seconds, but she wanted to stop, she wanted time itself to stop, she wanted to freeze the moment to give her time to think, to evaluate. What was it about Nollo's face? She couldn't say. There was the old condescension. As a child, she had thought that it suggested his exalted stature…before, in Chugrana. At least that is the way she remembered it. Somehow, now, it felt different. She had no idea how, or why. It flashed through her in only a second, then trickled off somewhere to be looked at later.

They were already walking down the concourse now, out to the baggage area, then to their car – well, their Aunt Jule's car, as Nollo explained. Somewhat boastfully, as if to let her know it was a mark of his stature, he said, "Jule did not want to leave the Emporiums – she has two stores now, you know, and she lets me drive her car whenever I want, if she doesn't need it, so Little Bratabraq and I decided to pick you up ourselves."

"Little Bratabraq." Nollo's old nickname. Memories of their childhood rushed into her mind...not that she had ever used Nollo's name for his brother. Braq wasn't "little" now; he was just about as tall as Nollo.

They got in the car, with Kaki in the front seat. Braq sat behind but during the whole trip leaned his arms over the seat, so his face was between Nollo's and Kaki's and he could be right in the middle of the conversation. It was so great to have Kaki here, he felt that he wanted just to jump right into the front.

Nollo kept interjecting, even interrupting Kaki or Braq, and sometimes even himself to call attention to this and that, like a pedantic tour guide who has to show off his erudition. He took a route from the airport that wound them through downtown D. C., pointing out the capitol, the memorials, the monuments. All of a sudden with scarcely a transition he thrust upon her the fact that he was the valedictorian of this year's graduating class at the Schaal Chugrana.

Kaki's eyes opened, and after a minute she said, "Nollo, that's wonderful!" A moment later, after she had fully taken in this piece of information, she said, "Your parents would be so proud of you."

He did not make any pretense of modesty. He looked over at her as he drove with a somewhat lordly glance, but his face fell when she added, "You must have had to study hard to get grades good enough to be valedictorian."

His mood was ruined.

He answered with a little bit of exasperation, "The Schaal doesn't give *grades.* We've gotten past that kind of old-fashioned thing – grading on individual-oriented measurement. The valedictorian is chosen by the collective decision of the faculty…and of *the whole Chugran community.*"

She gaped in confusion. "Of Chugrana?!"

"Well – you know – of Chugrans *here.*"

"All of the Chugrans here in America?!"

"The ones who really represent the spirit of Chugrana – of the original Chugrana."

She had no idea what he was talking about, no doubt because "the whole Chugran community" who had chosen was – Ku.

"What is the 'original Chugrana' ?" she asked

"Oh, Kaki!" By now he was getting very hot and angry. "Why are you cross-examining me? Why are you being so analytical? Are you disrespecting my accomplishment – even if it's not the same thing as stupid '*grades*'?"

She answered, "Nollo, I would never demean anything you accomplished…or…did. I'm just trying to understand what you're talking about."

Braq butted in at this point. "Kaki, what *is* going on now in Chugrana? Tell us more about Father and Mother!"

They were driving out of D. C. now, on one of the spokes that radiated northeast out of the city, but Kaki was no longer looking at the scenery. She turned to face Braq and Nollo more directly. "Your father is OK, as far as his health. He's lost weight, but we think he's OK. Your mother thinks that's partly because he was always so fit and healthy before they arrested him. And because of his spirit which never seems to fail, no matter what. But she only gets to see him about once a year." She described the nature of the visits Liz and Zaq were allowed.

"The bastards."

This came from Braq. Nollo looked over his shoulder at his brother in surprise. Braq did not use this kind of language often. Kaki too looked at him, startled, because he had said it with violent softness.

Kaki continued, "They still have him under tight security. Maybe even tighter than before. The Dryrugers are terrified of a revolution. Not that your father would be part of that!"

"Why not?" Nollo demanded.

"A revolution to do what?" Kaki said in answer.

"To get rid of the Dryrugers, of course."

"And replace them with what?" Her eyes were flashing now. Their bright darts of light shot at Nollo. He looked over at her, unused to a challenge of this kind, especially from a girl, and one younger than him at that.

"Wouldn't just about anything be better than the Dryrugers?"

"No!" shot back Kaki. "Not anarchy. Not a bloody chaos! Not random murder and revenge from all sides. Not everyone slaughtering each other in a civil war in which both sides fight to establish a racial dictatorship."

Braq's eyes were glowing. He said to Kaki, "You sound just like Father!"

She said, "I've been studying his ideas with your mother's help for the last four years."

Braq interrupted the conversation to poke Nollo in the shoulder. "Drive by Chamberlain," he said. Nollo had been silent, even slightly morose for a minute or so. He wanted to argue with Kaki, and he resented Braq's observation that Kaki sounded like their father. That tone of voice that was so *typical* of his brother – a tone of reverence.

"Reverence." A word Nollo even used from time to time: "reverence for Chugran traditions," for example. But he felt nothing when he said it. He had never felt such an emotion. It was merely a floating abstraction, a word to be used to subjugate other people. But he recognized the outward appearance of someone who "revered." He saw it in Braq's face. It made him even angrier.

For now, he thought that he would soft-pedal things, till he had a better idea of just what Kaki's position was – she seemed to be a kind of official spokesman for his father, being in charge of his book, or so the letter they had received implied. He thought he should first find out which way the wind was blowing before he "gave anything away." Those were the words that crawled across his consciousness.

He knew why Braq wanted to drive past Chamberlain, and Nollo resented that too. Nonetheless, he steered the car to the road that would take them in the direction of the University.

"So tell us about the book," he said.

Kaki leaned forward eagerly, and her voice became bright with excitement. "Your mother has collected your father's speeches, editorials, and articles. Hundreds of them – from twenty years ago till the last speech he made before he was arrested. She edited them. I helped her. We planned the whole thing. Then I brought the manuscript to the publisher in Boston. It's your mother's old company, Integra Press."

Braq's head was slightly tilted. His chin was resting on the back of his folded hands over the seat back. He was looking at Kaki's profile. He followed the slender planes of her jaw as they slanted back and upwards toward the delicate conch of her ear. The warm sun splashing through the window softly swiped a reflected light with a caress along the line of her jaw. He felt a sudden, immediate, and uncontrollable desire to paint her.

He said, "Whose idea was it?"

She said, "Mine. Your mother said she had thought of doing something like this, but it hadn't crystallized into a project until I suggested...well she laughs and says I whipped her into it. I guess I *was* pretty pushy about it. But it's so important!"

Braq said, "I *thought* it was your idea." His voice held an unusual tremor.

Kaki laughed.

Nollo drove on in silence. He felt that a young falcon was sitting in the seat next to him, with sharp beak and talons, and even sharper eyes glittering with purpose, a falcon whose wings he could not succeed in clipping. He had expected the same childish awe from her that he had enjoyed in Chugrana. He had expected worship. He had expected a continuation – of what he had been receiving from people for years. He had expected his feeling of safe satisfaction to go on. Instead, the actual feeling that was engulfing him was that the car might fly out of his control at any minute. He gripped the wheel more tightly, and slowed down. To the other two it merely seemed that he slowed because they were now passing through the community of Chamberlain.

At one end of the town the main road ran for a stretch along an immense wrought iron fence. Through this fence and past the soaring trunks of ancient oaks they saw at a distance the white columns and pediments of clusters of buildings in Greek revival style, a scene from some bucolic myth.

"That's where I'm going this fall," said Braq. "Chamberlain University."

Kaki raised her eyebrows. "Really? Are you finished with your high school, or whatever the system is here?"

"Oh, the education I got at the Atelier took care of all that," he said. "I passed all of my entrance exams with flying colors."

Nollo rejoined the conversation. "Little Bratabraq's being modest. They were fawning all over him to get him to come to Chamberlain. Calling him a boy genius, and a lot of other things. He's not the youngest student ever admitted, but he's close to it. There was some twelve-year old math prodigy that they had once. I think Braq's the second youngest."

He said all of this as if to impress Kaki. Certainly when he had told it to his pals in the Confraternity he had felt a kind of vanity – as if Braq's achievement was his too – as if, being the brother of a talented person, he shared in that very talent. As if talent leached into both of them from the same fountainhead of blood, or race, or genes or…who cared what. And the proof that one person had it was merely to see it in the other. The reassuring murmurs of his pals confirmed it. But here, now, he got no such reassurance from Kaki. As he extolled his brother to her, he felt instead…puny.

Kaki made it worse when she asked, "Where are you going in the fall, Nollo?"

He said, curtly, "I haven't decided yet."

Braq started to say, "Have you heard anyth– " but Nollo cut him off rudely. "Drop it!"

He had heard nothing yet. And it was getting late. Colleges by now had sent out their letters of acceptance. But Ku had told him that there was still a chance. Ku himself was working on it. If only those damned test scores had been higher. Or his grades – well, lots of schools had now dispensed with grades. And who cared?! Evidently, they still cared at Chamberlain, however much they professed to be liberal and modern and progressive. But he was banking on the premise that if your whole community could be inveigled into singing your praises, then you must be a very fine fellow, the kind of fellow the University would want. Why hadn't they seen it? Why had they admitted his little brother, and now were leaving Nollo to hang on a gibbet in the wind, humiliated? Did he have to beg? Well, he wouldn't! They could go to hell!

But no! He *had* to go to Chamberlain!

He did not ask himself why it felt so crucial that he go *there*, only *there*. He especially skirted the fact that he felt this compulsion most strongly whenever anyone brought up the fact that Braq was going there. "He's getting away." The same words that had echoed over and over when Braq first made his decision to go to the Atelier. The University was only a few more miles up the road. Why did it seem like Braq would be on another continent? And anyway Nollo had his own pals, he had the Confraternity, he had Ku, he was looked up to by all of them…and they were the people whose esteem he valued…didn't he? And after he left the Schaal, wherever he went he could surely boil up another pot of such people, couldn't he? As long as they were…Chugrans. And Chamberlain did have a few Chugran students, thank God! Why did he need anything else? Braq was less and less his pal anyway. They seemed to be growing further and further apart. Braq rarely called him his Big Brátano anymore. So why couldn't Nollo just let…him…go?

He looked over at the young falcon. Just behind her shoulder perched…another predator. A young eagle. Nollo did not know why he felt vulnerable.

The car seemed to find its own way to Old Rolling Road. Before long they were approaching the Atelier Derosch's entryway. Braq said, "This is where I've lived and studied for the last four years, Kaki. It's so great!"

He needn't have added that. She could tell by his tone of voice how ecstatic he was about this place. Nollo turned the car into the drive. He wished he didn't have to be here, but he had to drop Braq off anyway. "Braq's home," he thought with disgust.

Braq was eager to show Kaki the Atelier. He took her in the front door, then down the peripatos, to the main studio, introducing her to anyone they met along the way. Nollo followed along behind.

From her first step off the plane in Boston Kaki had felt a benevolent discrepancy. In Chugrana her racial identity was not just important, it was crucial, potentially a matter of life or death. It was, therefore, an urgent, ever-present fact one had to keep in focus – as one walked down the street, as one walked into stores. Here, this necessity seemed to have vanished. When she stepped off of Vasc Sulam's plane, she was met by his agent, one Mike McCormack, a ruddy, potato-faced man like none she had ever seen who prattled to her without stopping as if she were his sister. He roped the cab driver too into his conversational stew, and even though this driver's English was difficult to understand (he was evidently from Southeast Asia, his name tag identifying him as Pradik Binh), he instantly chimed in as if he had been Mike's lifelong chum. At the publishers' everyone she spoke to seemed to have little interest in anything to do with her race. Oh, there were the expected and natural comparisons of culture that any people from different countries inevitably make. But most of the time they appeared to be focused on her as an individual. They were interested in what she…*thought.*

As she walked about the streets of Boston, she noticed, occasionally, some person who would look through her as if she didn't exist, as Dryrugers often did in Chugrana. But here there was no way to know if it was the indifference which racial alienation nurtures or the indifference one might well feel for any stranger on the street.

The discrepancy between Chugrana and America was even stronger here in this studio of the Atelier. She couldn't put her finger on the reason. It wasn't just that the individuals Braq was introducing her to, the woman, Tressa, or her uncle, Benedict, or her grandson, Gideon, were not suspicious of Kaki, or that they were not standoffish or in any other way antagonistic to her because of her race. It was more that Kaki felt they *could not* be antagonistic to her for such a reason. They had spent each of them their lifetime *not* focusing on such a thing that to do so now would be impossible.

Kaki, first in Boston and now – even though it was only a few minutes since she had entered the Atelier – felt herself growing more and more attached to this American culture, felt it by virtue of: relaxation.

Physical therapists know how the body carries tension through the day or even for weeks at a time. These therapists press their fingers into rigid muscles, trying to persuade those hardened fibers to: *let go.* Yet they know that sometimes the rigidity is no passing tightness, easily dispelled in one or two sessions of soothing ministrations. For some people the tension is an armor they donned many years ago, so threatening were the perils of their world, or so they may have thought.

And so for those living under political tyranny there must be added to the ledger of crimes committed against them this *anatomical* tyranny, this physiological rigor mortis, this lifelong cuirass made of their own muscles. The blessed therapist which is freedom cannot always beguile them to let go of the fibrous fortress constructed of their own muscles. But Kaki was young. For the first time in nine years, she consciously felt herself relaxing.

She saw the love and admiration the people at the Atelier felt for Braq. They treated him in that easy, familiar way Americans had that was so different from the formality of Chugrans, yet they also obviously regarded him as someone special.

She also saw Braq's love and admiration for one person in particular.

"Here's Mrs. Derosch. We call her 'La Maestra.' I can't wait for you to meet her," said Braq enthusiastically.

Kaki saw a tall, gaunt woman with a severe face, of advanced years but as erect as a young cadet, entering the studio. As Antigone looked about the room, she saw Kaki and stopped, staring. Her focus became more intense. She walked up to them. Kaki felt that never had she been so searchingly examined – not even by Braq – than by this woman towering over her.

"You're 'the Freed Captive,' aren't you?"

Kaki was dumbfounded by this question.

"The girl in his drawing," said Antigone. She gestured toward Braq.

Kaki looked at Braq, still puzzled. Antigone said to Braq, "Go get it." Braq ran to get the framed drawing from its place on the wall in his work space. Antigone said, "You must be Kaki."

Kaki nodded and put out her hand. "Kaki N'Tosh."

Antigone gave her another searching look as she shook the girl's hand. Her eyes narrowed as she said, "I would've recognized you anywhere, from Braq's drawings."

"He's really good, isn't he?" said Kaki. "He was good when he was little in Chugrana."

"Yes," answered Antigone, and she looked intently at Kaki as she replied, "He's *good*." Kaki did not know why, but she felt that Mrs. Derosch meant something wider than just artistic talent.

Braq returned with "The Captive Freed." He showed it to Kaki.

She stared at it for a long time, then looked up at Braq. In the playful voice she had used with him in Chugrana, she said, "How did you know what I look like…without any clothes?"

There was an awkward silence.

But Braq smiled. "I made you up."

Kaki laughed. "That was cheeky of you."

Antigone put her hand on Kaki's shoulder with affection. "It's what we artists do when there is no model. Sometimes even when there *is* one."

This was all going way too far, thought Nollo. Everyone was just so damned chummy. He felt like spitting at them all. He controlled himself. If Kaki had not been there, he would probably have just let loose, as he had in the past; but then he wouldn't have felt this way if she had not been there. As Antigone removed her hand, Nollo put his own in its place on Kaki's shoulder. He said, somewhat smugly, and feeling as he did so that he was slapping every single one of them in the face, "This is my *wife*, you know."

There was a stunned silence from everyone. But Kaki broke the awkwardness by laughing and saying – though there was a scant little frown between her eyebrows – "Yes, that's right…from long ago…in Chugrana."

She laughed again, and no one – no one – could tell whether she was taking it seriously or not.

CHAPTER 56

An Inspired Race

"I can't believe that these white Americans were ready to listen to a fourteen year old Chuker girl!"

It was said with sneering bitterness.

"Rodit!" said Jule. She was appalled at his bigotry and at his use of the disrespectful epithet; she was angry at his disparagement of Kaki; she was saddened by his bitterness. But she had long become inured to this last emotion: her numbness, and a shadow of nostalgia, were all that was left of her feeling for her husband now.

Kaki answered, gazing at Rodit calmly but with a faint air of reflection, as if she were studying a new bug. "No one at the publisher's said a word about my being a girl, or about my age, or about my being from Chugrana. And no one called me that word you used. They listened to everything I told them…And...I guess...they're all Americans, but I couldn't tell you if they were all 'white.' There seemed to be all kinds of people working there – and I didn't think to pay much attention to it."

Rodit's face was sullen, and still held a remnant of skepticism.

Kaki added, "They listened to me because I know what I'm talking about." She said it without a hint of boasting, but her voice had the confident certainty of your arithmetic teacher reminding you that twice two is, still, four. "The publisher knows and respects your brother, Zaq. He knows and respects Liz. He knows and respects Mr. Sulam, who arranged everything to make it possible for me to get out of Chugrana with the manuscript, and then to Boston.

"And now the publisher knows and respects me."

Kaki, Jule, and Rodit stood around the dining room table, a pregnant tension holding each to his spot. From the doorway, Nollo watched his uncle and Kaki.

"Are you even going to look at it?" Kaki asked.

The first proof of Zaq's book had arrived by courier from the publisher several days after Kaki's arrival. It lay in galleys, a neat rectangular block of pages, on the table. Alongside were two sheets which were the proofs of the front and back cover art, two of Ander Churai's pen and inks created out of the whole cloth of his imagination when he, like his descendant Zaq, was in jail for this crime: that one day he said certain things while wearing the wrong suit – his skin.

Rodit's hand hung inert by the side of the table, near the cover proofs. He made no motion to pick them up. He stared at them as if their glossy sheen were a pane of glass through which he could look at the past.

How much had happened since he had been the respected patriarch of the Churai family, he thought?

Time, and disrespect for truth, can do this to a memory. While there are without question families who look up to one of their members the way that Rodit imagined, *he* had never occupied such a station. Yet, time having blurred the reality of their lives in Chugrana, he now had some such idea in his mind of himself, that he the eldest Churai, in some "good old days" of his memory, had been the recipient of an homage that had now been forever shattered. Everything about this book that lay offensively on his table – including its parturition through the labors of this – girl! – reminded him of his world that had collapsed – the world of family, of tradition, of comfortable submission to the answers to all of life's problems laid out by tribal traditions. This book represented everything he had clashed over with Zaq – Zaq who wanted to think for himself, to act for himself, Zaq who was the enemy of the tribal, collective way of life, Zaq who subordinated his family to his own convictions, Zaq to whom Rodit had given these drawings by Ander ("I should have followed my first inclination and just thrown them out," he thought), and Zaq who was now flaunting the sacrilege of using these very images as the cover for his book – almost as if he were going out of his way to defy the sacred values of the Chugran community. Zaq who married outside…not only outside of the tribe, but outside of the race itself…a white woman. Not that Rodit had ever had any complaint against Liz herself, a perfectly courteous, respectful woman…but not a Chugran. And now this girl, this child, presuming to do the kind of work that belonged to adults, to men, to the family. It was so typical of something that would issue from Zaq...his brother...that day many years ago, when Rodit had had to choose between his brothers, the day that had extinguished the glow of life within him. But perhaps there still smoldered one final ember, a bitter little nugget of resentment – that winked in the ashes of his soul.

Rodit put his hands in his pocket. "No. I don't think I *will* look at it. I got rid of these images years ago. I don't want to see them again. And as for the book...." He looked at the pile of sheets. "Why does Zaq always have to stir up trouble? Why can't he just leave things alone...leave them to the community to solve. The community knows best."

Kaki felt like shouting, "Where was your 'community' when the Dryrugers were slaughtering my family?!" But, eyelids very slightly narrowed, studying the bug that appeared to be crawling across her plate, at this moment, she realized that there was no point. That nothing she could say would change one Rodit particle. She shrugged. She felt a hand on her shoulder.

It was Jule. She smiled at Kaki, and said, "Well, *I* can't wait to read it. Having escaped that place of oppression, living in freedom now, I appreciate Zaq more than I ever did. I only wish I had given him more encouragement when we were all there in Fulon."

Nollo stepped up to the table. He picked up the manuscript. He said, "Mind if I read this?"

Kaki turned her entomologist's gaze to Nollo's face. "Your mother especially wanted both of you boys to read it. But this is the first proof from the publisher. I have to go over it word for word to make sure it's accurate. How about if I let you read each part as I finish proofing it?"

She held her hand out for the manuscript.

Nollo looked at Kaki for a moment, then said, negligently, "Sure." He handed her the hefty pile.

Kaki said, "I want to make sure that Braq gets to read it too. But I don't want this out of my sight. I plan to get it back to the publisher as fast as I can. We hope that this book will help bring Zaq's cause to the attention of the public – here and all over the world."

Nollo's face took a sarcastic tinge. "Do you think anyone will care?"

Kaki said, with complete sincerity, "Yes."

Nollo's mouth screwed up in a kind of resentful pout. "Why should they? Zaq – all of us – are a people that many of them have never even heard of. Why should anyone give a damn?"

Kaki said, "Because it's justice. They must."

"But...in the end, it's just words."

"Nollo! That means – 'it's just ideas.' Ideas are what your father lives by."

Nollo said nothing to this. Seeing that he was not going to reply, Kaki went on, "Do you think Braq can come over here to read it?"

Nollo said, "I don't know. He's very busy now, getting ready for graduation...me too, I'm working on my valedictorian's speech."

Jule said, "Yes, Braq is trying to finish several paintings, especially his entry for the Derosch Prize."

"What's that?" asked Kaki.

Jule said, "Each year the Atelier awards a prize to a currently enrolled student who has created the single best piece of work during that year. The whole faculty votes, although I think Mrs. Derosch gets to break a tie, or even overrule them all. Not that I think that usually happens."

"But you can bet she would if she wanted to," said Nollo. "She's the dictator of that place."

"Why shouldn't she be?" asked Jule. "It's *her* place."

"No, but do you think anyone has a chance with her little darling great grandson Gideon in the race? She fawns all over him."

Jule smiled. "Grandparents are like that."

Nollo scoffed, but Jule looked at Kaki and said, "Pay no attention to Nollo. I have no reason to think they aren't fair. But it's true that Braq is very busy. Not only finishing up all of his work for the year, but also did he tell you that he's getting ready to go on the Atelier's European trip?"

Kaki nodded.

Jule said, "He's been saving up for it for several years now. They take a group to the major museums of Europe each summer...They're leaving right after graduation."

Kaki still hadn't gotten over her shock when she had learned this from Braq. She had thought they would have time to spend together...she, Braq, and Nollo...until the book was published...then she would return to Chugrana...to Chugrana.... But – he was going away. Very soon! She didn't want him to go away from her.

Her face fell. Jule patted her on the shoulder. "It's just for six weeks, then he'll be back and the three of you will have the rest of the summer."

Kaki's only response was, "I must make sure he gets to read his father's book."

***

It was Kaki who suggested that they run.

They were at the Atelier, she, Braq, and Nollo, standing by the yew hedge. It was the last day in May. Kaki had now lived at the Churai home for several weeks, sharing Sue's room. She divided her time between gallivanting around with Sue, and, as their time permitted, getting together with Nollo and Braq. Sue Churai worked hard at her mother's two stores, but she was perfectly happy to take some time off to show the younger girl around, to take her to Washington or Annapolis or Baltimore, for sightseeing or window shopping.

Kaki appreciated the older girl's easy friendliness. She seemed to recognize something in her manner: Sue apparently saw nothing in her life but blessings – sights, sounds, and palpably pleasant accomplishments. Her manner was so different from that of Kaki's friends and acquaintances in Chugrana. Those Chugran girls were friendly enough: they could even occasionally laugh. Yet a guarding shield might come down on their faces, even over their bodies, in an instant, behind which shield they could take refuge. The American Chugran, Sue Churai, on the other hand, offered a direct, uncomplicated, open face to the world around her. Her glance was simple and unguarded. But it was not just the contrast between Sue and those Chugran girls. There was something more personally familiar to Kaki about Sue's sense of existence.

Discussing life in Chugrana, Sue answered a question Kaki put to her with this emphatic answer: "Never!"

Kaki's question had been: "Would you want to go back to Chugrana?"

Kaki did not need to ask why Sue did not want to return. The blessings of which Sue's life was full were so obvious. When Sue asked Kaki the same question, Kaki was appalled to find the word, "Never," stuck in her throat. She was appalled not that it stuck, but that it had even risen to produce that tentative contraction of her vocal chords. What was that word even doing there, lodged in her throat?! It seemed treasonous. Not treasonous to Chugrana certainly; she felt no such loyalty. No, it felt treasonous to Zaq and Liz.

Could a mere handful of weeks in this country suffice to subvert her values to the point of making the return to Fulon with Zaq's book in hand seem not a passionate commitment but a drear duty?

A duty. That was the leaden feeling she had experienced when Nollo had, as it appeared, praised her for everything she was doing, with the book, with the effort to free his father, with helping Liz. It all seemed clear and straightforward, and Kaki accepted his gratitude at face value. But then he had gone on to say that he and his organization, the one with the strange name – she still couldn't quite get it to slip easily off her tongue – were engaged in the same struggle, as all Chugrans were, that they all owed their lives to this struggle, and to the race. And they had "to help the great men of the race." Or words rather like that.

Helping a race?

Suddenly, for a moment, her purpose seemed less clear, less clean-cut, and less like the passionate moral quest she had been pursuing. Why did her revered hero, Nollo, out of that face that belonged on some ancient statue of god or man look at her in that peculiar way when he said, "serving the great Chugran men?" And why did it suggest something like a self-sacrificial duty?

She wished she could have a long talk with this man Bevol Stagri, professor of anatomy at the Atelier. He seemed to know a lot about Braq and Nollo, more than he had said to her in their first brief meeting. A week later, she visited the Atelier. Braq being too busy, Bevol took her on a tour of the place, told her its history, always interweaving references to Braq. He showed her Braq's private cabin, showed her the work projects Braq and Gideon had tackled on the grounds, showed her the paths where Braq ran. Back in the studio, he took a thick binder from one of the shelves in the library. It was a catalog of Braq's works at the Atelier, a labor of love that Antigone and Bevol had jointly assembled.

Kaki was stunned. This boy, her childhood chum – he still seemed a boy, especially in his carefree, open-faced benevolence – had already produced a whole body of works that simply amazed her. There were hundreds of photos of paintings, drawings, and sculptures. She paused for a long while on "Zaq's World," with its enticing grandeur; on the benediction of "His Sanction"; on the purposefulness of "The Unforgiving Minute"; on the thematic drama of "The Master Race" and "Slavery"; and on the drawings, "Thought" and "Action." These last two startled her. She could not say exactly why. Professor Stagri had said, "Thought aims at action, and action without thought is worthless," but this explanation did not really show her why this pair of drawings struck her so forcefully.

And why did Stagri look so closely at her, even urgently, when he said, "To act blindly, without knowing what you're aiming at, will lead you to failure, or to a success you may regret. And waiting passively for the world to write its mysteries on inert pages of thought is the work of no mind.

"Not everyone who acts or claims to act does so with intelligence; there is more than one motive for pursuing 'struggles' and 'causes.' "

"But Braq is pursuing *his* goals with intelligence!" said Kaki. She gestured at the catalog of his works.

"Oh, yes, *Braq* is," said Bevol. "And he'll succeed…if…." He stopped, and Kaki looked up at him.

"If?"

"There are two main antagonists to a man like Braq." (She did not find it strange that he said "man.") "One is indifference. From the people who say, 'Yes, it's great but who cares. It's just one individual's accomplishment, after all.' The other is envy. From the people who say, 'Yes, it is a great individual accomplishment, so I hate it.' The first type will ignore a Braq, which is still a crime. But the second will…attack him."

A chill of horror ran along Kaki's skin. "Who could be so evil?"

Bevol looked at her. He shrugged. "Kaki, there *are* such people in the world."

"Bugs," she thought.

This discussion had been two weeks ago.

Now, on the last day of May, she stood with Braq, Nollo, and Bevol Stagri in the main studio looking at Braq's painting – his hope for the Derosch Prize.

This contest, it must be said, was rather informal. The students did not have to submit any particular piece of work. All of the faculty knew everything that each student had done that year, and any piece of work might be selected as that student's best, to compare with all of the other students' works. But Braq had poured his mind into this painting like none he had ever painted.

The work depicts a scene within an art studio, rather like the Atelier. But really quite different. The denizens of Derosch would not have recognized it as the Atelier, and yet something about it would have seemed very familiar. Light floods into the space from a skylight. It is the kind of light a Vermeer might have painted, a cool radiance which ennobles and blesses with warmth everything it illuminates. The space this light washes over is calm, ordered, clean – laved not only by the light but also by its own reflection of the rational purposes of some Designer and of the people within the space.

Everything within the space is sensible and ordered because placed within that logical, measurable system of perspective discovered by the Renaissance. The architectural elements – the walls, the skylight, the tiles on the floor, even the chairs, easels, and stools were all so many facile tools by which Braq took your eye into his world, and led that eye where he wanted it to go. And everywhere he conducted it, there was order and clarity. The shadows, too, were limpid, concealing nothing murky or malevolent.

But the spot where Braq led your eye, over and over, was to one figure in the painting. It was not to the naked female model posing on the model stand. Nor to any of the students working at their easels. Nor to the glowing skylight. It was to the teacher, a gaunt woman who stood beside one student's easel, pointing, with a brush in her right hand, at his painting, while her left hand, in emphatic gesture that was a kind of salute, aimed at his chest. Her eyes looked intently at this student the back of whose head is to the viewer. We, the viewers, can look into her piercing eyes.

Not only did the perspective and all of the tools Braq had mastered seem to direct your attention, repeatedly, to this figure, but moreover all of the order and serenity in the space seemed to flow around and even from her. As if she *was* the creator of ordered space itself. The space seemed suited specially *to* her. As if *she* were the measure, and perhaps the measurer, of space, or even of all things. The painter of this work evidently seemed to feel that this woman was the Designer.

You felt that it would be a wonderful thing to be in this space with this woman, to be standing next to her, to have her looking into your face, instructing you as she was this student.

You felt that *here* anything could be accomplished, and was worth accomplishing.

The painting was like the lucidly harmonious melodies of a concerto such as men used to know how to compose, in the Age of Reason, expressed here not in sounds but in two dimensions of space. Evidently Braq, and the Atelier Derosch, had missed the news that the Age of Reason was past. His painting was Braq's tribute *to* that Atelier, and in particular, to Antigone Skye Derosch.

Bevol stood next to Kaki, looking not at the painting but at her. "He calls it 'The World Enlightened'. Of course, it's his own soul he's throwing a light on. He's showing the world his soul."

Kaki stood for what seemed an eon, her figure still and her face glowing with a solemn ecstasy. To himself, Bevol thought, "And you, Kaki, are illuminating *yours* by that response."

Kaki felt, "In *this* world, there are no vermin. In *this* world, there can *be* no vermin."

They were standing in the Atelier, so she was able to compare the real world around her with the world Braq had created. She could see that he had completely transformed it. He had made up many elements, changed others, deleted, rearranged. He had selectively recreated a world, *his* world. She had long known the story of Ander, so she had understood the process, in principle, but she could see now, in front of her, the way of and the fact of artistic creation.

She turned her glowing face to Braq. She said. "Braq, this is wonderful."

"Thanks, Kaki," he said.

As he directed Bevol's attention to a matter of anatomy in the painting, Kaki turned to Nollo to say, "Isn't this fantastic?"

Nollo rearranged the muscles of his face, pasting a polite expression over some other fleeting emotion that had just been there. He said, "Yeah, it sure is." He began to praise Braq in a strangely perfunctory way.

When Braq turned back again to Kaki, she said to him, "I can see that you changed *this* into *that*" (she gestured from the great hall to his painting), "but just how, I'm not sure."

He laughed. "It wasn't easy. You have to get used to saying, 'What if?' Here, I'll show you."

He walked further down the studio, taking Kaki with him explaining the perspective scheme he had used. Nollo stood by Braq's easel. He did not follow them. Bevol saw the disgruntled look on Nollo's face. Nollo fronted Bevol Stagri, almost accusatorily. Bevol looked at him and raised his eyebrows. Now what was this about?

Nollo began as if they were in the middle of a conversation.

"You said one time that Chugrans have to acknowledge their inferiority compared to other races."

Bevol said, "Those are not my words at all. I don't think of races that way. I do think that you must face up to the fact that slavery, maintained for generations, succeeds in making its victims inferior."

"OK, OK," said Nollo impatiently, "but you say that Chugrans carry the legacy of slavery with them, that they're slower, less educated, less skilled, less everything."

Bevol frowned. He had never said that, but it did accord with his thinking, to some extent, so he nodded hesitantly, his face screwed up with skepticism as to where Nollo was going with this, while he tried to remember when he might have said such a thing to Nollo. In fact, it was

Zaq's words Nollo was remembering, perhaps from Chugrana, perhaps from the book whose proof pages he had now read, but Zaq's and Bevol's views seemed to coincide so he attributed these words to Bevol.

Nollo went on. "And now, when one of them, one Chugran, who is better than that, who rises above the legacy of the past, who is the equal of other peoples, or even superior to those other peoples, goes among those others, he must *prove* himself." He gestured to Braq's painting. "This contest! It's insulting and degrading. Why should he have to prove his worth? Why should he have to be compared…to whites?"

Bevol said, "He isn't superior to other 'peoples.' He's superior, as an artist, to other *people*. You just can't help thinking in terms of collectives, can you, Nollo? In any event, I don't think Braq ever looks at it that way. I don't think he says, 'I'm proving myself to others.' He just thinks, 'What do I want to do with this problem in painting? How do I solve it?' or 'Here is my vision'. And he runs with it."

Nollo said, "That's fine for him. He's a genius. He can get away with that. What about the rest of us?"

Bevol answered, "Maybe *that's* what makes him a genius – that he always and *only* thinks *that way*."

Nollo said, with dripping sarcasm, "I'm not so lucky. I have only Chugran genes in me, not half white and half Chugran, so I guess I'm handicapped."

Bevol stared at Nollo silently for a moment to let him hear his own whining. Then he said, "And maybe that's another reason Braq is so successful – he doesn't blame or credit his genes for his actions – he just runs with what he has, and lets the results fall as they may. Although, I think if you asked him, he would say he doesn't have time – time for all this blathering you indulge yourself in, all this talk to explain why you can't do this or that. He has no time because he's busy doing."

Nollo came back angrily, "But he's so selfish! Why doesn't he ever look at his fellow Chugrans and see their suffering? Why doesn't he sympathize with them? Try to help them? Who will lift them up?"

Bevol said, with a faint sigh of helplessness, "To lift someone up, to inspire a person, you must show him that something is *worth* doing and that *he can do it. Every* Chugran who achieves something good inspires his fellow Chugrans – as he inspires anyone. If Braq has not done that, then no one ever inspired anyone. You, Nollo, you think you sanctify yourself by devoting your waking hours to your 'concern for other Chugrans?'…I think you will turn yourself into a parasite who needs the whip-scarred backs of your own race to feed your empty soul. If, by some miracle, every Chugran now on earth were suddenly raised to some state of temporal splendor and needed nothing, what would be left for your self-esteem to hang itself on? How would you greet the next day? I know what would be left for Braq – he would go on painting. What about you? Do you live for anything but people's misery?"

Nollo said, "So – no one should help others?"

Bevol said, "Help them to do what? Help people, as a teacher does? Wonderful. Help them to acquire the skill of living their lives? Oh, yes. Help them to be able to do something productive? Of course! Help them to see what a glory they could make of their lives?" His face was lifted now, and his eyes shone. "Yes! But help them to anger and frustration? Help them to bitterness and malevolence toward the whole world? Help them to envy and resentment? Help them to think they're the pawns of some outside power?

"Help victims of racial injustice wallow in more race-thinking forever?

"Help them to feel helpless?"

Nollo objected with a tepid wail, "But can a person climb out of a boat that's foundering, or even sinking, wade to shore, stride off into some career, not looking back at the people still in the boat who may sink and drown?"

Bevol said, "A person *can* – many do – Braq has. You can. Will you help them by staying in the boat and drowning with them?"

Nollo lowered a sullen face, and turned away.

Bevol reflected that the sullen look had never left Nollo's face during the whole conversation. He had not wanted to learn any truth, only to stroke his feelings. Bevol shrugged.

"Helping a race." What could that mean, he thought. If it had any legitimate meaning, any moral validity, it had to mean – first and foremost – removing irrational burdens and barriers – in other words, combating racism – race-thinking – on the part of the society the victims live in. So it was, and it had to be a task of negating.

As with so many things, the negation meant that one mainly needed to get out of people's way, to leave them free of coercion, and free of irrationality, in order for good to flourish. Beyond this, he supposed, voluntary programs might be beneficial – for example, promoting education, enterprise. But most of these things just required letting people who want to be so engaged go ahead and do it – that is, *laissez-*

faire. The modern idea of welfare, of some grand scheme to "help a race," was immoral, and it treated people not as responsible adult moral beings, but as metaphysical cripples. It was the very opposite of moral.

In any event, "helping a *race*" would mean trying to help each and every member – including the criminals and those who don't want to achieve anything. "Race," Bevol thought, "does not exist – only individuals exist."

He saw two individuals, Braq and Kaki, returning to the space. Braq seized Bevol's attention now, to ask still another question. Bevol, answering him, saw Nollo take Kaki's arm, strolling her toward the main door of the studio.

Outside, Nollo and Kaki walked along the neat rows of Braq's and Gideon's plantings.

"But, you know," Nollo said, "The world isn't really like that." He flipped his head over his shoulder back toward the studio.

"Like what?" asked Kaki mystified. The vibrations of her clear melodious voice resonated in the warm spring air.

"Like that painting!" he said with a rasp of animosity in his voice. Kaki could not figure out why she was puzzled. It was his tone of voice, and she could not figure it out because she could not grasp even the possibility of what that tone implied: hatred. The most that made its way through to her was that it sounded as if he did not *want* the world to be like Braq's painting.

They were approaching the hedge when Braq caught up with them. "Hey, you two!" he yelled. "Where are you going?"

Nollo said, "Just walking and talking with my wife…with 'Why Walk N'Tosh'...with 'Why wash n' talk.'"

They barely smiled at his old joke.

Braq said, "She talks *now.*"

Nollo scowled.

Kaki looked at Braq and said, "I know who the teacher in your painting is, but who was the model for the female nude? Did you make her up too?"

He said, "She's just a model we had in life drawing class."

Nollo said, with a smirk, "Little Bratabraq's unfaithful."

The other two looked at him blankly.

"He's married to the moon, but he's always drawing naked women."

If his remark was intended as a joke, it fell flat; neither Kaki nor Braq laughed. Nollo went on, feeling a furtive satisfaction of giving in to his feelings, of letting go. He did not know why but he wanted to goad these two people. "Naked white women."

He still had not gotten the reaction he wanted. They were looking at him with frowns now.

"Little Bratabraq has no use for women of his *own* race. He's too good for *them*."

Braq looked at his brother in shocked amazement. "I draw everyone!" he said. "And anyway…Nollo, don't you remember that night how Father told us that the color of a person's skin is not important, that when he fell in love, both times, the skin did not matter...when he said that race should *never* matter?"

"It *shouldn't* matter," Nollo said resentfully, "but it *does*. People force the issue of color on us. So it *has* to matter to us. And it will until the bastards…get what's coming to them."

"Who is forcing it on you...Which…bastards?" This from Kaki.

He stopped himself. He was on the verge of going too far. "The ones who commit injustices against us, of course. The ones who have put Father in prison. The ones we're fighting against, all of us…." He looked at Braq. "Or at least most of us are."

It was possible that Braq ignored the innuendo, but his reply was this: "Nollo, I don't want you to call me 'Little Bratabraq' "

Nollo said, "Why not?"

Braq said, "I'm not little anymore."

Kaki standing between them, looking from one to the other, seeing Braq Nollo's height, she thought that it may have been the way the two boys held themselves, Nollo's head sunk surlily into his shoulders, Braq stretched forward like a lance…like Zaq.

Nollo said, "Oh – too good for that too?… And I suppose I'm no longer 'Big Brátano?' "

There was a moment.

Then Braq's face softened. "No…Big Brátano...at least...I don't want that to change."

Kaki said, "Let's run."

Without waiting for an answer, she took off down one of the paths. Nollo glanced at Braq and then sprinted after her. Braq too took off, and for just an instant it seemed to him as if they were back in Chugrana running through their neighborhood. But in Fulon their running had been born of the joy of childhood – simple, unalloyed, self-sufficient. Now there seemed to be something more.

Kaki did not look back. She flew straight and purposefully, but relentlessly, as if her life depended on it. And Nollo too ran like a zealot, or a predator after its prey, a frown between his eyes, as if it mattered that he…catch…Kaki. And Braq, too, felt that more, much more, rode on this run than on any race before. But he did not frown. He felt his lithe body as a single whole, his muscles relaxing, with a kind of integrity, into their tension, as he sped into his ground-devouring lope.

Perhaps it was the fact that Nollo, for all his years of involvement in the plantchi "teams," had been somewhat sedentary. Perhaps it was the urgent stress in the way he ran. Perhaps it was Braq's frequent running that gave him such speed and stamina. Perhaps – but what does it matter – Braq caught Nollo. Nollo felt the rush of thumping feet behind him. He felt a rush and a pressure behind his shoulder. Then, as Braq sprinted past his brother, Nollo heard him breathe out, undoubtedly as a jibe, but friendly, without a tinge of malice, "Hey, Big Brátano!"

And Braq gained on Kaki. She was turning a corner for the last shot to the house, as he sailed past her with a grin. She caught up to him when he stopped by the hedge where they had started. He was scarcely winded. They both laughed. Then they turned and looked back down the path. After a bit, Nollo came, not running – walking up to them. He gave the two of them a cold, bitter look as he walked, without a word, straight past them to the car.

After a moment, Kaki shrugged and followed him.

CHAPTER 57

A Prize Won, A Prize Forfeited

Kaki rebelled at contradictions. At heart, she was a logician. Always A should be A. If A seemed to be not-A, her hackles stood right up. This explained her loathing for the "bugs." Human beings should treat each other with justice; the "bugs" did not. They were a contradiction of what humans should be. To such a logician, harboring a contradiction within herself was especially monstrous. Would not then she become a bug, too?! Any such inner contrarieties must be expunged, purged, rooted out. And this was why Kaki was in such turmoil. She could not solve the dilemma.

She knew that part of the conflict was out there – in Nollo himself. But hard as that was to understand the harder part was what *she* felt. She had never known such a conflict....If only, she thought, Nollo would be more – open. She wanted to ask him so much about what he had said in his valedictorian's speech at the Schaal graduation. Every aspect of that speech brought forth whiffs of the contradictory. But he was extremely defensive, and put off all her questions.

To begin with, what was this nonsense about his name? The strange man, Pranti Ku, gave a glowing introduction of "this divine Chugran." She could only understand half of Ku's bizarre locutions, and the other half seemed to be praise for Nollo that was so fulsome as to be ridiculous. Then, halfway through, Ku said that although some had known him in the past as "Nollo Churai," his true "race name" was "Nollifer Chiughalana." Kaki was baffled by this; she had never heard of any such thing in Chugrana. Nonetheless, her puzzlement was swept away, and she experienced a thrill of admiration when she saw Nollo stride so confidently to the lectern in the Schaal's small auditorium, to the pulsing swell of acclaim, the genuinely enthusiastic applause of teachers, parents, and students, only marked in a slightly disturbing way by the raucous, almost frenzied cheering, from the front rows, of that group of Nollo's special...people...the group he called "the Confraternity."

And then, as he began, his ringing tones filling the hall, she felt that here was an orator such as she had never heard, an orator who could sway minds. She felt at first, that it would indeed be "mind speaking to mind." His intonations, his pauses, his emphases, they all seemed born of some inner strength of conviction that would ring out to as large an audience as might be within his hearing, and yet he looked at each person in the hall as if he were just speaking to them alone, as if each idea had just emerged, newly coined to reach that person's mind in that moment.

Why, then, after it was over, wouldn't he let her look at his draft, or notes, or whatever he had used in preparation? There were many disturbing things in the speech, so many that she wanted to read the precise words, in order to ask him what he meant. But, afterwards, when she asked him if she could read the speech, he denied even having any notes, any drafts, any scrap of paper at all. Yet he had, for weeks, claimed to be busy preparing it, so how could he have nothing?

And it seemed very unlikely to her that any great speaker could have delivered such a well-crafted performance, purely impromptu; and well-crafted the performance was. She knew from Liz, by way of contrast, that sometimes Zaq had spoken without notes, but only after spending countless hours on draft after draft. She knew that a brilliant mind may – on dais or village green – extemporize a brilliant line or two, but not, she thought, an entire oration with nary a stumble, stutter, or hesitation.

Yet Nollo swore that he just got up and spoke!

And the phrases from Zaq! They *had* to be from him. Nollo had read the manuscript of the book. And he was Zaq's son. He had heard his father speak many times. Also, Kaki recalled from their childhood Nollo's phenomenal memory.

When, in his speech, Nollo said, "No man should be forced to be subservient to the values of any other man," but should be true to that "state of liberty he was born in, a free agent with a free mind," it was straight from the pages of Zaq's writings. When he said, "We must deny the merciful servitude of the racists," it was straight from the masthead of the Sovereign. These and many other inspiring phrases and sentences. When she asked him why he hadn't acknowledged his father's authorship even once, asked him why he had not even mentioned Zaq's name – why had Nollo become so surly, saying, "I don't know what you mean…I guess more than one person can come up with an idea besides Father, can't they?"

But it was that clash of ideas *within* the speech that was most upsetting. To a person for whom ideas matter, the *words* must matter. They cannot be tossed out lightly, cavalierly, thoughtlessly. And a person like

Nollo, a son of Zaqqaq Churai, could not speak for so long, about such topics – about what a human being is, about ideals – and then say that the ideas behind the words and the words that pricked out the ideas did not matter.

How could he rail against "the racists," in one sentence, and in the very next speak of "Chugran authenticity," and "the crucial need to develop a collective Chugran consciousness," (if she remembered that bizarre phrase correctly). How could he say "We are all alike, all men, all struck from the same divine mould," and only a few words later speak of "the unique and unaccountable spiritual power of the Chugran essence?" How *could* he say, "We must avoid both the despair of fatalism and the vicious injustice of holding each of society's pathetic victims responsible for their every choice?" How could he say that "the light of reason was being extinguished in schools made decrepit by racism," then turn in the next paragraph to say, "Reason unshackled from faith in the group to which you belong becomes shackled to distortion and rationalization," and that we need "a new language to clothe our thoughts, a new way of thinking, unbound by the constrictions of logic"?!

Did he not hear what he was saying?

If any of this was what he really said. Without the text it was hard to be accurate and fair, and Kaki wanted above all to be fair. But, listening to the speech, she could scarcely hold onto one sentence when its successor wiped out the meaning of its predecessor. She knew that for all of Nollo's plagiarizing of Zaq's phrases, this was a speech that Zaq could never have delivered. In Zaq's speeches and articles one thought led to another, the groups of thoughts packed together like solid bricks in the firm wall of ideas he was erecting, a solid wall for one to contemplate, and then accept or reject as one judged appropriate.

This speech was different. It almost seemed as if the ideas did not matter after all, that each phrase or sentence was merely to be *heard* by the audience, and was merely to *stimulate* that audience, independently of any other phrase or sentence. As if he intended his audience to be stirred up merely *by* the words, as if the words were no more than buttons he pushed, having no significance, no meaning, no truth beyond that reaction they produced, as if only the sounds mattered.

Not the ideas.

How could this be? Was such a thing possible? She had never met or seen or heard a person who could be so – insincere. The voice, the expressions of tone and face, the gestures were fervent, passionate, bespeaking conviction; the content was a seething clash of contradiction. Kaki and Braq stared in numb disbelief as if at a mocking specter – as if a horrid jester peered out from behind a mask on the face of their idol. Kaki was dumbfounded. How could one believe in a man's integrity who could not sustain it even for the length of a single sentence? But this was Nollo! The same Nollo who on a day in Fulon when she had first come to worship him had sworn so fiercely to Kaki that he would bring justice to the vicious people who had perpetrated the outrage on her family, and all people of that ilk. Could it be the same person? It was Nollo, the hero who had risked his life to save the Museum. How could such a hero become – dishonest?!

After the speech, Kaki, Braq, and Jule had looked at each other grimly. Jule said, "The three Churai brothers were as different as could be, in spite of having the same genes. I just heard *two* of them speaking through the same voice. How Jonni and Zaq could end up in the same speech, I couldn't tell you."

After a minute she said, "If Nollo weren't so well-behaved, I would swear he was going to become another firebrand just like Jonni."

And this was another of Kaki's conflicts. Nollo was well-behaved – in front of his aunt Jule and his uncle Rodit. Around the house, he was respectful, and even somewhat formally polite with Kaki herself, employing the traditional Chugran courtesies. But outside the house a change occurred. Like that time they had gone for a walk down to the river. Nollo had seemed to molt his manner as if it were only an annoying piece of dead skin barely veneering his preferred mode of behavior. He became cruder, and he looked at her in a way that made her strangely uncomfortable.

Perhaps this was the worst of her conflicts. Before she had left Chugrana, had anyone asked her then how she would feel if her beloved Nollo Churai expressed a sexual interest in her, she would have said that such a prospect was wonderful, intriguing, and perfectly natural. Hadn't she been the one to propose the "marriage" in the first place? These few weeks had changed all of that. She could not say that any one thing had done it. It was thousands of fine droplets adding up to a torrent. But the torrent hit the levee made of all her previous thoughts, images, preconceptions of Nollo, Nollo as she had...thought him to be...in Chugrana...when she and Braq had gloried in the fellowship of Nollo. The levee was cracking.

Now, Braq…she could hardly take in what *he* had become. He seemed so single-minded, rather like *her* really, when she thought about it. She wished they had more time together. But he was so dedicated, and his powers of concentration had only gotten greater. She had seen him at work, oblivious to all around him. Not that she begrudged it him. To the contrary, she did not want his concentration, his incredible work to be disturbed. And it seemed to her that nothing *could* disturb it.

She saw just how dedicated he was, not only to the grueling work of his craft, but also to the *truth* of his craft. She saw him use a rag soaked in turpentine and a piece of sandpaper to wipe out a painting he had struggled with for the three previous months.

She was aghast. She had never seen such a thing. To destroy what you had slaved over! How awful!

As he scrubbed out his work, sending the paint to oblivion with the sweet-smelling solvent and the gritty abrasive, he explained with impartial objectivity, "Kaki, I've learned a lot here – and one of the things La Maestra has told me is that it's not a…sacrifice…of your *self* to give up something that should never have been in the first place, something that was poorly thought through, or something that was just not *for you* – then and there. She says, 'Go on to something better, to something you *can* achieve.' "

He did not repeat the sentence that La Maestra had added, perhaps because he did not really understand it: "No unrequited love – for canvases or women."

Watching him wipe the last traces of paint off the canvas, Kaki supposed that it seemed reasonable. But what if the thing you wiped out really *should have been yours*?

All of a sudden she pictured with horror something crawling across his canvas…toward Braq. And he didn't see it slithering toward him. What a disgusting image! What had made her think that?...In a funk, her thoughts continued to stumble by her consciousness. Very soon, after his graduation, he would be going to Europe on the Atelier tour. Just as suddenly as before, she thought, "He'll be safe there!" There it was again! What an idea! What made her think that? How could there be any bugs *here*, for Braq, that he needed to be safe from? And why did she feel that, above all, it was Braq who needed protection from the bugs?

***

"In a few weeks," said Bevol Stagri, "we will begin hanging the year-end show. You all know, I assume, that the deadline for getting your work in is this Friday."

There were the usual shuffles of dismay from students suddenly faced with the inexorable doom of a deadline. They had to complete their work, or wait for another year for the next opportunity to be part of a Derosch Show, to which dealers and patrons came from all over the country. The Derosch Prize was to be awarded on the first day of the Show. The winner received a cash prize and also a write-up with photos in New Inheritors, a journal dedicated to publicizing new talent in many fields.

There was a hum of excitement, as there was each year. Thinking back, Bevol believed that nothing had ever matched the tension this year, the year that Braq and Gideon graduated. A debate ran through every part of the Atelier over who would win the prize. While all knew that these two youths had outdone everyone else in the school, their talent was so clearly superior that every other student resigned himself or herself to this inescapable fact, shrugged, and joined the debate, siding either with Braq's "The World Enlightened," or Gideon's best work to date, "A Course in Écorché." Gideon's painting was a tall canvas, on which a figure of a living man – the suggestion was of a teacher – was depicted with the distinct and separate presentation of each muscle, as seen on an écorché figure, but with the skin still in place, not flayed. The skin was somewhat dark, and more than one person thought the face of this figure resembled Bevol Stagri's although he denied, truthfully, having had anything to do with this painting, and he certainly had not posed for Gideon. The figure in the painting was holding the superior end of his own sartorius muscle, detached, as in the celebrated drawings of Vesalius, from its own bony origin, and at the same time the figure gestured toward that point of origin, the anterior superior iliac spine, on a skeleton standing next to him, as if lecturing to a class.

All of this was executed flawlessly, with dashing technique, and with no hint of gore or ugliness about the detached muscle. It suggested Gideon's usual impish humor, displayed with tour de force skill.

The debate was still raging when, on the morning of the first day of the Derosch Show, Kaki, Jule, Nollo, Sue, and Mark arrived at the Atelier. They strolled the premises, examining hundreds of paintings, sculptures, and drawings, installed throughout the main house, the peripatos, and the studio. The high professional standard produced by the Atelier clearly showed why this institution was so well regarded in the art world.

In the main studio, they found hundreds of people admiring the scores of works that hung in the radiant light. They quickly noticed two groups on either side of the long vaulted room, each group centered on one of the two main contenders for the Derosch Prize. On the long south side hung "A Course in Écorché." On the long facing wall, "The World Enlightened." A swirling current of bodies and arguments not always civil coiled back and forth between the two. Students debated with teachers, graduates from former years harangued more recent ones, dealers pointed admonitory fingers at clients. And some people stood just lost in rapt admiration of either work.

As Kaki, Jule, and Nollo mingled, they overheard the following remarks.

"There's no question that Gideon will win – he's got the whole Derosch tribe behind him!" "Antigone Derosch sees Gideon as the heir to the Atelier. I heard her say that. So what does that tell you about who will win?" "You can't take somebody out of some obscure country on the other side of the world that no one's ever heard of, where the people there don't even know the name of Raphael, and make that somebody into a top caliber painter, no matter how talented they are. It's either in your family's blood, or your people's blood – or it's not. And Gideon certainly has it in his blood!" "You heard, didn't you, that the whole Derosch family met last night to hash this out, and that they've already decided to award the prize to Gideon. He was even there at the meeting. I heard it from one of the students."

And between two visitors, this exchange: "How can there be any question. He's her great grandson. His father, Fritz Raeburn, and his grandmother, Tressa Raeburn, are voting too, along with a bunch of other close relations. It takes no brains to figure this out!" And the response: "No! You're missing the point. These Derosches pride themselves on being liberals. So they need to make a political statement by choosing a minority race, to show how tolerant they are. That's why they'll pick this little Brock Shry person. He's just a token."

Nollo felt as if a prickly rash were crawling over his skin. He was violently thrown between two contradictory emotions. On one side, he wanted his brother to win. He wanted him to conquer these bastards, to show them all, to smash them in the dirt. And for this reason he felt anxious that Braq might lose. Probably that is why he said to Kaki, with a quiet hiss of fury, "The deck is stacked against him. He hasn't got a chance. Look at the old lady, Ann, slobbering all over her little darling." Kaki looked but only saw that Mrs. Derosch had her hand on Gideon's shoulder.

On the other side was a quite different, even opposite emotion. Nollo kept this emotion to himself: even more he kept it *from* himself. It produced no open expression. Except for the rash.

Kaki was most disturbed by what Nollo said next. Conspiratorially, he leaned to her ear and said, "I happen to know that there is another reason Braq probably won't win. He has a problem. He can't paint people's skin. I've heard people here talking about it. It's because he's ashamed of his own skin. He doesn't like to flaunt being a Chugran for that reason. You know how he is. But the trouble is it makes him louse up his paintings. That's why he threw the figure of the nude model in his painting into the background–so you wouldn't even look closely at it and so you wouldn't see the problem."

Kaki was appalled at this information. "But the model is a white woman, so why would his being ashamed of his own skin...which I don't believe...cause him a problem with her?!"

Nollo said contemptuously, "It doesn't matter *whose* skin. And meantime that little jerk, Gideon – he's so superior about his race, about being white, that he thinks he can paint anybody!"

Kaki said, "But, Nollo, Gideon painted a dark skinned man, and he's done it beautifully. So what are you talking about?!"

Nollo snarled, "Kaki! Don't you understand anything?!"

A few minutes later, Kaki strolled past Tressa. Through the surrounding noise she thought she heard Tressa saying to a dealer, "…as far as comparisons…Gideon…the most brilliant painter in the school."

Intrusive laughter near her ear kept Kaki from hearing the rest. She wondered if what Nollo had said was right. But she forgot all that when she followed Braq and Gideon themselves. The two boys stood in front of and critiqued each other's works in the harshest, most excoriating terms. It is true that Gideon could find only one tiny patch of color, a speck of ultramarine blue down in the left hand corner of Braq's painting to criticize, but he did so in the most devastating and iridescent language. It is further true that Braq found only one minute brush stroke in Gideon's painting that was offensive to his critical eye, but he heaped on Gideon the rich condemnation his friend deserved for this egregious flaw. The two opponents having demolished each other's work, they proceeded to drag Kaki over to a punch bowl where the three of them stood for the rest of the time until the announcement of the winner.

It became apparent at some point that there were no longer any faculty in the room. They had all gone upstairs, summoned by La Maestra to select the winner of the Derosch Prize. In the drawing room, the faculty gathered around a burnished table. Gert distributed special ballots, that is, scraps of waste paper Thaddeus had just torn in half minutes earlier, to each of the faculty, which at this time counted nine: Antigone Skye Derosch, Benedict Skye, Thaddeus Derosch, Hara Derosch, Tressa Raeburn, Fritz Raeburn, and three non-family members including Bevol Stagri. Gert, who was not faculty but who had inveigled herself into the proceedings, marched with a self-important air behind each person's chair holding out "Tressa's brassiere" for them to deposit their ballots. At the end she brought the "brassiere" to La Maestra, who dropped her ballot in. The head of the Atelier Derosch began to take them out one by one, reading each aloud.

That the ballots were anonymous was a harmless fiction: Antigone knew everyone's handwriting, and in any event no one ever felt the need for secrecy. Still, this was their tradition.

The first ballot she read was this: "Braq Churai – 'The World Enlightened.' "

The second read, "Braq – 'The World Enlightened.' "

The third said merely, "Braq," while the fourth said, "The World Enlightened."

The fifth ballot she opened said, "Braq Churai."

The sixth said, "Braq, of course!"

And the seventh had these words: "The Chalk's 'World Enlightened.' "

The eighth said, "Enlightened."

The ninth read, "Braq's 'World.' "

The tenth – .

There should only have been nine ballots. Antigone frowned as she opened a tenth scrap of paper. She started to read, " 'Gid – '." She stopped abruptly. Her head swiveled like a howitzer to aim at Gert, who was standing at the side of the room, squashed against a large bombé chest that was somewhat reminiscent of her own figure. Perhaps she thought she might be ignored as another piece of furniture.

Antigone said in a metallic voice, "Gert, are you out of your mind?"

Gert took a little step away from her redoubt. Beet red, she protested, "But…he's your own flesh and blood!"

Antigone stood up so abruptly she sent two flocks of white birds flying – the scraps of paper ballots scuttling onto the carpet, and their reflections from the shiny table fluttering into oblivion. She stopped and took a breath. She said to the assemblage, "Thanks, everyone. We'll present the award in a few minutes."

The faculty accepted her dismissal, and began to file out, wondering what would happen next. Gert too tried to meld in with the abruptly mandated exodus, but Antigone said, "Gert."

The woman stopped.

Thaddeus and Hara Derosch abandoned their daughter to her aunt. Inexcusable dereliction of parental loyalty, no doubt, but, after all, there was no danger of Antigone actually killing the silly woman. And she was a big girl who could sink or swim on her own. Besides, they thought their daughter was a fool. There are a few such honest parents in the world.

Antigone waited until the last teacher, looking with dismay over his shoulder at Gert, had exited, and then she turned to Gert.

"If I had a family heirloom to give away, I might give it to my grandchild. If I was dispensing the last piece of my favorite blackbottom pie, I might give it to a relative instead of someone outside of the family.

"But the Derosch Prize is for merit, for achievement, for exceptional ability. This is what this school stands for, and what I stand for. It is what I have given my whole life to, and why I founded this school."

Gert attempted a mewling reply, but Antigone's voice overrode her. "Don't ever presume to judge a Derosch Prize again – especially by fraud! And if I ever hear of you injecting favoritism for family into official Atelier business, you'll be on the stoop quicker than you can say '*niece*.' "

She turned and went downstairs, leaving a humiliated, sullen-mouthed Gert.

There was tremendous acclaim when Mrs. Derosch announced to the roomful of visitors, in the main studio, that Braq Churai was the winner of the Derosch Prize. Gideon slapped his friend on the back. The other students too, and the faculty, congratulated him. Kaki gave him a kiss, which he felt as a burning spot for some long minutes afterwards. But she disappeared almost immediately.

Jule came up to Gideon. She complimented him on his painting. Then she asked, "What was this meeting that was held last night?" The boy looked puzzled. "Oh, we met to discuss the running of the Atelier this summer while most of the faculty are in Europe. Why?"

Jule laughed. She said, "It's not important."

Kaki had gone to find Tressa. She said, "Mrs. Raeburn, half an hour ago, I heard you say to some man that Gideon is the most brilliant painter in the school."

Tressa nodded. "I did say something like that."

Kaki asked, mystified, "And Braq?"

Tressa put her hand on Kaki's. She said, "Kaki, I think you must have missed *all* that I said. Gideon *is* brilliant – and certainly in *comparison* to all of the other students. But Braq – Braq cannot be compared to *anyone*. He is *sui generis* – one of a kind. He's a genius!"

***

Braq finished packing his suitcase. He had double-checked to make sure he had all of the drawing tools he would need. If all went as planned, they would visit some twenty or thirty museums, and see countless new sights. He planned to draw as much as he could.

He had sold many works now through the Atelier's gallery and through exhibiting in the annual show; he had saved the money earned from working for the Atelier. The result of all this productivity was that Braq Churai, aged fourteen, had amassed quite a large capital, far more than he needed for the European Tour, so much that he was going to be able to extend his stay there for most of the summer before he had to return to enroll at Chamberlain.

This meant that he would not see his brother, or Jule's family, for many weeks, but with the eagerness of a young man he only looked forward to the great adventure ahead. The only thing that caused him to stop for a moment, regretfully, was the fact that he would not be able to see Kaki. His hands held the lid of the suitcase open. He stood immobile.

He did not yet know if she would still be here when he returned. She had made one or two remarks that implied she was to return to Chugrana soon. He knew that this had been her intention, that she wanted to get back to Liz, and to take copies of Zaq's book to be secretly distributed in Chugrana. And he wanted that goal too. But once she had come to Maryland, and the childhood friends had been reunited, he had also begun to hope that she might stay...even though she and Nollo were "married."

He gave the barest hint of a smile, belied by a rueful twist of one corner of his mouth. He had long since dismissed the childish ritual of his "marrying the moon," but he had no clear idea if Kaki, or Nollo, still intended to honor the childhood pact, the pact formed when Kaki selected Nollo as her spouse to be. There had been a few allusions to it since Kaki had arrived – allusions that were less than whole-hearted it seemed to him, allusions that hung in the air, as if waiting for someone – Kaki, Nollo, or who knows who else – to say, "Yes! This is to be!" or "No! It was a horrible mistake!"

Nollo seemed to take it for granted, as a pledge he owned and was entitled to, yet perfunctorily, as if the promise of love that one would expect to see lying underneath such a pledge was itself not important. The pledge *belonged* to him, and it didn't matter its origin. And he almost seemed possessive, even jealous, when Braq was around. When the three of them were together, Nollo always managed to sit next to Kaki, or between Kaki and Braq. Sometimes it seemed that he was even more belittling of his brother than usual, just because Kaki was present. All of this implied that he regarded Kaki as "his."

But why should he regard Braq as a threat? Braq had never consciously suggested anything that would challenge Nollo's assumption; he could not understand his big brother's behavior. Nor did he realize that it was apparent to others, including Nollo, that Braq's voice took on an edge of enthusiasm greater than usual when Kaki was around. And that his eyes shone more brightly.

Braq stared at the suitcase. Kaki and Nollo "married"...Braq "married to the moon." Again his rueful smile, one corner of his mouth up, the other down, signaling a clash of emotions. He felt confused. Braq had bridled when Nollo had accused him, in front of Kaki, of "always drawing and painting naked white women." Nonetheless, it was true: he looked…there…with interest. Oh, being a fourteen year old boy, he looked at each of the female models with sexual interest, but he looked at the lighter-skinned ones with something more than sexual curiosity. It was almost as if over each one there hung a question barely whispered, as from some deep locale, buried under drifts of time, as if from under some ancient avalanche, the question: "Is this she?"

The one.

By falling in love with such a one he might reveal himself to be a person who set race and color aside…as his father had…by loving a woman who was *not* like him…not like him in that detested, trivial, unimportant feature of skin color. The one by loving whom he might reveal himself to be as good a person as his father…to be "the kind of man we want."

A conclusion was forming in his mind: wordless as yet, not framed with precision, as he would have preferred, and even the premises were unclear to him. The premises: Nollo regarded Kaki as his; Kaki had said and done nothing to disown the pledge. Moreover, to do what his father had done, to choose a woman *not* like himself, would that not be an admirable thing, as admirable as it had been for Zaq? The conclusion, implicitly taking shape: Kaki was not for him; he should look elsewhere, and especially at women who were not "like him."

As he moved to higher ground on the Chugran strand to build a new sand sculpture when the old one proved treacherously uncertain, as he wiped out a drawing poorly conceived, as he scrubbed down a painting that should never have been and then started a newer, better one, as he discarded all unrequited values, so now he wiped out – a possibility. Even before it could arrive in his mind in specific words: the possibility of Kaki.

Braq clicked the suitcase shut. He carried it outside. He looked up towards the main house and the studio, then back to his "slave cottage."

He knew he would miss all this. But he felt only excitement – at the trip he was about to embark on, at going to Chamberlain University, at continuing to build his life, at the paintings he was eager to create. He was excited to be alive, and in charge of his life. He felt that he could handle this business – his life. He felt that he was up to the job and well equipped for it. He knew that while nothing was guaranteed to him, he had the tools to achieve what mattered most – his work.

There were only two faint shadows hovering on the margin of his awareness. He had, he felt, just dismissed one of them. He would have to look for someone besides Kaki.

The other shadow he could not dismiss. Nor could he even frame such words to himself, not even as a question. Yet the shadow remained.

The shadow, the unutterable question, was this: "Do I still have a Big Brátano?"

Several hours later, at the airport, Braq felt that his wordless decision – to move on to an *attainable* value – was the right one. Braq had gone to the airport in a chartered bus with the members of the Atelier entourage and their luggage. Nollo and Kaki had said they would meet him at the airport to see him off. Braq and the Atelier travelers parked and walked into the airport complex through an underground concourse. They passed a subway stop, where clutches of commuters, shoppers, and students stood waiting, while others exited or entered the motionless subway cars. With a glance, an appalled glance, Braq took in the fashion of the day. On the subway platform, flocks of black storks which were people huddled in a massy silhouette; though the city was cleaner than it had been in many years, the clothing had become blacker – a dull, coalish black that absorbed any scrap of light – even aboveground in the sparkling sun.

Before he could register how or why, he was smiling broadly, gratefully at the girl who walked out of the drab mob. Heads turned, the women eyeing her resentfully, their glances following her. She wore a gaily-colored dress which swayed silkily with her walk and with her hips, without affectation, unself-consciously. She radiated amidst the black storks. She was a reproach.

It all happened in an instant. In the next, he saw that it was Kaki. Nollo was just behind her, holding her elbow.

Nollo and Kaki saw him, waved, and quickly came up. Together, they walked to the gate designated for their flight. Soon the departure was announced. The Derosch tour group moved down the corridor to embark. At the door, Braq paused and turned to look back. He waved once more at the girl in the brilliant dress, and at his brother. As he started to turn his face to the hallway that snaked around the corner out of sight, the last thing he saw was his Big Brátano putting his arm around behind Kaki's shoulder. The image stayed with Braq for some time afterwards. It was not an image he wanted to paint.

CHAPTER 58

The Tapestry of Morality

In the latter years of the twentieth century, people in America had daily – hourly if they so chose – exposure to the most depraved acts that people could commit. They had this access through television, newspapers, magazines, and – in time – the internet. No crime too bestial but they expended countless hours savoring its details of degradation. Future historians may wonder that these people did not expose themselves instead to those *exalted achievements* that men…committed.

It was a choice. But the choice was guided – as are they all – by men's fundamental premises. If one is convinced that man is, at root, evil, one will not only miss the evidence which might demonstrate the contrary, one will also in time ignore such evidence, and one will not only stare, smitten, at the evidence of men's evil and at nothing else, one will also *seek out* such evidence above all other considerations. One will seek it out in order to confirm one's estimate of his fellows…and of himself.

Nor was it just the ancient religious spirit which had always condemned man, and still did, but the secular worldly sophisticates too who joined even – it seemed – eagerly, the wailing chorus that accused the very species itself of innate depravity.

The cornucopia of choice, of wealth, of property, of health which had been made possible by some two hundred years of freedom and the guarantee of men's rights was thoughtlessly spilled onto the floor, and its fruits with careless abundance were rolled about the hall, no one asking where these gifts came from. People even were so brazen as to complain that more were not instantly forthcoming. Men produced abundance, yet people called *man* the evildoer. They did not inquire, though, into the nature of evil.

Never in the history of the world, had any creature had such a limitless range of choices spread before him – a Lucullan feast for all of life – with so little guidance from those, his intellectual standard bearers, who ought to have held lamps beside his path. Little was said, in all this ceaseless chattering, that would illuminate and alert one to the steps by which the walls of virtue, of morality, of civilization might be torn down within a human soul to bring a man to the point that he could commit depraved acts that people bemoaned while they watched…and watched.

The faintly flickering torches that *were* erected by his guides, the intellectuals, were such as these:

"There are no principles."

"Do whatever you want."

"Morality is an illusion (and a boring one at that)."

"Principles are to be made up on the spot, and abandoned on the next spot."

"Principles are the province of the group – any group – and the group can change those principles as it sees fit, with no other criterion than its own whim."

Occasionally, when some glimmer of conscience shone onto their paths, casting a faint shadow that they might with a little thought have identified as guilt or, who knows, even innocence, in regard to anything they did or thought, they ran away to *this* that they called an explanation – "Nature or Nurture."

But never would they stand still for a moment and face their own – responsibility.

Such intellectuals having shattered the guiding lampposts of every moral code by this point in time, one might be led to make excuses for the pathetic souls – the common man, the ordinary fellow, the guy next door – who relied upon them and to say, "Since they had no guide, one can hardly hold them to account."

But –

If, on the farthest reaches of moral discourse, there are complex, subtle questions – the kind that academic thinkers love to pose to befuddle their students – it remains true that there are also great simplicities which all those creatures we call human can know with the least amount of thought. To condemn murder requires no moral excavation, no careful sifting of each layer of some dig of the soul. To condemn theft requires no hard won discovery. Every person, and every society, knows the depravity of rape, the corruption of dishonesty, the turpitude of cowardice. From some primordial Cain to the present, there has breathed no man who could say "No one told me not to" when he was charged with – fratricide.

If morality is a tapestry hung as a wall of instruction, receding off into a distance, a tapestry full of rich, intricate, vibrant colors, designs, and textures, and if some men can see all of that for a long, long way, whereas others, being morally myopic, can see only for a few feet in front of them before the wall fades into obscurity, and still others perceive the colors of this tapestry but only washed out and faded, and others see the color but are squinty as to the patterns and designs, still they all see it, they all know that the tapestry *is before them.*

If someone cannot see the visual world, there is a blunt word in every language to describe him: *blind.*

If one cannot hear the auditory world, there is another word: *deaf.*

For someone who cannot see the tapestried wall of morality, a person who could commit fratricide, there is also a word.

You know it too.

Even in the modern world, some people recognize that ideas have consequences. But each strand, each piece of thread within the tapestry of morality is an idea. There are other ideas which oppose as pole to pole the ideas within that tapestry. Each corrupting idea snags, like a crochet hook, a thread that is part of the tapestry and plucks it out.

These were some of the crochet hooks lying loose in Nollo's soul:

"*We Chugrans* see the world in a certain way, *from birth.* By nature."

"We are all the slaves of something, something outside of us, or in us."

"Only the Race is real; only the Race is important."

"America stands for the individual – where is the glory in that for me? It means that I stand alone, and must *become* something."

"When my blood is up, I can do what I want."

"Knowledge and truth come from the Race."

"We need no heroes, no moral guides – blood takes care of that for us. And I am a hero of the blood."

"Race is the standard of the good, and Race should be the recipient of the good. For the Race the individual must sacrifice himself."

"Though individuals are to be subordinated to a Race, yet the Race then will be subordinated to one individual."

"If any of this, anything I say, or do, or think, causes conflicts among men, then physical force, even death, is the answer."

"Why do I have to keep trying to *figure out* this mystery – the world? Who cares?!"

It is not necessary to ask whether or not he "believed" each one of these hooks. To ask such a question is already to grant an assumption of honesty, of regard for the truth, of sincere conviction. Nollo picked these hooks up as he needed them, when a thread required unraveling. He stored the hooks in no careful order, but tossed them down in his soul when they were no longer called for.

Still, they ordered themselves.

Though not beliefs, in the honorable sense, yet they were who he was.

***

"He is safe," thought Kaki as Braq's face disappeared round the corner to board his plane. In the same instant, before her waving arm dropped from its farewell, she felt Nollo's arm circling her shoulder. She shrugged it off. She turned to face him. She said, almost as a challenge, "I'm going to miss Braq."

Nollo gave an angry lurch as he wheeled and began to walk to the exit, answering Kaki as he walked. "He's running away. He's given up…if he was ever with us anyway."

Kaki walked alongside him. She said, "Running away from what? He's pursuing his own goals, and why shouldn't he?! He's got so much to do with his life, with his great talent!"

Nollo said, "He's running away from our struggle." He was silent for a moment, then added, "*His* talent! *His* goals! *His* pursuits! I think self-centered personal accomplishment is an obsession that threatens the Chugran Race itself. We don't have the luxury of 'rugged individualism.' When we're being slaughtered, when men like my father are in prison."

Kaki said, her voice becoming hotter, "Is anyone here slaughtering you, here, now, in America, where you have the good fortune to live because your parents sent you here?!"

"No," said Nollo, "but you and I are still dedicated to helping Chugrana, and Chugrans, and helping people like Father. Braq is doing nothing!"

Kaki said, "What do you think – that every Chugran doctor, lawyer, engineer, teacher in America should drop their careers and run to join some organization like yours? That white people may live as simple purposeful individuals pursuing their right to happiness but we may not – we – individuals like Braq, for example. Or are you even saying that it's wrong for whites to do that too, that they also have to be slaves to their own racial causes? Or to ours? To…to you?!"

Nollo gave a curt wave of dismissal, at the same time making a noise of disgust. Some minutes later they got into the car and began the drive home. But they were not long on the way when Nollo began a conversation about the scenery and other innocuous things as if they had never had the previous discussion, as if they were just simple friends. He had even put a note of gaiety in his voice.

Kaki, however, was paying only scant attention to this. Her mind was elsewhere, prompted by Nollo's mention of Zaq. It was time, she thought, to get back. She wanted to bring the book to Liz, to show her the product they had worked for, to discuss what could be done next. They hoped that the publishing house's efforts to gain world-wide publicity would bring pressure on the Chugran government to free Zaq. It was what she had dedicated....

She stopped.

"Dedicated."

That was the word Nollo had used. Why did she suddenly feel repulsed by this word, "dedicated"? She did not feel a part of this same "dedication".

What was she dedicated to? "What" was a principle: individual rights. *Whom* was she dedicated to? "Whom" meant people: Zaq, Liz... and....

Who else? "And?" The little word she heard in her mind was a conjunction to – a thread connecting to – whom? Anyone like Zaq and Liz? Anyone? Was she giving her life to *the whole world*? Was she becoming a slave? What an ugly thought! No, not to the whole world, only to those who deserved to be free, those "suitable for liberty." To men who *chose* liberty. And not just political liberty. Who chose to live their lives *as individuals*. To men like...Braq.

And – if it was right for Braq to be free of the race, why not her too? Again, she thought, "dedicated" – to whom was she dedicated?

But Braq was married to the moon – that was her doing. He was entranced to his art – that was his doing. In any event, she thought, he had shown no...interest...in her. And still, there were Zaq and Liz. That was *not* her enslavement, it was her passion. She, herself, as a free individual, *wanted* to help them. It was not a duty inflicted on her from outside by Nollo, or Chugrana, or Race, or God – it was her free, rational choice.

She heard Nollo's voice beside her still prattling chummily, breezily, as if they were not just friends, but an old married couple who could take their affection for each other for granted. Why was he going on in that way? It began to make its way through to her. It was almost as if he was pressing her to notice his manner, to accept it, to join him in it, to join him in *something.*

They arrived home and pulled into the garage. Before Kaki could get out, and as if to forestall her from getting out, he turned toward her and said, "Kaki, have you ever thought that the women of Chugrana have a special role to play in this struggle? That they serve a very special need for the men of the Race?"

It was not just his voice – wheedling, cajoling, insinuating, and, faintly, threatening – that disgusted her. It was not just his hand that, as he uttered the word, "need," slipped under the edge of her skirt and grasped her thigh, high up. It was, more than any of these things, the fact that this handsome boy, the one Braq reverently called his Big Brátano – and Kaki, reverent too, had called him that on the day of the boys' flight from Chugrana – the one she had knelt to in her mind as an object of worship, that he should treat her now as a mere member of a race, that it was not Kaki, the unique person, he desired, it was some racial prize, a merely physical token of a collective, a group, to satisfy what he called his "need."

She threw his hand off of her. She jumped from the car and slammed the door. She walked into the house.

Nollo did not follow her.

Kaki walked quickly past Rodit to her room. As she did so, Rodit asked with vague apprehension, "Is there anything wrong, Kaki?"

Turning at the door to the bedroom, she said, "No. But I'm returning to Chugrana. I'll have Sue drive me to the airport."

He said, "Why don't you let Nollo drive you? He'd be glad to be of service to you."

She said, turning her back to him, "No. Sue will do it."

As she began to pack, she thought with a bitter shake of her head that she would, on a time, have been glad to become Nollo's love slave: she would never become his racial slave.

CHAPTER 59

What a Lord Gives He May Take

The stage was set, the script written, the parts chosen, the audience assembled. The director had only to lift the curtain. He was glad that Braq was gone. He was glad that Kaki was gone, unfinished business though he regarded her. Not but that he would, secretly, have loved to flaunt certain things before each of those persons. But not this, not what he surely intended. Not these crochet hooks, not these –

A sacrificial victim is needed, a piece of dung to be thrown in the fire. I have selected the piece of dung.

It is necessary to bind them together by an act of blood.

I must bind them but not be bound.

I am above the law. The law comes from me.

He had alerted part of his audience. He had told Ku that he thought the pals were not "devoted enough." They were not yet sufficiently "subservient to the Race." He said that "mere blood relation" is not enough of a tie. It is not surprising that this statement – on the face of it the height of hypocrisy – fell unchallenged at Ku's feet. Not surprising because, though they never tired of promoting the ideas of race and tribe, Ku and Nollo had by now spent so much time establishing that true racial relationship was the product of their own subjective decree that they now readily believed that mere genealogical tribal membership was perhaps just a bit shaky.

"Mere blood relation is not enough," Nollo said to Ku. "An *act* of blood is needed."

Ku's eyelids became a bit sleepier, and his fingers twitched on his belly. The statement interested him. It also scared him. He wasn't sure he was ready for this next step yet. Was there time to pull back? Should he raise an objection?

"Traitor!"

Ku gave a little jump. But Nollo was not referring to him. He was looking off, trancelike, as if seeing someone far away. "A false

Chugran....someone who has deserted his race. A traitor." There was a pause. Then Nollo came out of his reverie. He looked at Ku as if just seeing him now. He said, somewhat more matter of factly, "A false Chugran in our midst...is the same as a traitor! We will have to nifar him."

"Who?" asked Ku cautiously.

Nollo said, "Whoever is not like *us*."

He said nothing more about it except to mention a day, June 25, and a time, noon, and he dropped the word "grotto" into the conversation. He knew that was all he needed to do.

The date in June arrived, a crystal clear day, the kind so clear it hurt one's eyes. They were all there in the grotto. The last one had just walked into the dank gloom. A painfully bright wedge of light in the entrance behind them all told them that outside it was still a summer's day, a day of brilliant sunlight, warm air, and the carefree chirps of birds – it was still a world of innocence.

"We have come to pronounce the nifasta."

They heard Nollo's voice and turned their eyes away from the opening, squinting in the gloom to try to see his face better.

"You have all pledged your loyalty. Your loyalty to Chugrana, to your fellow Chugrans. To your ancient bloodlines. And to those who carry the true blood of Chugrana within them."

Only a few of them nodded enthusiastically, though they had all made these pledges before, in one or another of their meetings.

"You swore your loyalty, even to your own death – or the death of our enemies."

There were a few nervous shuffles. Some of them had giggled at this kind of language in the past. It was all very theatrical. It wasn't meant to be taken...seriously...was it? But this sounded different. Nollo had implied something very serious when he told each of them beforehand of the meeting.

"The true Chugran is not just born – he *earns* the right from his fellows to be called one. He is a union of body *and* spirit. Not just the mere physical blood, but the blood of his soul tells us who he is. And tells us our enemies, even if they look like us." He added, "Even if they be as close to us as our own brothers."

There were more nervous shuffles as they looked furtively around at their pals.

"And the true Chugran does not challenge his leaders, does not undermine them, does not question their wisdom, does not act like a little worm trying to gnaw holes in their authority."

His voice had taken on a sneering tone, and he was now looking directly at little Chompy. Now they had an object for their fear, their uncertainty, their anxiety, their resentment, their guilt.

They began, by degrees, to form into a circle around the quivering boy.

Chompy let out an almost inaudible squeak. "What?!"

Nollo loomed over him. "Did you or did you not interrogate me about why I let my secret Race Name be used publicly at the graduation?"

Chompy answered, his voice shaking, "N-no…y-yes…I didn't understand…I wasn't ch-challenging you…I just…I know I'm not on your level, so I just wanted to know…"

"It's not *for* you to know," said Nollo contemptuously. "I can divulge my Race Name whenever I decide that it's in the interest of Chugrans to do so."

He went on. "And then you – you! – decided to tell other people, outsiders, that *you* were going to be given a Race Name soon too! No one had ever told you that! I smelled you out a long time ago as an impostor! And you should not have been even discussing it outside. You did, didn't you?"

Chompy nodded. The little boy was crying now. "I thought since *you* let *your* name be used, it was OK."

"You hadn't been given a Race Name because you don't deserve one. You're not an authentic Chugran. I always suspected as much. Now we know.

"The collective consciousness of our race excludes you.

"You are the nifanto."

Chompy gasped in terror.

"We no longer recognize you, not even as 'Chompy.'

"We pronounce the nifasta."

Chompy's figure crumpled as if his spine had been snapped.

At this Fempy Lobbel, as if on cue, began chanting, "Nifar! Nifar!" He motioned to the others to join him. Some were reluctant, but no one wanted to stand alone, certainly not with Chompy.

The word had been made up by Ku for Nollo's use. It was a silly word, but now, lying prone on the ledge above, like a great deflated bug, ear to the crack, hearing this word echoing off the walls of the grotto, Ku found it very disturbing. His face turned even blotchier under the sun. He felt ill.

At a certain point, Nollo raised his hand. He looked around at all of them. "You know what this means."

No one breathed.

They knew *what* it meant, but not how. Would they use their hands, or some weapon? Some of them were having second thoughts. Their blood was up, they couldn't be stopped – but they wished someone would stop them.

Nollo produced from nowhere a rather long dagger. He raised it above Chompy, who was too terrified even to move.

Nollo looked around. He sized them all up. He decided to turn the screw a bit further. He said, "Hold him."

Fempy and another pal took hold of the shaking Chompy.

Nollo let a certain amount of time go by. When he thought that they could stand it no longer, he said, "The spirit of Chugrana speaks through me. And *to* me. It says to be merciful. To spare this poor mongrel who appears to be so blessed as to have a small portion of our blood."

Above, kneeling on the ledge, Pranti Ku almost rolled over onto his side, so astonished was he at this maneuver. To goad them, to incite them, to stoke them, to bring them to a pitch of emotion where they would accept as proper a heinous act, and then to claim the right and the power to transcend the law, that very law that would have sanctioned their act, to make oneself the source of the law – what a stroke! He always knew that Nollo Churai had the seeds of a kind of greatness in him. This clinched it.

Nollo had gotten them to agree to murder; but then *he* had spared them. They had not actually had to commit the deed, but it was *his* dispensation that had saved them.

They were doubly his.

Nollo was speaking to Chompy again. "You have been nifared. Never let us see you or hear from you again. And if you repeat to anyone what happened here today, our mercy will disappear."

Chompy staggered to the grotto's entrance. Nollo turned to the others. He said, "Now, some of you take care of that damned sign."

A few moments later, hiding now behind a bush a short distance from the ledge, Ku saw little Chompy crawl shakily up into view, like an insect making its feeble way on rickety legs across the rock. The boy ran, stumbled, and tottered past Ku. He ran away to the far side of the plantchi field. The others emerged also, in one's and two's, like moles blinking in the sunlight. They drifted past Ku, concealed behind the bush, some of them glancing furtively toward the receding figure of Chompy Screws. They walked in the opposite direction, toward the front of the Schaal.

Nollo came last, and Ku saw him spy Chompy's tiny figure in the distance. He saw Nollo look toward the straggling line of pals, and again toward Chompy. He saw him follow Chompy.

Only Ku saw this.

Stifling a shudder, Ku waddled as quickly as he could after the pals.

***

At the farthest edge of the plantchi field, Chompy Screws looked back. He saw skirting the edge of the field, coming his way, his revered Nollo, the god of his race. He looked around him terrified. He was far too far from the roadway – and what help was there in that direction anyway – that was where the pals had gone. The pals whom he had counted on for his protection against the world. Counted on to give him a secure racial fastness from which the members of other races could not hurt him. The pals who gave him...character...who made him what he was.

Nollo was still coming toward him. Panic-stricken, Chompy scurried into the woods. He stumbled along a faint path; surely it would lead to something. Through brambles and vines he kept looking over his shoulder where each time he saw Nollo following him steadily.

At length, he emerged from the woods. He was in a small opening on top of a bluff that lowered on the Severn River. There was nowhere else to go. He had boxed himself in.

Nollo walked out from behind a bush, saw the situation, and snickered derisively at Chompy. "You're hopeless, aren't you? And you wanted to be a Chugran!"

Chompy didn't know what to do or say. He nodded with a remnant of a smile and a trace of a whimper.

Nollo said, this time with still more contempt, "It's why I nifared you." He stressed the "I."

"You're of no use to anyone – not me, not Chugrans, certainly no one else. *Are* you?"

Chompy shivered.

"If you're of no use – not to a family, or a clan, or a tribe, or a race, or nobody at all – then – you have no reason to live. *Do* you?"

The sun blazed mercilessly above. Chompy shivered even more.

Nollo stepped closer to him. "What are you still standing here for? An individual is nothing, *nothing* against the Race. You're not even real. You're worth – nothing!"

He waited. Then he said, "Why haven't you gone?"

Chompy looked around him. Go…where? He looked behind him. He was on the edge. The drop was steep. It ended many feet below on jagged rocks glistening with froth from the river's chopping waves. He looked back at his tormentor.

Nollo had moved a step closer. He was going to say something more, going to keep applying the cattle prod of his voice, and his authority. He was enjoying this. His blood was up. He felt that nothing could stop him.

It wasn't necessary. Whether little Chompy just gave up, or gave in to his fear, or even just from clumsiness lost his footing, the next thing Nollo knew, the boy had disappeared over the edge. The last thing Nollo saw was Chompy's eyebrows crinkled with terror vanishing from view.

Nollo stepped to the edge. He looked down. He saw the body of the Chugran boy lying partially on the rocks, partially in the water.

Nollo raised his eyes to the horizon. Far in the distance he saw sparkling white chips of light which were sailboats glittering in the warm summer air. Nollo did not shiver. But a single, uncontrollable, writhing shudder went through his frame. He turned and hurried away.

It was a few days before the body washed onto a sandy margin some miles away. The death was the subject of concern for a couple of days within a small segment of the Chugran community.

The detective assigned to the case ascertained from Chompy's mother that on the day he had gone missing, he had left home before noon, saying nothing, and simply had not returned. She suggested that the detective speak to his friends. But when he questioned the boys on the list she gave him, they each denied having any knowledge of Chompy. "It gave me the strangest feeling," the detective reported to Chief Cutby, who included Sergeant Booge in on the discussion. "It wasn't just that they had no information. It's their group, or gang, or fraternity, or whatever they call themselves, I can't get a straight line on it. I'm reasonably sure from other witnesses that this Chompy belonged, or used to belong, to them. But they don't just deny that, they – several of them

– said 'I know no Chompy.' Almost like he never even existed as far as they were concerned. And almost like someone had told them what to say…or think."

"It was definitely a united front."

Cutby asked, "Do you know who's the head of this gang?"

"Oh, yes, there's no question about that. A young man named Nollo Churai."

Cutby's head came up, he thought for a moment, then he sucked in his breath. "Oh." Then he said, "I'd like you to stay on this a bit longer. I know there's no evidence of foul play. But see if you can turn up anything more. If the boy belonged to their gang, and they're denying it, it's fishy."

The detective was able to "turn up" nothing more. Many Chugrans distrusted the police. The Chugrans he spoke to seemed to resent his persistence. The members of the Confraternity closed ranks. Nollo had made it clear to them that, though Chompy had disappeared right after their meeting, that even though they had "spared" him, that even though he, Nollo, had no idea what had happened to Chompy, still they all knew the meaning and the consequences of their oath, their decision, their actions. He implied that though there was nothing to feel guilty about, they were all in "it" together.

He spoke to each one alone. And each one nodded, whether from conviction or fear, when Nollo said, "The Race is purer now. We don't need weaklings." And each nodded again when he added, looking intently into his eyes, "It's a lesson."

Ku said nothing to Nollo about what he had seen and heard. But in a talk to some of the members of the group, Prester Pranti Ku, their spiritual mentor, said, and as he did it he gave a sly sideways look at Nollo, "And the psychic violence our racist society heaps on us will produce justifiable and boiling Chugran rage. We will not be to blame for its consequences."

As usual, Ku's use of the future tense was ambiguous. Did he mean the past? Did he know something? Did he mean the future? Was he predicting? Was he just blathering? Nollo shrugged. Ku followed this by saying, "It's a shame that our traditions are not shown more respect." No one took him up on this, so he continued, "Tearing down the sign that way."

Nollo looked him straight in the eye. "What sign?"

"Didn't you know, someone tore down 'Let Mind Speak to Mind.' Nollo's cheeks sucked in ironically. "But 'Let Race Speak to Race' is still there?"

Ku nodded. Nollo said, "Good."

In another brief exchange, Nollo's lieutenant, Fempy Lobbel, said ingratiatingly to his leader, "You showed Chompy clemency, but it looks like Fate gave him what he deserved after all."

Nollo Churai cocked his head at Fempy. He raised one eyebrow and from his hooded lids he looked down at Fempy derisively. He said, with quiet but pointed sarcasm, "*Fate*?"

Fempy, after an uncertain snicker, shut up and said nothing more.

Nollo and Ku had one more important conversation near the end of that summer. Braq was expected back any day from Europe, and he would then enroll at Chamberlain University. Ku called Nollo up one day and said, "You're in."

Nollo said, "What?"

Ku said, "Chamberlain. They've finally accepted you. I just got off the phone with the Dean of Admissions. He said they didn't get the number of admissions they required so there were openings, and he gave me a lot of bilge about 'ethnic outreach.' I think it means they didn't fill their racial quotas to be able to prove to the government that they have met their social obligation. But whatever the reason, you're in!"

Nollo was insulted.

He was flattered.

He was angry.

He was pleased.

He felt all of these things. But one emotion overwhelmed all the rest. It was a secret exultation. If it had found words, this emotion would have expressed itself thusly: "Good! He won't get away from me after all!"

He could not say why but he felt an urge to do something. He looked around restlessly, feeling driven. All of a sudden, he went into his bedroom. He opened a drawer. From the bottom, underneath a pile of socks, he extracted a sheet of thick paper. It was an old piece of watercolor paper with pigments washed into its fibers by Little Bratabraq. It was the First Painting. He looked at the child's attempt to capture his own image of his heroic elder brother.

Nollo went down to the basement. Over in a far corner, he lit a match. He held it to the painting. He watched it burn, crinkle, and scatter into black shards on the floor.

Continued In Book Three:

Suitable for Liberty

SOVEREIGN *Book Three: Suitable for Liberty*

Contents:

Part V: No Power Outside

Part VI: The Kind of Man We Want

www.ingramcontent.com/pod-product-compliance
Lightning Source LLC
Chambersburg PA
CBHW030013180626
46810CB00001B/18

9780982836514